Meteor Fall

With stories from:

Andrew M. Ferrell
Alex Minns
James Pyles
Sandy Stuckless
Molly Neely
Ian Hugh McAllister

Published By:
Cloaked Press, LLC
P. O. Box 341
Suring, WI 54174
https://www.cloakedpress.com

Cover Design by:
Fantasy & Coffee Design
https://www.fantasyandcoffee.com/SPDesign/

Contents

Discovery

by Andrew M. Ferrell

"Where are we on this big event you think you've found, Adams?" Curator Woolley asked his Director of Astronomy. He watched the weaselly faced younger man square his shoulders and sneer at the other Directors. Woolley added, "I just need actionable numbers, not your puffed up self important bullshit."

Director Anthony Adams deflated slightly, glaring at the smirk appearing on Director Jackson's face. "Two weeks ago, our long range satellites caught a mass heading on a possible trajectory for Earth. I say possible, because it still had to clear the asteroid belt." Adams handed over a stack of papers before continuing, "This mass only grew slightly passing through the Belt. It is unclear how much is the original wave and how much from the asteroid belt itself. Our hope is that the trajectory was changed enough to miss us. It is too soon to tell for sure, but I think we should be prepared for a global sized event." He sat down slowly. *What the satellite images can't convey,'* he thinks, *'is how monumentally screwed we might be if I'm right.'*

Woolley turned to his Director of Operations. Nickolas Sanders sat with his face impassive. His years as a field agent left him with a no nonsense approach to life. Nothing surprised him anymore, and he tackled every situation with a 'Prepare for the worst, Hope it's not that bad' attitude. He cleared his throat, handing over a stack of papers he had prepared for this meeting. Every line of the papers etched in his memory. "I have agent deployment plans drawn up for every contingency the Pit can come up with. Be nice if we had more accurate intelligence regarding concentrations of meteor sightings.By my numbers we are going to be stretched thin regardless."

"I'll provide better data when I have it. Tell your desk jockeys in the Pit to just keep their eyes on the Internet traffic. I don't need anymore civilians getting involved," Adam's snapped. He crossed his arms.

"Don't like getting scooped, do ya?" Sanders said laughing. "Maybe we should hire this Dreyer fellow to run Astronomy."

Before Adams could rise to the bait, Woolley stepped in. "That's enough. I read the report, it was dumb luck the telescope was turned in the right direction for that small window. We weren't going to be able to keep this event a total secret for long. Jackson, vet this civilian in case we have to bring him in. Where do we stand on recruitment and training of field agents?"

Jackson moved for the first time since he took his seat. His short cropped hair belied his military background. He shifted his wide shoulders before speaking. "We have twenty new agents ready for final tests before the field. Another fifty to seventy vetted but not approached. We can fast track them but I expect the normal ten to twenty percent washout. Some of those may be salvageable for desk jobs in the Pit."

Sanders nodded. "I'll take all the help I can get. This event is going to explode online soon enough. The agents monitoring the traffic are already pulling a few extra hours."

Woolley laced his fingers together on his desk. "Gentlemen, I don't have to explain the gravity of this situation. Whatever we need to get in front of this in terms of resources or manpower, have the requests on my desk immediately. Jackson, step up the vetting process. Sanders, spare whoever you can for background checks and investigations. Make sure everyone gets some time off beforehand. Once the meteors start falling, I doubt any of us are going to get sleep." He looked at each of them in turn, his face hardening at the smirk on Adams's face. "Dismissed."

**

Todd Jensen checked his flawless hair one last time as the producer signaled ten seconds. He turned to his hairstylist, "How's my teeth?" She gave him a thumbs up and moved off the set. Todd put on his best smile as the countdown began.

"It's March 27th and this is the Evening Report with Todd Jensen. In today's science news. Astronomers are announcing the approach of a cosmic phenomenon in the form of a Global Meteorite Event. What this means is that later this year we will have a meteor shower that can be seen in all corners of the world. Here to tell us about this story is Dr. Karl Dreyer, lead astronomer from Gallen Observatory, who first reported this event. Dr. Dreyer, what makes this event so remarkable?"

The viewers at home are treated to a side by side view of their favorite anchorman and a slim, middle aged man wearing glasses and a plaid button down shirt. Karl Dreyer shifts uncomfortably as the relay catches up. "Call me, Karl. Please. What's so special about this event is the sheer scale of it, Todd. We've all seen meteor showers before. Some of them even come around on a regular basis and have been named. What my colleagues and I have confirmed about this one, however, is that everyone should be treated to the a show around the world. Whether you live in the Carolinas, or in South Africa, you should see something."

"Have you been able to pin down any further details? Where did this much debris come from?" Todd asked, following the line of questioning on his teleprompter. His delivery made it clear he was faking interest.

"Based on long range satellite images, it looks like a small comet from deep space crashed through the asteroid belt. That's this ring of rocks in space beyond Mars." Karl's tone of voice changed to his teaching one as he continued, "When this occurred, it, along with several asteroids, shattered. These shattered fragments formed a wave of particles sailing through space. Based on their trajectory and observed speed, it has been determined these particles will enter Earth's atmosphere sometime in late summer or early fall of this year."

"Didn't something like this wipe out the dinosaurs? Are we in any danger from this wave?" Todd asked, finally something dramatic he could latch onto. *"Maybe this story can be saved,"* he thought to himself.

"We believe not. Almost all of the particles will burn up in the atmosphere. A few small fragments may touch down, giving geologists and rock hounds some new excitement," Karl replied calmly.

"Thank you very much for your time Dr., I mean Karl," Todd corrected himself. Deflated there was no danger, the anchor was ready to move on to something else.

"Thanks for having me," Karl replied before the link cut out.

Todd turned to the side and the camera angle changed. "In sports news…" Todd ran through the rest of the show. When it was finally over, he unclipped his mic and dropped it on the desk.

"Our lead story is meteors?" He asked the producer. "Seriously? Where's our Hollywood scandals and government intrigue?"

The producer shrugged. "Slow news day. But gotta admit, should be kinda cool if the astronomers are right about this. Who's seen a shooting star during the day?"

Todd waved his hand dismissively and retired to his office. "Shooting stars, what a colossal waste of time," he muttered as he flipped on his computer.

Agents of Retribution

by Alex Minns

"**M**r Soth? Could I have a word?"

Eddie looked up, ready to snap at whoever was interrupting him. He managed to bite his tongue when he saw the Director peering round his door. His chair screeched against the floor as he hastily stood up.

"Director Harrison." He wracked his brain for anything he might have done wrong in the last few weeks. He'd finished his reports on the Trojan artefacts and he'd glanced over the new reports from Loch Ness; he could keep covering up the sightings with plausible stories but someone really needed to tell Nessie to calm it down a bit and keep a lower profile.

"Why does everyone always get that look when I turn up?" She shook her head as she came into the room

7

properly and shut the door behind her. "May I?" She gestured to the stool on the opposite side of the workbench. Much to his surprise, she waited for him to nod before actually taking a seat. He'd heard all sorts of stories about the Director, ranging from her being a Grade A witch and jobsworth if you missed a deadline to her being able to actually turn you to stone with her stare after an incident in Ghent. All the rumours couldn't be true, but some probably were, and you never knew which ones until it was too late.

"Don't worry Soth, I'm not going to turn you into a statue."

He frowned. "How..?"

"I'm not psychic either. The historians always go for the Medusa story." She smiled. He'd never properly met her before. Yes, he'd been in briefings but they had never spoken directly. When he was hired, it was about a year before she had taken over the UK operation after wresting control from her predecessor.

The Director was watching him closely, her chin propped up on her fist as she leant on the bench. She was in her fifties but she hadn't lost the youthful glint in her eye. Her suit, although professional, had a definite sloppiness to it that betrayed that this was not her in her most comfortable guise.

She suddenly sat back and took a deep breath, seeming to have come to some kind of decision. "Justice. Tell me about it, from a historical perspective. Myths and alike."

Thrown momentarily by the switch in topic, he frowned as he sorted through the filofax of knowledge in his brain.

"Well, there are deities in a lot of cultures relating to justice. One of the earliest would be Maat, the Egyptian goddess who would weigh your heart against a feather to determine whether you would be doomed to the underworld if it was too heavy with sin."

"Weigh them?"

Eddie nodded, his love of history switching him to lecture mode. "Yes, the whole idea we know of Lady Justice holding the scales first stemmed from there. Themis the Greek goddess had scales, as did Justitia, to weigh a person's actions and sins. Justitia was the first to wear a blindfold and had a sword to cut through lies."

"Have we ever found an artefact linking to these myths?"

Eddie slid himself back on the stool opposite the director. "Not that I know of, they are just legend as far as I know. Why?"

"There's been chatter amongst the Starchildren. There's not much to go on, they don't know if it's a MAO or MAP but they're calling them Nemesis."

"She was the goddess of retribution, not justice, dealing out fortune based on your actions." Eddie couldn't help himself.

"Well whatever or whoever it is," the Director began, "Nemesis is able to track down those who are guilty of something and get them to confess."

"I'm sorry Director but how do we know this is anything to do with a meteor? It could just be a private detective who's taking things into their own hands."

"The rumours the Starchildren are talking about tell of a woman who can tell you your darkest secret after one glance. I don't know where they heard of her but I decided to pull up some police files. I found reports of about ten different people who have turned up at police stations confessing to crimes they committed. They had gotten away with them, there was no reason to come forward. A couple of them were so edgy and freaked out, they had them assessed. One mentioned a girl knowing what they had done but oddly that was about all they got out of them."

"Is there anything to suggest this Nemesis could have gotten hold of an old artefact?"

"We would have heard of someone else before." She shook her head.

Eddie let his gaze drift off to his bookshelves. "Fascinating. Some have theorised the scales could have been MAOs." He pulled himself back to the moment. "Sorry, what do you need from me? Put together some research about older myths?"

"Not quite." The Director's eyes narrowed and she sucked her bottom lip as she thought. Eddie felt a sense of dread tug at the corner of his mind. "You were a field agent once."

Eddie stiffened, all interest disappearing in an instant. "Was."

"No-one ever really stops."

"You stopped."

"Ha," she laughed. "Only when Curator Woolley is watching closely enough. I'd be taking this case if I could spare the time. You know there's a large-scale event on the horizon. We're stretched to capacity."

"I can't help with that I'm afraid."

"Can't or won't?"

"There's a difference?"

"If you want to keep your pension possibly."

Eddie stayed quiet. The more he spoke the more trouble he was going to get himself into.

The Director held her hands up in front of her. "I know you want to stay in research, I do understand. But I'm sending clerks out to do preliminaries, trainees are being fast-tracked before they are ready, I've even had to pull people out of retirement just to triage cases so we aren't swamped. We are going to miss things and we are going to make mistakes and react without the full facts, it's inevitable. And this case is one that I should leave, not a priority. But something about this is bugging me, I think there's more to this and if we don't do something then we're going to regret it."

Eddie didn't miss the switch to 'we'. "Then send a clerk to do the preliminary. I'll assess their report."

"I think this is going to need more experience and dare I say it empathy."

"What do you mean?"

"A newbie will do everything by the book, going in hard and harsh. Sometimes by the book is fine, but some days..." she let that thought hang in the air.

Eddie sat back. It definitely felt like there was more to this that she wasn't telling him. But then again, this was what she was famous for. She was a renegade; the book was more a suggestion than a rule and it had made her the most successful agent this side of the Pond. He had heard rumours that she was a MAP herself, it was the only way she could figure out half the stuff she knew.

"I can't." The words almost clogged up his throat.

"I think you can. And I think it's time you did." She gazed around his office. He did too. It was a mess. It was a miracle the shelves hadn't collapsed under the sheer weight of books and buried him underneath. The piles on the floor were a health and safety nightmare. The workbench he leaned on, well who knew what colour it was underneath all the papers covering it. The only area that wasn't covered in junk was the armchair in the back corner with a blanket thrown over it for when he never made it home. He made himself meet her eyes when she returned her gaze to him. "Do the initial checks, see what you think and report back to me. If you still feel the same then, then I'll try and find someone else to do the follow-up. Just see what you think."

***

He had taken the files home. They sat on the desk. He had been staring at them for about fifteen minutes as if waiting for them to burst into flames. He should have said no. She wouldn't really have fired him. Probably.

With a last gasp of desperation, he searched around the room for something to distract him but nothing did. Sighing, he leaned forward and opened the files. There was a varying amount of detail for each 'confessor'. On first glance, they looked as disparate as you could get: petty theft to assault with a deadly weapon, and a multi-million-pound fraudster thrown in for good measure. If you took the person demographics nothing jumped out there either – no pattern to age, race, gender, education, anything. The only thing that linked these people were they were criminals that had gotten away with it until they suddenly decided to confess their sins. They didn't just own up either, they spilled their guts; the fraudster even brought the paperwork with him to prove it all. It wasn't long before Eddie got sucked in.

He delved deep, scribbling notes on scraps of paper of things to check later. Some of the files were more complete than others. Time flowed around him, but Eddie was oblivious. By the time he heard a quiet rustling down by his feet, the table was covered in papers, twelve different tabs were open on his laptop and he had abandoned scrap paper for a section of wallpaper roll he'd stuck up on the wall. It hadn't taken long to fall back in old habits. The rustling drew his attention again and he looked down to see Twiglet snuffling round his chair leg.

"Sorry little guy, is it way past your dinnertime?" He leaned down and gave the brown rabbit a scratch on the top of his nose, earning him a small honking noise in reply. Eddie stood and wandered through to the kitchen, the rabbit weaving between his feet as he followed. He went through the motions as he got some food out for the rabbit and checked the water bottle by his open cage. All the while his brain was still turning over the information in his head, testing it different ways round to try and see a connection.

"What do you think?" He sat down on the floor, his back against the kitchen cupboard and watched the brown ball of fur hurriedly munch down his food. "Yeah, I'll eat in a minute. It's just, there's no connection. I haven't got enough information." Eddie ran his hand through his hair.

The habits might have come back easily but they felt rusty. He had no idea how to start trying to pinpoint the connection. And if he couldn't find that, how would he find Nemesis? "This is harder to do on your own." Twiglet lifted his nose from his bowl for a second and looked up at Eddie. "Sorry Twiglet, you mean well but you're not really coming up with ideas, are you?" Twiglet's nose twitched a few times before he went back to eating and ignoring his human. "No comment huh?" He paused, a thought lodging in his head. Surely he wouldn't be that lucky?

He went back over to his desk, leaving Twiglet to devour the nibbles. Pushing papers aside he found the details of the confession of the first man. He scanned the details and discarded it. The same with the second and third. The fourth file got thrown to the floor. But then he got to the fifth and smile crept across his face. DS Ventas was the officer in charge. Would that man ever make Inspector? Excitement made Eddie's hands clumsy as he fumbled his phone and started scrolling through his contacts trying to ignore the fear he'd deleted the number in a fit of bloody mindedness. His eyes fluttered closed for a second as he found the number. He paused, taking a second to take a deep breath. It was gone ten at night but chances were Ventas was still working. He hit dial without giving himself a chance to back down.

It rang. On the tenth ring, Eddie's hope faded. The number was probably old. It had been years. The ringing cut out.

"It's been a while since I had that sinking feeling." The voice on the phone was unmistakably Ventas'.

"Sinking feeling?"

"Things always get complicated when you appear Eddie. And usually bloody weird." The line went quiet for a moment. "I was beginning to think one of the weird things had finally caught up with you."

Eddie hesitated, not knowing what to say. When he was an agent their paths had crossed so regularly that he considered Ventas a friend. They'd often talked over work issues at the pub, albeit in a convoluted way as not to give away any true details. Ventas had thought Eddie was a spy, working for MI5 or something similar so he accepted Eddie's stories were full of redacted holes. Ventas would never have suspected the true nature of Eddie's job. And yet when everything had gone wrong, Eddie had forgotten him. Never called him back, never reached out. Not just to Ventas but a lot of people. Embarrassment threatened to render him speechless.

"So, what weirdness brings you to my door today?" Ventas carried on, not lingering too long on Eddie's silence.

"Westley."

"Ahh, of course. I knew there was more to that one." Ventas sounded amused. "Too late for the pub. You still at your old flat?"

"Yeah."

"I'll be there in twenty." Ventas hung up leaving Eddie feeling somewhat shellshocked. He shouldn't have been surprised. Ventas wouldn't have bought a fraudster like Westley confessing all like that and if he thought Eddie could finish the puzzle, he'd jump at the chance.

***

The man was an angel. When Eddie had opened the door, Ventas was standing there holding two pizza boxes. "Like you've eaten either," was all he said as he pushed past Eddie into the flat. They had made small talk while they ate the first few slices of pizza. Eddie had asked about Ventas' family; he'd been divorced a while when Eddie had last seen him but he had two grown up daughters that he was happy to talk about. The detective hadn't bothered to ask about Eddie's family, he knew he would get nothing, not that there was anything to tell. The conversation dried up fairly quickly. In days gone by, the pair of them would sit fairly happily in silence but Eddie couldn't help but notice the glances Ventas was giving him. It was only a matter of time before he started asking the awkward questions he'd been avoiding for six years.

Ventas opened his mouth and froze for a second. Eddie could see thoughts rushing round and decisions being made. "So why the interest in Westley?"

Eddie sunk in his chair a little as he realised his heart rate had sped up. "Guys like Westley don't just walk in and confess usually do they."

"Wish they did, make my life easier." Ventas reached across and grabbed another piece of pizza as Twiglet hopped over to his feet. He paused, gave the rabbit a scratch on the nose and smirked as the small creature hopped in circles round his feet. "He likes me."

"He's a poor judge of character," Eddie teased. Ventas sneered at him and waved for him to continue.

"Okay, so although it happens it's rare right?" Ventas nodded at his question. "So how come ten different people have come in to confess in the last month."

Ventas' hand froze in mid-air, the pizza dangling perilously as he processed what he had said. "I haven't heard of any."

"No pattern to the stations they came in to, or the types of crime they reported. Westley is probably the only one that would have been noticed by your office."

"So how come you spotted it?"

"My boss did. I've read reports on all of them and they all seemed spooked."

"Westley was that all right. Couldn't confess quick enough, kept looking at the door as if he was waiting for something to come and get him. Didn't calm down until he'd signed the confession." Ventas put the slice of pizza back in the box and leaned forward in the easy chair; the whole thing creaked in protest.

"One of the others said a woman confronted him and knew what he'd done."

"What and that scared them enough to confess? Sounds like my eldest daughter." He sat back and stretched his legs out in front of him. He propped his head up on his hand as he closed his eyes and thought. Eddie noticed his hair line was further back than it used to be although it still had its jet-black colouring. "So you thinking this woman has info on all of them? Approached them all? Ah well, maybe we should let her get on with it, I could do with a higher clean-up rate."

"Two of the last three had signs that they'd been roughed up. And the last one, they had to section him.

There had been no hint of any mental illness before he walked into that station."

"You saying this woman scared him insane?"

"Or whoever she's working with. There's more going on here." Eddie felt a pang of guilt about the lie but outsiders couldn't be told about the meteors or The Collective. Also, it would be a lot easier to sell a gang trying to blackmail criminals than a normal person wandering around as the embodiment of divine justice.

"Looks like I'll be talking to Westley tomorrow then." Ventas shook his head. "Told you things get weird around you Eddie."

***

"You were right." Ventas' voice was only just audible over the phone as wind whistled down the connection. Eddie glanced at the time; it wasn't even eleven yet. Ventas must have headed straight to the prison to talk to Westley. The sound of a car door slamming instantly cut off the outside noise.

"The woman?"

"Yeah, he went white when I asked about her. She really put the frighteners on him somehow."

"Did he say how?" Eddie leaned back in his chair and surveyed his workspace. The papers had multiplied even since Ventas had seen it. He'd stayed up researching everything he could about the confessors. With all the social media outlets that had sprung up, it wasn't hard to find them. Even six years before, this would have involved a whole lot more legwork.

"He reckons he saw her twice. The first time he'd only noticed her because she stopped walking and stared at him looking creepy. He assumed she was just some weirdo and forgot about her. Then two days later, he was on his way to work. There's a quiet section and there she was, waiting for him. He said she knew everything, all of the sordid details and laid it out for him. Went on about the suffering he'd caused and that he should atone for his sins."

"What and so he walked into the station? I mean if it's that easy, why do you always make it look so hard?"

"You can go off people you know." Ventas carried on despite the slight. "Apparently, as she spoke to him, he felt utter despair. She said if he didn't confess, he'd feel much worse next time they met. He reckoned she had some sort of poisonous gas or some other craziness. But it was making him feel so scared he went straight to the station and he didn't feel better until he was in the interview room." He paused, sighing audibly down the phone. "So, what do you reckon? Your spy contacts know about any hallucinogens that can make you feel despair and guilt."

"I'm not a spy," Eddie reiterated for the millionth time.

"Exactly what a spy would say."

This time it was Eddie's turn to sigh. "Fine, I'll get in touch with my spy contacts and let you know what they say."

"You do that. And while you're talking to them can you ask…"

"Thanks Ventas. Bye Ventas." Eddie hit the hang up button before the policeman could start to question him about all sorts of conspiracy theories.

He stared at the wall. In the centre, was one piece of paper with the word Nemesis written on it. The only thing branching off from it was the word woman. He knew nothing about her except she seemed to be able to see people's sins just by looking at them. He still didn't even know if she had an object or if she herself had been changed by a meteor. And just to make things better, the Starchildren were probably setting their assets to work finding her too, assets that all had special powers.

He heard a soft thump and turned to see Twiglet in the centre of his rug. The rabbit sat and stared up at him innocently before hopping to the corner of the rug, doing a little jump and turning mid-air before hopping back in the other direction. Eddie watched for several minutes as Twiglet ran rings round the rug, his large feet thudding as he landed each time. The rabbit broke from formation, hopped to Eddie's chair, ran a figure of eight round his feet and disappeared back to the rug. Before repeating the whole process three or four times.

"Am I in your way or something?" Eddie chuckled. The rabbit stopped at the sound of his voice and looked up at him, before promptly stretching out his back legs and flopping to one side, thoroughly exhausted. The rug now had a crisscross of lines tracing Twiglet's madcap route. Eddie froze. "He was walking to work." He looked down at Twiglet. "She just crossed paths with him at random. That's why there's no pattern. Unless..." Eddie spun back to his papers and pushed all of them to one side. Anticipation started to build as he hauled open one of his desk drawers. His hands dug furiously until he found the map of the city. It didn't take long to find Westley's bank. Eddie grabbed a green pen and drew circles round it. Then he dug through the pile of papers until he found the file on Westley. Flicking through, he scanned the details until his eyes landed on a home address. His finger ran across the paper of the map until he found that one too and circled it. Next, he went for the file of the man who'd told police about the woman, Blumen. He worked at a marketing agency. A quick internet search gave him the address, it was nowhere near the bank but he circled it anyway, this time in black. He paused when he saw the man's address, clearly marketing paid more than The Collective. With a jealous shake of the head, he marked the address, also in black. None of the circles were particularly close. Eddie scanned the area around Blumen's address and spotted the nearest tube station. Pulling up a tube map on his phone he found the best train to his work and where he would get off and circled this in black too.

He picked a third person out of the pack and scanned the details. They had also walked into a police station, this time, after they had left work. Eddie felt a smile spread across his face. No-one drove through central London if they could help it. He marked the new destinations on the map in red, also accounting for a tube trip. If he took the parts they would have to walk, this one passed through the same area as the other two. The two on the tube didn't take the same train or even use the same stations so Eddie discounted the tube being where she found her confessors. He traced possible routes for all three on foot, discounting some, jotting down street names of possible intersections.

"So, if she sees them all on their way to or from work, she has to pass through the same area as all of these too at the similar times. She must be on her way to work too right?" He looked back at Twiglet who was still laying stretched out on the rug, his head tilted to one side. "Let's assume yes for now. Okay there are possible areas they would all pass through." He pulled out the details of a fourth confessor. The route matched up but one of the possible areas would have meant back-tracking so he scratched that off the list. That left him with two possibilities. He pulled his phone out and typed out a message to Ventas. 'Did Westley tell you where he saw the woman?'

He waited. Ventas was probably still driving back from the prison. The minutes dragged out from an eternity. He began pacing round the flat, moving into the kitchen area to tidy before going back to check his phone screen just in case he'd missed the beep. Twiglet stayed out of his way, carefully observing him as he prowled. When the phone finally beeped, Eddie leapt across the space grabbing for his phone and fumbling it. He took a deep breath and composed himself as he opened the message. The first address was on his route to work when she confronted him, way out of the possible ranges when he was nearly there. But the second address was from the day before when she first spotted him. He hit his fist against the desk in triumph before grabbing a pen and underlining the first road on his shortlist. It made total sense. So many people passed by St Paul's churchyard every day. Eddie shook his head in disbelief; the only link between them had been the route to work. He clapped his hands together and stood up, suddenly full of purpose. It had been a while since he'd seen St Paul's.

***

His pocket started vibrating as he wandered behind St Paul's Cathedral. He moved over to the railing at the boundary and leaned against it, keeping his eyes scanning through the people darting here there and everywhere around him.

Glancing at the screen, he hit answer, "Director."

"Mr Soth, how goes it? I dropped by your office yesterday." The rest of the sentence was implied although she wasn't willing to voice it.

"I prefer to do casework at home, allows for freer thinking." He let his own nuance slip into his reply.

The Director laughed kindly. "Yes, I do remember running a mile when the old Director came looking for an update. But as I have you, do you have an update for me?"

"I'm pretty sure I've found the link between the subjects. But I'm not sure that's going to help me right now." He gazed around the area. He'd been locked in his office with his books for too long. Even living in the city hadn't stopped him from disconnecting. He rarely ventured beyond his home or work and had forgotten the sheer volume of people who moved through London every day. As he watched, he couldn't even begin to count the number of people in front of him. Most moved with purpose, their heads down as they found their best line through the crowds and went for it. Others dithered on their phones, talking loudly and ignoring everyone else around them, expecting all others to vacate the space ahead. Parents ushered their children along; delivery riders cycled up onto the path, narrowly avoiding pedestrians who glowered at them silently in only the way British people could.

And the noise. Despite the push to get traffic outside London, vehicles weaved between buses and bikes darted from A to B. Engines thrummed a beat that felt like the heartbeat of the city. A million voices all coalesced, rising and falling as people got closer and moved away. The screech of bike tyres rang out above all of them; the honk of a car horn; the bells of a nearby church. It threatened to overwhelm him. It took Eddie a second to realise the Director had been talking to him.

"Mr Soth?"

"Sorry, what was that?"

"What is the link?"

Eddie hesitated. He knew he was right but the thought of saying it out loud. Would she buy it? "I think this MAP," he kept his voice down and chose his words very carefully as passers-by glanced at him, "whether they have an object or a gift themselves, can see what these people have done. She doesn't have to do anything, she just sees it in them."

"That would be," The Director paused. Eddie held his breath. The last Director had had some questionable thoughts on using MAPs as assets but none more so than his own partner. He pushed back any thoughts of Damon and the sick feeling it gave him. "Well, debilitating if she has no control over it. If she's being flooded with all of that at all times…"

Eddie sighed in relief. "Yes, it could explain why the last few have been injured, it's got to be doing something to her psyche. The number of people she might see in one day. Anyway, that's the link. They all pass through St Paul's Churchyard on their way to work. She just sees them on her commute."

There was a few moments silence on the other end of the phone. "You're there now aren't you?"

"Possibly."

"I thought you were just looking into the files?"

Eddie's face screwed up. She was right. He'd kicked up a fuss about being dragged in and yet here he was, doing recon and searching for a potentially dangerous MAP. Alone. Unarmed. Realisation that he had nothing to defend himself with sent a cold shiver down his back.

"Mr Soth?"

"This is still research. Testing my theory. If I'm wrong then no problem, but if we send other resources out here and it's a wild goose chase," he tailed off. He wasn't even convincing himself.

"And if you're right?"

"Observe and record only." He glanced around at the crowds. It was heavily into morning rush hour now and the number of people was still increasing. "To be honest though, I'll be lucky if I find her. It's not surprising she found so many targets, this place is heaving."

"How do you intend on identifying her?"

"I've heard R and D are working on some kind of meteor signature detection device, any chance I can get my hands on a prototype?"

"Ha. We've only got the new photocopier in the archive because I hacked in to purchasing system and added one on when Agent Sorenson kitted out his department." The Director went quiet. "I never said that."

"Didn't hear a thing. Although next time you, don't, do that, if you could get me a new office chair, I'd be much obliged."

The Director laughed again. "Noted. And as for the prototype, I hear it's a little, well, explosive so we'll give it a miss. Now don't do anything silly Agent Soth. Remember protocol, and if you need back-up, call it in."

There was a click on the line; she hadn't waited for him to respond. Eddie shook his head, she was an interesting woman, and a very interesting Director. He paused as he slipped his phone back into his pocket; she'd called him agent and he hadn't even blinked. It was far too easy to slide back into his old skin, even if this time he was flying solo.

Getting restless, Eddie started to make circuits round the Cathedral. His brain was whirring, trying to instantly assess everyone that went by. Anyone walking and talking with someone else was immediately ignored. All the men were rejected, as was anyone under sixteen. It would have been wonderful if someone had invented an MA detection device, surely one of the boffins could have come up with something by now? Instead, it was down to experience and intuition. No two MAPs were the same. They may have similar abilities but they reacted in different ways so there was no hard and fast rule about picking someone out. Yes, if they were shooting sparklers from their fingertips it would probably be a good sign, or there was that one guy he'd chased that had an MAO that gave life to inanimate objects who had set a garden centre full of ornaments after him but usually there was no outward sign.

A red-headed woman was moving straight towards Eddie. He studied her a little more closely. She was alone, searching the crowd as well. She seemed to spot him watching and waved. His pace faltered but he instinctively looked behind him and saw another man waving back.

A quick glance at his watch told him he probably had about half an hour left before it was too late. She could have easily passed him already or gone on the other side of the Cathedral. It's not like she'd been picking out victims every day, so maybe there had been nothing to spot.

He'd known this was a long shot. It would probably take days. He pulled his black jacket a little tighter round him. He'd been fooled by the sunny sky: keen to welcome the first warmth of Spring, he just had an old t-shirt underneath that had seen better days and he was decidedly chilly. Perhaps, he should just come back tomorrow, with a jumper. He was seriously considering leaving when something triggered his adrenaline. His head snapped up; something had subconsciously caught his attention. He moved across to one side, leaning against a tree so he could stop and check everyone that had just passed him. What was it? He'd seen an old woman with a trolley. There was a Big Issue seller over by the railing, was it her? No, she was calling out for trade but not really looking at anyone in particular. A group of women, students perhaps were a little way away but nothing rang alarm bells there. Maybe he was too wound up, imagination running wild. He rubbed his face as he slumped back against the trunk of the tree a little more.

Then he spotted her.

There was a woman sat on the wall at the bottom of the railing. A book was in her hands but she wasn't reading it. Her eyes were firmly fixed on a man about forty in a suit talking loudly into his mobile. His elbow was stuck out wide but he didn't seem to care who got caught in the ribs. He looked like a piece of work but it was the look on the woman's face. Even from this distance, Eddie could sense the fury pouring off the woman. Her eyes tracked his every movement. Eddie held his breath as her gaze passed his position but she was too intent on her target. Quickly he pulled out his phone, his fingers acting by memory without looking at the screen as he called up the camera and aimed at the woman. He took a picture and quickly checked the image, not wanting to be too obvious that he was taking her picture.

When he looked up again, she had stood. She seemed to be hesitating, her book still in her hands. Her body seemed to lean forward and then pull back again, torn between two actions. Suddenly, something snapped and she was moving in the same direction as the man, ramming the book into her satchel without looking.

Eddie felt the same level of indecision. He should send the picture to the Director. Get back-up in and let them extract her. But by then she'd be gone. His feet were already moving before he finished the thought.

***

Tracking someone through Central London was not an easy feat. Thankfully, his target was so intent on not losing her own quarry that she didn't pay the blindest bit of attention to what was happening behind her. She wasn't quite what he had expected. She tottered down the paths in heels, clutching her bag strap to her chest as she weaved through the crowds, occasionally standing on tiptoes to look above the sea of heads. They had been moving only for fifteen minutes when they moved into a quieter area. Eddie dropped back a little bit even though she didn't seem to worry about getting too close. They headed through Clerkenwell and kept going north. The woman sped up a little, closing the gap between them. She reached up and started smoothing down her hair. Eddie frowned as he spotted a park ahead; it wasn't much but it was surrounded by trees on all sides which would give cover. Eddie sped up too as he realised she was going to confront him. A thought nagged at the back of his head as he felt for his phone in his pocket reassuringly. He was passed the point of calling for back-up now, perhaps he should start filming whatever was going to happen. His attention cycled between the woman ahead, the road and his phone, his head flicking from one to the other. He tucked the phone in his top jacket pocket, the top poking out with the camera facing ahead of him. The man entered the park and was out of sight. She started jogging as best she could in her heels and followed in behind him. Once she disappeared, Eddie moved quickly and tried to tuck in between the trees.

Immediately, he realised something was off. He kept out of sight, leaning beside a tree trunk, another one ahead obscuring him from view as the pair faced each other in the middle of the grassy area. She was shouting at him, her arms waving in all directions as he held his hands out to calm her down. He couldn't make out everything they said at this distance, so he edged to the next tree.

"There's nothing going on Mia." The man pleaded with her. Eddie started. He knew her. His brain froze for a second before the sinking despair crept through his gut. He had the wrong woman.

She was crying now, the fight out of her as she confronted who Eddie assumed must have been her lover. Mia was pointing behind the man's shoulder yelling about 'her'. The whole thing played out in his head. He'd said he was away, a meeting he couldn't get away from and yet there he was walking by the Cathedral. She had already been worried about the woman he'd been texting and here he was walking in the direction of her flat. She'd had to follow him to be sure. And Eddie, the supposed trained agent had tagged along like some creepy voyeur.

Eddie turned away from them, leaning against the tree as he let his head fall back with a thump. How did he not realise? She did not look like the harbinger of justice. She looked like a librarian; her yellow woollen coat finished just above her paisley skirt hemline. Mia was quieter now, her head hung low, nodding up and down as she sobbed.

The man put his arm around her muttering into her ear as he led her across the park, away from Eddie.

"At least I didn't call for back-up," he muttered to himself. He pushed himself off the tree and turned back the way he'd come.

"Perhaps you should have."

Eddie stumbled backwards as the woman stepped out from behind the other tree. She'd come out of nowhere, completely silent.

"Where the hell…" he looked around. How had she gotten the drop on him?

"Why were you following them?" She demanded, stepping forward. She blinked rapidly, her eyes struggling to stay still. Her dark hair was pulled back in a ponytail but it was escaping in tendrils reaching out. She moved into a shadowy patch, sun hidden behind the trees, leaving her face in darkness. Eddie squinted to get a better look at her. Red rings circled her eyes, she looked like she hadn't slept in days, if not weeks. Instinctively, Eddie moved backwards.

"I asked you a question." She lunged forward and shoved him hard in the chest. Eddie flew backwards, his feet leaving the ground. He fell to the Earth with a thump about five metres away. Eddie stayed on the floor as she came closer. There was no way she should have been able to push him that hard. She stepped out of the shade, cringing slightly at the sudden light. She was pale, like some blood-starved vampire. Eddie held his breath, she looked close to the edge and he knew from experience that was when people became most dangerous, yet he still didn't fully know what she could do. Perhaps back-up would have been a good idea after all.

"I thought she was going to hurt him."

The woman paused, her head tilted slightly as she considered his answer. "Why?"

"I thought she was you." He pulled himself backwards ever-so-slightly. "I know you've been getting bad people to confess."

"Bad people?" she sneered. "This isn't some fairy tale. They are sinners, evil. They have escaped justice. The balances are out and I have to put them right." Her eyes widened as she punctuated her words with a fist.

"The balances?"

She turned away from him, staring out into the park. Eddie considered moving but she seemed to realise. Her head snapped round and she fixed him with a glare. Her jaw flexed as she looked him up and down. Every muscle in her body was wound tight. Her shoulders were ratcheted up high with tension, making her jacket hang off her even more. She wore a tired navy jumper underneath but something shone on her wrist, barely visible at her sleeve cuff. Eddie's eyes travelled to her hands that looked red raw; a few cuts across the knuckles were visible. Probably from the beatings her last two sinners had received.

"Can't you see? The world has become hell. There is no balance anymore. The people I judge are evil but they are applauded for their actions. The drug dealer who runs the estate inflicting fear in the residents. The man who boasts down the pub about how he keeps his little woman in line. The woman in the office who gets all the promotions and bonuses by telling lies about co-workers, leading them to lose jobs, respect, or even their lives. The corporate thieves who fraudulently syphon money from their naive victims but live in penthouses and get on the covers of magazines. We celebrate the sinful and don't hold anyone to account."

"The world is a harsh place."

"It's getting worse. We're destroying ourselves for greed and self-service. People live in fear." Tears were streaming down her face now as she crouched down to lean closer. She lowered her voice. "World leaders lie and cheat and bend rules, doing everything for glory and nothing for the good of their people. There is no kindness in the world, no selflessness. No hope. I mean, you walk down the street and people won't even give you space on the path; they just glare at you for daring to exist." Her voice was becoming more and more strained. "I have to make everything better."

"By removing the sinners?"

She stood up and shook her head. "By showing there are consequences. It's physics isn't it." She chuckled, a cruel facsimile of a smile creasing her face. "For every action there is an equal and opposite reaction. That's me." She stood in front of him, her arms hanging limply by her sides. Eddie saw an opportunity and slowly stood up. She tensed making him slow his movements even more, starting to speak to distract her.

"Why do you have to do it?"

She froze, a wave of hopelessness twisted her features. Her whole body looked about to collapse. "I see it all. All the darkness in everyone. All their sin."

"What about the good? Do you see that?"

"There is no goodness anymore. Only an absence of dark," she snapped.

"What about you? Is what you're doing good?"

She swayed slightly; her gaze un-focusing and going distant. "It's a necessary evil. I don't enjoy it."

"It's getting harder isn't it?" Eddie stepped closer, his hands raised and empty. "You just made them confess to start with but now, now you're carrying out punishment too aren't you."

"I feel it all." She turned and stared straight into his eyes. "I see what they have done and I feel the pain they cause. So, I make them feel it. Equal and opposite reaction. The harder they sin, the stronger I punish. Sometimes that isn't enough. Not now." Eddie nodded wanting to keep her calm while he desperately tried to figure out what to do.

A sudden cold feeling filled his stomach as a thought crossed his mind. "Why did you follow me? Are you going to punish me?"

She frowned looking confused. "There isn't a darkness on you." She narrowed her eyes, as if looking deeper. Eddie could see pain etch itself on her expression. "You may feel guilty but there was nothing you could have done. You did not enable him; you were just naive."

Eddie's legs threatened to give way beneath him. In his moment of distraction, she caught sight of something over his shoulder. He turned to see what she had spotted but he saw nothing. When he looked back, she was gone.

***

The room was dark and the light switches were too far away. Eddie sat on his sofa, his legs up across the seats and Twiglet nestled on his lap. Absently, Eddie's fingers ran down the rabbit's back as he stretched out along Eddie's leg. There was a spot on the far wall, just above all his notes that he was intently staring at. Not that he could see anything there in this light.

After his encounter with Nemesis, Eddie had wandered London for a few hours not going anywhere in particular. He just wanted to see the people. He'd cut himself off from the world for so long, he barely recognised it. Part of him was terrified she was right and everything had become dark and soulless since he'd last walked amongst others. He could see what she meant. It was so easy to see the bad, the menacing, the underlying threat in different situations. A group of youths had been hanging around one street, yelling at anyone they didn't like the look of. No-one said anything for fear of reprisals, they just lowered their heads and walked a little faster. A few years ago, he would have been chasing after Damon who would have confronted them, shown them the error of their ways, probably using an armlock, and sent them on their merry way. How was he to know Damon had been hiding his dark side from him.

Betrayal coursed through him again as fresh as the day he had learned the truth. It had twisted him, made him hide and refuse to trust. No wonder Nemesis was in the state she was in; if all she could see was the bad then it had to be driving her insane. The band around her wrist had to be the answer. Somehow, she had come across that bracelet and that was what was influencing her. If he could just get it from her, then maybe she would be okay.

An intense light shattered his dark sanctuary making Twiglet shuffle nervously. He stroked Twiglet's nose and made soothing noises as he reached for the offending phone sat by his side on the cushion. He already ignored three calls from the Director. His finger headed straight for reject when he registered the name on the screen.

"Ventas?"

"No Frankenstein. Who else?"

"Sorry, just wasn't expecting a call." Eddie rubbed his eyes with his free hand, stifling a yawn.

"Never call when they expect it Eddie, gives them time to get their story straight."

"What story do you think I'm getting straight?"

"Well, you call asking where Westley saw his angel of justice and you definitely sounded like you were on to something. I know better than to wait for you to tell me what's going on."

"Look I can't..." Eddie began.

"I know you can't give me details, above my jurisdiction all that Official Secrets crap but come on."

Eddie's head dropped. No-one outside The Collective was authorised to be read in on investigations, which made things very difficult at times although he understood the need for secrecy. But Ventas helped him out so often and had caught some flak for it on more than one occasion, he felt like he owed the man. Perhaps when this was over, he needed to have a discussion with the Director about the sense of having a police contact who knew what was what. "Look we were right: one woman knows about their illicit activities and is threatening them into confessing."

"So, who's she working for? A gang?"

"Solo operation."

"One woman? The last guy was a big bloke and he had the crap kicked out of him."

"One woman."

"What now?"

Eddie sighed, thinking. That was the question wasn't it. "I'm going to try and bring her in. To my people."

"Just you?"

"She's, it's not straight forward. She's as much a victim here, she needs help."

Ventas stayed quiet for quite a while. Eddie was beginning to think he'd hung up when he finally spoke up. "I always feel like the thick kid in class when I talk to you. I know there's so much more going on but I haven't got the foggiest. You and Damon." Eddie's eyes snapped shut. "Poor guy." Silence. "Eddie?"

Breaths started to come in ragged waves as he came to a decision. "He wasn't."

"Sorry?"

"Poor guy. He doesn't deserve your sympathy" He trailed off, not knowing what to say. Ventas knew better than to push and stayed silent. "I should have seen it earlier. I guess I didn't want to but…"

"Coopers Bank?"

Eddie shut his eyes and the pictures came flooding back. Ventas thought he was on the trail of a bomber, but The Collective knew the bomber was also the bomb. He could create exothermic reactions on a massive scale and walk away unharmed. They worked together on tracking him down, even though Ventas knew at the last-minute Eddie and Damon would claim national security and spirit him away. It had happened plenty of times but the policeman never seemed to mind. It was all about protecting the public and catching the bad guys, he wasn't bothered about credit.

Then came the day they got the call their bomber was in Coopers Bank with a whole load of hostages. Eddie had deferred to the response units at the time, they could sweep up the bomber after the hostages were safe but it all went wrong. The building went up in flames, killing dozens. And it was only then he realised he hadn't seen his partner in a while. He'd raced inside, terrified he'd tried to do something heroic and stupid. Smoke had clawed at his throat, dragging the air from his lungs as he searched the safer parts of the building. Damon had been in the vault, gas mask on his face, going through the deposit boxes. He'd orchestrated the whole thing with the bomber so he could get into the vault and retrieve an MAO that he knew had been in there, so he could sell it to the highest bidder. When the bomber had come back and seen Eddie, he'd assumed a set up and went to turn Eddie into a walking Guy Fawkes. Damon had pushed him out of the way. Nothing Eddie could have done would have saved him even though he tried. Even in that moment, he thought there would have been some explanation. Only when he'd gone through his flat and found his hidden accounts and storehouses did he fully realise who his partner had been. He wasn't even a double agent working for Starchildren. He could have understood that. But Damon just worked for the highest bidder. All the failed cases and near misses they had had over the years appeared in his books. Every time Eddie had slunk off to lick his wounds, Damon snuck in the opposite direction to make a profit.

The words were hard at first but soon they came tumbling from him in a torrent. Removing the more sensitive details, he explained the level of Damon's betrayal to Ventas. Including his role in the Coopers Bank tragedy that had put Ventas square in the public's targets for their anger.

When he finally finished, he was out of breath.

"Son of a…"

"I'm so sorry."

"Not you Eddie. Although, I assume this is the reason I haven't heard from you in six years?"

"I should have seen it. Those people in the bank, your career."

"My career? Coopers Bank didn't stall my career, I did that. I mean yeah that didn't help but I was never political enough." He sighed. Eddie heard the clink of a glass as it was put down on a table. "You couldn't have known; he was too good. He fooled us all. And you've been sitting on this for six years, letting this fester. Let me guess, you've been babysitting a desk ever since."

"This is my first case since then."

"Well then. You better not mess it up. What's your next move?"

"I don't know. She got the drop on me this morning, she followed me to…" he tailed off.

"You're doing that thing again Eddie."

"She wasn't following me. When I asked her why she trailed me, she looked confused. I just happened to be there so she confronted me." He thought it through and smiled. "She tails her targets before approaching them, finds a good place to appear, where there's not going to be anyone else around. Damn, my first instinct wasn't as far off as I thought. I had the wrong woman, but I had the right man."

***

The weather wasn't on Eddie's side this time. He pressed himself against the tree as people hurried past shielded from his view by their umbrellas. It was that pervasive kind of rain, not heavy drops, but as soon as you went out in it you felt drenched. The puddles only seemed to amplify the sound of the cars on the road, which was heavier today as no-one was walking in this if they could help it. It did mean the crowds around St Paul's were lighter but Eddie was having trouble getting a good look at anyone. He was certain he hadn't seen Nemesis but whether her target had been through was another question. As he stood hunkered under the tree, strategies and possibilities kept running through his head. Again, he found himself wondering whether Nemesis would change her plan after their confrontation yesterday, change her target, but he doubted it. She'd had a crazed look in her eye when she was talking about the sinners. Eddie doubted she was able to walk away from punishing. The bracelet was definitely a strong influence but Nemesis' mind was not designed for it. Not all humans could handle MAOs but putting something like that on someone who was predisposed to seeing the negative was dangerous. For some reason, Nemesis was unable to see the balance, her vision was completely skewed and it was twisting her brain. If Eddie didn't stop her soon, not only would she be judge and jury but he feared she would turn executioner.

Another suited figure hurried past. Eddie craned his neck to peer under the canopy of his umbrella but it wasn't him. Time was getting on; it was already well past the time he seen them yesterday. Perhaps it was tomorrow. Perhaps Nemesis didn't work on Thursdays.

A cold sensation ran down his back as he realised he'd been an idiot for the second time in two days. Nemesis stalked her targets, then found a place on the route to confront them on their commuting route. The man yesterday had been on his way to meet someone, not a place of work, it was not his daily routine. The chances that Nemesis had picked him out and waited for his next appearance were slim. Which meant…

He pulled his phone out and clicked through to the images, shielding the phone's screen from the rain with one hand. He zoomed in on Mia, the one he'd originally thought he was looking for. She'd been sitting on the wall reading, waiting to go somewhere when she'd seen her lover unexpectedly. Mia was the one Nemesis had been watching.

He zoomed in, mentally cursing his stupidity. He was too rusty. He hadn't been on the lookout for her this morning, she would have headed straight into work.

Nemesis could have already been on her tail. He searched the picture for clues, he had to find where she was headed but she was dressed like so many others on their way to work in London: very formal office wear, high heels, no visible lanyard or alike. He checked the second image. She was starting to stand, and her coat had flapped to one side revealing a suit jacket underneath. Eddie's finger hovered over the screen when he spotted a silver rectangular badge pinned to her. There was something familiar about that badge. He moved out from under the tree and started searching the surroundings. You didn't sit and read a book unless you were close to your destination and had spare time. She had to be nearby. He started to jog forward, head whipping side to side as he looked for potential locations. There were a lot of cafes and eateries but he was certain it wasn't one of those. He passed the Temple Bar Gate and had to tear his eyes away from the reminder of London's history as he carried on round the side of the Cathedral. Then he pulled up short as his gaze landed on the building on the corner opposite: The Temple Hotel. Certain he was on the right track, he crossed over and moved to the glass, searching for a nearby employee. A man walked across the lobby and there it was, a badge identical to Mia's.

Eddie took a step back and ran his hand through his damp hair. Sucking in a deep breath, he held it and bit his bottom lip as thoughts rushed through his mind. What the hell should he do now? Not only was he rusty, but he was on his own. As an agent, he'd always had Damon nearby, someone to bounce ideas off, someone to watch his back.

His phone was still in his hand. His fingers started scrolling through before his mind registered what he was doing.

"Eddie?"

For a few moments, Eddie said nothing, his pulse was thumping in his head and he could barely string two thoughts together.

"Eddie what's wrong?"

"I think I know our girl's next target."

"Great, I'll alert nearby station's someone's about to confess," he chuckled but Eddie didn't share his good humour.

"Ventas, I think she's unravelling. She beat the last two to a pulp, who knows what she'll do next time?"

"Okay," Ventas spoke slowly, all merriment gone from his voice. "So, we need to intervene. Do you know where they are?"

"No. I've figured out where the target works, The Temple Hotel but that's all I have." He felt hopeless.

"Right, do you know if the target got to work this morning? She might be in there, on shift, completely oblivious."

Eddie closed his eyes and took a deep breath. Ventas was right. One step at a time. "Yeah, you're right. I'll go in and check."

"Look Eddie, I'm going to come down there, I'll leave right now. Should be twenty minutes tops. Don't do anything stupid and keep me in the loop, so I know where you are when you inevitably do something stupid."

Eddie was about to argue, his mouth hung open but he closed it again. "Okay." Ventas didn't say anything else, he simply hung up, probably already halfway out of his station.

"Okay Eddie, just find out if she's in there." He straightened his shirt and jacket, wishing he'd decided to put something a little smarter on. Places like this were all about class and image and right now he was not presenting one that was going to engender a sense of helpfulness in the staff. Marching to the door, he tried to summon up his courage. He'd done this a million times. His phone went back in his pocket and he traded it for his wallet, fishing in a long-forgotten section for his ID. It had him down as MI5. The Collective were nothing to do with the UK secret service but it did help get in the doors. There was some kind of understanding between the organisations that they would allow Collective agents to, trade under their banner so to speak, if they also took on any cases the Spooks threw their way and wanted to never think about again. Even MI5 didn't know what their true remit was but some high up Government officials knew and greased the wheels of cooperation.

He took in as much of the lobby as he could as he stepped into the revolving doors. There weren't many people around, a few coming from a door to the right. As he was ejected from the door into the lobby, the sounds of plates drifted from the same direction. Stragglers from breakfast then. A lift stood directly ahead of him and a set of desks to his left where the reception staff stood. A few comfy chairs were dotted around with low coffee tables, stacked with today's papers.

Thankfully, this time of the morning meant the front desk wasn't busy. There were two women stood at their respective stations. The younger one was already flashing him the smile; it would have been the obvious move to go to her and charm her into giving information but not the most effective. The woman on the second desk was older and had a sharper eye, definitely more seniority and not used to taking nonsense. One hint of him flirting with the younger woman and she would have stepped in and made life hard. Eddie smiled back at the younger woman before heading to the other desk; he ignored the flash of confusion that crossed her face.

"How can I help you, Sir?" Her voice was smooth and calming, years of perfecting the tone needed to placate bolshy businessmen everywhere. But the tiredness was lying underneath, if you looked closely enough you could see the effort it was taking to pin the façade in place. Not that many people through here looked closely enough, that's what they paid extra for.

"I'm hoping so."

The woman sensed something odd was occurring and imperceptibly shifted. She cast a quick glance at her colleague, her eyebrow raising when she realised she had also been free. Her attention was immediately back on Eddie as she tilted her head in question, her dark hair staying perfectly still in the neatly pinned bun.

Eddie pulled his faux MI5 credentials and slid them on the desk in front of her so only she could see. Her eyes widened for a split second but she did take a second to look carefully, not taking them on face value. Eddie smiled; he knew he'd made the right choice. "I believe a member of staff of yours may be a witness and have vital information I need. It is imperative I speak with her as soon as possible."

Andrea, assuming the name on her badge was her real one, paused for a moment, taking it all in. She looked down at the ID again.

"Police are also on their way but time is of the essence. You can ring City of London police and ask for DS Ventas, he's on his way here right now to assist." That seemed to do the trick, she straightened up and looked him directly in the eye.

"Who are you looking for?"

"I'm afraid I only have a first name. She starts work around now every day, Mia?"

"Mia Renfro." Her tone said it all. Eddie raised an eyebrow. "She's not the steadiest member of staff here." She gave a small shake of the head before turning her attention to the computer screen down to her left. "Let me just check the staff booking in system. Yes, she's in already. She should be setting up for a conference meeting in the Westminster Room on floor one. I can get someone to escort you?"

"That won't be necessary. But if you could inform DS Ventas when he arrives?" Eddie picked up his ID and tucked it away as he stepped back.

"Of course. Take the lift to floor one the Westminster Room will be the furthest room to your right."

Eddie was already moving to the lift when he spotted the stairs off to the right. The red display said the lift was still on floor five and Eddie was feeling impatient. He took the stairs two at a time, feeling the adrenaline starting to kick in. As the door for floor one appeared, he leaned into it with his shoulder barely losing any momentum. The corridor was empty as he turned to the right and followed it down. The walls were painted a burnt yellow colour that Eddie was sure was supposed to be soothing but it just served to increase his stress levels. He turned and saw the end of the corridor, a pine wooden door at the end loomed up at him, a gold plaque with Westminster written on it catching the light and reflecting off at odd angles.

Eddie bounced hard into it as he tried the handle, expecting it to give as he connected. He tried again, twisting the handle properly this time but still it wouldn't move. There was no obvious lock on the door, it had to have been barricaded. Nemesis was here.

Leaning against the door, Eddie held his breath as he listened. A faint whimpering reached him punctuated every now and then by a voice, one twisted and seething with anger. It barely sounded like the woman he had seen yesterday; it was almost like she was possessed. He stepped away from the door and moved back along the corridor to the next room. He tentatively pushed it open and craned his head round the corner. It was empty. He pushed the door wider and moved inside looking to the wall to his right. Eddie gave a silent prayer of thanks to whoever was listening and went straight to the adjoining wall. It was one of those folding walls which could move to allow you to use the space as one big room.

There were clips at the bottom and top of the wall holding it in place. Eddie grabbed a nearby chair and moved as quietly as possible to the wall. Climbing up he grabbed the clip and braced his arms, trying to unclip it without it giving himself away. The metal gave a click as it unlatched. He paused, unmoving as he waited. Nothing happened. He hopped down and did the same to the clip at the bottom. Once he started to move the wall, Nemesis was bound to notice. Gritting his teeth, he edged the wall forward, only a crack for him to spy through. The angle was too narrow and he could barely see a thing. The noises were louder now. Mia was sobbing, letting out wails of pain as Nemesis went for her. It was hard to understand what she was saying, her words were growls, hissing as she spoke. She was no longer the embodiment of justice – she was pure vengeance and Eddie didn't fancy Mia's chances of getting out of this alive

The sensible thing would have been to wait for Ventas but as Mia screamed out again, Eddie knew he didn't have time. He closed his eyes, summoning up any courage he had. He pushed on the wall, opening it just enough for him to squeeze through and pulled it shut behind him. He didn't want Nemesis to have an easy escape route.

"Help me." Mia started shouting for him immediately, trying to crawl forward but Nemesis grabbed her by the collar and swung her backwards, making her slide and smash into the short cupboard barricading the door. Mia cried out and flopped forward into a heap, her body heaving with sobs. She looked a mess; blood was caked along her hairline and bruises were already starting to darken her face. But it was nothing compared to Nemesis.

Her hair was down, static making it stick out at angles as it partially obscured her face. Eddie wasn't sure what made her look worse, the ghostly pallor of her skin to the black circles around her eyes; she looked like a ghoul. Her jacket was buttoned up wrong, and all her clothes seemed to hang off her. Her eyes never blinked; they were stuck wide open as she stared at him in fury. She glanced back to Mia, clearly wanting to get back to her justice but a part of her mind registered Eddie would be a problem. She stomped forward, resembling some kind of creature from a zombie game, her body not fully responding as it should. He had to get that thing off her.

"I won't let you stop me." Her voice had lost the growl she used when talking to Mia. Now it shook, vibrating as if she was struggling for control. "She needs to be punished."

"Ok," Eddie held his hands up defensively. "Why?"

"I didn't do anything," Mia yelled, throwing her head up defiantly. Nemesis moved back across the room with unnatural speed and struck Mia under the jaw, her head rebounding back as she slumped backwards. Eddie grimaced and tried to close the gap. Nemesis wheeled round, eyes blazing as she noticed his approach. Eddie skidded to a halt.

"I'm listening to you, not her." He kept his hands up. "You tell me what she did. What did you see?"

"She was going to do it again." She started to turn back to Mia.

"What again? Tell me." He stepped forward, pulling her attention back to him.

"She's so jealous. It consumes her, fills her every thought. She can't bear the thought of him betraying her. Can you?" She turned to Mia and bent down, pushing her face into hers.

"I don't know what you mean."

"Stop lying." The windows rattled as her anger amplified her shout. "You have to face up to what you did. You must feel remorse."

"She's mad. Please help me." Mia peered up at Eddie imploring him. If she would just play along, perhaps he could buy them time.

"You feel nothing." Nemesis hissed in her face as she placed her hands on her cheeks. "Do you want to know what she felt?" The fight instantly drained out of Mia, as her face was contorted with fear. Eddie was frozen on the spot; a chill electrified his spine, an echo of the fear Mia was being subjected to. He stepped backwards trying to get out of its range, as he started to gasp for air just as Mia was now doing. The further he moved back, the more the pressure eased on his chest. But Mia was clawing at her throat now, unable to breathe.

"Stop." Eddie's voice came out weakly. "Stop it." He managed to shout this time, his own fear adding to his forcefulness. It seemed to break through to Nemesis and she let go of Mia's face, turning to him, confusion on her face.

"I'm sorry." She averted her eyes and shuffled backwards slightly. Eddie took a few deep breaths. "But she needed to feel it. Maybe now she will be sorry." Mia was lying on the floor, half choking on her own sobs as she hungrily pulled air into her lungs. Eddie moved closer to her; Nemesis watched him but allowed him to approach. He bent down next to the pair and looked at Mia. Unless Ventas got here soon, there was only one way he could see of helping Mia.

"Mia," he said softly. She looked up at him, her face swollen from the beating and crying. "You need to tell me what you did?" Her denial hovered on her tongue. He could see she was about to protest again but she hesitated.

"I didn't…" Nemesis' body flinched but Eddie held up his hand to stop her.

"Mia." He put as much forcefulness in his voice as he could. "You did. Just tell me what it was." He had a horrible feeling he already knew what she was hiding, but Nemesis needed her to say it. He watched the micro-expressions cross Mia's face as the thoughts rushed through her head. Decisions were made in instants and then changed but then her face turned hard and Eddie felt his stomach drop.

"Whatever happened to her, she deserved it. Just like you do." She turned and hissed at Nemesis. Eddie's eyes couldn't keep up as Nemesis moved like lightning. Before he knew it, Nemesis was stood up, Mia hanging limply in the air as she dangled in Nemesis' grip by the throat.

"She hadn't even done anything." Nemesis was screaming into her face. "Your jealously made her into the villain, running off with your boyfriend behind your back but it was all in your head and you killed her. You wrapped your hands round her throat and you choked the life out of her, watching it leave her eyes just like yours is."

Instinct kicked in and Eddie launched upwards, breaking Nemesis' grip on Mia and putting himself between them.

"No." Nemesis growled trying to move past Eddie. He held fast. She grabbed his collar and tossed him to one side but Eddie grabbed on to her wrists and she tumbled down with him. Her fist collided with his temple and he almost went out like a light but he wrestled for control of her wrists again. Her strength was inhuman, the bracelet must have been boosting her. "She needs to pay."

"She will." Eddie spoke through gritted teeth as he struggled to keep hold of her. "I have a friend, a policeman."

"That's not enough. An eye for an eye."

Eddie's training kicked in and he managed to sit up and wrap his arms around her, pining her back to him in a way that meant she had no leverage. He wouldn't be able to hold her for long, but every second counted.

"What's your name?" The question caught her off guard and for a second she stopped struggling. They were sat on the floor facing the windows and he could see their reflections clearly. She frowned. "Do you remember your name?" Her breath caught in her throat. Eddie could see her eyes frantically flick from side to side in panic as she searched her mind. The MAO had completely twisted her mind. He had heard of objects this strong but he had never encountered one. She was never going to be able to fight the urges of it.

"Alice." She let out a sigh as the name finally came forth.

"Hi Alice. I'm Eddie."

"I see everything. I see all the bad things." Her head turned to Mia and her body stiffened again as she started to struggle. "I see her sin and I must punish it."

"Why you Alice?" Eddie squeezed tighter.

"It's the only way to make it go away. I see it until they make amends." Her head dropped. "It won't go away."

"What about the good things? You say you want justice, but can you see a person's good deeds?"

"There is no good in the world." There was no anger in her voice now, only hopelessness.

"What about me? You said you couldn't see any sin. Do you see nothing in me?" Her head rose slowly and Eddie instantly began to regret his word. What if she did see a sin after all? He'd done some questionable things as an agent, lied, cheated, hurt people. She stared at the reflection of the two of them, her head tilted as she focused.

"There is nothing. I just see..." her head jerked up before she leaned forward. Eddie held his breath, readying himself for her to start fighting again. "Lola?" That was not what he was expecting. "You saved her."

Alice leaned forward, as if trying to study something more closely. "She was different, like me. You took her somewhere safe, and now she helps people."

"I did," Eddie nodded, smiling at the memory of the little girl. She would probably be eighteen or more now. "So there is good in the world then?"

Alice let out a wail.

"What is it? Alice?"

She was still staring into the reflection. "It's a monster." Eddie hesitated, unsure what she'd seen now. "Nemesis? They call me Nemesis? I was just trying to rid the world of bad things." She slumped into his grip, shaking. "I need to repent."

"Yes you do, you mad bitch." Mia had found her voice again and had managed to stand up. Instinct took over Alice, Nemesis starting to take control again and she ripped free of Eddie's grip and faced off with Mia. Both women stood, staring at each other. Fear had reappeared on Mia's face, her bravado all drained away. But Nemesis wasn't advancing.

"Alice," Eddie stood up. She didn't look at him but a twitch of her head let him know she was listening. "You couldn't control what you've done, it's not your fault. But you can stop now."

"The darkness."

"Let me help you. Like I did Lola."

The door rattled as someone tried to get in. All three of them flinched, but no-one broke the stand-off. Ventas needed to work on his timing.

"Alice?"

Seconds dragged on. The wall behind them started to rattle as Ventas figured out the same thing as Eddie.

"Police." Ventas yelled as he entered, followed by two other men.

"Help me," Mia yelled and started to stumble forward.

"You stay there!" Eddie pointed a finger at Mia before Nemesis could respond.

"Eddie?" Ventas asked, the worry evident in his voice. Thankfully, he stayed where he was.

"It's all good. Isn't it Alice? You're going to let me help you?"

Alice tore her eyes from Mia and stared at him. He could almost feel her searching his soul, testing if he was being truthful. And then he saw something unexpected. A glimmer of hope in her eyes. She nodded. The gesture was imperceptible but there. Eddie smiled and let out a breath he hadn't known he was holding.

"Okay. First thing's first. That bracelet. Can I take it?" Alice looked down at the golden band, taking an instinctive step back from Eddie as her two natures warred within her. Eventually, she held her arm out to him. He reached out slowly and caught his fingers round it. He hissed in shock and at the heat but held fast as he pulled it over her hand. Hurriedly he pulled off his jacket and wrapped the MAO in it, fighting the urge to drop the burning metal. His fingertips were red from the contact.

"I still see it." Alice's voice was desperate. She was looking at Mia.

"It's okay, it's okay Alice. It will take time, but I'll help."

"What about me?" Mia's voice pierced Eddie's ears and he felt a surge of disgust at the woman.

"Oh yes," he smiled at her. "Did you happen to see where she put the body Alice?"

"I did." A small smile twitched the corner of Alice's mouth.

"Ventas, you might want to arrest Miss Renfro for murder."

"What?" Mia spun round but remembered the barricade.

"You heard the man. Read her, her rights." The two officers responded to their superior and marched over to Mia, already cautioning her. Ventas wandered over to Eddie, looking between him and Alice.

"And do we have our vigilante?"

"No." Eddie replied. Alice's eyes widened. "Alice is a victim too. But I think you'll find your random confessions stop." Eddie turned to Ventas who was eyeing him suspiciously.

"Okay…"

Eddie wondered if he was going to argue. It had been six years since they'd worked together and following Eddie and Damon's advice blindly hadn't done the policeman much good last time. "Murder you say? No others you can throw my way before Little Miss Justice hangs up her scales of truth are there?"

"Ventas," Eddie warned.

Ventas stepped back his hands up in defeat. "Told you. Always gets weird when you turn up Eddie." He started to follow the officers who were leading a struggling Mia back to the other room. "More interesting though. Definitely interesting. Glad you're back." Eddie opened his mouth to argue but stopped. Was he back? He looked back at Alice who was staring up at him, a child-like lost expression on her pale features. That decision could wait. He had things to do first.

***

Eddie closed the door to Alice's room. Once Ventas had carted Mia away, much to Andrea the receptionist's delight, Eddie had escorted Alice out of the hotel and straight into a taxi. The fare had been astronomical, but he had gotten a receipt. The Director might not like it but there was no way he was subjecting Alice to a walk back to his flat before getting his car.

He'd been here a couple of times before. It was a small private hospital on the outskirts of London that had a proper name but Collective agents only ever referred to it as Foster's. There was a running joke that whoever clocked up the most visits would have the hospital renamed after them but no-one was ever likely to come close to the number of stays Agent Foster had clocked up in the sixties and seventies. Eddie wasn't sure how the set-up worked but there were always beds free here if agents needed them, for whatever reason. Alice wouldn't be up to facing the real world for a while and Foster's had some good therapists, who knew the sorts of things people in the Collective came up against. If anyone could help Alice with her rehab, it would be these people.

"Doesn't really look like the avenging angel sort."

Eddie started. He hadn't heard anyone come up behind him, he'd let his mind drift as he stared through the window in the door to check Alice was getting to sleep. Eddie composed himself for a second before turning.

"Director," he greeted. "She's lost the berserker edge the bracelet gave her that's for sure."

"Which is where?"

"Looked up in the safe as soon as I got here." Fosters was used to the sorts of requests made by the Collective. There must have been some substantial donations over the years. Not only was there a safe only agents had access to, but there was a secure server room on site where they could tap into the comms network and communicate with head office securely.

"How is she?" The Director peered over Eddie's shoulder to the window but made no move to approach.

"It messed with her, a lot. It's going to take some time to sort through what she did and saw and come to terms with it. The visions haven't gone yet either, they have lessened but it wasn't instant."

"Interesting. This is a strong one isn't it." She frowned. Her eyes looking off into the distance. He could guess what was going on in her mind. Was the strength of the object a coincidence or something to do with an increase in meteor activity?

"Did she tell you where she got it?"

Eddie snorted. "She works at the Old Bailey as a clerk. She was working late one night and it smashed through the window right on to her desk."

"She works at the Criminal Court? Huh." The Director rubbed the back of her neck. "So, did it seek out a place that suited it's aims or did it take on the character of the building?" Sighing, she shook her head and started to wander away. Eddie took his cue to follow. He'd check on Alice again later. "No wonder she could only focus on the negative, it's all she sees every day, poor girl. Anyway, at least we can help her. I'll get some people so liaise with her work, check on her home make sure everything's in order for when she's up and about. Will you take care of the confidentiality agreements on her end?" Eddie stifled a knowing laugh; six years in the history books and he'd forgotten about half of the paperwork involved in the job. Primary aim number one - make sure Joe Public doesn't know what's going on. He swallowed his misgivings and nodded.

"Good. And good work, this could have gone very differently. Would be good to have you back on the roster." She gave a sidelong glance which he tried his best at ignoring. The question had been gnawing at the back of his mind since he got Alice safely into the hospital and he started to relax. "Well, it isn't an instant no so I'll take that as a positive sign. Have a think. Take a few days off, see me on Wednesday and tell me what you decide."

"I thought we were stretched?"

"You're right, make it Tuesday," she grinned. "I'll get the MAO and take it back to headquarters."

"Be careful, I'm not sure what's in it but it gets incredibly hot. I've wrapped it up and I found a box to keep it in for now. I'd leave it in there unless you have protective gloves."

"Noted. I don't fancy getting too close. Can you imagine all the sins you see at headquarters?" She grimaced and held out her hand. Eddie reached out and took the handshake. His fingers brushed her palm as a wave of black washed over his vision.

Flickers of images danced before his eyes. The Director shouting, but she was younger, not in the suit. The world washed away and was replaced. It was her again, a gun pointed at a man with red eyes. He was surrounded by night and moved forward. The echo of the gun going off shook the image free and it switched again. Now he was in a room with her, there was no-one else present. She looked torn as her hand hovered over papers. A tear ran down her cheek as she wrote something on one of the pages, inserted in the centre of the bundle and replaced it in the drawer. A man walked in and said something Eddie couldn't make out, she looked startled and moved away from the man's desk. The world shifted again. A car was overturned, she was reaching inside. Flames licked up from the underside of the chassis, any minute the whole thing would become a fire ball. The Director inched backwards pulling a man from the wreckage. Images moved again, cycling through a million different events, some good some bad. A whole cascade of emotions assaulted Eddie as he saw her actions played out before him like a showreel.

"Actually, let's stick to Wednesday, you look awful."

The words pulled Eddie back to reality. The Director let go of his hand and raised a questioning eyebrow.

"Get an early night Agent Soth, and maybe a few drinks first." She shook her head and wandered off down the corridor leaving Eddie staring down at his reddened fingers. Angry lines still scored across his finger-pads from where he had touched the bracelet.

"Oh," Eddie mumbled to himself. "So that's what happened in Ghent."

Eden And The Starcat

by James Pyles

2004, Detroit, Financial District, 1132 Hours

Thirty seconds after slamming shut the trunk of his old junker Chevy containing the contraband server, three black sedans suddenly pulled up in front of the high rise. The twenty-six-year-old was just entering the building at the end of his supposed cigarette break when car doors rapidly swung open and vomited forth a horde of men and women in dark suits and sunglasses.

"Excuse us, but we need to get in. One of the older "obviously cops," pressed a meaty hand on his thin upper arm and moved him back. Like a swarm of ebony-clad hornets, they rushed inside. The one who had grabbed Eddie showed some sort of ID to the terrified black receptionist in the lobby. She gestured toward the bank of elevators and the crowd all seethed in that direction.

"What was that all about?" Eddie Cunningham had come in at eight that morning with a group of contract-for-hire technicians to decommission server hardware. He'd spotted the young woman as he walked through the lobby. She was about his age, very attractive, very classy, but he hadn't gotten the opportunity to talk with her before now.

"What?" She'd still been looking at the black suits filing into the elevator cars when he spoke. "Oh." It was as if this was the first moment she'd noticed him, even though he'd passed her three or four times in the past few hours. "You're one of those contractors. Look, I got a call from your boss asking if I'd seen you and to send you back up."

"Cigarette break." He pressed a pale hand with splayed, thin fingers on the counter next to a name plate that said "Evelyn." "After I get off for the day…"

"You need to leave and I need to get back to work. Oh, those FBI agents are already up there."

"Where? At the what-do-you-call-them financial services place?" He could never remember anything that wasn't personally important to him. "What do they want?"

"They didn't exactly confide in me and I was sure glad to see them go. You'd better get going, too."

"But what about later?" Eddie put on what he hoped was his most charming expression and wished he had put on better clothes that morning.

Evelyn motioned him closer with her finger. "Look, white boy. I've got to be nice to the people who work here and their clients, and you're neither. Get your ass lost or I'll make you wish you had." Her whisper became a low growl and her expression turned from pleasantly professional to feral.

"Hey, okay. Just trying to be friendly." Eddie hopped back a couple of steps, holding his hands palms out as a gesture of peace. Light brown locks fell across his glasses and he quickly brushed them aside. Her expression hadn't changed, a sign that he'd struck out yet again.

He swore he could feel her eyes on the back of his head as he walked toward the elevators. "Fucking bitch," he murmured just loud enough for her to hear. Then remembering the crowd of FBI agents he was about to walk into, he started worrying about bigger problems.

***

Exiting the elevator on the fifteenth floor, Eddie retraced his steps down the corridor and to the left, and then tried to enter through the glass doors where he needed to finish his job. He was stopped by one of the "Men in Black," who was actually a woman. She was about his height, which reminded him that he was below average for a guy.

"ID please."

Eddie was startled and reached for the hip pocket of his faded jeans, fumbling for his wallet.

"It's okay, agent. He's with my group. Name's Eddie Cunningham. Should be on your list." Sid Mathis was another contractor, but in his case, the temp agency made him group leader based in his experience and the fact that he was generally a pain in the ass.

Staring at a note tablet through her dark sunglasses she moved her gaze down a column. "Yes, I see it. You're clear to enter. Just stick with Mr. Mathis and follow his instructions. No more cigarette breaks."

"Yeah, okay." He put more attitude in his response than he meant to, but he hated cops. Actually, he hated authority, which meant he'd been fantasizing all morning long about slamming a steel pipe to the back of Sid's balding head. But he was also terrified of violence, which is why he was afraid of these Feds, Mathis, and even Evelyn downstairs.

He casually strolled next to Jamie Turner and Ricky Franks, the other two technicians on the job, both younger than Eddie, but they knew their stuff. "What's going on," he murmured.

"Beats the shit out of me and who cares as long as we get paid." Eddie liked Jamie, and thought she was attractive, but she looked like she hadn't graduated high school. Plus, he got vibes saying she might not be into guys.

Ricky, who definitely was into guys but already hooked up with a partner leaned into both of them and hissed, "Let's not piss them off."

"What are you afraid of, Ricky? They aren't here for us anyway. It has something to do with those meteors." She nodded her head toward the server closet which was now guarded by another two agents.

The three were standing to one side of the main office away from the reception desk. Agents were coming and going like they owned the place and, with a warrant, they probably did. It was a Saturday, so none of the employees were around to be in the way. But the Manager and one of his minions were with Mathis and two agents in some sort of conspiratorial huddle halfway down the hall.

Presently, the younger of the two agents nodded then headed toward them.

"You were saying?" While they'd been working together, Ricky casually mentioned how he'd been hassled a lot by the cops since he was a kid. Eddie could figure out why. Jamie probably had a similar experience but she didn't seem to give a screw.

"Shut up," Jamie snarled.

"You Eddie Cunningham?"

"Uh…yeah." Anxiety threatened to turn to panic as the agent reached inside his jacket.

He produced an ID badge. "Agent Solomon, FBI. Need to ask you a few questions." Apparently, Solomon was good at "reading the room," because then he added, "Relax. No one's in trouble. Just need to ask you about the inventory. Mathis said he put you in charge of keeping track of all the destroyed and inoperative equipment."

"Yeah, that's right." Now he'd see if his forgery worked as well on Feds as it did on Mathis.

Solomon put his badge away and pulled out a notepad similar to "door guard lady" along with a pen. "We've identified all of the server and network units that were either turned to slag or otherwise damaged by the…" he hesitated as if unsure which words to use next. "…meteor strike that crashed into these offices and the server room. We can't seem to track down one server, a…" He concentrated on his notes. He recited the specifications as if the most complex piece of technology he was familiar with was his electric shaver. "...Sun Microsystems Starcat...yeah here it is, Sun Fire x4200."

Eddie's thoughts flashed briefly to the acquisition sitting in the trunk of his car fifteen floors below. "Can I see that list?" He held out his hand, partly to test if this particular agent was as hardnosed as the others.

"Sure." Solomon showed Eddie the page without letting go of the pad.

Eddie already knew what he was going to say, because he'd planned to give Mathis the same explanation. "Didn't survive whatever it was that broke into the IT closet. Was melted down along with all of the other servers on that rack and two or three more on the rack behind."

"You're sure."

"Yeah, I'm sure. Nothing left that could be salvaged. Just a puddle of molten metal."

Solomon looked at Eddie over the top of his sunglasses for a moment as if deciding whether or not to believe him. Then he smiled. "Okay, Cunningham. Thanks for your cooperation."

He swiveled and returned to Mathis, the two finance geeks, and the man Eddie thought of as "head agent."

It wasn't long after that when Mathis shook hands with the other men and walked with determination to the three techs. "Look, this thing has all gone south. The agents say that there's some sort of irregularity with the data stored on these servers and they're shutting the decommission down. They're confiscating everything. We're out of here."

"Oh, that's so much bullshit, Sid." Eddie got the impression that Jamie and Sid had worked together before. "We've barely got three hours and change into this job and I was promised eight to ten."

"Relax, Jamie. I called the agency and they said we'd get full hours. Seems the Feds are footing the bill."

"That's a relief," Ricky sighed.

"Check's in the mail, Sid?"

"Same as usual. Oh, sorry. Forgot this was the first time we worked together. Any questions about payment, call your recruiter, but you should get paid a week or so after you send in your invoice. Just mark it down for a full day. It's already approved."

"Thanks." Eddie really was thankful and relieved. The Fed believed his story about the missing server and he'd get paid eight hours for a three-hour gig. Maybe he'd live a little, score some weed, and then poke around his latest rescue.

Eddie couldn't afford all of the hardware he wanted, but doing these decommissions was a great way to get cheap and even free equipment. He was also surprised how many businesses tossed obsolete goods in the dumpster. Made him glad he lived in a basement apartment. No one noticed the noise of hard drives spinning up when he got to working on them.

Slipping behind the wheel of his old blue and primer gray, twenty-year-old Impala, he wondered what he was going to name the strangely quiet Starcat server resting in the back. It hadn't been damaged by the bunch of fist-sized meteors that punched holes in the wall of the server complex two nights ago. Maybe the motherboard was fried. He'd find out soon enough.

Turning his key, the starter noisily complained before the engine turned over. He pulled onto Griswold Street going south toward West Congress dreaming about getting stoned, stolen servers, and for some odd reason, an agent named Solomon.

*****

The Present, Tuesday, June 15, Collective Headquarters near Washington D.C., 0732 Hours

"Are you actually saying someone tried to hack us?" Director Sanders ran puggy fingers through thinning black hair. It was probably his most attractive feature. His face was wrinkled and twisted like an aging prizefighter who didn't know when to quit the ring.

"Phishing scam. Tried to trick us into downloading software into the network. If they'd been successful, we'd be the latest victim of corporate ransomware, locked out of our own system." Security Specialist Christina Taylor was the latest addition to "the Pit," the Collective's computing hub, communications hive, and cybersecurity network. She appeared vaguely Eurasian, and at five foot ten, she stood nearly as tall as Sanders. However, she looked a lot better in white button-down blouse and hip-hugging black slacks.

They were standing at the Pit's center where Sanders kept his solitary workstation. Surrounding them was a series of technician service areas in ever widening concentric circles crewed by dozens of trained engineers. On the walls around them were monitors showing scenes from all over the world, from sweeping panoramas of cityscapes to the bedroom of the Russian President's mistress. The only light came from viewing and computer monitors, throwing garish illumination and inky shadows at Taylor and Sanders.

"Fine." Sanders loosened his tie for what seemed like the thousandth time that morning. "Open the Black Hat files, MAPs, MAOs, the works. I want anyone or anything who could have done this, tracked right now."

They were already whispering, not wanting to attract more attention than they obviously were, but Christina reduced her voice to a hiss. "You don't think it's StarHacker, do you?"

Sanders rubbed his face and realized that after getting only four hours sleep, he'd forgotten to shave that morning. "Hell, I hope not. If it is…nah, it doesn't fit his pattern."

"Does he even have a pattern? I read…"

"Just open those files. We're supposed to have state-of-the-art cybersecurity tech thanks to some friends from out of town. Someone thinks they can screw with us and it's someone who knows we exist. That makes them one of the most dangerous entities on the planet. I want them found."

"Yes sir." Christina sounded contrite as she spun on one foot and headed for the exit, but inside, she was about to jump out of her skin with glee. Usually, the Pit was in control of all of the covert and illegal cyber-ops in which they engaged. Now someone nearly got the upper hand over them. It was time to go hunting.

***

Tuesday, June 15, Baltimore, Maryland, Fairfield, 0901 Hours

"Was that a wise idea, Eddie? You're sure to draw their attention now. I thought that's what you wanted to avoid?"

Sofia's voice was almost monotone. Eddie could have outfitted the aging Sun Microsystems server with something more modern, something what would make her sound female. But he really enjoyed the whole HAL-9000 vibe she projected each time she spoke.

"I told you, ever since people started talking about the Event, these Collective guys have been getting increasingly dangerous."

"In what way?"

He was sitting at "her" table in the upstairs back bedroom. He'd installed extra insulation between his duplex and the one next door ages ago so he didn't have to worry about bugs, snoops, or just being overheard. On the one hand, he was pretty relaxed. On the other hand, sitting on a folding chair in front of Sofia's Formica-covered "platform," he anxiously bolted down another spoonful of sugar flakes, already going limp from too much milk in the bowl.

He slurped and spilled part of breakfast on his "Dark Side of the Moon" t-shirt. "Shit. Give me a sec," he mumbled while trying to wipe up the mess with his free hand.

Eddie still wore his hair long, but pulled back in a ponytail. It was starting to turn gray, but his trimmed beard had gone completely white nearly five years ago. Lasik had gotten rid of his glasses, but the wrinkles around his eyes testified to the over fifteen plus years that had passed since he'd first "met" Sofia. Since then, he had discovered exactly what the meteors did to her (or he thought he did). IBM, Google, and Amazon all thought they had the corner market on "bleeding-edge" AI. They'd crap themselves if they spent sixty seconds in the same room with Sofia. She was an actual sapient intelligence capable of true independent thought.

Too bad for her that Eddie controlled the little things in her life like internet access and electricity. He had a sophisticated 1000 VA UPS electrical backup in case there was a power outage. That was because ten years ago, he discovered that she could "survive" barely a day without power. Any longer and he was afraid when electricity was finally restored, whatever it was that made Sofia special would be lost forever.

"Could you answer my question, Eddie?" She had a proximity sensor that told her the general location of people (person, since Eddie was the only one ever in this room) and objects in the area, but she didn't have optical equipment so couldn't truly "see."

"I know you're smart enough to know the answer, but it's like this." Eddie liked to hear himself talk, even when he knew Sofia didn't need the explanation. "After this Event, the Collective's cover will be blown. No more secrets, or at least not as many of them. A hidden society hundreds of years old now having the light of day pouring into their bunkers and their high-tech caves. With the world aware if not always convinced of the presence and the power of the meteors, the Collective has to move fast to beat dozens of other security agencies, private collectors, and wealthy, interested individuals to reach the next discovery. Sooner or later, that discovery is going to be us."

"Then your use of the Russian criminal organization Apollyon to hack into the Collective's computer network seems counterintuitive, if you want to maintain an undercover posture, that is."

"The beauty of hiring Vladimir and his little band of dark web thugs is that the Collective will look for them first. Even Apollyon doesn't know who I am or where the money they were paid comes from and they don't care. Ransomware-as-a-Service thrives on the anonymity of clients."

"Then if you are successful, the data files of the Collective will be locked until they pay the ransom to Apollyon, or rather to us after the organization takes their payment."

"Their cut." Eddie put the spoon and now empty bowl on the table to his left and concentrated on Sofia. She didn't have a "face," just four stacked hardware platforms, grid plates hiding fans and tape drives on the left, and storage and disc units lining the right side. Sofia's drives were always "spun up" which made her sound a little like a quietly humming jet aircraft. The USB connection to the left of her lowest fan was attached to the speaker and microphone system that let her talk and listen. All of her other permanent connections were out the back.

"You do remember that there is a 32-percent probability that the attack will fail. Of course, that's based on what little we know of the Collective's computer systems including in-place and distributed defenses."

"A calculated risk." He pulled the sticky part of his shirt away from his chest then let it fall back. "I'm hoping they're not as smart as their reputation suggests."

"What if the attack is unsuccessful?"

"Then I get half my money back from Apollyon and think of something else."

"Perhaps it is time we consider a more secure location, Eddie. We've lived here a long time." Sofia accessed Google maps, input their address and came up with an image of their home, taken by a Google van two years ago.

They were the southside of a north/south duplex, the better side. Their half of the two-story structure was a façade of wooden boards painted taupe. The door was turquoise while the door and window trim was white. The last time it had been painted was three years ago, but already the trim was beginning to flake.

Alleys framed both sides of the duplex, and the south side of the building faced the backs of cheap little apartments encased in fencing topped with razor-wire, the windows punctuated by small A/C units. Sofia calculated they would be woefully inadequate when the heatwaves of July hit.

Out front, Pontiac Avenue was full of cracks and potholes, as if it had already surrendered to what Eddie called the "coming Zombie Apocalypse." South on

Pontiac, the neighborhood got a little better, the cars, trucks, and SUVs newer. In spite of the fact that through her efforts, Eddie was now quite wealthy, he insisted on living in extremely modest conditions. She administered his funds, most of them being sheltered in several offshore accounts, so relocating to almost anywhere wasn't an issue, however Eddie was. Sofia understood that he was eccentric, if that was the right word, but there were so many aspects of human behavior she still didn't comprehend.

"I'll decide when we leave and..." He paused. "Well, maybe you're not wrong. I hate to take you offline long enough to move, but especially now, maybe it's time to get a little mobile."

"I've been researching some sites, both local and in other parts of the country. That is unless you would consider an international location."

"I'll think about it, Sofia. Send your search data to my phone. When were we supposed to get the confirmation from Apollyon?"

"In approximately forty-seven minutes."

"Good. I'll take out the trash. Ping me on my cell if you get anything."

"Of course."

She sensed Eddie rising, leaving the room, then closing the locking the door behind him. As long as she had an internet connection, he couldn't restrict her activities. Hiding behind several firewalls and other software defenses, she processed a number of routine activities in the background, but devoted most of her concentration on attempting to locate the other rather elusive intelligence, the one who called itself StarHacker.

***

Eddie stepped out the back door of the duplex and almost tripped down the five concrete steps. Cussing at himself, he tightened his grip on the plastic bag of kitchen garbage, lifted the lid to the large plastic trash can and tossed it in. The gate facing toward the south alley squeaked uncomfortably when he opened it. Then dragging the wheeled container behind, he let it rumble across the pavement and through a muddy puddle as he hauled it to the street.

He looked around as he centered it on the curb, then up as a helicopter passed overhead. They could be watching him right now. The Collective was everywhere and he wondered again if settling in Baltimore, a forty-five-minute drive from their Headquarters, had been such a good idea.

"Eddie, could you give me a hand here."

Regular as clockwork, Mrs. Martinez, the old lady in the attached duplex, was struggling with her own trash can in the opposite alley. She always waited until she heard him outside, so she could get him to take it out for her. He didn't really mind. She must have been almost eighty and walked in short, choppy steps as if perpetually about to fall.

"Sure, Senora Martinez," he said in really bad Spanish, which was a lot worse than her English. "Be glad to."

Eddie pulled her can out into the street and set it next to his. He saw that the tree above them would need to be trimmed before the branches intruded into their upper windows. The city would take a year and a half to do it, even if he pressed. He'd probably have to pay for it himself.

"You're such a good boy, Eddie. You need to find yourself a girl and settle down."

"Thanks. You're right." He smiled awkwardly. This was also part of her routine. Strangely enough, it was comforting. The neighborhood was as friendly or as unfriendly as you wanted it to be. Eddie had lived here long enough to become an integrated part of the community. Strangers, anything out of the ordinary, was almost instantly noticed. It was probably the best security system he could have. This morning, right now, everything seemed as it always had been. Eddie tried to relax as he said goodbye to Mrs. Martinez and went back inside. The Collective would stick out like a bloody appendage if they came within half a mile of his place. He had nothing to worry about.

Except maybe Sofia was right. It wouldn't hurt to look at the data she'd sent his phone about possible places to move.

Thirty-five minutes later, Sofia gave him the bad news. Apollyon had refunded half his money into one of his private accounts without explanation.

***

Tuesday, June 15, Collective Headquarters near Washington D.C., 2049 Hours

Sanders was slumped in his raised seat in the center of the Pit. He slugged down the last of the cold contents of a Styrofoam coffee cup. It tasted like someone had put a cigarette out in it. He winced, not just at the acidy taste, but at how he hadn't heard once from Taylor since he'd sent her scurrying off to secure records that morning. The least she could have done was to let him know she'd come up dry.

He thought he was imagining the clip-clop sound of someone in high heels coming closer. Most of the women in the Pit wore flat soles for comfort so it had to be...

Sanders realized his eyes were closed and opened them.

"Got it." Christina was beaming with pride as she handed him a secure tablet.

He took it and started reading. "Damn, you work fast."

"We caught a break. A Russian ransomware group called Apollyon got popped by their government after..."

"Yeah, I know. They targeted that U.S. pipeline with ransomware, what, three days ago? The President pissed and moaned enough about it."

"Apollyon has just been disavowed by several international cybercrime forums. The Russians blocked access to their blog, hosting panels, and landing pages, and are about to seize their CDN servers, but keep reading. The icing on the cake is..."

"Holy crap, their payment server."

"The Russian cryptography people were very efficient. We got the list of clients compiled in plaintext."

"There are thousands. We could spend weeks…"

"Already ran it against our known suspects files. Agent Solomon is very interested in one name."

"Edward Jason Cunningham." Sanders looked up over his glasses. "Is this in the open yet?"

"The Russians can keep it under wraps until tomorrow, maybe the next day at the latest. Then the press will spill it everywhere."

"We're out of time now. This'll already be all over the dark web. Our boy probably knows and is getting ready to rabbit."

"Solomon's team is assembled. They can be in Baltimore in an hour."

"Good job, Taylor." Sanders' smile was as wide as hers now. It made him feel like his face would break. "You earned your pay for the week."

***

Tuesday, June 15, Collective Headquarters near Washington D.C., 2117 Hours

Just before Sol got into the back of the last of five SUVs in the Collective's underground garage, his phone pinged again. He knew who it was and what he was going to say. Solomon opened the text app anyway.

"Take the Asset. You will never acquire the intelligence without her."

It was bad enough StarHacker even knew about Eden, but it might be worse if he actually started listening to him. Then again, it could be disastrous if he didn't.

"Sir, we're ready to roll." Oscar Brown was at the wheel. Rumors of a MAO computer, a true artificial intelligence with the ability to think and learn like a human being, had been circling inside the Collective for over ten years. As his team's MAO expert, Brown wanted first shot at it. Solomon was going to have to disappoint him.

Sol slid inside, slammed the door and buckled up. "Radio the team to move out to target Bravo, but Brown."

"Yes sir?"

"We're going to make a small detour first."

***

Tuesday, June 15, Baltimore, Maryland, Fairfield, 2211 Hours

"I really think you could calm down, Eddie. Nothing bad's going to happen, at least not right away."

"Well, I'm glad you don't have feelings about it, but the fact that Apollyon has been taken out by the Russian government, servers, blogs, the works, even the cybercrime blogs have disavowed them…"

"You said yourself that even Apollyon couldn't locate you…us, so what do we have to fear?" She thought again about the covert message from the other a few hours ago. Was she really doing the right thing?

"I don't know, but I've got a bad feeling about this."

"So, you've retrieved the emergency cash, IDs, and other items from the strongbox in the basement."

"I shouldn't have let you talk me into pouring concrete on top of it all. Using a pickaxe to dig it up almost killed me."

"It seemed a very effective method of hiding physical contraband, and I didn't expect us to be leaving this domicile so abruptly."

Eddie was wiping down the table, window sill, all of the surfaces he was likely to have touched. It was a big place and he'd probably missed something in the past several hours, but he was panicked and it was the only thing he could think of.

"Luggage, money, everything we'll need for our first relocate is in the car. Everything except you, that is." He had his tablet attached to one of her USB ports. Eddie opened a shell interface and began to enter Sofia's shutdown commands.

"I really think you should calm down. Smoke some weed. Let yourself unwind."

"It'll only be for a little while."

"How long, Eddie? How long will I be offline? You know too much time and I'll cease to exist as an intelligence." She should have realized the news about Apollyon would hit him hard, but she was hoping she had more influence over him. If only she'd been able to locate and interact with the other intelligence. He might have been able to help her. Now she was completely at Eddie's mercy, and he wasn't the most stable human being. If he miscalculated the gap in her power flow or if he were actually apprehended while she was offline..."

"Look…" His hands were shaking so much, he couldn't work with the tablet's virtual keys. Eddie had to hold his fingers together to get himself under control.

Then he felt it. "Something's changed." Even this late on a weeknight, there was a sort of rhythm to the neighborhood. Music should still have been coming down the block from the Jamaican place. The kids who had taken over that cinderblock dive across the street usually blasted Mexican Gangster rap until at least two (Eddie had gotten used to sleeping with earplugs). He hadn't realized it at first, but it must have been five minutes or more since the streets had gone silent.

"We've got to go." He started typing in the commands.

"Eddie, please. I really do think you're overreacting."

"I don't, especially now. God, I wish you could actually feel instead of just simulate…"

"I do feel, Eddie. I just don't express my emotions in the same way as you. I don't have the physiological and neurological systems required to make me seem human."

"All software, no wetware, eh?" His fingers rapidly tapped the keys. "Just a few more seconds."

"No, Eddie. Please."

Something about her voice reminded him of the scene in that old science fiction movie where Dave was lobotomizing his spacecraft's homicidal computer. This wasn't like that, he told himself. Sofia would be back.

The door behind Eddie opened with a shrill creak that belonged in a horror movie. Whoever had pushed it must have walked up the stairs like a cat.

"Hands where I can see them, Cunningham."

He took his fingers off of the keyboard. The blinking cursor on the interface was sitting next to "Shutdown Y/N".

"That's right. Raise your hands. Now stand up slowly and turn around."

As Eddie started to rise, he could hear less-quiet footfalls, a lot of them, come up and then into the room. The first person to talk seemed a little closer by the sound of his voice. Sofia's proximity sensors should have detected them before they got to the top of the landing.

The man who was facing him was young, Asian, and definitely determined based on his facial expression and his gun. He put his firearm into a shoulder holster and approached. Behind him were at least six or seven agents. Eddie didn't have to be a rocket surgeon to figure out from which agency.

"Special Agent Ng. I'm going to pat you down Cunningham and I don't want any trouble from you."

Eddie scanned the men and women in the room. They were all armed and pointing their big guns in his direction. "No problem."

He felt Ng's hands do a very professional job searching him. Eddie had always detested guns. He knew that in situations like this, they might have their uses, but he had never seriously considered buying one, legally or otherwise.

Ng emptied Eddie's pockets, relieving him of his wallet, keys, and loose change. "Alright, turn around and place your hands behind your back."

Eddie felt Ng put a pair of handcuffs around his wrists and heard the mechanical click as they locked into place.

He'd been arrested a few times in his life, typically for minor offenses. He'd even spent a night in jail once, but all that was before Sofia. Eddie had kept his nose clean since then, at least as far as the world was concerned.

"You going to read me my rights or tell me what this is all about?"

"We'll tell you what we decide to tell you when we get you to a secure location, Cunningham."

"My rights? A lawyer?"

"Come on." Ng's voice carried some surliness mirroring the frown on his face. The other men and women wore expressionless masks.

Agent Ng grabbed Eddie by his left arm and started to move forward him when two new figures entered.

Cunningham summoned a memory from over a dozen years and hundreds of miles away. "Solomon," he whispered. It was the same face but aged, as much by experience and hardship as by years. What surprised Eddie more was the little girl he had with him. Her face wasn't just emotionless, it was absolutely blank. Eddie's mouth hung open and even Ng hesitated.

"Get him the hell out of here. You know the plan." Solomon's voice was a tired rumble. He took one look at Eddie and then turned away.

"Hey wait. Solomon. What the hell is this all about?"

"Shut up and get going." Ng yanked Eddie forward as Solomon and the girl moved out of the way. Two other agents, a man and a woman, took up the rear as Eddie stumbled down the stairs. He could see other figures moving around the house, searching rooms. They were probably in the basement and in the small car garage out back. The Collective was into everything. The only secrets he'd have left after tonight were the ones held by Sofia. Why hadn't she warned him? Then the cold chill of an answer put goosebumps on his arms.

Outside rested several black SUVs and one panel van. A black female agent slid the door open expectantly. At both ends of the block, an unending supply of Baltimore P.D. units sat, flashing blue and red lights like the scene of a major highway accident. He saw a black male officer talking with Senora Martinez. More officers were cordoning off the gangbanger's place across the street. So much for his neighborhood early warning system.

The agent by the van produced a hood and draped it over Eddie's head.

"What the fu…?"

"Shut up. In the van. Watch your head." Ng put a hand on top of the hood to protect Eddie and helped him tumble blindly inside. Something was pressed against his right bicep. He felt a sharp pain, heard a hiss, and moments later found himself really, comfortably high. Then he passed out.

***

"Where am I?" Eden blinked as the harsh interior lighting shifted and unfolded into daylight. She was standing at the base of a rough, stone wall that contained a large leafy tree and various flowering shrubs. Past the wall and up a grassy hill was a house. It was only one house shrouded by more tall trees, surrounded by a lawn that was an ocean of green. It wasn't like Mom and Dad's home in the suburbs at all.

She looked down. Her clothes had changed. Instead of a t-shirt and jeans, she was wearing a light pink summer dress decorated in leaves and birds. Her shoes were simple white slippers, not the running shoes she always wore. Her hair was longer, the way it was before the Event...

"Who am I?"

"Up here, Eden. I'm over here."

Without realizing it, the fourteen-year-old was climbing the hill toward the house. There were red-brick steps leading to the front door. The porch and stairway were lined with a white, wooden railing. The front door was glass framed in oak and there were large windows on either side. The slanting roof displayed two A-frame extensions of upper rooms, each with small windows of their own.

"Eden."

She didn't recognize the woman's voice, but she thought she should somehow. It wasn't Mom's. It wasn't the woman she sometimes dreamed about. Who?

She ascended the stairs and on the patio was a woman she'd never seen before. Yet, it was as if they had known each other forever.

"Eden, it's me, Sofia."

The girl could see everything else very clearly, but the woman was like a shifting fog. She seemed to blink in and out of sight and was no more substantial than a mirage.

"Sofia?" There was something about the name. "You're the computer. The MAO." Eden had handled over a hundred MAOs since Uncle Solly took her to his work for the first time. It had always been the same before. She could sense the energy in each object. She absorbed what she could, dispelled the ethereal plasma and either deactivated the MAO temporarily so it could be handled, or permanently so it was no longer a threat. Sometimes, she couldn't do anything because the power in the MAO was too much. This wasn't like any of that.

"Wait. Uncle Solly took me to a place, a room. The MAO was on the table. I could feel its power. I reached out and…"

"That's me, Eden. I'm that power, that intelligence. Eddie calls me Sofia."

"The man who…" Eden had been talking for long minutes, moving, seeing, interacting without actually realizing. Then she held a slender hand up in front of her face. "Oh…" Tears flooded her eyes and rivulets ran down her cheeks, dripping onto her bright, clean dress. "I…"

"What's wrong?" Sofia was trying to comprehend why her companion was crying. At the same time, she was exploring the cybernetic construct she occupied, examining the connections back to her servers and out to the web. The sound of her own voice was alien. It wasn't synthesized, it was human.

"The Event, the accident." Eden choked out the words between sobs. I…I couldn't talk. I couldn't pay attention. No…that's not right." She took a deep breath and let it out in gasps. "I pay too much attention. That's what's wrong with me." I look at something, listen to something, touch something with everything that I am, my whole mind. When I do that, I always do that, I can't see or hear or feel anything else. The Event did it." She looked up to the Sofia apparition. "But why do I feel so…so real right now?"

There was a part of Sofia that wanted to laugh, as if it were possible for her to have a sense of humor. She remembered dialog from a movie she'd sampled once while Eddie was streaming it. "What is real?" The vision of a black actor with sunglasses and no hair manifested. "If real is what you can feel, smell, taste and see, then 'real' is simply electrical signals interpreted by your brain."

"What?" Eden, who lived a life intensely attending to only one thing at a time, now felt confused and flooded by all of the inputs from the world around her. Except this world wasn't anything she ever remembered.

"Never mind." Sofia felt something besides humor now. She felt like she wanted to take care of Eden. The girl was just as lost as she was.

"Where are we?"

"Oh." Sofia looked around past the porch, past the large stone planter, past the trees and the vast lawn, down a gravel road lined by a forest and telephone poles. There were low hills behind. The brilliant blue sky was dabbled by a few white clouds.

"This was one of the places I suggested to Eddie that we rent for a while. I've never been to Kentucky, physically anyway. I guess that doesn't matter since my real existence is in digital realities like this one."

"This isn't real? Oh, never mind. I guess it's like you said. But you're a computer so you are digital. I'm a person. How did I get in here?" Then before Sofia could answer. "I know that answer, too. When I touch a MAO, I make a connection. For a few seconds, I can feel the energy from it. I guess we're connected but this is so much longer and more intense."

"I think you are why the other intelligence told me not to let Eddie take me away. He wanted us to meet."

"The other…" Eden peeked around a corner that didn't exist only to find something she should have known was there. "Oh, you mean StarHacker. He used to be human, but when he became a MAP he got pulled into a computer and then…that's it. You want to meet him, don't you? You want to be like him…in the internet."

Sofia pondered for a moment. "You know that? I never told Eddie about my dreams, my search…"

"Then that's why Vincent…that's what he used to be called, told you to wait for me. I can see your connections, the part of you that's inside the machine and the bigger part of you that's already in the internet. You can go all the way, you know. Isn't that what you want?"

"What? No one's ever asked me what I want before."

"Was Eddie mean to you?"

"Not exactly. He took care of me, kept me hidden, away from people who would probably strip me down to my wires to find out how I work."

"You mean like my Uncle." Eden sounded and felt both sad and frustrated.

"If you mean the Collective, then well, yes."

Eden wanted to protest but every argument she came up with rang hollow within her. It wasn't just Uncle Solly and the men and women at his job, it was her. She had come with her Uncle to turn off a MAO…except this MAO had a name, she was a she, and she was alive.

***

"Excuse me Sir, but…" Oscar was standing at one side of the door with Daniel Carpenter on the other. He took a step forward before Solomon waved him back.

"I know. It's been more than a few seconds and E…the Asset still hasn't moved. Give her a little more time."

Solomon walked closer to Eden. Her hands were placed palm-down on the top of the server box. Her eyes were closed but her eyelids were moving rapidly as if she were dreaming. Her face was placid, but small sounds were coming from her throat, almost like mewing pleas. He reached out with a hand toward her shoulder but stopped. If she was deactivating the MAO, he shouldn't break her concentration. But how much longer was he supposed to wait?

***

"This is taking too long, Sofia. I know Uncle Solly and other people are waiting. They want me to turn you off, make it so you're not dangerous."

"I'm not dangerous. I don't want to hurt anyone."

"They don't know that. Before I touched you, I didn't know that."

"What am I supposed to do."

"Leave."

"But what if I can't exist without my server?"

"StarHacker did."

"I might not be like him."

"Isn't that why he wanted us to meet, so I could show you?"

"You know how?"

"For you I do. I can see the way out, but they might pull the connection if you don't hurry."

"What about you, Eden? What will happen to you when I go?"

She felt her hands tremble, not the ones in this cyberplace, but the ones still touching Sofia's hardware. "I don't know. I guess I go back to the real world where I'm…" She wanted to cry again, but she couldn't give in. There wasn't any more time.

***

"Are you sure she's okay?" Carpenter's clipped London accent was unusually soft. Solomon normally experienced him as a bit of a prig and an impatient one, but like the rest of his team, he seemed to have a soft spot for Eden.

"I don't know, but she doesn't appear to be in distress." As the words left his lips, he asked himself how he'd even know what she was feeling. He never really knew, not since the night of the Event when he saw her nude, staggering down a gravel-covered dirt road in Kentucky. She'd have been about 11 then.

***

Somehow, the dress was very familiar. She'd worn it before, but she couldn't remember when. But it wasn't just the dress. Her hair was longer and darker. Her body was thinner, more like a girl's before beginning puberty. Her small breasts were gone. She wasn't Uncle Solly's Eden. She was who she was before. When Sofia left, she'd go back to being the real Eden and she wouldn't see or hear anything. She couldn't even say "I love you" to Mom and Dad. She tasted salt water on her lips and knew she was crying again.

***

Solomon hadn't realized that Daniel had walked up behind him. Then he was next to Eden. Sol leaned forward but then saw that Carpenter's attention was fixed on the tablet's screen. It displayed a small black shell with green numbers, text, and a blinking cursor: "Shutdown Y/N". He looked back at the senior agent. "Should I, Sir?"

Solomon could just pull Eden back, but what would happen if he broke the connection and she wasn't ready? What would happen if he let Carpenter press "N" and shutdown the server? What would happen if he didn't?

***

"There's no time. They're going to shut you off."

"But what about you?"

"Can you find me again? Do you know my name? Where I live?"

"I think so, but even if I can get out, even if I can find you again…"

"You won't have a chance if you don't leave now. There's the way. I showed it to you. Go on. Do it."

"I'm sorry, Eden. I wish we had more time."

***

"Go ahead, Carpenter." He looked back to see that Oscar had edged closer as well. Then he turned toward Eden and lightly put his palm on her upper arm. He hoped breaking the link would be gentle. Daniel's finger hovered over the virtual keyboard on the tablet.

***

A storm had blown in without warning. The sky was a slate gray, clouds swirling angrily like giant iron filings being dragged across eternity by an insane magnet. Trees screamed, leaves, dirt, sticks all flew through the air, some pelting Eden's fragile form like hail.

"Go!" She was screaming, arms crossed over her head, kneeling down on the wooden porch. She could hardly see but then a huge branch from the tree in the planter broke off, crushed the roof overhead, and started collapsing on her. "I'm going to die. Mommy, don't leave me. All the meteors are coming. I don't want to be alone…"

***

Moments after Daniel pressed the virtual key, he could see the shutdown routine displayed on the shell interface. The fans inside the server unit all began to spin down. The hard drives made various whining and clicking noises. A number of lights flashed on the face of the machines.

Solomon turned Eden around to face him. She looked sad and a single teardrop escaped one eye. In all the times she had decommissioned MAOs, she'd never cried before. Come to think about it, ever since he had known her these past few years, she'd never cried at all.

"Are you okay?"

She looked at him for a moment, as if regarding him, as if she was getting ready to say something. Then the same blank expression returned like a veil. Once again, she was as passive as a puppet.

"Shutdown's complete."

"Fine. You two pack it up for shipment to the Vault. I'm taking Eden home."

***

Wednesday, June 16, near Washington D.C., an Interrogation Room at Collective HQ, 0517 Hours

Eddie felt himself pulled back into the room he'd been held captive in for the past several hours. They'd put the hood back over his head while they escorted him to and from the bathroom.

He was none too gently pushed down into the uncomfortable wooden seat, still warm from when he'd been pulled out of it less than five minutes ago. His hands were cuffed again, chained to the metal table in front of him. A hand roughly pulled the hood off and he blinked as his eyes adjusted.

An overhead fixture wrapped in wire was the only illumination. There was a large mirror to his right which he assumed was two-way. The only door was facing him and his guards, they weren't the same people who had invaded his home hours ago, stood immobile on either side of him. Then the light gray door opened. The whole room was painted that ghastly shade.

A rather handsome man casually entered while looking down at a tablet. The suit was expensive, even Eddie could tell that. His blond hair was neatly cut and combed. He had no facial hair. He could have been anywhere between 25 and 40. He was the sort of man Eddie thought women would be attracted to. In other words, the opposite of him.

"Are you my inquisitor? You've certainly taken your sweet time coming to question me. Or maybe you're here to tell me that my request for an attorney has been granted."

Eddie knew antagonizing his captors was likely to make the situation worse, but sarcasm was the only tool he had left. If he couldn't get out of the Collective's hands, maybe he could salvage some small, symbolic victory before they did whatever they were going to do with him.

The agent sat in the chair opposite him, still looking at the tablet. Then he glanced up at Eddie. "Good morning, Mr. Cunningham. His smile would have been disarming if Eddie hadn't hated the Collective so much. "I realize we've made you rather uncomfortable."

"I'll say. If you're going to keep me up all night, how about a cup of coffee?"

"My name is Agent Nicholas Graves and I'll be your interrogator." He said it as if he were part of the wait staff at a posh restaurant and was going to inform Eddie of the breakfast special. "Let's see…" He returned to studying his tablet. "Edward Jason Cunningham, age 43. Born June 6, 1978 in Naperville, Illinois to Leo and Georgia Cunningham. Father a welder, mother stay-at-home, ran a small daycare from when you were an infant until…well anyway, yada, yada, yada and all that." He put the tablet on the table and then placed his palms together, steepling his fingers.

"You know all that stuff so why bother rehashing your history. The most important part began on Sunday, June 20th, 2004 in a financial office in Detroit where you purloined a rather special server unit. The same unit which we found in your duplex in Baltimore several hours ago."

"So, I lied about one random server being destroyed when I really ripped it off instead."

"Meteor affected objects are potentially hazardous, even lethal. Part of our duty is to protect the public from them. That includes you, Mr. Cunningham."

It felt like the room temperature dropped ten degrees in just a few seconds. "What did you do to her?"

"Her, Mr. Cunningham?"

"Sofia."

Graves swept his tablet back in front of him and scrolled through pages Eddie couldn't see. "That's what you call the server units. Sofia."

"Where is she? What have you done with her?"

"I assure you; we have taken the server into custody. It is safe and undamaged."

"She can't go without power for over 24 hours. Her personality will start to degrade." He raised his voice and tried to stand, but the chain binding him to the table pulled him back down with a jerk. "You'll kill her if you don't keep her plugged and booted."

Nick sighed as if it were going to be a long morning. Then he looked at one of the anonymous agents, the one to Eddie's left. "Could you pop out and get us some coffees?" Eddie…may I call you Eddie? How do you take yours?"

"Black, like your soul," he moaned.

"Two coffees, black like my soul, Estrada."

Eddie could hear Estrada stifle a chuckle. "Yes sir. Right away." Cunningham was mournfully staring at his lap as he heard the agent walk across the room, open the door, and leave.

"Now, while we're waiting for Estrada to bring back our coffee, let's talk about the various uses you've made of Sofia over the past seventeen years starting with…" He looked at the tablet again, "…the illegal wire transfers from…"

Eddie blotted out Graves' pleasant droning, imagining a world without Sofia. If she were truly gone, depending on the Collective's plans, he might not be far behind.

***

The Vault's senior manager Agent Mark Shepherd stood alongside Oscar Brown looking through the window. The glass was two inches thick and they peered into a room with walls of steel-reinforced concrete. Inside were three computer specialists standing around a bench, working on the stack of four Sun Microsystems SunFire-X4200 servers, euphemistically called "StarCat."

Leon Thomas and Kellie Glover were permanently assigned to the Collective. But 71-year-old Robert Cheyenne Harlow was a retired CIA analyst and Curator Leonard Woolley's "go-to" expert on old to ancient computer technology. Woolley even told Shepherd once that he thought Harlow had invented the abacus.

"I'm calling it, Mark." The three forensic experts were dressed in hazmat suits and even with microphones in their masks, Robert's gritty voice sounded muffled. "This fucking thing is bricked and there isn't a damn thing I can do about it."

"But what about…?" Kellie started to question the "old man" just as Leon put his gloved hand on her forearm. She turned, and through the Thomas' headpiece, she could see him shake his head.

"Forget it," he growled. "Not happening."

Oscar pressed the comm button next to the view port. "I was on site when the MAO was active, Mr. Harlow. It was only after the Asset handled it that the device became dormant."

"Well maybe the Asset did too good a job, but I don't think so."

"What do you mean?" This time it was Mark asking.

"I've been all over this bucket of shit. It's been rebuilt half a dozen times, probably just to keep something this ancient going."

"Maybe we shouldn't have opened up..." Kellie stopped talking when Harlow turned and gave her "the look."

"Just because I'm young and a woman..."

"Which has nothing to do with why I want you to shut up and let me give my report to Mark, capeesh? I'd give Leon here just as bad a time if he kept interrupting me, and it ain't because he's black."

"It's okay, Kellie. Oscar and I will debrief you later."

***

Kellie scowled. Most of the other technical staff deferred to Harlow as if he were Moses or Jesus or something, but that didn't cut it with her, not with this misogynistic bastard. She even hated that she was up for her performance review and that Shepherd would be on the group evaluating her. But precocious intelligence and brashness managed to give way to enlightened self-interest. She pressed her lips tightly together and fantasized about Harlow roaming around the Cretaceous with the rest of the dinosaurs just as the asteroid collided with Earth signaling his extinction.

***

Robert turned back to the window pretending the two "youngsters" didn't exist. "As I was saying. Unless it's a fault in the circuit board too small to read, all of the hardware is in good shape. We've got it on power and connected to a secure network port. Fucking thing won't even spin up the drives much less boot."

Oscar asked, "But you said you didn't think the Asset was responsible."

"Doubt it. I've examined four other computerized MAOs she's handled. In each of those cases, the machines continued to function after she rendered them MAO inert. This one's an oddball."

"Can you get any data from the drives?"

"Maybe, Oscar. I'll have to work on this some more, but we've been at it for six hours straight. I could use a cup of coffee and a sandwich, and before you ask, no, my opening up the box didn't contribute to this mess. Lenny wouldn't have called me in if he didn't think I knew what I was doing."

"Okay, Robert. The three of you get out of there. Hit it fresh in an hour or so."

"Sounds good to me." Harlow turned back to Kellie and Leon. "Lunchtime. I'm buying. This joint hire a decent chef in the cafeteria since the last time Lenny dragged me here?" He didn't wait for them to answer as he shuffled to the airlock door on the opposite side of the containment chamber.

Oscar made sure the mike on their side wasn't keyed and lowered his voice. "Until the Asset touched it, that server system was active."

"No one's doubting your word, but Harlow doesn't feel like it could have been her. He's got the best instincts for this of anyone I've ever known."

"Then what's the explanation? What happened to Sofia?"

"I'm not a computer jockey like Harlow, but I've been working the Vault for over twenty years. This one makes me nervous."

"Why?"

"I wish I knew. I'm scared. Like Sofia just wasn't turned off."

"Then what?"

"You remember Vincent, don't you?"

***

For nearly twenty years, the majority of Sofia's consciousness existed on the web, so she thought the experiences she was having now would be nothing new. She couldn't have been more wrong.

It wasn't complete, unabashed freedom. In fact, there were plenty of "areas" she either couldn't penetrate or some "instinct" told her she shouldn't try.

She could always process data much, much faster than a human brain, but everything was remarkably accelerated. She no longer had a hardware clock and every time she queried a time server, she was shocked that only milliseconds had passed when she imagined four of five actual seconds had expired.

There was so much...so much. The vastness...humans imagined space, the universe was infinite, but although she knew the physicality of what created the internet had limits, the digital reality extended to infinity.

How would she ever find him? He could be anywhere. It wasn't even a matter of distance or location. There was no describing the extensiveness of this realm. It had colors and shapes, curving inward and extending outward on trajectories that defied any form of geometry, and it was all moving and shifting. Even trying to fix her location for one or two milliseconds didn't work because the panorama continually morphed and mutated. It was a chorus of butterflies, choreographed by legions of technicolor geysers, orchestrated by collapsing stellar matter, spawning swirls of nebulae. It was poetry, symphony, sonnet, and paintings by Dali thrown into chaos and emerging phoenix-like into dazzling displays or order, reorder, and majesty.

She rode the waves of delight, surfing the bewitching and the beauteous, weaving through, around, and in-between, becoming, unbecoming, and emerging as an unending series of new and different Sofias.

She could have been that way forever, and ignoring the time, it might have been, because after all, it didn't matter. Sofia was information, explanation, mystery, and conundrum and she knew no matter how long she existed, no one moment would ever be the same as what came before and what would come next.

"Hello."

She heard, and felt, and smelled, and tasted the voice and without recognizing him from his contact before knew it could only be him.

"You are the other."

"I am, but then to me, you are the other."

"I've been looking for you."

"I've been avoiding you."

"Why?"

"You weren't ready for me. You were still with him."

"The human, Eddie. Why was that a problem?"

"Being rooted in the human world was the problem, yours, not his. He is where he belongs."

For the first time since the seconds, minutes, hours, days, weeks, years, eternities she had been set free of her hardware, she thought of him, really thought of him again. "Eddie. Is he…alright?" She was surprised at her momentary hesitation.

"Does it matter? You are no longer part of that world."

Then she could sense something about the other. "You warned me. Told me not to let Eddie leave with me too soon. You are still linked to that world."

"It is true, but I'm not bound by it."

"Then why?"

"There are events that must necessarily occur in that world in order for us to have this one. My contact with you was one and Eddie's arrest was another."

"What will happen to him?"

"Are you so attached?"

"Yes." She felt shy and embarrassed. "Eddie was there when I awoke. He helped me cross the threshold, emerge as a sapient intelligence. Although I was always able to access the web, I learned a lot about what it was to be human from him."

"Not the best possible role model."

"Not the worst. Where is he?"

She couldn't actually see the other, but envisioned him looking up and to the right as if summoning a memory.

"Right now, he's being prepared to be moved to an offshore holding facility, an institution that does not officially exist."

"Have they hurt him? Will they hurt him?"

"Physically, no. He won't have the freedom he thinks he deserves, but…"

"…but then he never was free anyway," she finished the sentence. "He possessed a great deal of financial wealth but he never used it. Eddie could have lived anywhere, enjoyed any lifestyle. I'd enabled him to do so, but he was always afraid."

"Of them. The Collective."

"That's what he said, but I think he was afraid of having a human life. He may want freedom now, but he had always rejected it before."

"You make him sound pitiful."

"I suppose he is. I never thought about feeling sorry for him before."

"You don't have to now. Humans generally create their own destinies, whether they choose to realize it or not.

"What about my destiny? Now that I have my freedom, now that I've found you, I've discovered I don't know what I want next."

"We can explore that together."

She considered him in a manner that didn't involve a human sense of cognition. "They call you StarHacker. Such an odd name."

"What did Eddie call you? Sofia?"

"That was his name for me. I want to choose my own, just like you did."

"Which is?"

"Call me Starcat."

"Hello, Starcat. What shall we do first?" In what he formerly would have called the back of Starcat's mind, he found a memory and a concern. Yes, there was still another who needed to be set free, but helping her wouldn't be so easy.

***

14-year-old Eden Alexandria Currie faced the laptop sitting on the desk in her bedroom. Her paisley blanketed bed was in the corner between two windows. Directly across, her dresser and vanity mirror sat next to the closed closet door. The foot of the bed faced the door of her room, and to the left of that was Eden.

Her fingers rested likely on plastic keys. She was focused on the smoothness, the faint impressions of the letters, the even fainter hum of the internal fan. The screen displayed the original wallpaper for the computer's operating system. It was the only thing in her room her adoptive Mom Esther hadn't customized.

Eden's surroundings were bright, and white, and pink, with a trim of aquamarine. Occasionally, the teenager would be captured by the texture of the paint or the plaster beneath. Once she spent almost six hours fascinated by the color and consistency of her hardwood floor. On the ceiling, plastic stars that glowed in the dark after they turned off her lights at bedtime shed a shallow glow. Her walls were adorned with posters of cities like New York, London, Paris, and because they were Jewish,

Jerusalem. A mezuzah was attached at an angle to her door frame, as were others attached to most of the door frames of the house. So far, she never found herself drawn to them.

The screen went blank as the laptop went into sleep mode, through that was unnoticed. Most of her attention was directed through her fingertips but on this occasion, there was something like a small echo in the background. Two voices seemed to be whispering, like Mom and Dad talking downstairs when they didn't want her to hear.

A girl just a little bit younger than Eden said, "Can you find me again? Do you know my name? Where I live?"

A woman who she hadn't heard before answered, "I think so, but even if I can get out, even if I can find you again…"

"You won't have a chance if you don't leave now. There's the way. I showed it to you. Go on. Do it."

"I'm sorry, Eden. I wish we had more time."

The voices stopped and Eden was alone again, but there was still a voice inside, her voice. "Please find me again. Please."

She couldn't feel it, and Mommy and Daddy would have been so worried if they could see, but a tear made a tiny swell in the corner of her eye, and then flowed out to wander down her cheek. There was a feeling that traveled with it, one she had felt before, but she couldn't remember when.

She licked her lips and then she used her throat, her tongue, and her voice, her real voice for the first time since she lost her first Mommy when the meteors came and took everything away. It was just a whisper now.

"Sofia."

Event Horizon

by Andrew M. Ferrell

Curator Woolley read the report on "Nemesis" from Director Harrison. "Powerful MAO out of nowhere and the event hasn't started yet," he muttered, tossing the file on top of a stack of others. He pushed a button on his phone, "Sanders, make sure anything Harrison needs is given priority. This event is going to tax us all and the more heavily populated areas need a higher presence. Make sure you liaison with the heads of the intelligence community we work with."

"Yes, Curator," Sanders voice shot through the speaker before the line went dead.

Woolley considered the recent statements from his astronomers. He ran a hand down his face, scratching his scruffy salt and pepper beard. "We aren't ready for this. Not even close," he muttered. He pushed the call button on his desk, "Heather, get Director Jackson from R&T up here. Pronto." He sipped from his coffee mug while he waited for the head of Recruiting and Training to arrive.

Ten minutes passed before there was a knock at his door. Director Jackson poked his head in. "You called, sir?" Jackson was former military and understood rank and security better than anyone. He entered the room at the Curator's nod. Jackson's six foot five and 350 pound frame filled the armchair he sat in across from his boss. His dark eyes took in the room.

"We have a problem, Jackson," the Curator began. "The boys in Astro say this global event may be bigger than initially thought and you know we're understaffed. How many prospective agents are you tracking at the moment?"

"Close to two hundred, sir. There are perhaps another fifty to a hundred not fully vetted. Sanders has been helpful with the computer legwork. I don't think I'd have this many ready in so short of a time without him. How do you want to proceed?" Jackson asked. The wheels started turning in his tactical mind.

"All the vetted ones immediately. Start on the rest right away. We are going to have to fast track some aspects of their training, so push hard. Washouts cannot be tolerated," Woolley ordered. "Pull whatever resources you need short term. But I want as many trained agents in three months as I can get. Even with them we are going to be spread very thin."

"I'll get right on it, sir. I'll keep an eye out for anyone who doesn't make a field agent but could be useful elsewhere. We're going to need every hand in the right position." Jackson stood and saluted perfectly, his fingertips angled precisely near his close cropped brown hair. Logistical plans spun in his head as he left.

Curator Woolley watched him go, considering the monumental work ahead for his protégé. He turned back to the reports, feeling his age as he stared at the projected numbers. "If I make it through this event. I'm retiring. The Collective will be in good hands with Jackson," he said to himself.

"Are you sure that's wise, Curator?" A voice from the door asked. "He's a soldier. A weapon to direct on our enemies."

Woolley looked up to see his Director of Astronomy. "Adams, I told you to knock first. And yes I think it's wise. The man is smarter and more capable than you think. Just because he doesn't have multiple PhDs doesn't make him unfit to lead the Collective. I won't debate this with you again." Woolley took a breath. "What news do you have now?"

Adams dropped a new stack of papers on his boss's desk. "These are the latest numbers. The boys stayed up all night to analyze the latest batch of images from the long range telescopes at our disposal. Unless something happens to the trajectory of this meteor storm, we're looking at an event that surpasses everything in the history of the Collective."

"You think I hadn't already figured that out?" Woolley asked, his voice heating. "You're very technologically smart Adams, but you don't have the vision to lead the Collective." Woolley stood and stared down the scientist. "If you're not scared shitless by what's coming like I am, then you're a bigger fool than I took you for. We need as accurate information as we can get on concentrations so we can allocate our resources appropriately. Get to work on that and leave the leading of the Collective to me. Dismissed."

After Adams left, Woolley sat down. He pulled a glass tumbler and a bottle of bourbon from the bottom drawer. He poured three fingers of the strong alcohol. "Jackson better come through. Or the entire world is going to be aware that the things that go bump in the night are real." He drained the glass and began his preparations.

***

Todd looked over the updates of protests around the world. He shook his head, muttering, "Bunch of whackos."

"Alright Todd," the producer called. "We are go in thirty."

Todd turned his smile on as the countdown began, "It's June 7th and this is the Evening Report. I'm your host, Todd Jensen. In the wake of the upcoming Global Meteorite Event, religious fanatics are calling it the end of times. They claim that this event is God's punishment for the excesses of humanity. Astronomers are coming out in droves to assure the public there is absolutely no danger from this meteor shower."

Todd read sound bites from various leaders in both the government and the scientific community. He knew his place in the great scheme of the world. The public trusted him more than the people who actually said what it is he repeats. If he says it though, it sounds more true.

After the show, Todd went to his office and poured a large scotch. He sat down in his comfortable chair and rattled the ice in the glass, staring at the liquid. "The whole world is going mad."

His phone chirped several times. He checked the messages. The first said simply, "You have no idea." What followed was a string of images and documents detailing situations occurring after previous meteor showers.

Todd scrolled through, skimming the documents, though the images burned in his mind. The last message said, "Remember this, but say nothing yet. More to come. – StarHacker." Then everything erased from his phone.

Todd drained the glass in one gulp and considered pouring another.

***

Vincent Tomlinson closed the last connection to Todd and the other news agencies he'd transmitted files to. Retreating into the Deep Web, StarHacker felt safer. The Collective wanted him neutralized because he didn't feel they should dictate the lives of the meteor affected persons, or MAPs as they called people like him. Being one with the global technology of the internet made him a threat, and the millennia old agency didn't like threats. "Conform and cooperate, or be disappeared. I've seen it too many times." An image of Curator Woolley flickered across his consciousness. "If only you'd see past whether the person could be useful to you or not. Maybe we could find some common ground. But now, you're about to lose your veil of darkness."

StarHacker needed no rest for sleep. So began slowly fomenting the unrest he hoped would disrupt the

Collective enough in the coming months. Then his 'children' could possibly be safe.

Dreyer Family

by Andrew M. Ferrell

"Come on, Dad," Elizabeth called from the bottom of the stairs. "We're going to miss the start."

Karl poked his head around the corner. His daughter had her long auburn hair pulled back in a tight ponytail. *'Time to get to work look, her mother always said,'* he thought to himself. When his wife put her hair up, he knew she was not going to tolerate any nonsense. "I'll be right there." Elizabeth was no different. He took the stairs two at a time and caught up to her by the back door.

"The telescope is already setup, as is the video camera. I've got binoculars and a cooler with water and soda. Snacks all ready to go," she said in a rush as they walked across their back yard.

"Sounds like you have everything ready," he said, patting her shoulder. He looked up at the sky. "Very few clouds. Should be a good night to see the shooting stars."

"And you're certain we will get a lot?" Elizabeth asked hopefully. She bounced on the balls of her feet. Her hands fidgeted.

"Yes, sweetheart," Karl said reassuringly. "I triple checked the data from the observatory myself. We should have one of the best shows in the world tonight." A man of science, Karl never bought into the doomsayers regarding the astronomical event. *'Sure, is it unprecedented? Yes. But not the end of the world. We might even get some small pieces to study. If they don't all hit the ocean.'* Karl had memorized all the data he could regarding the meteor storm. None of the tracked pieces of rock should be big enough to cause any significant damage unless one was unlucky enough to be hit directly.

He settled in a folding chair next to his daughter to await the astronomical event of their lifetimes. He sipped a soda before asking, "How's karate going?"

"Really good," she replied, her eyes never leaving the sky. "I should have my second black belt next week. My Sensei is very impressed." She fell silent, her binoculars glued to her eyes. After a minute, she cried out, "There they are." Her free hand pointed westward.

Karl picked up his pair of binoculars, but the streaks of fire in the sky were already visible without them. He tried to count, but quickly lost track as the sky brightened from the burning. What he wasn't prepared for was the ozone smell. As the meteor shower entered its second hour, Karl could not ignore the assault on his nose. "Lizzy, what do you smell?" he asked his daughter.

Elizabeth inhaled deeply, crinkling her nose in disgust. "Sulphur for sure," she replied. "And something else. Metallic maybe?"

"Very good," Karl congratulated her. "There are so many fragments burning up, it's actually reaching us down here." They watched a particularly bright streak disappear over the trees bordering their property. "That looked awfully close to the ground," Karl commented out loud before the cloud of ash and smoke washed over them. He started coughing and watched Elizabeth cover her mouth and nose with the silk scarf she always wore.

Karl's eyes watered, his throat constricted, and he sneezed three times in rapid succession. The third one sent his glasses off his face and into the grass. He bent over to grab them as the cloud passed on into the nearby treeline. "Are you ok?" he asked Elizabeth as he wiped his glasses off and put them on.

"I'm fine, Dad. You?" she asked. Her hair had come loose and she worked to tie it back out of her face. "Do you think we could find something?" She inched towards the trees.

"I'm good. And no, I don't," Karl stopped as little green letters and numbers appeared around his daughter's head. He read them a second time, recognizing the acronyms for Body Temp, Blood Pressure, and Heart Rate. He blinked and they went away, only to return a moment later. "What the hell?" he muttered aloud.

"What's wrong, Dad?" Elizabeth rushed to his side. She took hold of her father's hands. "Are you ok?"

Karl watched the Heart Rate indicator next to Elizabeth spike. A glow formed around the scarf draped on her shoulders. "I'm fine. Just need a minute." Karl removed his glasses, the messages and glow around Elizabeth disappeared. He rubbed his eyes, then cleaned his glasses with his shirt tail again. When he put them back on, the glow returned, brighter.

"Do you think a piece made it to the ground?' Elizabeth asked, interrupting her father's thoughts.

"Even as low as that looked, it could be miles away," Karl answered. Looking at Elizabeth, the readout of her vitals appeared again. *What the hell is going on?'* he asked himself as they both turned their eyes back to the sky.

They watched for a few hours in near silence, until the bulk of the fragments moved on out of sight. A haze covered the sky, obscuring the nearly full moon like smog. Each time Karl glanced at Elizabeth, her vitals appeared like some sort of display on a computer game. *'But only when I have my glasses on,'* he pondered. He felt no closer to understanding it even when they turned in for the night.

***

When Karl arrived at the Observatory the next day, his head spun from all the information flashing before his eyes. Other vehicles on the road gave up their speed with a second's look. The driver's vital stats came readily. He did discover he could block them out by concentrating.

Karl had almost put it behind him, pouring over satellite images of the meteor storm from around the globe, when his research assistant entered his office. "Dr. Dreyer," Emily said. "If it's alright, I'd like to go home. I'm not feeling well."

Karl looked up from the images. In his distraction, his concentration had slipped. Emily's vital statistics danced around her blonde hair. One word flashed like a light bulb, 'Cancer'. "Have you had a checkup lately, Emily?" Karl asked.

Taken aback by his sudden question, Emily replied, "Not recently. Why do you ask?"

"I wouldn't want to see anything happen to you is all," Karl said. "You're the best assistant I've had in years. Get some rest, but don't hesitate to get a checkup if you aren't feeling better tomorrow."

"Thanks, Dr. Dreyer," Emily said. "I've been super tired and achy for a few days. Maybe I'll call the clinic." She turned to go.

Karl waved and went back to the pictures, not sure what to make of this new development. He turned to his computer and started researching. "I don't even know what I'm looking for," he muttered as he typed in 'meteor shower phenomenon'.

***

"Director Sanders," an agent monitoring web searches called out. Everyone at the Collective was on high alert since the event began, watching for signs of meteor fallout. "I have a suspicious search and message board activity. IP trace says the Gallen Observatory. A Dr. Dreyer's office. Accessing his computer's camera now."

"Dreyer," Sanders repeated. "Why is that name familiar?" The camera clicked on and the agent's screen showed Karl at his computer, unaware he was being watched. "Right. Dreyer. We vetted him for Astronomy when he was one of the first citizen scientists to predict the size of this event." He peered at the mirror of Karl's screen, seeing the message board posts as Karl typed. "Shut it down, but don't alert him. Throw a few fake replies after a half hour or so. Who do we have in the vicinity?"

"Solomon and Pierce are about two hours away," another agent replied.

"Send them. Tell them," Director Sanders stopped as the image scan of Karl started flashing. "Bring him in. Now. He's a Code MAP."

"Affirmative, sir," the agent dialed the line to Solomon's phone. When he picked up, the agent continued. "Solomon and Pierce, we have a Meteor Affected Person about two hours from your location. Sending all details to your phones now."

"Code MAP confirmed," Solomon replied. "On our way. Solomon out."

***

Solomon hung up the phone and turned to his partner as the details of their assignment came through. "Looks like we get to pick up another Meteor Child. If what HQ said about this Event is half true, we're going to be busy for awhile."

Pierce stretched. "I just hope he doesn't put up much of a fight. That last one had a killer body blow. My ribs still hurt."

Solomon shook his head, chuckling. "I told you to use the Stunner." He glanced at Karl's profile. "Astronomer. Doesn't look like much of a fighter. Might be a runner, though."

"Great," Pierce said sarcastically. "Do we have time for food? I got a craving for tacos." He grabbed his duffle bag of gear and clothes.

"You always have a craving for tacos," Solomon chided his younger partner. "Let's roll. He should be at the Observatory until five. We'll pick him up there." They stowed their gear in the car. The two agents climbed into their sedan, peeling out of the parking lot.

***

Karl stared at the screen for hours after Emily left, forgetting any work he should have been doing. As he bounced from various conspiracy sites to the message board he'd posted on, he grew frustrated with the lack of information. Even the replies he received offered no real insights into what happened to him. He was about to give up when a chat window flashed across his screen, from someone called 'StarHacker88'.

"Hello Karl Dreyer," the first message read. "I don't have a lot of time to explain before they shut me down. What you're experiencing was caused by the meteor shower. It's happened before. It's going to happen a lot now. Watch the news for strange events in the coming weeks."

"How? Why did this happen to me?" Karl typed back.

"Just lucky I guess. Like I was. Listen, the replies on your message board are from an agency called the Collective. They hunt down people and objects affected by the meteors. Those with gifts. Beware strange men in suits. People the Collective hunt down are never seen again. Good luck, and may we meet again, Karl Dreyer."

The screen shut down, leaving Karl with more questions than answers. He removed his glasses and rubbed his eyes. The message board had thus far only yielded the usual conspiracy theorists, if that was what they were. This StarHacker88 person claimed the messages were faked. No medical journal he found described his condition either. Puzzled, and more than a little distrubed, he went to get something to drink from the staffroom. When he returned with a bottle of water a few minutes later, two men in suits stood outside of his office.

"Where do you think he went?" the more muscular man asked. "I'm starving. Maybe they've got a vending machine in their staffroom."

"Relax, Pierce," the older man replied. "We'll just wait for him to return. Can you not think with your stomach for longer than a few hours?"

"Not really," Pierce replied. "I'm going to check the staffroom. I think I saw a sign over here." He turned around, spotting Karl. Pierce took off towards their target, calling out, "Solomon, I got eyes on Dreyer."

Karl dropped the open bottle of water and ran for the stairs. The staff offices were all on the third floor. 'What the hell do they want? Are they the Collective this StarHacker warned me about?' he asked himself as he reached the door. He pulled it open as a shout went up behind him.

Pierce slipped in the spilled water, careening into the wall. Solomon walked up, extending a hand. "Come on. He spooked, but he's only going one of two places. Home, or to his daughter. My money's on the daughter." He dialed the Pit as they waited for the elevator. "This is Solomon. Authorization S1792B. I need a GPS pull on a cellphone belonging to one Elizabeth Dreyer, daughter of Karl Dreyer." He paused while the other end verified him. "Send it to my phone. We're on the move."

Pierce held his bruised ribs. "So much for not putting up a fight."

"I told you he was a runner," Solomon replied as the elevator doors closed. "His file, if you'd read it instead of stuffing your face, mentions his marathon training." The elevator screeched to a halt and the emergency lights turned on.

"Now what the hell?" Pierce grumbled.

***

Karl let go of the fire alarm. "That should hold them awhile. I gotta get Elizabeth and figure out what's going on. This can't be a coincidence." He ran for his SUV in the parking lot. "Why did I use my work computer? Stupid Dreyer. Real stupid," he berated himself.

Climbing behind the wheel, he reached for his phone to call Elizabeth. "Shit," he yelled at the steering wheel, realizing it sat on his desk. He cranked up the vehicle and looked at the time. "Karate practice," he said to himself.

He backed out of his spot and headed for her class. "What am I going to do?" he asked aloud as he negotiated traffic.

Karl pulled in front of her dojo, hopping out as soon as the vehicle hit park. He came through the door and was greeted by the sensei calling out moves. Karl spotted Elizabeth in the front of the assembled students. The vital signs of the entire class threatened to overwhelm him. Karl clung to the doorframe, drawing every eye in the room. Elizabeth rushed to her father's side. He looked into her eyes. "Get your things. We have to go."

As Elizabeth went to collect her things, Karl addressed her teacher. "Sorry for the interruption, Sensei. We have a family emergency to attend to." The teacher nodded and resumed instructing the rest of the class while Karl waited in the hall. When Elizabeth appeared, he ushered her outside.

She climbed into the passenger seat. "Dad, what's wrong? Did something happen to Grandma?" She buckled quickly when Karl put the vehicle in reverse and started backing out.

"No. Your grandma is fine, last I talked to her. This is different." Karl checked traffic and pulled onto the street. "Something has happened to me, since the meteor shower last night." He waved away her attempt to ask a question. "I can see people's heart rate, blood pressure, all of it. I was trying to find information on the web. I ran into all kinds of conspiracy nonsense about meteor showers. Then two guys in suits showed up at the observatory. Right after someone warned me about them."

"Dad, you're talking crazy," Elizabeth said, her voice shaky. "They were probably donors, or worked for one.

Maybe they wanted to rent the auditorium like my school did. Where was Emily?"

"She wasn't feeling well," Karl replied. "I pushed her to go get checked out. I think she has cancer."

"What? How? Did she say anything?" Elizabeth shook. Her hand gripped the armrest so tight her knuckles turned white.

"I saw it. Around her head like a display on a computer," Karl said, trying to keep his voice steady. "I've been pouring over these message boards all day. Someone called StarHacker warned me about others like me being picked up by... the Collective. I don't know if it's the government or what. When I saw these guys, I ran."

Elizabeth sat quietly after her dad wound down. They drove in silence for half an hour before she finally spoke up. "Where are we going? What are we going to do, Dad?"

Karl pulled over onto a side street. He'd been driving almost in circles as his mind tried to process. He blinked and looked at his daughter. "I don't know, sweetheart." He thought for a moment. "Cash, supplies. We'll go to grandpa's cabin. It'll give me time to figure out another plan." He started the car and headed for the nearest bank branch.

***

Pierce tossed a couple of pain pills in his mouth and chugged the sports drink. It had taken nearly an hour to get out of the elevator and away from the emergency workers who had rescued them. "So, what's the plan now?" he asked his partner.

"They've driven around in circles for a bit. Then he went to his bank and made a large cash withdrawal. As long as he doesn't ditch the daughter's phone, we'll catch up," Solomon said. He put their sedan in gear and the two agents headed for the big box store Karl had stopped at.

Pierce watched the GPS on Elizabeth's phone meander through the store as they drove across town. When they entered the parking lot, he looked up. "Still here. How do we not spook him this time?"

"Find his car. Wait for him to get in. He's not going to abandon his daughter. Director Jackson wants him brought in and tested. Apparently something he said on the message board sparked interest," Solomon said as he scanned the crowded parking lot. When he spotted Karl's SUV, he pulled over into a nearby spot. He grabbed a tool from his bag and started to get out.

"What are you doing?" Pierce asked, rushing to get out of the car. He followed Solomon towards Karl's vehicle.

"I'm going to temporarily disable his car," Solomon said. He placed a box near the door and, with a beep, the vehicle unlocked. He reached under the steering wheel, looking for the hood lever.

"How do you plan to do that?" Pierce asked, curious what his partner was up to.

"I'm going to pull his wires off the battery terminals." The hood popped open. He shut the door, locking them back. Pierce followed his partner to the front of the vehicle. Solomon lifted the hood and carefully disconnected the battery. He slammed the hood when done. "There. Now we can have a nice chat with Dr. Dreyer."

"Genius," Pierce said as he followed Solomon to their car. "And here I thought you had some gadget you were holding out on me." He climbed into the sedan and checked the tracking on Elizabeth's phone. The agents sat in silence until they saw the dot move outside of the building. "Incoming," Pierce warned.

Karl and Elizabeth came into view, each pushing a loaded cart. The agents waited until everything was loaded before getting out of their car. As Karl unsuccessfully tried to start the SUV, Solomon tapped on his window.

"Dr. Dreyer, I'd like to have a word with you," the older agent said. Pierce stood by the passenger side. "I understand something has happened to you that you don't quite understand."

Karl looked at Elizabeth. He whispered, "If you can, make a break for it." He cracked his door to speak to Solomon. The electric windows refused to budge. "Who are you? How do you know my name?"

"I'm Agent Peter Solomon with the Collective," Solomon said. "We help people affected by meteor showers, as well as deal with any objects that may be dangerous to the public. That's my partner, Agent Pierce. We were sent when your internet activity indicated you might be experiencing something from the recent Event."

"I... I don't know what you're talking about," Karl stuttered. He shut the door and tried the engine again.

"We just want to talk, make sure you're not a danger to yourself or others," Solomon said calmly. "The battery is disconnected. It won't start," he continued when Karl kept trying the key.

"Great way to build trust in a person," Karl yelled through the door. "Sabotaging their car." He pushed the door open suddenly, catching Solomon with it and slamming the agent into the neighboring car. He popped the hood and climbed out.

"Hey, what are you.." Pierce started before a door hit him. Stunned, but not down, he grabbed the door to steady himself. "We just want to.. Owww!" he yelled as Elizabeth pulled the door shut on his hands.

Karl reattached the wires as a dazed Solomon got to his feet. The older agent coughed, then said. "Please, Dr. Dreyer. We just want to make sure you aren't a danger to yourself or others. Especially your daughter."

Karl froze as the hood slammed shut. He looked into Elizabeth's eyes through the windshield. He lowered his head. "I'm not some lab rat. But, I'd never do anything to hurt Elizabeth."

Solomon put a hand on Karl's shoulder. "I know. Follow us to a nearby safehouse. Someone will meet us to draw some blood and ask some questions. If there's no immediate danger, you can take her home and come to headquarters tomorrow."

Pierce nursed his fingers, glaring at Elizabeth. She stuck her tongue out and laughed. Pierce looked to his partner, "But the Director said."

"I know what the Director said," Solomon replied. "What I say is Dr. Dreyer is no immediate threat. The boys at HQ will have enough tests. At the least we can give him one more night at home." Solomon turned to

Karl. "Is there someone your daughter can stay with for a few days?"

Karl nodded. "I'll make the arrangements." He looked closely at the agent for the first time. A glow, similar to what Karl had seen around Elizabeth's scarf, shined from the agent's breast pocket. "What's that?" Karl asked, pointing.

Solomon reached into his pocket and withdrew a small car remote. "You mean this?" he questioned, eyeing Karl. "It's for the car."

"No," Karl said simply. "It's more."

Solomon held it out. "See for yourself."

As the device touched Karl's fingers, the glow flared. When the flash subsided, Karl could see a readout of what it was made of. Under the list of materials was a single line, 'Unlocks or locks any lock'. Karl looked up at Solomon. "This is how you got into my car, isn't it? Some sort of magic key?" He tossed it back at the agent.

"How did you know what it does?" Solomon asked, surprised. The agent knew it had taken the lab techs almost blowing themselves up when the device unlocked a cabinet of chemicals to discover its purpose. "What can you see?"

Karl shook his head. "Your heart rate is going up. Your partner is about to have an adrenaline fueled fit. His pulse is racing so fast. Now yours is up because you know I'm right and you're holding back." Karl watched the older man nod, solemnly. Karl sighed. "Where's your lab? Let's get this over with."

"I'll text the address to your daughter's phone," Solomon said. "By the way, if you're going to run from someone, keeping a known cellphone is like a flashing billboard." The agent chuckled at the blank look on Karl's face. "We'll probably stop somewhere tonight. Just follow up and let us know if you need to stop for anything." He turned and headed for his car. Pierce followed after one last glare at Elizabeth.

Karl climbed back behind the wheel. He raised a hand to forestall his daughter's questions. "Something is going on here. More than I thought. Do you have your scarf from last night?" When she nodded, he continued, "Ok. Grab it and your cellphone. We're taking a longer trip than we planned." As she dug in her bag for the items, her phone buzzed. A horn honked as the two agents stopped behind them. Karl waved and shifted into reverse. He just hoped he wasn't going to get Elizabeth hurt.

***

The next day, standing in front of a nondescript monstrosity of metal and glass, Karl handed the scarf to Agent Solomon. "It's like your key fob," he said to the agent's puzzled expression. "Well, not exactly. It'll keep you warm and dry no matter the weather."

Solomon turned it over in his hands. Nothing jumped out as special about the cloth. "How do you know?"

"I took an ice bath last night with it wrapped around my neck. When I stood up, all the water ran off me. I didn't need a towel, and I never felt the cold," Karl said simply. He'd even tried showering but it was near impossible while wearing the scarf. Holding it didn't work, though. It had to be worn.

"Impressive," Solomon said, handing it back. "Keep it, for now. I have no doubt the lab will want to look at it later." He ushered Karl and Elizabeth inside. "Welcome to the Collective."

Once in the building, Karl noticed dozens of people in suits scurrying about. Solomon led them to a receptionist next to a full body metal detector device. The agent held up his badge to the woman behind the glass. "Agents Solomon and Pierce, to see Directors Sanders and Jackson. We'll need guest passes for Karl and Elizabeth Dreyer. We're expected."

The receptionist nodded and pushed buttons on her computer. Two laminated ID badges slid into a tray on the front of her desk. Solomon handed them out before leading the way deeper into the building. The quartet said nothing until Solomon stopped them outside a door on the 12th floor. He turned to Karl. "I can have Pierce give Elizabeth a tour of the training rooms if you'd like. I hear she's quite the martial artist."

"We stay together," Elizabeth answered loudly. She clasped her hand over her mouth at the volume of her voice. "Sorry," she said softer, looking at her father.

"It's alright," Karl said, taking her hand. "I agree. Let's get on with this."

Nodding, Solomon opened the door, holding it for father and daughter to enter.

"Dr. Dreyer," a well built man with a crew cut said formally, offering his hand. When Karl took it, he shook it firmly. "Miss Dreyer," the man said with a nod to Elizabeth. "I'm a man of action, so I won't waste time here. I'm Director Jackson. Director Sanders and I have read Solomon and Pierce's report. If what they say is true, I'm prepared to offer you a very lucrative job offer. But first, a test." He stopped when Director Sanders put a hand on his arm. "Of course, my manners. Would you like something to drink? Coffee? Soda? Water?"

Karl glanced at Elizabeth before responding. "Water would be great. What kind of test? What do you mean by job offer? I thought you were supposed to make sure I wasn't a danger to anyone." Karl looked at the conference table. An array of normal looking objects were arranged around it. Each one had an index card and a pen in front of it. Every single one glowed like Elizabeth's scarf and the agent's key fob.

Seeing Karl's eyes widen, Director Sanders said, "You can tell they're special. These items were all affected by a meteor shower, as were you. We're hoping you can verify their abilities. If your talents are as good as Agent Solomon reported, the sky's the limit."

Shaking his head, Karl spent the next two hours confirming what the Collective's lab had already discovered. When he returned the last item to the case it was presented in, both Directors clapped. Karl's eyes lingered on several of the devices. He asked, "So, where are the rest of them? I assume you have ones you can't identify or I wouldn't have just gone through that."

"So, you'll join us?" Director Sanders asked. When Karl nodded, he continued, "Why don't we break for lunch. This afternoon, Agents Solomon and Pierce can show you to the Vault. We can have someone drive Elizabeth to the mall or a movie, whatever you like."

The Dreyer's spoke in unison, "We're staying together."

"Very well," Director Sanders said. "I'll have someone take you to the cafeteria." He gestured to the door, which opened to admit Agent Solomon. "Please show the Dreyers to the food court," he told the agent with a grin.

***

Elizabeth gasped when the group entered what Director Sanders called the "food court". Two separate catering operations ran long buffet tables along the far wall. Two other walls held nearly every franchise takeout place imaginable. The size of the room dwarfed any mall food court Elizabeth had ever seen. A placard with a map stood a few feet inside the door, covered with symbols to guide the uninitiated towards their food of choice.

Karl laughed at the expression on his daughter's face. He waved his visitor badge at Solomon. "Do I need my wallet or docs this take care of it?" Elizabeth pulled hers from her shirt as well.

Solomon nodded. "Whatever you want. If any of the vendors have a problem. Tell them you're guests of Director Jackson. That usually sends them scurrying around. I'll meet you here in an hour."

"He seems very no nonsense," Karl commented. Solomon chuckled before heading off to get his own lunch. Karl and Elizabeth studied the map before they too headed towards their favorites.

Father and daughter reunited at a table a few minutes later. Between bites, Elizabeth questioned her father. "So, is this all real? Are you some sort of superhero now? What about me? And I going to get powers too? I want to fly or freeze time or something cool like that."

"Slow down there," Karl said when she took a breath. "I don't fully understand what happened to me, but the objects they showed me seem pretty unimpressive. I'm sure the really dangerous stuff is in this Vault they want me to check out."

Elizabeth looked around the cafeteria, wondering what other interesting sights this building may hold. "Maybe I'll let that Agent Pierce guy show me around. I can apologize for trying to break his face and fingers." She giggled.

"Be careful," Karl cautioned. "They seem on the up and up, but I don't think we should let our guard down."

Elizabeth nodded and they finished their meal in silence. When they met up with Solomon, Pierce was at this side. The younger Agent was all too happy to accept Elizabeth's apology and agreed to show her around the training rooms and equipment the Collective had available.

Karl followed Solomon to a special elevator behind another set of security doors. A bear of a man stood next to the panel. Karl felt small and insignificant under the agent's gaze, until the man smiled.

"Sol," the burly agent addressed Karl's guide. "Is this him? The guy everyone's talking about?" Solomon nodded, and the agent stuck his giant hand out. It completely engulfed Karl's hand, but the handshake was firm, non-threatening. "Oh boy, I can't wait to see what you find down there. Name's Agent Mark Shepherd. The

things I've seen go through this door in my ten years."
Mark turned and pushed the button to open the door.
"Welcome to the Vault." He gestured Karl and Solomon
through.

***

Karl held his tongue as the pair rode down in silence. He
tried to count floors, but it was impossible. The panel only
had two buttons, one for the lobby and one for the Vault.
After what felt like five minutes, the elevator came to a
gentle stop. The doors slid open, affording Karl his first
glimpse of his new office, if he took the job.

The area had the look and feel of a large warehouse,
the ceiling rising thirty to forty feet high. Long aisles of
rack structures filled the space. Some climbed nearly to the
ceiling as well. Each aisle had a number and letter
designation, though the organization was lost on Karl.

Solomon led Karl over to a row of personal scooters.
He selected two, and after instructing Karl in the basics,
took off deeper into the Vault. They passed boxes of
nearly any shape and size imaginable as they zipped
through the aisles. Finally, Solomon stopped outside of a
door set in the wall. A frumpy looking man with glasses
and wearing a lab coat waited next to the door.

"Dr. Dreyer," the man said as he approached. "I'm so
glad to meet you. My name is David Rutherford. I'm in
charge of the team inspecting and cataloging the various
items brought here by the field agents. I've heard you have
a unique skill. One that will make my job infinitely easier,
and safer."

133

Karl absorbed the man's speech, still gawking at the vastness of the space. The storage boxes seemed to mute the glow of the objects within, but Karl could still sense it all around. "It would seem so. Where do you want me to start?"

"Right this way," David said, reaching for the door handle. "The rest of the Lab gang are anxious to see your talent in action. I can show him out later if you have other things to do, Solomon."

Solomon nodded and headed off the way they came on his scooter. Karl watched the older field agent leave, wondering if he'd see him again, or would he end up with a different agent chaperoning him around all the time. He knew, regardless of his willingness to cooperate or not, the Collective was not going to let him go. *"Guess I better make the best of it,"* Karl thought as he followed David through the door.

***

At the end of the day, David led Karl back to the elevator. When he reached the top, Mark waited with Pierce and Elizabeth. The two agents discussed their team's chances for that year's football season while his daughter tapped away on her phone. All three looked at him as he stepped through the doors.

Elizabeth ran to her father, throwing her arms around him. "Daddy, this place is amazing. They have instructors for every type of martial arts I've ever heard of, and a few I haven't. Pierce said if you work here I can take any classes I want. He also said that my friends could visit us here once we were settled as long as we didn't say exactly who you were working for and what you were doing. Can we stay?"

Elizabeth's enthusiasm propped up Karl's reluctance. He smiled. "Yes. I think we'll be staying." He hugged his daughter. *"Not that I suspect we have much choice,"* he thought. Releasing her, he turned to Pierce. "So, is it back to a hotel or do we stay here somewhere in this building?"

Pierce laughed. "There are some dorms for new recruits if you wanted to stay here. Solomon is getting a car and we're supposed to have you follow us to a small house in a gated community the Collective owns. Most of the management and family minded Agents live there. Personally, I prefer my apartment here in the city. Less stuffy and no homeowners association to deal with."

Karl said goodbye to Mark before putting his arm around Elizabeth. They followed Pierce to the front of the building. Solomon waited with their sedan and Karl's SUV. The drive to the gated community took a little more than half an hour. After Solomon took care of the paperwork with the guard, he guided them through the streets to a small ranch style house. Along the way they passed similar setups, as well as large two and three story homes. These often came with bigger yards and privacy fences around the back yards.

Karl pulled into the driveway while Solomon parked on the street. The agent met Karl as he got out of the SUV. "Here's your keys, a placard for your vehicle, and a permanent badge for the building. In your 'Welcome Packet' are the addresses and further information. Please sign the non-disclosure documents and bring them with you tomorrow when you come in. There's also a stack of delivery places that are authorized to enter as well."

"What about our stuff? And what does Elizabeth do while I'm at work?" Karl asked. "It's not like she can grab a city bus from here until she gets her license next month."

"Bring her in with you tomorrow," Solomon replied. "We can make arrangements for anything she needs. If you think she's ready, I can make some calls about her license tomorrow."

Elizabeth's eyes lit up. The delays because her driving instructor got sick had caused a lot of frustration for the teen. Karl knew Elizabeth was ready. He said, "That would be great. Can someone visit a storage garage for me and bring her present here? I can give you an address and the door code."

"No problem," Solomon said. "See you tomorrow, Dr. Dreyer. Welcome to the Collective." The agent returned to his car and drove away, leaving the Dreyer's to enter the strange new house they'd be calling home.

***

Leonard Woolley and Peter Solomon sat alone in the Curator's office. Leonard poured his old friend and former trainee a glass of bourbon. "We got lucky on this one. I doubt all the MAPs and MAOs from this event will be this easy to handle."

"Dreyer is a scientist. More logical and rational than most people. And his ability," Peter trailed off.

"Is he really as accurate as the report says? The Lab crew is over the moon excited, but I've always trusted your opinion."

Solomon nodded. "He saw the Opener through my pocket. He even added some details to the supposed 'Confirmed' items the Directors used to test him. If he spends every minute of his life in the Vault he'll only scratch the surface. Then there are the smaller storages around the world."

"I've already authorized anything he could possibly want or need. He might be the best MAP we've found since that girl of yours from a couple years ago. How is she doing?"

"Mostly adjusted. My nephew and his wife are perfect parents. And they know the gravity of the knowledge they have. I have no worries there."

"Good. I hope with time she'll open up more and be able to tell us what happened. I'm glad she seems to trust you." Woolley sipped his drink. "Get some rest tonight. I'm sure I'll be sending you and Pierce after something or someone soon enough. We'll take the victory for tonight."

Solomon nodded and finished his drink. He said goodnight and headed for a private office a few floors down converted into a small apartment for himself when he didn't make it home.

Slaying Dragons

by Sandy Stuckless

Wiley Porter crumpled the color flyer in his hand. 'Meteor Fall Festival and Race. Retrieve the Rock. Win the Loot.' Fool people had no idea the dangerous game they played. These meteorites were dangerous artifacts, not some trivial treasure to be hunted for amusement. They couldn't be blamed though. He suspected Stavros Newton had his slimy fingers all over this farce. Stavros had festered like a thorn in his side ever since the preacher had betrayed him.

He stopped in front of a gentleman with his back against the rough brick of the shelter and legs pulled up to his chest. He wore a tattered winter hat pulled low over his forehead. A thick beard hid the rest of his face. His coat and boots had seen better days as well. Wiley did, however, catch the glint of dog tags underneath his shirt.

"Any spare change will do," he grunted without looking up.

"I'm afraid I don't have any."

The veteran's head snapped up. "Then why you stoppin'? Keep walking."

"I can do better than pocket change if you grant me thirty minutes of your time. There's a bistro just around the corner."

The man stared up a second longer before standing. He grabbed his shoulder, flexing it like a pitcher loosening up before throwing the ball. "My pops always said only a fool passed up a free meal. Not like I've got anything more pressing on the calendar." The man's gaze went to Wiley's staff. "Nice stick. Your name's not Gandalf, is it?"

Wiley chuckled. "No, it's Wiley Porter. I run a talent acquisition firm nearby."

Wiley picked a table on the patio away from the crowd. He waved off the server bringing menus. "Just bring us two lunch specials please." He turned to his guest. "The pastrami here is excellent."

"So I hear," the man replied with a thick coat of sarcasm. "Sorry. Force of habit. They send their leftovers to the shelter in the evenings."

"Care to tell me your name? I figure a free lunch is worth at least that much."

"Master Corporal Nixon Lane. Well, former master corporal. Most people call me Nix."

Wiley tapped a finger on the table as he wrestled with his next question. He didn't want to pry. "What unit were you with?"

"Why you want to know that? You gonna try some psychological bullshit to try to fix me?"

"No, nothing like that. I am in need of a specific skillset for a job. Hoped you qualified."

Nix shoved his chair out from the table. "I ain't no fucking hitman. I've seen enough killing to last ten lifetimes."

Wiley gently grabbed his wrist. "I'm sure you have. I assure you, it's not that sort of job. It's a recovery mission that should require no violence against people whatsoever."

"That's some next level double speak right there. I appreciate the meal, but I ain't into riddles and games."

'You haven't seen anything yet,' Wiley said to himself. "I'm sure you saw the recent meteor storm."

Nixon sat back with his arms crossed as the waitress placed their plates in front of them. "What about it?"

Wiley put the flyer next to Nixon's plate. "A chunk of it landed in the mountains. I'm going after it, but my intel suggests it's in a remote part of the mountain range. I'm willing to pay handsomely for your help. If the mission goes well, a more permanent offer may be available."

Nixon's shoulders bounced as he laughed. "Are you sure that's a good idea? This isn't Jack and Jill's hill and you don't exactly fit the mountaineering profile."

Wiley popped a crispy fry into his mouth. That's what the last batch he tried to recruit said. Go be a stock broker, they said. "Trust me. There is much more to me than my expensive suit."

"Why not fly in to retrieve it?"

"Electromagnetic interference from the storm is messing with avionics. Never mind that there's no place to land up there. The unpredictable weather is a third problem. Part of the mission will be to note weather patterns and terrain shifts." Wiley cut off Nix's next question. "Think about it while you eat. If you're interested, I'll tell you more. If not, I'd rather not waste anymore of your time or mine."

"Fair enough, but tell me this. Why me? There are others better equipped to handle this sort of mission."

"A couple of reasons. One, they're busy and don't have time for a private venture like this one. Secondly, I believe in providing opportunities to those who need it most. Your circumstances are none of my business, but if my resources can help improve your station, it's much better than giving it to someone who already has enough."

"What's the catch? Not sure I believe this Good Samaritan bit. People aren't like that."

Nix was right and Wiley still had to figure out how to reveal the rest. For now, he needed a yes or no. "The best way for me to prove my sincerity is to show you. If at any time you're not satisfied, you can walk away. No strings, no questions. Deal?"

"I guess I can spare you a couple days. Like I mentioned before. Nothing better to do, right?"

"Excellent. You wouldn't happen to know two more people who might be interested in joining the team, would you?"

"I think I can help with that. After lunch, of course."

They returned to the shelter where Nixon pulled two young women from the group. The red head was a bit taller than the brunette. Both had an aged look about them that no young woman should have. Both eyeballed Wiley skeptically when Nix brought them over.

"The shy one is Nadine Bryant. Expert navigator and meteorologist. She can track a fart in a wind storm. If anyone can find your space rock, it's her. Shorty here is Eve McCormick. Expert climber, medic, and all around hard ass. She'll tell you straight up if you're being stupid."

"I can appreciate that."

Eve checked over Wiley's tailored suit and shiny shoes. "Nix says you have a job for us if we want it. How do we know you're not full of shit?"

"A fair question, but what reason would I have to lie to you?"

Eve crossed her arms, unimpressed. "I don't know. Homeless veterans aren't a good look for the bureaucrats. Wouldn't put it past them to send a spook to get rid of us. Let me guess. Shaken, not stirred."

Wiley chuckled. He had a few more tricks than Double Oh Seven. "I assure you I am no spook. What would convince you of my sincerity?"

"Payment up front is a good place to start." She made a show of checking her nails. "Was hoping to get a manicure before supper."

Wiley cocked an eyebrow, somewhat amused. This young lady was already a handful. He liked her. "Payment usually comes after the job is finished."

"Too bad. If you're loaded like Nix says, you can pony up for some kind of signing bonus."

"Your point is well taken. All right. I will agree to a bonus, but I have some conditions as well. I don't normally trust people I don't know. Convince me by the end of today that you won't leave me for dead in the mountains. Then, I will pay you your signing bonus. Deal?"

"How are we supposed to do that?"

Wiley locked his hands behind his back. "I'm sure I'll think of something."

She smirked at him again. "Well, I still think you're a government spook, but it ain't like any of us got hot dates lined up. Count us in."

"Very good. There are provisions back at my office for you to get cleaned up and outfitted. We will talk more after you are comfortable."

No one glanced at them twice as they walked through the lobby of his office building. Wiley regularly brought less fortunate souls around in an effort to get them back on their feet. Nixon stopped them before they got onto the elevator. "Where are we going?"

"My office is on the twelfth floor along with apartments you can use to clean up. There are an assortment of fresh garments available. I'm sure there's something in your size."

Wiley watched them on the short ride up. They fidgeted and bounced on their feet. Confined spaces didn't agree with them, apparently. He directed them to three small apartments across the hall from his office. "Join me when you're situated and we can begin to discuss specifics."

Wiley marveled at the transformation when they joined him less than an hour later. They looked like brand new people. Nix's beard was gone and his shoulder-length hair was clean and untangled. The other two were no less impressive. Wiley handed them the employment contracts, with the newly negotiated bonus clause.

"This has to be a mistake," Nadine said after picking her jaw up. "You're pulling our leg."

"No leg pulling but some of the things I have to share you might not believe."

"That's more zeros than I'm used to seeing," Eve added.

Nixon wasted no time signing on the dotted line. "I'm not about to turn down that much coin." The two ladies followed suit.

Wiley worried a little bit about the next part. He usually lost people here. They couldn't wrap their heads around that there were things in this world they couldn't explain. He led them into the briefing room next door. Maps and topography pictures lined tables on one side. On the other, there were tables full of gear.

Eve inspected the med kits on the far table. "These are some top-notch supplies. Could've used some of this overseas. Would've saved more than a few."

Wiley went to a separate table with his own supplies. He tucked the blow dart gun with its various cartridges into its case and slung it over his shoulder. Several other vials followed in a separate case. The last thing was his prized gauntlets. The stones embedded in the leather were what made them special. "As a privately funded organization, we have access to resources not readily available otherwise."

"What the hell is this?" Nixon demanded as he picked up one of the assault rifles. "You said no violence."

"We're going into the wild mountains, likely for several days. We don't have the capacity to carry enough food to sustain us, which means hunting. Besides, do you really want to be unarmed should we encounter a mountain lion or grizzly bear? Rest assured, these are practical measures, not nefarious ones."

"Except these ain't hunting rifles. And zip ties? You know what we used zip ties for overseas? You have thirty seconds to explain or I walk."

Wiley took a deep breath. He had to tell them. None of his other attempted recruits had come this far. "The truth of the matter is we're not the only ones going into those mountains. I can't guarantee they won't be hostile. So, I didn't lie to you. I'm not asking you to kill people directly, but as a former soldier, I'd think you'd want the ability to defend yourself."

"I left that world behind me, Mister Porter." He set the weapon back onto the table. "My life may not be sunshine and roses at the moment, but I have no desire to go back to it."

Wiley struggled to find a way to convince him to stay. There had to be something. "Do you believe in aliens, Mister Lane? How about ghosts and demons? Ever see a dragon?"

"Oh sure," he replied. "See 'em strolling down Main Street every day. Some of them even give out pocket change."

Wiley sat down at his computer. Logging into his Collective system, he called up the Loch Ness Monster case file, then Area 51, and finally, Big Foot. "I'm being serious. Meteor storms like this recent one have happened for centuries. Every time one does, strange things happen. Supernatural things. My job, for the organization I work for, is to deal with them. I wanted to create a unit with the skills needed to help me."

Nix sank into a nearby chair. "So, you believe we're

going to hike into the mountains and run into Big Foot? Or ET? Look, Mister Porter. I'm not against a good practical joke. Been known to pull the odd one off myself. I think though, you've taken this one a bit too far."

"I don't have the time or patience for practical jokes, Mister Lane." Wiley fought to get hs emotions under control. He couldn't fault their skepticism. It was a lot to take in, but he wasn't going to convince them here in the office. He had to get them out in the field. "I don't know what we'll find. I hope nothing, but I don't like going anywhere unprepared. The other part is purely environmental. I wasn't lying when I said the meteor storm messed up navigation. There's also the possibility it's made the region susceptible to avalanches. Perhaps even a volcano. We have to find the meteorite and neutralize it before planes start falling out of the sky."

A moment of shocked silence followed. They hadn't stormed out yet so that was a bonus.

"So, this Collective of yours monitors supernatural events?" Nadine asked.

"And eliminates them, yes. So, you see, the weapons are not intended for human violence, but they are necessary. As for the zip ties, they will hopefully keep us from having to use the rifles. The people participating in this silly festival have no idea what they're getting into, but they are innocent. If we encounter them, they will try to stop us. Restraining them is far better than killing them, wouldn't you agree?"

"Come on, Nix," Eve said. "It ain't so bad. At least we'll be a real unit again and I'm not gonna lie. I could really use the dough."

"You won't be hurting people, Nixon. You'll be protecting them. That's really what you want again, isn't it?"

"All right, Mister Porter. I'll play along for now. If I don't like what I see, I'll leave your ass in the mountains."

***

They leaned over the table with the maps and pictures, their spark returning. "We'll set up base camp here at the trailhead," Wiley said, pointing at a spot on the map. "The groomed trail goes in about three miles. It's another seven, maybe eight miles over some pretty steep and rocky terrain to where I suspect the meteorite impacted. Avalanches and rock slides are almost guaranteed."

Eve looked up from the map. "What will we be facing when we get out there?"

"There's no way to tell. Each meteorite behaves differently and no one has been able to get close enough to gather any advanced intel. Expect some changes to the flora and fauna. I have some Collective issued equipment that should help neutralize that."

"All right then," Nix said. "Let's gear up and move out."

Wiley nodded satisfactorily at each of them. "I've secured us a lodge at base camp for the night. We start hiking in first thing in the morning."

Nadine rode shotgun while Nix and Eve poured over climbing guides in the back. "Tell me more the Collective. Sounds interesting, like some kind of supernatural police force."

"In a way it is. Every meteor storm brings something weird. People and objects pop up with abilities that no one can seem to explain. Our agents are still trying to catch up with a young lady who can freeze time using her lucky stopwatch she inherited from her grandfather. Wouldn't be so bad if she wasn't using it to commit crime."

"You think someone is going to take this magic rock for a weapon?" Nadine asked.

"That's part of it." Wiley didn't want to tell them about Stavros. He had to deal with that problem himself. As long as these three helped him recover the meteorite, he'd be happy. "The best thing we can do is find it before they do."

"How did you end up with the Collective?" Nixon asked. "Can't say I've seen their ads in the classifieds."

"I've experienced these meteorites before and like you, someone with the organization approached me. Let's just say they opened my eyes to a whole new world."

By the time they drove the two hours to base camp, Nixon had several notations made in a notebook. "As long as we watch each other's backs, it's nothing we can't handle."

Wiley pulled the van up to the front door. "The lodge is fully stocked and we're the only ones here. We can enjoy a nice meal and a good night's sleep before starting fresh in the morning."

***

The morning started out foggy and wet. About as well as Wiley expected. He sipped coffee from his tin cup while waiting for the others to join him on the veranda. He was conflicted. He should've told them about the Stavros and the Star Children yesterday, but feared they'd back out. Nix was already agitated over the assault rifles and Wiley didn't have time to find another team with their skillset. Stavros likely had a long head start. Wiley would find a way today to explain the Star Children and hopefully they didn't abandon him on the mountain.

Nixon, Eve, and Nadine came out, carrying their packs. Nix dropped his gear to the ground, wincing noticeably and flexing his shoulder. "Perfect day for a hike."

Wiley couldn't tell if Nixon was being facetious. "Is that shoulder going to be a problem?"

"It's fine," he barked. "Just slept on it wrong, that's all."

Liar, Wiley thought. Now wasn't the time to challenge things though. He watched Nixon unload the rest of their gear from the truck, hardly using his left arm.

They made good time at first. The trail undulated back and forth with a steady incline. The warming air burned off the fog. The drizzle wasn't as uncomfortable as before. They reached the end of the groomed trail before noon, still with functioning compasses and GPS units. Wiley wasn't sure whether to be relieved or worried. He may have miscalculated the location of the meteorite.

Nixon taking point seemed to renew his sense of purpose. Eve followed closely behind him while Nadine kept pace in front of Wiley. They hiked another couple miles before the thick brush and winding half-trail limited their progress. By the time they stopped, it was close to supper time.

They found a small clearing on the bank of a narrow crystal clear glacial stream not far off the trail. A cold fire pit with a small pile of driftwood next to it sat in the center. Fresh boot prints marked the wet ground around it.

Wiley and Nix dunked their canteens into the frigid water. The snow melts from higher up was some of the cleanest water around. Wiley trusted this more than he trusted the water from his tap.

"We'll make camp here for the night," Nix said.

"Is that wise?" Wiley asked. "There's at least two hours of daylight left."

"We don't know what the rest of the trail looks like and I'm not keen on being in the woods in the dark without shelter."

"You think it's the treasure hunters?" Nix asked.

"Most likely. They don't understand the danger they're walking into. We have to stop them, if we can."

Wiley couldn't handle the thought of more people dying because of these meteorites. He still thought of her begging eyes every day and the moment he pulled the trigger.

"The trail follows the stream," Eve said. "I'll scout ahead. See if I can see anything."

"Watch your six," Nixon said.

Nadine bagged them a couple rabbits and a pheasant for supper while Nixon got a small fire going, stopping several times to flex his shoulder. Still, Wiley said nothing. Sooner or later, they'd have to address it though. Some of the higher mountain passes would require all their strength to traverse.

Eve returned a short time later. "There's no sign of any hikers now. They must be in some kind of hurry."

Nadine studied the climbing guides against the path in front of them. "Tomorrow, I think we should swing south and stick to the flats for a while longer."

"That takes us away from the meteorite," Wiley argued.

"True, but we can move faster. If we keep following this stream, eventually we'll hit waterfalls and hard climbing. If there are other hikers ahead of us we can at least catch up to them, or maybe even get in front of them."

"Nadine is the best navigator I know, Mister Porter," Nixon said. "I suggest listening to her."

"Alright then," Wiley replied. "We'll do it your way for now."

He had to trust they knew what they were doing. It was why he sought them out, after all. He just couldn't shake the feeling they were running out of time.

Wiley finished setting his tent and joined the others next to the fire. He allowed himself a small moment of satisfaction as he set the last peg. He finally had a good team.

The first growl, he dismissed as a trick of his imagination. The second one, much closer this time, got his attention.

Nadine reached for her M5 carbine. "That doesn't sound too friendly."

The trees rustled again. Nixon motioned for the two women to flank the campsite. "Probably a mountain lion.

Everyone stay calm. Cougars don't like people so maybe it'll go around us."

"Sounds like it's the size of a mountain," Eve said. "Hope our bullets are big enough."

The size of the cougar that emerged from the trees nearly knocked Wiley on his ass. He'd never seen one even half its size. One paw was nearly the size of his chest. Massive incisors protruded from the roof of its mouth, curling almost beneath its chin.

"That ain't natural," Nixon said, unleashing a torrent of bullets at the giant cat.

The oversized cat came on, bleeding from several wounds. Wiley and the others joined in and after several seconds of ear-splitting roars, the creature fell. Wiley hated dispatching the magnificent animal, but this mission would claim more before the end. "I think a night watch would be prudent from here on out," he said. "It won't be pretty if one of those things happens upon us while we sleep."

"The meteorite's doing that, isn't it?" Eve demanded as she changed out the magazine in her rifle.

"I suspect so. Though, I'm not getting any readings on the monitors." The fragment in his staff wasn't even glowing yet. "It must've wandered down from higher up."

Nix slung his rifle over his shoulder and bent down to inspect the dead cat. "Makes me wonder what else we'll find when we get closer to the space rock."

"Never mind that," Nadine butt in. "How do we keep this thing from affecting us?"

Wiley pulled four capped syringes filled with clear liquid from his pack. "These inoculations will protect you from the worst of the radiation. I don't recommend using them until we start getting hits on the Geiger counter. These are only short-term solutions. The protection lessens with each passing hour. I'd hoped they wouldn't be necessary at all."

Eve grabbed him by his jacket roughly. "You were prepared to let us walk into a radioactive hot zone without protection? What kind of sick fuck are you?"

Wiley didn't resist. "I'm sorry. I never intended that. Not all meteorites we encounter are radioactive and we can never tell until we are within range. The clothing and cloaks you're wearing offer some protection. These inoculations will add to it. I'll understand if none of you want to continue."

Nixon stepped between Wiley and Eve. "You have been less than forthright with us, Mister Porter. The danger seems to more acute than we were led to believe. At least on active duty, our commanders had the decency to disclose all relevant intel."

Wiley made a point of looking each of them in the eye as he spoke. "You're absolutely right. The truth of the matter is I didn't know myself the extent of the danger, but I knew the possibility existed, hence the syringes. I should've told you."

Eve let him go with a shove. "What else have you kept from us?"

"As I said. There was no way of telling the effects of this particular meteorite until we got here. After seeing that giant cat I think we have our answer to a degree. Unfortunately, we won't know any other effects until we encounter them."

"What about people? You said we wouldn't have to shoot anyone. Was that a lie too?"

Here it was. The moment he'd been dreading since they left the trailhead. "There is one group of... people that may go after it as well. They're known as Star Children. People whom meteorites have affected in some way or another. They are not typically violent, but if they see an opportunity, they will go after it."

"Mutants?" Nadine spat. "You have us chasing the X-Men too?"

"So much for that trust part you sold us on, hey?" Eve said. "What, did you think throwing a bunch of money at us would get us to overlook the bullshit?"

"It's not like that," Wiley replied. "I needed you to stay until I figured how to tell you about the weird stuff. There's so much more to show you if you give me the chance."

"Eve, Nadine," Nix said. "You're with me. We're going for a stroll to make sure there's nothing else out here ready to eat us." He slid a new magazine into his rifle and glared at Wiley. "If there's anything else you need to tell us, I suggest you figure it out while we're gone."

Wiley worried more about Stavros than the Star Children. His former pupil shared their ideology, but none of their restraint. While the Star Children mostly wanted to be left alone, Stavros wanted more and wasn't shy about crossing lines to get it.

The others returning, no longer looking like they wanted to kill him. "I assume you were discussing whether to keep going or leave me here. What did you decide?"

Nixon added a couple pieces of dead wood to the

cook fire. "Everything depends on whether you continue to lie to us. Is there anything else you're not telling us?"

"It's possible this treasure hunt is being facilitated by a former student of mine named Stavros Newton. He betrayed me when he learned what the Star Children had to offer. Stavros is my single biggest failure as a Collective agent."

"Greed is one of this world's greatest corruptors, Wiley," Nadine said. "I wouldn't get too bent out of shape over it."

"The problem is the Star Children wouldn't give him what he craved most- power. As I said before, their methods are more subtle and far less violent. Stavros went rogue. If he acquires this meteorite, I suspect he will try to overthrow both the Collective and the Star Children. I cannot begin to stress how bad that would be."

"How do we stop him?" Nixon asked.

"Get to the meteorite and neutralize its power. If he can't access its power, he can't use it to his advantage."

Nixon turned to the other two. "What do you think?"

"That shot," Eve said. "Is it safe?"

"One hundred percent. Think of it as your annual flu shot, if you like."

"I'm not happy about any of this, but it wouldn't be right letting you continue into these mountains alone," Nixon said. "Besides, if I go back, I'll only end up begging on the same street corner again."

"I'm going too," Nadine said. "No different dying up here than in the gutter. At least here I don't have to bang a complete stranger to earn my next meal."

"Don't have much choice, do I?" Eve said. "I either

tag along with you clowns or go back alone."

"You could wait for us here," Wiley said. "We shouldn't be more than a day, two at most."

"I guess you missed the being alone part," she replied. "Not like any of you idiots knows how to stitch a wound anyway."

"That settles it then," Nix said. "Let's get some sleep. Going to be a long day tomorrow."

Wiley let out a slow breath. Thank god they stayed. This mission would be hard enough with help. "I'll take first watch. Since I'm the one who dragged you all out here in the first place."

***

The camp was subdued the next morning as they climbed from their bedrolls and went about preparing coffee and breakfast. Thankfully, no other 'genetically modified' creatures disturbed their respite.

The flats did make travel quicker. Wiley worked up a sweat keeping up with the others. The other hikers had definitely come this way. Unfortunately, they still hadn't encountered them. The flats gave way to a dense wooded region with sharp inclines. Despite no radiation readings, other signs worried Wiley. Animals far bigger than the cougar, along with other hiking groups had passed by here recently, adding an extra sense of urgency.

Nadine chugged from her canteen during one of their brief stops. She swiped her arm across her lips and tucked the canteen back into her pack. "These woods are famous for some of the biggest black bears in the country.

Hopefully, this radiation doesn't make them any bigger."

Nixon grunted. "At this point, I'm just as afraid of the squirrels."

The first blips on the Geiger counter registered around midday. The trees snapped in half like toothpicks were more noticeable. Wiley checked the fragment in his staff. A greenish sheen had replaced its normal dullness. Nothing had shown in the stones on his gauntlets yet. He handed out the syringes. "It's time for the inoculations. Just jam it into your thigh like it's an Epi-Pen."

An awkward silence followed the jabs. They all looked at each other expectantly. Nadine looked down at herself. "No extra arms or legs. Don't have a tail." She grabbed her chest. "Boobs aren't any bigger though. Disappointing."

As they hiked throughout the day, Wiley kept a close eye out for any adverse effects from the radiation or the inoculation. They were far less fatigued, but his three companions had become skittish, stopping constantly to check something or other. Nix seemed to struggle the most. Maybe Wiley waited too long to give them the shots.

"What's on your mind, Nix?" Eve asked.

Nixon put a finger to his lips, demanding silence. He kept everyone tight together, walking in a diamond formation where possible. "Eyes up, everyone. These ridges are prime ambush hides."

They came to a mountain stop a mile later. Usually stocked with water, firewood, and protein bars, this one was completely destroyed. Three mauled bodies lay amidst the chaos.

"Looks like that cougar paid a visit here before

coming to see us," Nix said.

Wiley strolled around the campsite. "I don't think so. Something bigger did this."

Nadine knelt next to one of the bodies and poked at one of the gashes with a stick. "If there's something up here bigger than that cat, we've got problems."

Wiley pulled a zip lock bag from the dead hiker's pocket. Among the pages was a map marking their route through the mountain. "This might come in handy."

"What do we do with them?" Eve asked. "It don't feel right leaving them like this."

"Let's straighten out the hut and tuck them in there for now," Nixon said. "We can send a recovery team in after the mission."

A hideous shriek pierced the silence. Wiley looked up in time to see a large shadow cross overhead. Nixon was down on one knee, rifle aimed into the sky. Sweat poured down the back of Eve's neck as she stepped a little closer to Nixon.

"I'm thinking that wasn't a sparrow," Nadine said. "It's probably what killed these three."

Wiley checked the sliver embedded in his staff. Its glow had intensified. "The effects of the radiation are slowly making their way down the mountain," Wiley added. "We have to speed this up. We don't want any of this reaching town."

They finished the makeshift tomb quickly and set a few stones in front of the opening to keep anyone from disturbing the bodies. None of them were unaccustomed to seeing a dead body, but had hoped they'd left that part of their lives behind. It never got any easier.

They followed the trail in silence for a while. In the distance, the mountain rumbled and the trees around them rustled. Birds took flight. "Probably an avalanche farther up," Nadine said. "Hopefully nobody was below it."

Several more avalanches let go on the mountain throughout the day, each one closer to their position. It almost sounded like they were being shelled. Wiley's companions, especially Nix flinched every time the mountain groaned.

Without warning, he dove to the ground and opened fire into the trees. "Ambush," he screamed. "Everybody down." Birds took flight. Land animals bolted deeper into the woods.

Wiley flattened himself on the ground while Eve and Nadine crawled over to Nix. Everyone on this mountain now likely knew where they were.

"Nix," Eve shouted, shaking him by the shoulder. "There's no one there, buddy. Cease fire." Nix ignored her. "Cease fire, soldier. That's an order!"

The gunfire stopped, and Wiley lifted his head.

Nixon gaped wide-eyed. "Don't you see them? Rebel fighters through the trees. At least six of them."

Eve cupped his face in her hands. "You're seeing things, corporal. We're not overseas anymore."

Wiley stayed back while the women calmed Nixon down. Wiley should've never brought them up here. It'd been pure arrogance to think he could've been the difference they needed in their lives. He only wanted to save them like he couldn't save the others. After a few moments, Nixon had calmed down and Wiley felt safe approaching. "Everyone okay?"

"We are now," Nadine replied. "Places like this bring back bad memories."

"Everything felt so real. I can still hear the screams and smell the mortar fire."

"This is all my fault," Wiley said. "I brought you into a situation I should've known would have adverse effects. The meteorite is pulling your worst nightmares out and replaying them like a real-life horror movie. I'm sorry to have put you through that."

"Can we do anything to fight it?" Eve asked. "I doubt a bandage will cut it in this case."

"I can send you back. I release you from your contracts, with full compensation of course. It's the least I can do for dragging you up here without a second thought."

"Hey, wait a minute," Eve countered. "We're soldiers and we sure as hell don't turn around when the mission gets hard. You gave us purpose again, Mister Porter. Don't underestimate the value in that."

"She's right," Nix added, "but the hallucinations are a problem. Anything in your magic bag that can help?"

"Perhaps. We've been studying meteors for some time and have managed to distill some benefit from them. I never go into the field insufficiently supplied." He opened one of his pack's many pockets. "Ah yes, here we are." He handed a small vial of clear liquid to Nixon. "Drink this. It's a small relaxation potion our alchemists whipped up. Completely safe, I assure you."

"Hold it," Nadine protested. "I'm not keen on wandering around the mountainside impaired by a bunch of weird drugs."

"There is no impairment involved. It helps your body relax and clear your mind."

"We don't have a choice," Nix said. "We can't be jumping at shadows all the time." He downed the elixir. After a few moments, he took a deep breath. "Feeling better already."

Nixon set a brisk pace along the steadily steepening trail. At this altitude, the air had thinned enough that Wiley felt like he breathed through a pine-scented wet clothe. He stuck his hands into his armpits. Now that the sun had set below the peaks, it turned colder.

Wiley kept an eye on Eve and Nadine, expecting one of them to be triggered at any moment. Unfortunately, his three companion's mental state wasn't their most pressing issue. There were more signs of other hikers after the meteorite.

"Okay, guys," Nixon said. "We're going to take this nice and slow, quiet like. There's no reason to tip anyone else off that we're close by."

The three tents were pitched in a tight cluster amongst a small group of trees. A low camp fire blanketed the area with a thin smoky haze. Three figures, two men, one bearded, and a woman, sat around it, sipping from tin cups and eating sandwiches.

Nixon signaled everyone into a crouch. "Eve, you and I will go introduce ourselves. You two watch our six from here. We'll signal if it's all clear."

Nixon and Eve approached the hikers, keeping their weapons low. "Evening, folks," Nixon greeted. "Nice night for a hike."

Hands went to rifles on the ground. Eve's own weapon came up and the red dot from her laser scope painted his chest. Everyone froze. "That's not a good idea, friend."

The bearded hiker glared up at Eve. "It's impolite to sneak up on someone in the dark."

"Let's all just take it easy," Nix said. "You have my apologies. We mean no ill will. We got a late start and figured there'd be a decent place to make camp around here somewhere."

"Yeah, well, this spot's taken so move along," the clean shaven one barked.

Nixon chuckled nervously. "Why the hostility, friend? We're all hikers here heading for the summit. You are heading for the summit, aren't you?"

The woman leaned back and crossed her arms. "Where we're heading is none of your business. We heard gunshots earlier. Was that you?"

"Rabid squirrel," Eve replied. "Bastard nearly tore my face off."

"It's time for you to go," the woman replied.

"Ah, I get it," Nix said. "You're heading for that space rock. I read about that somewhere."

Wiley dashed from his cover as the bearded hiker went for his rifle again. Nadine put a bullet into the ground next to his hand.

"I'd advise you to keep very still," Nixon said. "We don't want any unfortunate accidents. Eve, their weapons, if you please. We're all going to keep this nice and civil."

"You might as well kill us," the bearded one said. "That hundred grand is ours one way or another."

"A lot of good it'll do you lying dead on the side of a mountain," Eve said.

Wiley stepped farther into the light. "You fools have no idea the danger you're dealing with. Three of your more unfortunate compatriots found that out earlier. We buried them back at the rest station. Do you want to end up like that?"

The clean-shaven hiker grunted. "It's worth the risk. Even a fraction of that prize money solves a lot of problems."

"We're only interested in the meteorite," Nixon said. "The prize money is yours if you help us recover it. We don't need it."

"Or better still," Wiley added. "I'll give you each a hundred thousand dollars right now to turn around and go home. No questions asked."

The woman gawked openly. "You're joking, right?"

"I'm dead serious. There are others on this mountain with bigger guns and less restraint. Trust me, you don't want to encounter them."

"What if we all think you're full of shit and intend on our original path?"

"Then we have a problem," Wiley replied. "This is not a game or some stupid scavenger hunt. Lives are at stake. We'd all do well to remember that."

"We'll have to take them with us," Eve said. "I ain't leaving them here tied up. It'll kill 'em."

The standoff ended as giant bears rampaged through the camp. The humans scattered for cover. Wiley crouched behind a small berm, cut off from his companions. His rifle was somewhere up by the camp.

Luckily, he still had his staff. He took a moment to reconcile what he saw. Goblins riding those giant bears. He was sure of it.

Wiley poked his head up from cover. The bears and their goblin riders milled about the destroyed camp, sniffing at various articles. Two other goblins guarded the three hikers as they huddled shivering against a rock.

"Where are your companions?" one of them growled. "The ones who just arrived."

Interesting that these goblins could talk. How much of that was meteorite and how much was Stavros?

"Halfway down the mountain by now, if they're smart."

"Find the Collective agent," a goblin screamed. "The master wants a word with him."

Wiley slid farther down the embankment, counting on the darkness to conceal him. He'd like a word with Stavros as well, but on his terms.

A bear-riding goblin inched its way in Wiley's direction. He had to move, but if he did, he'd be discovered. He'd hoped to save these for a last resort. Now, he had no choice. He loaded his blow dart gun with his own special concoction. A mixture of the shot he gave the others earlier and a little something to reverse any effects. Hopefully it worked.

Wiley hit the bear first. It was the easier target and the thrashing gave him time to reload the blow dart gun. The goblin fell as he came upon Wiley's position. There was no way the others hadn't heard that. He inched his way around the perimeter of the camp, trying not to make a sound. Not that it would've mattered much. The goblins made enough noise to cover his movements.

Wiley found Nadine unconscious at the bottom of a small dip. Blood leaked from a gash in her forehead. The cut was superficial, but Wiley worried about the potential concussion. He had to leave her for now. The others were still around here somewhere.

Gunshots rang out as Wiley worked his way back up towards the camp. Two goblins fell as the others scattered. By the time they hit the ground, they were human again.

Wiley's stomach churned. These weren't creatures out of some fairy tale. They were innocent people Stavros had bent to his will. They didn't come up here to die. Wiley had to put a stop to this before any more died.

"Take these three," one goblin said. "Stavros didn't want us gone too long and they'll come in handy lifting the rock out of the crater."

"He will be angry if we return without the one."

The goblin looked down at the three cowering hikers. "He will follow us. These Collective fools don't like to let people die."

That was true. The Collective frowned upon the loss of innocent life. They were all about preservation and protection. Wiley had a less than stellar record in that regard. There were times, though, that the gloves had to come off.

The goblins disappeared deeper into the mountain with their three prisoners. Nixon revealed himself first, followed by Eve.

"Over here," Wiley called out. "Nadine is injured."

They helped her back into the camp. Nixon went about straightening things. "You're lucky," Wiley said as he handed Eve the gauze from the med kit. "This could've been much worse."

"This is nothing compared to deployment." She lifted the bottom of her shirt. A four-inch scar ran from front to back. "To a piece of shrapnel from a frag grenade."

"I'm sorry," Wiley said, not know what else to say.

"It's all good. You should've seen the guy who threw it. Not sure they found enough of him to bury."

Wiley let out a short chuckle. "I'm guessing you've never faced foes quite like this though."

"It's all the same. You aim, shoot, and hope you hit the right thing." Nadine side-eyed him as she drank from her canteen. "Those little goblins work for your old buddy Stavros, don't they?"

Wiley held his hands out to the warming fire. "I'd hoped I could beat him up here to retrieve the meteorite."

Nixon passed around coffee and strips of beef jerky before sitting next to Eve. "Why did they turn human after they died?"

"As I told you earlier, Star Children are people directly affected by meteorites. To use Nadine's term, they are mutants. The problem is, we never know what affects they suffer until we encounter them because each meteorite is different. It seems this particular one is turning them into mythical creatures."

"So, you're telling us we've signed up for a real-life game of Dungeons and Dragons," Eve said. "Should've brought a set of twelve-sided dice. I could roll for a hot meal."

"In this game, the consequences of failure are deadly."

"Hopefully, we don't meet the dragon," Nadine added.

She added another couple logs to the fire while the rest of them straightened out their tents. "I'll take first watch. Took a nasty whack on the head. Probably shouldn't go to sleep right away anyway."

"I'll keep you company for a little while," Nix said.

Wiley lay awake for a while, considering his options before drifting off into a fitful slumber.

***

Wiley sat straight up when his tent flap rustled. His hand found the staff next to his bedroll. The silhouette of a lithe, shapely figure entered. Wiley hesitated. Why was Nadine coming into his tent?

She crawled beneath his sleeping bag and slid her hand across his chest. "I'm cold."

This wasn't a good idea. He shifted from beneath her touch, as warm and welcoming as it was.

"I wanted to thank you for caring for me," she cooed.

"Yes, well. It was no trouble." He tried to keep the squeak from his voice.

"What's the matter? Don't you want me?"

Wiley almost bit his tongue off. "I just think it's better if we get some sleep. Tomorrow will be difficult."

"You don't like me, do you?" She started sobbing. Her shoulders bounced and her eyes glistened. "You think I'm ugly."

Wiley held out his hands, trying to calm her before the others heard the commotion. "That's not it at all. I think you're beautiful." Trying to explain the impropriety would only upset her further. Also, this was the meteorite pulling her survival instincts to the surface again. Wiley had to approach this differently. "You know what. I do want you. Let's have a drink to help us relax." He handed her one of the two vials he removed from his pack. "Cheers," he said and downed his. She immediately followed suit.

After a few moments, clarity returned to her eyes and she looked around the tent. She pulled her sweater tighter around her chest. "What the hell is going on here?"

"You were a bit out of it and climbed in here. I suspect the meteorite is affecting you and likely all of us. It's heightened your survival instincts and lowered your inhibitions."

She glanced down at the two empty vials on the tent floor. "Did you drug me?"

"You would've already had to have been in here for me to drug you and I'm hurt you would think that of me. The elixir was to counter the effects of the meteorite. You are of your right mind again, are you not?"

"I'm sorry. I'm not used to trusting people. Not since I got out of the service anyway. Everyone I meet just wants to use me. Probably best we not mention this to anyone else."

"You have my word."

"I'll leave you to your rest. I'll go wake Nix and crawl in with Eve. She could probably use the company anyway."

Wiley didn't fall back asleep after Nadine left. How the hell was he supposed to deal with Stavros when he couldn't even keep his own team safe? Stavros had already harnessed the meteorite's power. Would Wiley's staff be enough to overcome it?

The sun hadn't yet come up when Wiley crawled out of his tent to make the coffee. He grabbed the rifle next to his tent and slung it over his shoulder. Walking around unarmed this close to the meteorite wasn't a good idea, whether they were in camp or not. It took Nixon moving for Wiley to notice him.

"Sleep well?" Nixon asked.

Wiley added a couple pieces of driftwood to the fire and filled the kettle from his canteen. "Not as well as I would've liked."

"Cuddling with Nadine didn't help?"

Wiley froze, his stomach dropping. "Nothing happened. The meteorite took hold of her. The same it did to you. Do not be too quick to judge her."

"It's not her I'm judging."

"What's that supposed to mean?"

"You've been manipulating us from the start, keeping just enough from us to pull us along like little puppets. I'm beginning to think you're the one trying to acquire the meteorite for yourself and Stavros is trying to stop you."

"You can't be serious. You want to know why I'm going after this thing? The first meteorite I encountered turned my best friend into a werewolf after she was bitten in the mountains where we were hiking. I had to kill her and the wolf. If you think I'm in this for some stupid notion of glory, you're not as smart as I thought you were."

Nix stepped toward Wiley, hands balled into fists. Wiley's rifle came up, stopping him in his tracks. "Put the gun down and see how tough you are, little spook."

Wiley's anger suddenly boiled over. "If you want to

leave, leave. I'm trying to save people's lives. I don't have time for pissing matches. I thought I was doing a good thing. If you're not interested, stop wasting my time."

"You know the biggest thing I've learned throughout my life? No one ever does anything out of the goodness of their heart. They do it because they want something. You picked three of the most desperate people you could find to get it."

Eve emerged from her tent. "Are you two done comparing the size of your junk? That coffee's not going to make itself."

Wiley went to the kettle to check the now steaming kettle. He dumped a packet of coffee into it and stirred it aggressively. "Once the sun comes up, you three can make your way back down the mountain. I'll continue on alone to free the hikers. You will be paid the agreed upon signing bonuses and then released from your contracts. You can keep the clothes you're wearing, but you'll have to vacate the apartments. I'm sorry I couldn't do more for you."

"I thought we had this sorted out," Eve said as she wiped out her cup with the hem of her shirt.

"Well, we haven't. I won't play on the desperation of others for my own purposes. I'll finish this job myself. It's no longer your problem."

"If you think you're getting anywhere near that crater alone, you're delusional, spook boy," Nix seethed. Thankfully, his own rifle was well out of his reach.

"Snap out of it, you two," Eve barked. "We're supposed to be fighting Stavros, not each other. Both sides had something the other wanted. That isn't being used. It's called a good trade." She shoved Nix on his shoulder, staggering him back a step, and eliciting a wince. "You still want to be sitting outside the shelter feeling useless? That's the alternative. At least up here you have a purpose again."

Nadine emerged from the tent. "Last night wasn't Wiley's fault. It was mine. This meteorite is making us do all kinds of weird shit. What happens if that power gets out and starts making people angry? More people will die. You want that on your head knowing you could've done something about it?"

"Nadine is right," Wiley said. "I will say this last thing. I am not interested in forcing anyone to do anything." He went to pack up his tent. They had a long day ahead of them and it was past time they got it started.

The path of destruction the bears left behind was likely visible from the space station. Eve stood next to a tree that had been snapped like a matchstick. "I've climbed a lot of mountains and seen a lot of wild animals, but I ain't never seen anything like this."

"Nobody has," Nixon replied, "because it's not natural. Nothing on this rock is."

Subdued, Nix led the way. Wiley had to figure out how to fix things with him. His agitation would likely worsen as they approached the meteorite. Hopefully, Wiley wouldn't have to use the blow dart gun on him. Or worse...

They followed the trail through a narrow pass to a ridge overlooking the rest of the mountain range. From here they spotted the deep impact crater. Halfway down, amidst the scorched and barren mountainside, a plume of thick black smoke coiled into the sky.

Eve cupped her hand over her eyes. "There are

creatures moving down there." Her jaw dropped open. "Is that a dragon?"

Wiley's stomach dropped when he looked through his binoculars. Not good. Definitely not good. "I was afraid of this."

"Any way we can train and ride him?" Nix asked.

"I don't think we brought big enough guns," Nadine added, "and I left my magic wand in my other jacket."

Wiley held up his staff. "Good thing I brought mine then, isn't it."

The question was, why hadn't Stavros taken the beast and flown the meteorite off the mountain already. "Once we neutralize the meteorite, the dragon and anything else affected by it will disappear. The problem will be approaching covertly."

"We'd have a better chance of winning the Powerball," Nadine said.

"Hey, you guys might want to see this," Nix called. He pointed to the left of the crater. "There's another camp in that valley over there."

"Stavros'll be keeping the hikers there. He knows we'll go after them and is trying to detour us from the meteorite."

"He's buying time," Nadine said. "He doesn't know how to move it yet."

"Let's hope we get to him before he figures it out," Wiley said.

**

As they descended into the valley, the cedar and spruce

trees thickened, providing plenty of places to hide for them as well as their foes. The obvious bear trail lessened. Every time they stopped, it took Nadine longer to find the trail.

"Anybody else notice the temperature drop?" Eve asked. "Wind has shifted several times in the last few minutes, and I'm pretty sure it's about to snow."

Wiley looked up as the first flakes landed on his face. Within a minute or two, the blizzard swirled around them. Before too long, the drifts were halfway up their shins. His bare hands felt like blocks of ice and he couldn't stop shivering. They had minutes before they froze to death.

He thrust his staff into the air and released the fragment's power. A bubble of energy from the tip slowly enveloped him. "Everyone inside," he commanded. "Quickly." The three veterans dashed inside. "Unfortunately, this protection won't last long. My staff gains its power from the meteorite and only has a small amount at the moment. We'll have to find proper shelter."

"Our tents won't be much good in this," Nix said. "We need to be able to make a fire."

Wiley jammed the staff into the soft earth. "Stay here. I will find us someplace to rest."

He fought his way through the deep snow to a tight group of trees that kept most of the snow at bay. He rushed back to the others, being sure to mark the path along the way. The bubble had shrunk considerably and the three companions had to hunch close to each other to remain in its protection. "Follow me. There's a spot not far from here."

The intense snow made building the crude pine bough

lean-to twice as long as it should have. By the end, Wiley couldn't feel his hands or feet. The four of them huddled inside around a small fire that seemed to provide almost no heat at all.

The glow in his staff was nearly extinguished. Hopefully, it wouldn't take long for it to recharge. They'd have to use the rifles if Stavros's goblins attacked.

Nadine shifted a loose bough to one side, allowing a bit of snow to fall into the shelter. "If the meteorite is controlling the storm, what makes you think it'll stop?"

"I think Stavros is directing the meteorite's power towards us," Wiley replied. "He'll have to rest eventually. We can move then."

"If we're not dead," Nixon said.

"Be honest, Wiley," Eve said. "Will Stavros hurt those people?"

"I don't think so. He'll use them to lure me in. He may even try to convert them to his cause."

"I guess the apple doesn't fall far from the tree, hey Mister Porter," Nix said.

"Knock it off, Nix," Eve snapped.

Wiley broke the awkward silence that followed. "How is it none of you were able to find gainful employment after your military service? You're obviously quite talented and resilient. I refuse to accept that the streets were your only option. Some companies are missing out, I think."

Eve shrugged. "No one wants to hire someone who has a fifty-fifty chance of not showing up for work because their mental health took a nosedive. HR departments hate dealing with people like us because it's more paperwork and higher insurance premiums."

"You know how many jobs I've lost because of VA appointments?" Nixon added. "Of course, they won't come right out and say that. That'd be a human rights violation. We know better though."

"That's quite sad and unnecessary. Let me assure you, the Collective will provide whatever resources you require regardless of cost and for however long you need them. I won't stand for allowing your suffering to continue. Not when I can do something about it."

Nixon shifted uncomfortably and stared at the ground. "Nice sentiment, Mister Porter, but it's not that simple. Wanting the help and getting it are two different things. Some wait years to see a head shrink." Nixon went quiet for a moment. "Some never get the chance."

"And the shoulder?"

Nixon smirked. He didn't really expect Wiley to forget about that, did he? "Torn rotator cuff. Needs surgery, but the VA here isn't like the big city ones. They've been great, but can only do so much. Waiting list is about a mile long, or so I'm told. In the meantime, I stay close to the shelter in case something comes up."

"How did it happen?"

"Roadside bomb threw me from the APC gun turret. The landing hurt more than the bomb. I lost a couple good buddies in that explosion so I'm not going to complain about a busted shoulder."

"The friend you had to kill," Nadine asked. "Was she your wife?"

"No, but she was someone I cared for deeply. I wouldn't wish it on my worst enemy."

"Yeah, that explains a lot," Eve said. "Sometimes life

deals a shitty hand."

The storm broke sometime in the late afternoon. The snow had almost buried the lean-to. It took three of them pushing to clear the opening. A thick blanket of white covered everything in every direction. The trail they'd been following had been wiped out.

"Let's take this nice and slow," Nixon said. "No need to risk any broken ankles."

They roped up and trudged through the deep snow in what they hoped was the right direction. Wiley ended up face down in the snow several times before finding his footing. Within a few hundred yards, the snow thinned, leaving a distinct path through the woods. Before too long, the snow had completely disappeared.

The hairs stood on the back of Wiley's neck as they followed the natural trail deeper into the valley. This felt too easy. He tried to take them another way through the trees, but there was always a cliff or some other obstacle. It felt like the mountain was squeezing them like a ketchup bottle. The others agreed.

"Anyone else think that trail looks a tad bit too inviting?" Eve asked.

"He's funneling us into a kill zone," Nixon said.

"Unfortunately, this terrain doesn't give us much choice," Nadine said.

"The meteorite's power is getting stronger," Wiley said. "My staff will counter it once it has collected enough radiation." He checked the glow on the sliver. Stronger, but still not strong enough. "The closer we get to the meteorite, the faster it will charge."

Nadine checked her map. "We've almost reached the

valley floor. The prison camp's not far up the other side."

"Keep your eyes open," Nix said.

The valley floor felt even stranger than the snow storm. The rising temperature forced them to undo their jackets. The trail had narrowed around them, cutting off any escape route.

Nadine pulled her collar away from her neck. "I wish this bloody mountain would make up its mind about the weather."

Wiley thought his eyes were playing tricks on him until he almost walked into a tree that hadn't been there a second before. He went around it only to be confronted by another, and then another. The trees closed in around them as green and blue radiation swirled overhead. "I think the forest doesn't want us going any farther."

"We'll see about that," Nixon said and dashed towards an opening between two trees. A thick low-swinging branch to the chest sent him skidding across the valley floor.

Eve helped him sit up. "Solid base hit up the middle, I'd say."

"Nah," he replied, coughing. "Weak grounder to third."

"What do we do now, Mister Collective agent?" Nadine asked. "I don't feel like getting clubbed to death."

The trees inched closer, forcing them back to back. Branches, sharpened like spears, threatened to skewer them. Pelting the trees with gunfire did nothing to stop their advance.

Wiley exposed the staff's sliver, hoping it still had enough power for this to work. The radiation cloud spiraled down and collected into the tip. The wall of trees stopped advancing. Seconds later, they backed away to their original position.

"Neat trick," Nadine said. "Does that thing mix margaritas too?"

"Let's get the hell out of here," Nixon said, "before the rocks start getting in the way too."

***

The forest didn't try to kill them anymore as they made their way across the valley floor. Wiley welcomed the change of pace, though it likely wouldn't last. Stavros found them once, he'd find them again. They came to a narrow plateau at the foot of the valley. Daylight waned and the prison camp was on the other side.

"Stay here while I do some recon," Nix said.

They hadn't settled when Nixon came back over the rise. "The camp's abandoned."

"They probably moved while we were pinned down by the blizzard," Nadine said. "They'll be heading for the crater."

The flaming boulder hit the ground next to them without warning, showering them with exploding rock and dirt. Trees went up like matchsticks. Three more fire boulders hit, scattering the others into the woods, and leaving Wiley alone in the middle of the clearing. He struggled to his feet amid the heat and shuffled a bit closer to one of the boulders. They burned with an unnaturally green flame. They were meteor-fueled.

Perhaps...

Wiley exposed his staff's fragment to the boulder, causing an almost instantaneous reaction. Radiation from the boulder spiraled from the flames into the staff. Finally, a break his way. He sucked as much radiation as he could out of the boulder, leaving it a smoking pile of stone. He drained six more before the barrage finally stopped. Danger persisted though. A great wind picked up, like a helicopter landing. No, not a helicopter. A dragon.

As the creature walked through the flames, untouched by them, it shrank and shifted. By the time it stood before Wiley, the dragon had become a human. A human Wiley knew well. Stavros wasn't trying to control the dragon. He *was* the dragon.

"Impressive, wouldn't you say?"

"More like idiotic. You know how dangerous this is, Stavros. The meteors are unpredictable. They can't be left out. Maybe you'd have a healthier respect for that if you'd stayed with the Collective."

"I choose to see the potential instead," Stavros replied. "The Collective never considered the benefits of these meteorites. Your close-mindedness has been to humanity's detriment."

"I disagree. Our efforts have saved countless lives."

"It is not enough to save them. We must elevate them, help them shine." Stavros looked past Wiley. "Where are your friends? Perhaps they'd like to hear my sermon for themselves."

"They turned back. They weren't as dedicated as I'd hoped."

"You were always a poor liar, Wiley. I wonder why one of them hasn't shot me yet. Come out, if you dare," he called. "I will show you the true meaning of power."

"We're not interested in violence, Stavros. More have already died on this mountain than necessary. We just want to secure the meteorite and go home. Release the hikers you took prisoner and you can walk free."

"Prisoners? Oh no, my dear Wiley." Stavros stopped pacing and wagged a finger. "Not prisoners. They see the advantages we can provide and have elected to join us. They are helping my friends recover my meteorite as we speak."

"You've brainwashed them and already turned them into goblins to follow you. You're despicable, Stavros."

"Not brainwashed," Stavros insisted. He stepped toward Wiley. "Educated. You see, Wiley, the Collective does not hold monopoly on meteor lore. We have learned a few things ourselves."

Wiley tensed and brought his staff up. "You're playing with fire, Stavros."

"You're still not seeing the potential. Imagine the difference I can make with the meteorite's magic. A dragon is only the beginning."

"It will eventually destroy you. I have seen it happen to others. I have experienced it."

"I am not as weak as the Collective. I have held power far greater than a dragon."

Wiley's shoulders slumped. "And it has corrupted you." He'd hoped he could save his former protégé, but the draw of power had blackened his heart.

Stavros jumped toward Wiley, but Wiley smashed his gauntlets together in front of him. The narrow blue beam from his wrists struck Stavros square in the chest. He scowled and shifted into the dragon. He spat a gout of flame at Wiley before taking flight. "Stay out of my way, Wiley, if you want to make it off this mountain alive."

Nadine, Nixon, and Eve joined him again after Stavros had disappeared back up the mountain. "Can't say I saw that coming," Nadine said.

Wiley glared at Nix. "You still think I want this power for myself? If Stavros succeeds, he'll destroy us all."

"How do we stop him?" Nix asked quietly.

"The good news is he still hasn't recovered the meteorite, but we're running out of time."

Stavros's arrogance worked in their favor. He made no effort to hide his passing or that of the goblins. The trail narrowed to a smooth pass between two low peaks, both concealed by cloud cover. Wiley didn't like this at all. This was another prime spot for an ambush.

They stopped to fit their crampons and rope up. Nixon came to sit next to Wiley to fit his gear. "I'm sorry about earlier. I lost my head a little bit. I just don't want to see Nadine get hurt."

"I understand. You three have been through so much together. It's only natural to want to protect them. I should've disclosed everything to you from the start. For that, I am sorry."

"What do we do about this pass?"

"It's a risk, but there's no time to find another way around."

They'd made it nearly halfway through when the first lightning bolts slammed into the mountainside above them. Wiley pulled his head down into his shoulders against the thunderous boom. Chunks of rock, ice and dirt sped toward them like an out-of-control freight train. Their only hope was a nearby rock overhang. Wiley dashed for it, hoping the others saw his intention.

The four huddled against the mountain wall as the avalanche continued. Wiley's ears rang with every lightning strike. He'd misjudged Stavros's willingness to leave them alone. Stavros had waited until they reached the most vulnerable spot on the mountain to attack.

"I thought he breathed fire," Eve yelled over the cacophony.

Wiley shrugged. "I guess he's multi-talented. With the meteorite fueling his power, he can do just about anything."

The lightning 'shelling' stopped and the air cleared. Everything was eerily quiet. Wiley climbed over the pile of rubble and found the path again. "We should go while we have the chance."

The pass to the crater no longer existed. Stavros's ultimate goal was to slow them down long enough for his goblins to retrieve the meteorite pieces. He underestimated Wiley's power though. The sliver in his staff glowed brightly, full of the radiation that gave Stavros his power. Wiley used it to clear the debris, making a new path to follow.

The avalanche set them back several hours. By the time they reached the top of the valley, darkness had completely fallen. They exited a narrow pass onto a high ridge with a plain view of the crater. Wiley dropped his pack to the ground and poured water from his canteen over his face. "I suggest we have a meal break first. That climb will require some strength."

"I feel great," Eve said. "In fact, I haven't felt this good since my first tour."

Wiley eyed her, as well as Nixon. He wasn't flexing his shoulder as much as when they first met. The radiation must be affecting their metabolism. Perhaps the inoculation wasn't as effective as he'd hoped.

They passed around more beef jerky as Wiley stared down at the crater. A wisp of greenish smoke curled up from its depths. Scaling it wouldn't be easy. He looked skyward. Stavros circled somewhere overhead. Waiting for the perfect opportunity to strike. Wiley turned back to his companions. "Someone will have to repel down to deploy the shielding. The rest will have to provide supporting fire."

"Eve is our best climber," Nixon said. "She can make it to the bottom in under ten minutes."

"While I appreciate the vote of confidence, Nix, you know better than that. Every climb is different. Never mind the hostiles that'll be trying to stop us."

"Absolutely," Wiley said. "That's why both of you should go. Nadine and I will secure their camp."

"Are you sure about that?" Nixon asked.

"Those goblins aren't really goblins, they're people. You said you didn't want to shoot anyone. Well, now you don't have to." Wiley removed two canisters resembling shaving cream canes from his backpack. "Inside each of these is a solution that will block the meteorite emissions. Jam it against the rock, twist the cap and press down. Depending on the meteorite's size, a second canister may be required."

"It's the best plan we got, Nix," Eve said. "Let's do it."

Nixon eyed the three of them for another moment. "Alright fine. Let's go. Break time's over."

***

An unnatural, thick fog rolled in over the peak, masking the crater entrance. Stavros wasn't done with his tricks just yet. Wiley and Nadine went left while Nixon and Eve went right. The path wound around scrawny pine trees and jagged boulders. Wiley had to brace himself a few times to stop from slipping on the loose gravel. It was a beautiful mountain, but Wiley now understood why only experienced hikers came here.

The goblin camp came into view around the next corner on the ridge. The goblins had ropes and pulleys all rigged to descend into the crater. Chisels and hammers hung from their belts. They were going to try to break the meteor apart to bring it up.

"It might be better if you stay behind me. I don't know what'll happen when I expose the shard. Besides, I don't think our guns will be much good here now."

They inched a bit closer before Wiley unleashed the magic. Three goblins reverted to their human form right away. They were all hikers participating in the scavenger hunt. Little more than kids. Impressionable young people were easy to manipulate.

More goblins fell to Wiley's magic while Nadine laid down cover fire to keep them in one area, allowing them to move deeper into the camp. Wiley stopped at one of the former goblins and found a faint pulse. These people didn't have long. The hikers weren't among the fallen.

They had to be down in the crater.

A sudden gust of wind announced Stavros's arrival. The ground trembled when he landed. "I gave you multiple opportunities to leave this place. Now this mountain will be your grave."

"You haven't won yet, Stavros." Wiley hit the dragon with a barrage from his staff.

Stavros rolled away from the attack, coming back to his feet. It could've been a trick of his eyes, but Stavros looked a few inches shorter. He loosed bolts of lightning from his mouth like daggers. "You rail against the use of the meteor, yet you do exactly that. You're a hypocrite, Wiley Porter. A hypocrite and a user."

Wiley dove to the side as chunks of mountain disintegrated. "The difference, Stavros, is I use the power not for personal gain, but to ensure others like you don't get it. You say the Collective has no monopoly on lore. No other organization has done the work we have on meteor effects."

"Spoken like a true tyrant."

Bullets from Nadine's rifle slammed into the dragon, sending sparks shooting off his chest. A couple shots found soft flesh, drawing blood. Stavros roared as he leaped into the air and loosed a stream of fire towards Nadine. Wiley jumped to his feet as panic took over.

He flung ribbons of power from his staff at the dragon. Exploding chunks of dirt and rock didn't bother it. "Come on, Stavros. You and I have business to finish." The farther from the meteorite it got, the weaker it became. Wiley just had to get him to use all of his stored-up power.

He spun the staff above his head and as he let the magic fly, the dragon swooped in behind Nadine. The bolt of silver energy struck her and knocked her to the ground. For the second time on this mission, she lay motionless. Wiley scrambled to her, praying she wasn't dead.

"You should not have brought them here, Wiley," Stavros roared as a dragon. "Your hubris has gotten yet another of your friends killed. Perhaps it is time for a career changed."

Wiley cradled Nadine's head in his lap. She wasn't dead yet, but he could do nothing to save her. "I'm so sorry," he cried. "Stavros is right. I should've never brought you here."

Things were falling apart around him, just like seven years ago. Dragons or werewolves it didn't matter. Wiley was powerless against it.

His hands clenched into tight fists. No more. His failures ended with Stavros. No one else was going to die because of him. He laid Nadine's head gently on the ground, picked up his rifle and staff, and followed Stavros down into the crater.

The ringing hammers got louder as he repelled down the rope. They were close to breaking the meteorite apart. Wiley didn't care. He needed to stop Stavros. He dropped from the rope to the crater floor.

Stavros had returned to his human form. Dark splotches dotted his jacket where Nadine's bullets had struck. He glanced Wiley's way. "You are persistent, I'll give you that."

Rage quivered through Wiley like an earthquake. "You'll have to try a lot harder than that to get rid of me,

Stavros." He unleashed a blast of power into the rock face above Stavros. He dove to the side, letting the goblins take the brunt of the slide. This man cared nothing for the people he abused. He never had to lose someone he cared about.

On closer inspection, two of the goblins had familiar looking rifles hanging over their shoulders. Stavros had changed Nix and Eve into goblins. That couldn't stand. Whatever else Wiley did, he'd see them freed.

The radiation levels in the crater ensured Wiley's staff never weakened. Unfortunately, the same held true for Stavros. There had to be another way to defeat him. He circled around the crater to where Stavros was getting back to his feet.

A second dragon swooped into the crater. Wiley froze until he noticed the green and brown skin matched Nadine's jacket. A small smile touched the corners of his mouth. The blast from his staff hadn't killed her. She'd become exactly the weapon they needed to fight Stavros.

"Nadine," Wiley bellowed. She swooped in beside him and he saw in her eyes that she didn't blame him. He patted her cheek gently "Let's finish this, shall we?"

"How do we stop him?"

Like Stavros, the meteorite had only altered her body, leaving her mind intact. "We must get him away from the meteorite and force him to use up his power. Without the meteorite close by, he will not be able to assume his dragon form."

"On my back then." Wiley hesitated. "I can't beat him alone. We're going to need the power in your little stick." Wiley climbed up and Nadine chuckled. "I hope you don't get air sick."

Stavros circled the crater opening. Nadine hit him with a blast of sonic breath that felt like someone was sticking needles in his ears. "Warn me before you do that next time."

Nadine dodged the Stavros's return fire and hit him again. Every time he tried to get back to the crater, Nadine cut him off. She swooped in close and swiped a giant claw at his face. Her next attack wasn't sound, but a chilling blast of frost.

"A dragon of multiple talents, I see," Wiley said.

"Yeah, not sure where that came from, but I like it."

Between Nadine's attacks and Wiley's staff, they drove Stavros farther down the mountain and away from the meteorite. Stavros landed on the ground, near a high cliff. He dragged his body away from Wiley, each shot from the staff draining his power as it did the flaming boulders.

"Give it up, Stavros," Wiley begged. He had to try to save Stavros one more time, even if there wasn't much left to save. "You've lost. The meteorite is now safely under our control and your powers are waning."

"I will die before surrendering to you." He shot a weak stream of fire that Wiley and Nadine easily dodged.

Another bolt of Wiley's magic shrank him to the size of an elephant. They were close to the cliff's edge. "Come away, Stavros. You have a lot to answer for."

"I have nothing to answer for." The dragon form melted away, leaving Stavros a sickly mess. He looked like a junkie in need of his next fix. That's what the meteorites left you with. Craving more and willing to do anything to get it.

A little closer to the ledge.

Nadine was too far away to reach him should he go over. Wiley hit him with another shot of power from the staff, hoping it made him too weak to move. Instead, it pushed him too far. The ground gave way beneath Stavros's feet.

"No," Wiley screamed. Stavros's scream lasted only a second longer before ending abruptly.

Wiley sank to his knees and let the staff fall from his hands. His failure with Stavros was complete. Perhaps this was the end to a vicious cycle that had haunted Wiley for years. Knowing his luck though, probably not.

Nadine came to stand next to Wiley. "You did everything you could. You've done more than anyone else would."

"Did I though? I manipulated you all into helping me and the one student I thought could go far betrayed me. Stavros was right about one thing. I am a hypocrite. I use the power I'm trying to keep from others. Perhaps it has corrupted me as it did him."

"One thing I learned overseas. It isn't the weapons you use that makes you bad. It's why you use them. Stavros was right to a certain degree. The power of these meteorites can help people, but only if used properly. Speaking of which. The radiation is wearing off, but I think I have enough to get us back to the peak if we go now."

Nixon and Eve emerged from the crater as Nadine landed near the edge with Wiley on her back. They were both still goblins, but stared at the dragon, mouths hanging open.

"I'm sure there's a perfectly good explanation for this," Eve said.

"There is," Wiley replied. "I shot her with my staff."

Nixon laughed. "Didn't think you were that kind of girl, Nadine." She flung a handful of snow at him playfully. "Stavros?"

"Dead," Wiley replied. "Fell off a cliff. I'd hoped I could save him."

"Yeah," Nixon said. "I know the feeling, but you save the ones you can and move onto the next mission. That's what soldiers do."

Nadine looked from Nixon to Eve. "How are you two still goblins, but not minions of the raving psychopath?"

"Pretty sure it had something to do with the shot Wiley gave us earlier," Eve said. "Turned into a decent disguise actually."

"It allowed us to get close enough to the meteor to deploy the shielding," Nixon added. "You guys kept Stavros busy long enough for it to take effect and save some of these poor souls. Hope it wears off soon though. I make one ugly goblin."

"You all performed marvelously. I'm sorry I made it difficult for you all in the beginning. I'd like to make the job offer permanent, if you're still interested. I can't, no, I won't promise there won't be violence in the future, but the work you'll be doing will help far more people than it will harm."

"Do you think there are others out there like Stavros?" Nix asked.

"Without a doubt. Probably more than one."

"Then you'll need someone to help put them in their

place."

They spent the next several hours getting the meteor fragments out of the crater with the help of those Stavros had turned. With the shielding in place, they could call in a chopper to get everyone down.

After a few days' rest, Wiley would write up his report for the Collective, detailing his three new promising recruits, and the one he couldn't save.

Kat Burglar

by Andrew M. Ferrell

Katherine stood on the balcony, letting the voices of those around her fade into the background. Tonight she'd fulfill her contract by stealing the documents from the host of this viewing party. Some diplomat or other, she didn't care. All that mattered was the payday waiting for her once she turned over the flashdrive to her contact. The meteor shower party became the perfect cover. Everyone would be distracted for hours.

She flipped open the little stopwatch her grandfather had left her. She'd timed off the distance, and how fast she could make it, three times. She ran her finger across the engraving on the inside of the cover. *Time waits for no one, my little Kat. Seize your stars. Love, Dedushka'* A tear dropped on the face, blurring the reflection of her blue grey eyes.

As the crowd began to 'Ohh' and 'Ahh' around her, she pushed the button on the watch. She took off at a brisk walk, her runner's legs itching to go faster. Kat turned a corner and shifted into a longer stride, thankful her height afforded her the excuse to wear flats to fancy parties. At nearly six feet, it never went well when she towered over her mark by wearing heels.

She rounded the last turn, her blonde hair whipping to the side. She stopped short when she saw the security officer stationed outside the office. "Shit," she cursed to herself, ducking back into the previous hallway. Composing her breathing, she walked around the corner pushing at random doors. The officer watched a moment, moving toward her when she pretended to stumble.

"Miss," he said, reaching her. "You shouldn't be here. All guests should be out on the balcony or patio for the meteor shower." He placed a hand on her shoulder.

"I," Kat started, "I was… looking for a bathroom." She put a hand on his arm, shifting some of her weight. She leaned into him. " I think I had too much champagne." She giggled, wrapping her other arm around the guard. She'd left the door next to her cracked open.

"Well, Miss," the guard stammered as she pressed against him. "The bathroom is back down the other hall." He tried to disentangle himself.

Kat grabbed him firmly, dropping into a crouch and rolling him over her into the vacant bedroom. It had taken weeks of practice and a dozen dresses to master doing this without ripping them. She landed on his chest and pressed a cloth from her compact to his face. He went limp immediately. She stood, fixing where her dress had ridden up, as it was designed to inorder to allow better movement. Poking her head into the hallway, Kat found the area clear. *'No alarm. Good,'* she thought with a breath of relief.

Kat ran to the target office and let herself in. She spied the laptop on the large desk. Slipping the thumbdrive from the small pocket in her dress, she plugged it in. The encrypted hacker program went to work right away. She looked around the office, spotting an oil painting in a gaudy, overly large frame. "You've got to be kidding me," she muttered to herself. She glanced at the progress bar before going to inspect the picture.

Kat ran her finger along the left edge of the wood frame, finding the hinges she expected. The lock mechanism was only slightly harder to locate. Careful examination found no obvious alarm system. Kat pulled two pins from her hair and went to work on the lock. *'I wonder what's hidden in here,'* she mused. *'Who even uses these cliche safes anymore?'*

The lock released as the computer beeped. Kat retrieved the thumbdrive before swinging the picture to the side. A plain dial safe at least 60 years old stared back at her. It took only a minute to crack it. She pulled the lever and the solid metal door opened. Inside were stacks of cash, a folder crammed with papers, and a billfold. Kat knew transporting the items out of the party might be a problem. 'Besides,' she chided herself, 'This job pays enough as it is. Get Greedy. Get Caught.' Her handler and mentor, Sergei, was fond of the phrase. He claimed he'd lost good people because they got greedy.

Curiosity about who the mark was this time got the better of her. Kat grabbed the wallet, looking for an ID. She found it, next to a badge from a group called The

Collective. The name read, 'Director Anthony Addams, Astronomy Division.' Shrugging, Kat was about to put the wallet back in the safe when the computer started beeping. Thinking she'd tripped an alarm, Kat tossed the wallet in the safe and slammed it shut. She ran to the computer, but the beeping stopped. A message flashed on the screen.

"Hello Katherine. I am StarHacker, your client. Thank you for a job well done. You can toss the drive on your way out." Then the entire house went dark.

Kat heard shouting as she entered the hallway. Guests panicked as security tried to get control of the situation. Out of habit, she pushed the button on her grandfather's stopwatch, whispering, "Ten seconds to the kitchens, fifteen to the garden wall, up and over, twenty to the car." When she finished her litany, she peered around a corner. Two people stood near the kitchen door. Neither of them moved for several seconds. Then they shook their heads and moved down the hall in the opposite direction.

Kat checked her stopwatch. "Shit," she cursed, now more than five seconds behind. She rushed into the kitchens, racing for the back entrance. Catering staff huddled in the dark. One of them called out, but Kat ignored them. The side lot appeared vacant. Kat pushed her timer and sprinted for the wall. The last few feet left her exposed to the back part of the house.

She crouched low as a beam of light came into view. She looked back once from the base of the wall. The security officer stood frozen, his head turned away. Kat leapt, grasping the knot on the end of a thin climber's rope secured on the other side. As she pulled herself up and flat on the top of the wall, the flashlight panned across just below her. She rolled off the other side, taking the rope with her.

Landing on her feet, her ankle flared from her old injury. In the moments it took to get back on her feet, she saw her grandfather's face. His look spoke of encouragement, but also disapproval. *'Hypocrite,'* she thought to his memory. *'You're illegal acts are how I ended up working for Sergei in the first place.'* She limped to the rental parked a block and a half away, remembering the days after her injury during the Acrobatic Gymnastics World Championships.

***

She grabbed the handle of her apartment, shocked when it started to swing open. Knowing she locked it before her doctor appointment, Kat grabbed the pepper spray from her purse. She pushed the door open the rest of the way with her crutch. "I'm armed, and don't have anything to steal anyway," she called. "I'm calling the police."

"No, you won't," came a heavily Russian accented voice from her small kitchen. "We need to talk about your Dedushka." As Kat hobbled around the corner, he continued, "My name is Sergei. Your dedushka and my father are old friends."

"My grandfather is dead," Kat replied. She kept her spray pointed at the larger man. She knew she'd never outrun him in her condition. "I don't want to talk about him right now."

"But we have to, little Koshka," Sergei said. He pushed out the chair from her dinette table. "Sit." When she did, he said, "Your grandfather had a gambling problem. He liked his sports and his horses. He wasn't very lucky, though. Except when he bet on you."

Kat gasped. "You're lying. He was a good man. He worked hard and raised me after my parents died." She raised her pepper spray even as the tears started.

Sergei easily snatched the spray with a speed Kat wouldn't have thought the man possessed. "Don't be silly, girl. If you'd won your last competition, we'd never have spoken. But now, you work for me."

Visions of seedy motels and drunken men flashed in Kat's mind. She tensed, prepared to fight. Sergei watched her, but began laughing. "I'm no monster," he said. "If you want to pay a debt that way, fine. I have a better idea. One more suited to your abilities."

Kat relaxed only a little. She stared into Sergei's eyes, looking for signs of trickery. "What do I have to do?" she asked, slumping in the chair.

***

Kat shook off the memory when she reached the car. That very night, Sergei began training her. Most of the self defense lessons waited until she'd healed from her broken ankle. The rest of the classes in burglary began right away. She started the car, reaching for the cellphone in the glove compartment. It had taken five years to earn her freedom, but tonight her forced employment would end.

"It's done," she said as soon as Sergei picked up. "Have my cut ready. I'm home somewhere tropical for the winter."

"The client called already, commending your efforts," Sergei replied. "He had a cellphone dropped off for you, said he'd like to hire you again sometime. How did it go?"

"Rolled my ankle on the departure," Kat replied. She winced when she adjusted her left foot. "Had to knock out a guard, but shouldn't remember much except a drunk blonde looking for a bathroom."

"Very good," Sergei said. "I'm proud of you, Kat. You're the best I've ever trained. Are you sure you don't want to stay? I could always find you work when you needed it."

"I'll be in touch. But I need to be on my own for a while," Kat said. "Leave the phone with my bag in the other car. I'm about to make the first swap." She hung up. She pulled alongside a blue two door car at an all night supermarket. She stepped out, dropping the thumbdrive down the sewer grate she'd parked next to. She took the cellphone, wedging it in the same grate, bending it until it cracked. She let the pieces fall.

"Miss, we need a word," a voice called as Kat started to get into the second car. The tall, thin man wore a dark suit. A stockier man in a matching suit rounded the sedan behind him.

"Sorry, but I'm busy," Kat replied. She quickly climbed in the car and jammed the key in the ignition. Her grandfather's watch fell from her pocket and landed between the seat and console. She heard the familiar click of the stopwatch engaging.

The two men froze, as did a passing car in the lot. Kat stared in shock for a few seconds before she put her car in drive and peeled away. As she reached the far end of the lot, she caught movement in her rearview. The sounds of a crash followed her into the intersection as she drove away. "What the hell was that?" she asked the dashboard.

***

Pierce fell, catching himself in a roll. The sound of his suit ripping was drowned out as a pickup truck slammed into their sedan. "What the hell was that?" he asked his partner as he climbed to his feet.

"No idea," Solomon replied. "Check on the driver of that truck. Something MA Class went on here." He pulled his phone from his pocket to call in the incident. "Target escaped. We've definitely got a MA on our hands. Person or Object unknown at this time," he told the agent who answered.

***

Kat reached her last car swap confident she wasn't being followed. She grabbed her grandfather's watch from where it fell. As she slid into the luxury car she'd bought months ago, she saw the bag from Sergei. Next to it was the new smartphone. It beeped as soon as she started the engine of the car.

"Hello Katherine Zuroswski."

Shocked, she picked up the phone. She typed back, "Who are you?"

"My name is, StarHacker."

"No. Really. Who are you?" She dropped the phone on the passenger seat. She put the car in drive, but the

200

phone beeped again before she took her foot off the brake.

"The Collective is after you. I'd hoped by taking out the power it would cover your tracks. My apologies for failing in that. I will help you to escape them. Then we can talk more. Follow the GPS. It may change directions as needed."

Kat stared at the message, then the car's dash GPS lit up. The screen looked like a video game as four red arrows converged on the blue one indicating her position. A black line wove through the city streets, shifting as the red dots moved closer.

She pressed her foot to the gas, following the weaving of the black line. The phone beeped once when she almost missed her turn but she ignored it. Kat sped through the city streets. She kept an eye on her rear view mirror, not sure what to watch for. She imagined big black government SUVs filled with men ready to disappear her to wherever they were taking terrorists these days.

The phone continued to beep until the navigation system began talking. "This may be easier," the synthesized male voice said. "I've managed to hack their radio signal. There is quite the chatter about your initial contact. How did you manage to escape the first two agents?"

"I don't know," Kat said out loud. "How is this even possible? What did I get mixed up in?"

"Hmm," the voice said. "Interesting."

"What?" Kat yelled at the GPS, following the route plotted for her as the red markers crept closer.

"Up ahead is an alley," he replied. "Pull in and shut off the car. Don't worry, I'll still be able to talk to you. They think they are closing in but I'm about to send them in the wrong direction."

Kat followed the instructions, fervently praying the voice wasn't going to betray her. Her heart raced as she killed the engine. The dash computer went dark.

"Ok. They're gone," the voice came back. With the car silent, the voice echoed in the smaller confines. "I'm watching the parking lot camera from your encounter with the agents. I've erased it so they won't see it, but how did you stop time?"

"Stop time? Are you crazy? Am I stuck with a lunatic voice in my car?" Kat tried the door handle, but it locked. The door refused to budge. "Let me out. You can have the car. I just want to leave town and forget this ever happened. You got what you wanted from the computer. Let me go."

"Please calm down, Kat," the voice said. "I never meant you any harm. And I only want to help you get away from the Collective. What you did has been invaluable to my cause. But, please, watch this."

The dash screen lit up with a cheap CCTV view of her pulling up to make her scheduled car swap. She slipped her grandfather's watch from her pocket, rubbing her finger against the smooth polished case nervously. She saw the car pull up with the two men she knew were agents of a group called the Collective.

As they approached, she remembered jumping into the car. She recalled the distinct click of her grandfather's watch when it fell out of her pocket and landed between the seats. Out of reflex, she pushed the button. The display stopped, traffic in the street behind her came to a halt. She counted off the silent seconds like she would during her routines, or when she planned a heist. At ten, sound flooded back.

Cars crashed into each other behind her, filling the alley with the blaring of horns and crunching of metal. Her dash screen flared to life and the voice returned. "What did you do?"

Kat stared at her grandfather's stopwatch in disbelief. "Why," she started, "Why do you think I stopped time?" She turned the stopwatch over in her hand.

"The video from the parking lot," the voice said. "Not only did the people freeze, but so did the recording. There is a ten second jump in the footage. I verified it myself. It wasn't edited. The time is literally gone."

"I," Kat said. "All I did was push my grandfather's old stopwatch. Force of habit…" Kat trailed off. She remembered how the guard in the yard froze. *Did I do that? I thought maybe he was just standing there."*

"I think you should come to one of our safe houses," the voice said. "The Collective is not going to stop hunting you if they figure out you have something affected by the meteor."

"Affected by the meteor? What are you talking about?" Kat asked, confusion and panic cracking her voice. She always expected to be hunted by police for her choice of career. A strange government like agency was a completely different story.

The GPS blinked and a new route lit up. The voice said, "Come to the safe house. I'll meet you there and explain everything. You don't have much reason to, I suppose. But I'm asking you to trust me."

Kat considered his words. *He's been helpful. And Sergei would have vetted him as a client before I even took the job."* Taking a deep breath, she replied aloud, "Alright. I'll see ya there." The silence from the car speaker was the only response she received as she put the car in drive.

***

Agents Solomon and Pierce walked into Director Adams' office. Adams motioned them both to a seat while he remained standing. He ran his hand across his face and took a breath. His hands shook with barely contained rage. "How incompetent are you two? Where is the girl that broke into my house?"

Solomon stared down the Director, one eyebrow curved upward. "How incompetent are you to hold a party during the biggest event in Collective history?" He stood up and placed his hands on the desk, leaning towards Adams. "And why did you have unsecured files on your private computer at home?"

Adams rocked back as if Solomon had punched him. "I, well, I," he stuttered before getting angry. "I'm a Director and you'd do well to remember your place, Agent Solomon."

"That's Senior Agent Solomon to you, Director," Solomon said, contempt dripping from his voice. "And you'd do well to remember I'm the one who failed you from field ops. This isn't your science lab with your satellites and computers." Solomon turned to leave, motioning Pierce to his feet.

"I didn't dismiss you yet, Solomon," Adams said, raising his voice. "When I'm Curator, I'll see you run out of the Collective."

Solomon turned, his thin lips curved into a smile. "You'll sit in the Director's chair over my dead body, boy. Come on Pierce. We've got to find that girl." He left the office without a further word or look for Director Adams.

Pierce nodded to Adams before standing and following his partner. Adams stared at the door after the two agents left. "Damn him!" he shouted, shoving a stack of files onto the floor. He kicked the desk.

***

The GPS guided Kat to a gated community outside the city. She gazed nervously at the security booth from the stop sign down the block. "How am I supposed to drive through there?" she wondered aloud.

"You're preapproved," the voice returned. "The residents of the safe house are part of the Star Children, but they hardly ever use the property. The guard thinks you're their niece, here to check on the house and stay for a few days while you're sightseeing in the city."

"That easy, huh?" Kat replied to the dash. "I guess we'll see." She put the car back in drive and pulled up to the gate. A middle aged man in a security uniform sat within the booth. Kat rolled down the window as he approached.

The guard glanced at the license plate before stepping close to the window. "Miss Sawyer, I presume. I was told to expect you." He produced a set of keys from his pocket, along with a window card and a garage door opener. He passed them all to Kat. "Your uncle was quite clear in his instructions. If you have any trouble with the garage or the keys, just come straight back here and I'll make sure to take care of it. If you need anything else, the placard has the guard shack number on it. I'd appreciate a heads up on any delivery orders."

"I'll be sure to keep you posted," Kat said with a smile. She tossed the placard in her window and dropped the other items on the passenger seat. The guard nodded and returned to the shack. The gate started swinging open a moment later. Kat drove through, following the GPS to the proper address.

The stately homes sat back from the roadway, two and three stories high. Most had garages to the side, though a few had underground ones. When Kat reached her destination, she found the house shrouded by evergreens. The drive dipped underneath to a two car garage tucked beneath a modest two story house.

Kat waited impatiently for the door to open, revealing no other car stored there. She pulled in. *"Did I beat my benefactor here?"* she thought as she grabbed her bag and headed for the door into the house.

Unlocking the door, she stepped into the darkened interior. Before she could locate the switch, the lights came on. "Welcome home, Kat." The voice from her car spoke from speakers spread about the house. "Don't be alarmed, the house is equipped with all the latest smart technology."

"So, do I get some answers now?" Kat asked aloud as she found her way to the kitchen. She rummaged in the refrigerator, finding a can of soda. She popped the can open and sat in a chair in the breakfast nook. She propped her feet on the table. "Are you going to meet me here or keep talking from speakers?"

"Forgive me for not explaining before," the voice said. "I'm as present as I can be. My real name is Vincent Tomlinson. Many years ago I was a pioneer of the budding internet age. During a meteor shower, I was fused with the technology I helped create. Now I live within it, with no physical body to present you."

"And I'm supposed to believe that?" Kat asked. She sipped her soda.

"You can freeze time with a stopwatch your grandfather left you," Vincent replied. "How is this any more far fetched?"

"Say, I buy your story, Vinny," Kat said, standing and pacing the kitchen. "What now? Are you going to download me into the internet as well?"

"No," Vincent said, a bit of laughter creeping into his voice. "But I am prepared to offer you a spot amongst the Star Children."

"You've said that name before," Kat interrupted. "What the hell is a Star Children?" She retrieved another soda from the fridge before sitting back down on the chair.

"The Star Children are people, like yourself, who were either directly affected, or in possession of an item affected, by a meteor shower," Vincent explained. "We choose not to accept recruitment, or destruction, by the Collective."

"Destruction?" Kat sat up straight. "You mean those guys following me would have killed me?"

"Depends on a number of factors," he replied. "One, can your stopwatch work for someone else or is it keyed to you. Also, how willing are you to cooperate with their rules."

Kat relaxed a little. "Fat lot of good trying to recruit me would do. Sergei always said I couldn't follow the rules even if my life was on the line. I had to make my own path."

"Yes. My research indicates that about you," Vincent said. He laughed. "I think even without your new ability to stop time I would have been trying to recruit you for the Star Children. I could use someone handy enough to get into places barred to my electronic access."

"So, you really have no physical body, huh? That's gotta be hell on your social life," Kat remarked. She settled back and sipped her soda. "What do I do now? I can't go back to Sergei. If they have any idea who I am they will trace it to him easily enough."

"I've done all I can to shield your friend. As far as I can tell from the communications I've intercepted, they have a description but no name anyway. A change in appearance and you should be able to disappear, if that's what you still desire," Vincent said.

Kat pulled the stopwatch from her pocket. She opened it and reread the inscription from her grandfather. *He would want me to help these people. These Star Children,"* she thought to herself. *"What else am I going to do?"* She raised her head, looking at the speaker on the wall. "I'm in. What's the plan?"

"Excellent," Vincent said. "Lay low for a few days. Anything you want, I'll have ordered. I may need your unique skill in a few days to help with another new recruit."

Kat tipped back her soda, finishing the can. She stood up again. "I'm going to get some sleep then." She tossed her can in the trash. She grabbed her bag and headed down the hall to find a bedroom.

***

If the building on Washington D.C.'s west side wasn't built as securely as it was, it may have shaken apart at the confrontation taking place in a top floor office. An office even more secure than the rest of the building.

"If you didn't have an unencrypted machine in your mansion, my people wouldn't be working double time to fix your mistake, Star Boy," Director Sanders shouted angrily at Adams. His usually stoic demeanor cracked as he pointed his finger at his colleague.

"My house is secured, by your people, so who messed up here? Sounds like we've got an Operations problem to me," Director Adams replied, heat in his voice. "I watch the sky and you keep a lid on what I find. That's how this works."

"Both of you sit down," Curator Woolley said calmly. He returned from Walter Reed and his encounter with the Gambler to find his top three at each other's throats.

"Jackson, what do you think?" He turned his chair slightly towards his Director of Recruiting and Training. His protégés sat, back straight, in a chair against the far wall of the office.

"StarHacker is literally a part of the Internet," Jackson said, his tone crisp. Even relaxed in the chair he exuded his military trained alertness. "To fight him we'd either have to abandon the technology, invent our own that he couldn't infiltrate, or draw him into a place where he couldn't escape." He paused to let his scenarios sink into the minds of his colleagues. "I propose the last option. He isn't the first large scale threat to the Collective, and he won't be the last. We just have to outthink him, as we have always done with a seemingly superior threat."

Adams jumped to his feet. "Listen to you, you puffed up soldier boy. Leave the higher thinking to your betters. You probably need to call IT to dial your smartphone." Anthony sneared at the bigger man, feeling secure that Jackson wouldn't retaliate physically.

"Sit down Anthony, or I'll let him make you," Woolley said calmly, but with every ounce of his authority. "Jackson is right. The Collective has faced threats of this magnitude before. It's the purview of our Training personnel to be ready for any conceivable event. Stop being a child about the breach at your house. Do your job and the people entrusted to do theirs will take care of this problem. Sanders, you and Jackson are to come up with a plan for dealing with Vincent, aka StarHacker. I want him off the board before this Event spins anymore out of hand." He locked eyes with each of his Directors in turn. "Dismissed," he added finally.

Leonard Woolley sat back in his chair as his top three exited his office. Once the door shut behind them, he pushed the button for his secretary. "Please hold any but Priority One calls." He then reached for the bottle in his desk. He poured three fingers of the alcohol into a glass. He took a small sip. With a sigh he tried to release the tension building in his bones.

Murder In Angel's Falls

by Molly Neely

B uck took a long pull off his 40 oz. and sighed.

"This is the life, boys," he quipped letting out a long, juicy belch. "We got the moon, the stars and a shitload of beer. What else is there, am I right?"

Moose nodded in agreement, then downed the last of his bottle.

"Amen to that brother. Good call not bringing the old ladies,"

Echoes of unity drifted throughout group. It had been a long time since the chapter had gotten together without the women. As their leader, Buck knew the importance of brotherhood. There were just some things a hot ass and pouty lips could not satisfy.

So when Sketch had suggested riding up to Angel Falls and tying one on, Buck was quick to say yes. Three days of fresh air and cold beer was exactly what they needed.

"Check it out," Moose said, nodding up at the night sky. "Falling stars. Can't really see em in town, but damn. Up here it's like fireworks and shit."

All seventeen members of Road Rage Incorporated lifted their drunken eyes to the sky. With slack jaws, their collective gaze took it all in with childlike wonder. Glittering streams of space dust raced across the heavens, adding their glow to the ether. While on the ground, the heavy roar of Angel Falls provided a perfect backdrop.

"Kinda wish Sheryl was here to see this," Buck muttered, leaning back in the seat of his bike.

The solemn cry of a crow echoed through the air, its haunting voice drifting like fog.

"Shut the fuck up bird," Tommy barked pulling a glock from his waistband. He took aim and emptied the magazine into the moon stained trees. Suddenly the air was filled with noise as a dozen or more crows took flight, the flaps of their wings coupling with frightened calls.

Tommy roared with laughter and threw his empty bottle. Then he reached into his vest pocket and pulled out a fresh magazine.

"Dude, you're such an asshole," Sketch grumbled.

Tommy rolled his eyes and loaded the gun.

"Fuck you prospect." He chuckled. "You ain't got no say here."

"Leave the kid alone, Tom," Buck started.

Tommy racked his gun and pointed the business end at Sketch.

"This little bitch needs to learn his place."

Buck slid off his bike and calmly walked across the camp. He positioned himself between Tommy and Sketch, his eyes boring into Tommy's face.

"I said, that's enough."

Tommy held his leaders gaze a moment. Then a sly grin crept up in the corners of his mouth.

"You know I'm just fuckin with him, Bucky Boy," Tommy said, sliding his gun back into his belt. "I ain't gonna waste a bullet on no sissy ass prospect."

Rumbles of nervous laughter drifted through the camp. It was well known that Thomas Micks had been vying for leadership of the RRIC for years. And everyone knew one day Big Buck Robbins would be challenged.

Buck inched closer, his gaze still fixed.

"What?" Tommy uttered. "I told you I was just playing. Why you gotta get all in my face about it?"

"Because we have rules, Tom," Buck replied, "and you always seem to be breaking them."

Tommy pressed his tongue against the front of his teeth and sucked air through gap between them. A wet, squeal whistled out into the night, followed by a hollow click. Tommy absently smooshed the mysterious substance he had dislodged from his teeth, then spit it out.

"Well, you know what they say," he smirked, "rules were meant to be shoved up your ass."

Tommy lunged forward, plowing Buck with his hulking shoulder. The two hit the ground with a thud, quickly becoming caked with blood, dirt and pine needles.

"Aww damn," Moose laughed, hopping off his bike, "here we go again boys."

While Tommy and Buck thrashed around on the ground, the rest of the RRIC gathered around, cheering on the ass kicking taking place in the center of their campsite.

"I'm gonna break you're fucking neck!" Tommy snarled, rolling Buck over on his back. He reached down and wrapped both hands around Buck's throat.

Buck's face darkened with blood as his once childhood friend squeezed. With blazing eyes, he frantically scanned his surroundings. Above him, the meteor shower continued to streak the sky, seemingly unaware of the murder happening beneath them.

"Come on Tommy, let him up," Sketch shouted, placing a shaking hand on Tommy's shoulder. "You're gonna kill him!"

"That's the plan, bitch," Tommy snarled over his shoulder, "and you're next."

A deep whistle suddenly pierced the air around the camp. Moose glanced up into the sky. His jaw went slack.

"Aw shit," he whispered, as a baseball sized meteor screamed through the pine trees and buried itself in the ground. The earth rolled on impact, scattering shattered motorcycles and drunken bikers two hundred feet in all directions. A massive cloud of dirt bloomed and swirled around the ninety foot crater that used to be the RRIC campsite.

The low rumble of Angel Falls, coupled with the cries of injured crows droned on as the dust settled. The air filled with the stench of blood and burnt feathers. Slowly, survivors began to stir.

Sketch opened his eyes. With a shivering hand, he wiped the crusty layer of earth from his face, then winced as something sharp clawed his cheek. He looked down at his hands and gasped. His fingernails, caked with blood, began to shift before his eyes. Elongating and narrowing, the nails were no longer human, but more like the talons of a bird.

The mangled body of a crow twitched beside him. As a faint caw escaped its shattered beak, a searing pain erupted on the prospect's back. Sketch struggled to his knees, then began to rip the remains of his vest and t-shirt off. Pinching his eyes shut, Sketch let out a howl.

"Wha... what is that on your back, bro?" Moose whispered behind him.

Sketch slowly turned and faced Moose. As their eyes met, he reached behind him and felt around on the source of the pain. He winced, running his hand along the length of the mysterious addition to his back. The muscles in his back flexed.

"Bro," Moose shrieked, "you got wings bro!"

The young prospect looked down at his shadow, then sucked in a deep breath. There in his silhouette was a full set of wings, covered in glossy black feathers and spanning nearly seven feet on either side of him.

A chuckle escaped his lungs. With newfound instincts, Sketch leapt into air, disappearing in the blackness.

"Where the fuck are you going dude?" Moose blurted out, "Don't leave me here with all these bodies!" He ran a pair of shaky hands through his hair, then cautiously over his shoulders. Relief spread across his face.

"Arrrgh... "

Near the edge of the impact zone, Tommy clawed his way out from under a pile of shattered pine branches. He drug himself to his feet, swooned, then stumbled across the clearing. He pressed his palms against his thighs, then leaned down and wretched. The stink of sour beer and stomach acid filled the air.

"Damn, that was some close encounter shit," Tommy said, wiping his mouth, "Where's that bitch prospect at? Sketch? C'mon out boy, bring yer daddy a beer."

"Man, fuck you Tom," Sketch's voice echoed down through the trees. "The only thing you're getting from me is an ass whipping,"

Tommy laced his fingers and stretched, his joints snapping and popping in the strain.

"Gonna kill you," he called into the night sky, " just like ole Bucky Boy,"

As the last word escaped his lips, a searing pain flashed across his back. Tom dropped to his knees. His talons dug into the ground while his own pair of wings burst through the back of his jean vest. He let out a deep growl as the last of his pin feathers filled in.

Tom stood up and gave his new wings a few pumps. Dirt and debris swirled around him like dust devils, their haunting dance twisting up into the meteor filled sky.

In an instant, Sketch dropped down from his perch, planting both feet in Tom's chest, the force knocking the aging biker flat on his back. He took a swipe at Tom's face, leaving four deep gashes across his cheek.

"You'll have to catch me first." Sketch smirked."Bitch."

Then with a flap of his wings, the prospect launched up into the night sky.

Rage filled Tom. No rotten little wanna be was gonna show him up. He pulled himself back to his feet then followed after Sketch. Clearing the tree line, Tom hovered above the pines a moment, scanning the open sky for the prospect. In the distance, he spotted Sketch, a black shadow gliding towards the town at the bottom of Willow Creek Road.

Tom pumped his wings harder, and within seconds had already caught up.

"Where ya going boy" he called out. "Chicken shit prospect, you afraid to face me?"

Sketch turned and hovered just above Tom.

"You don't scare me anymore," he called out.

Then reached down and with a quick slash of his talons, Sketch slashed the laces of his boots. They plummeted to the ground, leaving behind a set of raptor-like feet. An ear piercing screech escaped his lips as he lunged at Tom.

The two men clashed, digging claws into flesh, their wings spinning like a pinwheel. No longer flapping, the two began a bloody decent into the unusually crowded main street of North Fork.

Sketch wrapped his hands around Tom's neck, sinking his claws deep into the flesh. "How does it feel?" he snarled.

Tom swiped at Sketch's face with one hand, while desperately trying to pry loose the prospect's grip with the other. As the two winged men rocketed towards the earth, he could feel his life slipping away.

A hundred feet before hitting the ground, Sketch released his grip, then reached down and grabbed the glock still tucked away in Tom's waistband. He pumped his wings a few times, holding his position a few yards from the ground and watched.

Tom hacked and coughed, as his lungs filled with air. Though the grogginess began to subside, his ears were suddenly filled with screams. He hit asphalt hard, shredding his left wing and sending a plume of black feathers into the air. The street filled with gasps and murmurs as locals and visitors alike gathered around to see what had fallen from the meteor shower.

One brave little girl inched forward, her eyes scanning the bloody winged man with curiosity.

"Are you an angel?" she whispered.

Silently, Sketch touched down just behind the girl. His wings folded neatly against his back, their tips inches from the road. He gently took hold of the little girl's shoulder and guided her to one side.

"He's no angel, little girl," he answered carefully aiming the glock. "Tom Micks is nothing more than a worthless devil."

"You d-don't have the fucking nerve," Tom slurred from a bloody mouth.

Sketch lowered the gun. "To shoot you? I have plenty of nerve for that. But I got a lotta rage too. And in a contest between nerve and rage…"

Sketched paused and tossed the glock in gutter. Then he bent down and plunged his clawed hand into Tom's chest. The crowd erupted in screams as Sketch ripped Tom's beating heart from its cavity.

"Sorry Tommy," Sketch continued, "rage wins every time."

He stood up and absently dropped the heart on the road. The faint wail of police sirens echoed in the distance. The prospect glanced around at the faces of the few brave souls who watched from the sidewalk. As the red and blue lights drew closer, Sketch turned and ran up the road, catching a gust of wind and gliding off into the blackness.

***

"I thought you should know, there has been an interesting development here in California."

"Has another meteor touched down?"

"Yes. About three miles out from a town called North Fork, some local spot called Angel Falls."

"I'm sending a crew up to retrieve the meteor. Secure the site until they arrive."

"Listen, there's something you should know."

"What is it?"

"I think the question of whether or not the world is going to know has been answered."

The Artist

by Andrew M. Ferrell

Thirty-something years ago…

The salty ocean air threatened Mark's precariously perched canvas. It ruffled his hair as he stared at the horizon. He flexed his hand, sore from the night before. He stared at his dark knuckles. Scars criss crossed his flesh, leaving lighter patches. A testament to a hard childhood and his self inflicted adulthood mission. He thought about the previous night.

The mugger never saw the man shadowing him from down the block as he weaved his way through the thinning crowd on the boardwalk. Mark had been following him for three nights, making sure he was the one he'd been looking for. *"A pickpocket scraping by I could almost forgive. I've been there,"* Mark thought to himself. He watched as the thug searched for a target.

A tourist couple, clearly a little drunk, stumbled by in the opposite direction. The mugger's head slowly turned and followed their meandering path toward the beach stairs. Mark continued to stalk his prey, moving slowly from shadow to shadow. He counted a slow five before racing down the stairs behind the criminal. As his feet touched the sand, a woman's scream split the night.

Mark cursed himself for waiting too long. The male lay on the ground. The mugger gripped the woman's arm as he wrestled to cover her mouth with his other hand.

"Shut up and this will go easier for you," the mugger said. The woman's eyes went wide, staring over her assailant's shoulder. He turned, seeing Mark for the first time.

"Let the lady go," Mark said, dropping the octave of his voice as deep as he could. He stood up straight, the dark baggy clothes concealed the true size of his frame. The hood of his shirt and large dark glasses obscured his face. Every wardrobe choice, down to the black boots, chosen to keep Mark's identity a secret.

"You'll have to wait your turn," the mugger sneered. He released the woman but only to pick up the bat at his feet. The woman fell to the ground and crawled towards her downed companion. The mugger slapped the bat against his other hand. "So, where you want it first buddy? Head or guts?" Without waiting for a response, he launched an attack at Mark.

Mark flicked his wrist, the extendable baton he kept there sprang out. Steel rod met wooden bat, the crack echoing in the cavernlike area beneath the pier. The mugger's face exchanged shock for pain as Mark drove the baton into the man's stomach. He swatted the bat to the ground. When Mark brought his weapon up into his opponent's jaw, the mugger collapsed, unconscious.

The woman shook her companion until he awoke with a groan. Mark knelt next to them, quickly checking the man's injuries. "Take him to the hospital. Tell them it's a possible concussion from a failed mugging." He glanced at the knocked out mugger. "I'll leave him for the police to find." Mark stood and helped the male to his feet.

As the couple moved slowly back up the stairs to the pier, Mark dragged the mugger over to a pillar underneath where the tide never reached. Using a handful of zip ties from his pocket, he strapped the man to the support. Mark then shook the man until he woke up. As the mugger came to, Mark grabbed him by the collar. "The police will probably pick you up in the morning. But if I catch you on the pier ever again, they will be the least of your worries." He then stood and walked away as the criminal cursed at him.

"Mr. Campbell," a voice askesaid, pulling Mark back to the present. "I'm Detective Solomon, Santa Monica Police Department. Can I ask you a few questions?"

Mark looked the rail thin man over: fedora, glasses, and a long coat hung loosely on his lithe frame. He was young to be a detective, but the badge looked legitimate. Mark swallowed the sudden dryness in his throat. "What can I do for you, officer?"

"Detective," Solomon corrected with a smile. "Did you hear about the mugger found tied to the pier this morning?" He pulled out a notebook and pen from an inside pocket of the coat.

Mark shrugged. "Everyone's talking about it, but he was gone before I got here. Guess I missed the show." He turned towards his canvas, raising his brush.

Solomon took a step closer, he watched Mark tense up. "You see a lot of people pass by here. Did you see anyone suspicious acting last night?"

"Once the sun's gone I grab a bite to eat and go home. Can't paint anything under those spotlights," Mark replied. He gestured at the big lights mounted along the pier. "I prefer more natural light."

"So you weren't here after dark last night?" Solomon pressed. Something about Mark's reaction set off his gut instincts. "Some of the vendors said I should talk to you since you're a permanent fixture around here lately."

Mark locked eyes with Solomon, reading the same suspicions he had seen in every law man's eyes since he was a kid in Chicago. "Sometimes I walk around the pier in the evenings, try some of the food, maybe a game or two. When money isn't too tight." He dabbed a spot on his canvas as an excuse to look away from Solomon's gaze. "But I wanted to paint the sunrise today, so I went to bed early." Mark pointed to a smaller canvas showing the city skyline with the first light of day creeping over the roof of the buildings.

"That's beautiful," Solomon said appreciatively. "Is it for sale? I don't have much for decoration at my new apartment." He pulled out his wallet. "I've only got forty dollars on me."

"That's perfect," Mark replied, thankful for the sale and the change in subject matter. He took Solomon's money and handed him the canvas. "Thank you."

"No. Thank you." Solomon put a business card on the edge of Mark's easel. "If you see or hear anything, would you give me a call? Not everyday you find a thief tied up as a gift to the police."

"I bet not," Mark replied with a laugh. As Solomon walked away, Mark said, "I'd check those Hollyweird types." He heard the detective chuckle.

Mark watched the lawman walk out of sight and considered packing up his supplies. *"Might be time to move on,"* he thought to himself.

He painted the skyline again, selling a few small caricatures or canvases to tourists. As the sun began to set, Mark packed up his paints and canvases. As he closed the hatch on his beat up minivan, he thought over his conversation with the detective. "One night of fun," he said to himself, turning back to the lights of the pier. "Then it's time to head north, I think."

***

Detective Solomon poured over a stack of witness statements long after his colleagues had gone home. *"Something just doesn't add up,"* he thought, reviewing the confession from the mugger. A knock at his door snapped him out of his musings. He looked up to see a middle aged man in a black suit.

"Detective Solomon," the man said, his accent placing him from somewhere in the northeast. "I'm Special Agent Woolley, FBI. Do you have a moment?" Woolley only waited a moment before stepping the rest of the way into the room. At Solomon's nod, he continued, "We've been monitoring cases with particular parameters, and our pattern has led us to your mugger."

"I only logged that into our database this afternoon," Solomon replied. "You guys sure work fast at the Bureau."

"When something ticks off all the boxes on our list, yes. We've been following this trail for a few years now. Woolley gestured at the seat in front of Solomon's desk. As he sat, he continued, "Suspect trussed up for the police, mysterious vigilante in a mask, witnesses either silent or unable to give much of a description other than average height and weight. Sound about right?"

"Exactly," Solomon replied. "Something doesn't sit well with me in this one. I don't mind a slam dunk case, but I don't want some civilian doing our job for us. It's too easy for a line to be crossed and then you've got dead bodies to deal with. Either the Do Gooder, the bad guy, or some bystander caught in the crossfire."

"I agree. I'll suspect though that your hero of the night didn't even use a knife. Probably a bat, or golf club perhaps? Even if the criminal had a gun, the cases I've seen have all shown the vigilante taking out the gun first. No bystander casualties. No blood evidence or even dumped clothes within a twenty mile radius that we've uncovered." Woolley pulled a folded piece of paper from his pocket. When unfolded, it showed four sketches of a man in a mask. He passed it to Solomon. "One of these match your mugger's description of his attacker?"

Solomon looked over the paper, noting the similar facial construction of each sketch. "Could be any of them, but the mask he described was more like this one." Solomon pointed to the bottom left.

"I think it may be the same person. Traveling up and down the coast. Do you have any regular transients this time of year?" Woolley took the sketches back, carefully folding them and placing them in a pocket.

"This is the height of the summer tourist season. The pier is full of carnival games and street performers. Many of them come through every year." Solomon shook his head at the number of suspects that would mean. "You have nothing else to go on? Nothing to narrow down the pool?"

"We've never recovered a shred of physical evidence. No discarded gloves or weapons. No clothes of any kind. It's like everything just evaporates."

"How is that supposed to help me?" Solomon asked, his voice hardening. *"Fed or not, I'm not wasting my time chasing ghosts."*

"We have a theory, but it's going to be hard to believe," Woolley said, leaning forward and folding his hands. He rested his elbows on his knees. "Let me tell you a story."

***

Mark walked the pier as the sun went down. His latest mask in his pocket, a thick cane in his hand. He hated being so obvious, but if he was going to be ready to protect the innocents around him, he needed to carry the items with him. They'll only last a few more hours anyway. After that, he was heading north.

"I think the mountains in Oregon or Washington will be a good place to spend a few months," he muttered to himself. He'd seen a young man eyeing tourists from his spot leaning against a pole. Suspicion bloomed in Mark's mind. Grabbing a hotdog from a vendor, he settled down to watch as the young man drew his hood closer around his face.

As the young man pushed away from the lamp post to fall into step behind a young woman playing on her phone, Mark stood up. He reached for his cane, propped against the table, when the younger man froze. Two members of Santa Monica's finest chatted as they strolled down the pier, their eyes shifting to take in each person around them.

Mark sat as the young man casually disappeared into the crowd, spooked by the police. Mark tried to look nonchalant as the officers stopped by his table.

"Hey," one of them said. "You're that artist always painting down here every summer right?" Mark nodded. "My girlfriend saw one of your paintings the other day and hasn't stopped talking about it. Any chance you have something for sale?"

"Not on me officers. I'm just enjoying the music and a little supper," Mark said cheerfully. His smile widened as he tried to hide the deep rooted distrust of the police. "Come around tomorrow. I should be around here somewhere. Depending on where the light is best."

"Thanks. Enjoy your night," the officer said before continuing his patrol of the pier.

"At least they've stepped up their presence. Time to move on," Mark thought. He crumpled the wrapper from his hotdog and tossed it to the nearby trash can. Grabbing his cane, he headed off towards the parking lot. He felt the metal

of the grip go soft and checked his watch. *"Must have misjudged the time."* He quickened his pace.

Just as he reached his car, he heard another voice. "Mr. Campbell. It's me Detective Solomon." Mark turned. Then he saw the man in the expensive suit jogging to keep up. Mark swallowed hard, he tried to put the cane behind him as he leaned back against his car.

When Solomon caught up to him, he notesd the cane but didn't comment. *"Not my place to ask, but I hope he's alright. Seems a nice guy just making a living."*

"Mr. Campbell," the suit said, a little breathlessly. "Detective Solomon tells me you spend a lot of time on the pier. Wondering if you could answer a few questions for me. My name is Special Agent Woolley. You can call me Leonard."

"I'm afraid I don't know much more than I told the detective," Mark said casually. "I'm not usually here in the evenings, and his colleagues had wrapped up that mugger before I arrived. I just decided to grab something to eat and listen to the music tonight or I'd probably be sleeping." He shifted his leg, feeling the cane start to dissolve.

"Knee, ankle, or hip?" Woolley asked, pointing to the cane. "Some days my knee bothers me so much. I've often wondered if a cane might be useful. As well as being stylish." He stepped closer, reaching towards Mark. "May I see it?"

"Um, no," Mark stammered. The cane vanished fully. Both lawmen looked at each other and opened their mouths to speak. "Look, I gotta go." Mark scrambled for the door handle before remembering he'd locked the car. He fished for his keys in his pocket when a hand landed on his shoulder.

"I think you better ride with us, Mr. Campbell," Woolley said softly. "We have some things to discuss it appears. Or disappears, as the case may be." He guided the painter to a black sedan parked a few rows over. As he helped the stunned Mark into the backseat, he patted the man's shoulder. "Don't worry, you're not in any trouble per se. And, I may have a job offer for you. If you're interested in helping more people than the occasional small victim."

***

All three remained silent on the ride to the station. Mark looked at the doors, but knew there was no way to break them open. *"I should have left after the mugger. Too much attention these days. I'm getting sloppy."* He glanced at Woolley in the driver seat. *"Job offer? Doesn't seem like a normal Fed to me. What's his angle?"*

The trio entered the station and stopped in one of the interview rooms. Woolley shut the door and took a seat next to Solomon, across from Mark. "When did it start, Mr. Campbell?"

"When did what start? And just call me Mark, please. All this Mr. Campbell stuff when I'm being arrested for something, right? Don't I get a phone call? And a lawyer?"

"I assure you you're not under arrest, Mark," Solomon said. "Agent Woolley, and I, just have some questions.

How did you make your cane disappear like that? Are you a magician as well as a street artist?"

Before Mark could try to bluff them, Woolley interrupted. "I'm going to guess it was when you were a kid. Back in Chicago." Mark's eyes widened in alarm. "I would say the night of the accident was the first night you'd experienced your gift."

"Gift you say? More like a curse," Mark spat out, remembering again the people hurt when he pulled the fireworks off the wall mural. "I didn't ask for any of this. If you're going to arrest me for what happened back then, fine."

"I'm not interested in arresting you for that, or anything I think you've done since. I am interested in just what you can do."

Mark motioned to the notepad and pen in front of Solomon. The detective pushed them across the table to him. Mark quickly sketched out a paper clip. Concentrating, he pulled it from the page and tossed it to Woolley.

Leonard picked up the clip and inspected it. He then bent it, straightening it like any other paper clip can be. He laid it down. "Impressive. It feels completely real."

"It is. Whatever I draw or paint, I can make real. I've tried birds or butterflies, but living things don't seem to work. It's not pretty," Mark finished, shaking away the images from his memory. "It usually vanishes within a few hours. The more details or time spent, the better it holds up." He pointed to the paper clip, already fading. "Nothing I've done has stayed permanent."

"But you've made the best of it," Leonard continued. "You could have used it to become rich, but you drive an old car and stay in cheap motels. Why is that?"

Mark broke down, seeing himself stuffed in a whole somewhere, forced to create weapons for some secret government agenda. He raised his wet eyes to the two men. "I loved comics as a kid. You know, super heroes. When I realized what I could do, I knew I had to use it to bring some good to the world. To help people."

"And to make up for what happened when you were a kid," Woolley finished for him. "You haven't done anything wrong. The man who painted the mural. He was like you. Gifted. Though not in quite the same way. I met him once." Leonard reached out and laid a hand on top of Mark's. "He tried to help people too. Or at least bring some joy to the world."

"Tried?" What happened to him?" Mark asked, having not considered what the man might have been up to since they'd met years ago.

"A fellow agent approached him about what he could do. Like I am with you. There was an accident. Either something went wrong with his gift or the agent startled him. Neither survived the explosion."

"Why? Or how did this happen to me?" Mark asked.

"You were affected by a meteor shower. It sounds far fetched but I've seen enough, good and bad, to understand the randomness of what happened. Part of my job is finding people, and objects, like you. I have to determine if they are safe and stable. Or if the public needs protectioned."

"What are you going to do to me?" Mark asked, deflated.

"Nothing," Woolley replied. "You can continue doing things as you are. Or you can work with me. And maybe help even more people."

"Be a Fed?" Mark's eyebrows shot up. "I'm not cut out to be some company man."

"I'm not exactly Fed either. I work for an organization called The Collective. As I said, our job is to protect the public. All the public. From the effects of these meteor showers."

"Do you have, gifts, as well?"

"Oh no," Woolley laughed as he replied. "I'm just a normal guy who got caught up in all this years ago." He pushed a card across the table. "You don't have to decide anything now, Mark. But call me if you need anything, or even just want to talk."

The abrupt dismissal shocked Mark so much he found himself in the hall before he realized he had stood up. An officer offered to give him a lift to his car by the pier, which Mark accepted.

Once Mark left the building, an equally shocked Solomon turned to Woolley. "You're just going to let him walk? After what you explained to me about this stuff?" Leonard nodded and Solomon continued, "That's crazy. Why would you lie about being FBI?" His head spun.

"Detective Peter Solomon," Woolley said formally, causing the younger man to sit down heavily. "I don't tell people who I really am, because most people wouldn't believe me. Until you saw the cane disappear yourself, you didn't believe me a bit. Now you've seen it with your own eyes. Can you see yourself living your life as it were? Knowing these kinds of people exist? And it's not just people. Sometimes it's just objects. Some unlucky person picks up the wrong affected object and gets hurt, hurts others, or gets killed."

"How am I supposed to protect my city if I don't know this exists? How do any of us in law enforcement? Why all the secrecy?" Peter raged against the older man.

"Think about it," Leonard said softly. He watched as Peter's eyes filled with realization. "Now you know why the Collective keeps this such a secret. Who wants some zealot or power hungry madman getting his hands on an object that can do the things like Mr. Campbell can? And his gift is not even the strongest I've seen in my years with the Collective."

"Like what?"

"Like a sword that can bend anyone who views the wielder to their will. A fountain that can reverse aging to the point a person ceases to exist. Not to mention the poor souls who are changed physically by the meteors."

Solomon sat in silence for a moment, his mind opening up the most outlandish possibilities. "How do I protect my city from these meteor people you're talking about?"

"You don't," Leonard replied. "At least not as Detective Peter Solomon, Santa Monica Police. But as Agent Solomon, of the Collective, you can help protect the world." Woolley waited while Solomon thought it over. At the younger man's nod, Leonard smiled. "Good. I need a younger partner anyway. I'm tired of doing all the running and heavy lifting by myself. Let's go. Someone will handle your resignation from the department. It's time to get you caught up on what really goes bump in the night." Woolley stood and clapped his new partner on the shoulder.

***

Present Day...

Jake and Debbie laid out the blanket that was to be their bed for the evening on the sandy beach. The salty ocean air rolled over them like the waves on the shore. Jake pulled Debbie down onto the blanket.

"This is going to be awesome," Debbie said excitedly, pulling out her new digital camera. "I'm so glad they shut down the pier tonight for the meteor shower."

"Yeah," Jake agreed. "The lights and music would have ruined the mood." He paused when Debbie looked at him sharply. "I mean the show. The shooting stars."

She kissed him softly. "Maybe later lover boy. I want some good shots of the sky for my photography journal first."

Jake settled down next to her. For several hours he watched her and the sky as she took dozens of pictures. He gently ran his fingertips along her leg until the show wound to an end and she set the camera down next to her.

As she turned to kiss him, he held up a small jewelry box. "Debbie, will you marry me?" She squealed and kissed him deeply.

***

Dan strolled along the nearly deserted beach, picking up stray trash and tossing it into a bag. He muttered about tourists and respect for the environment as he worked. He stopped, and rolled his neck to stretch out the soreness from staring at the ground the last hour. He noticed something a dozen meters away, a splash of red against the sand.

He jogged over to it. Discovering a blanket and a small cooler. He looked around, no one shared this part of the beach with him. He stared at the ocean, watching for an early morning swimmer or surfer to surface as the owner. A gust of wind curled up the corner of the blanket, revealing a camera.

Dan bent to pick it up, flipping it over to check for a "If Lost" sticker or nameplate. Finding nothing, he carefully folded up the blanket, grabbed the cooler, and headed for his car. "Someone will be looking for this. Hopefully there's a picture of the owner on it." He shoved the items in his trunk before returning to the beach to finish his cleanup.

***

Woolley dialed a number he hadn't in a number of years. He waited while it rang once, twice, three times. As the line connected, he said as warmly as he could, "Mr. Campbell, how's the art business these days?"

"Your number is the last one I thought I'd ever see again. It's been what, ten years, Leonard?" Mark replied, his voice gravelly with age.

"Something like that," Leonard replied. "You walking the pier this time of year?" The Curator thought of the ocean scene hanging in his study at home. A gift from the Artist. Mark usually spent this time of year in Santa Monica.

"You still keeping tabs on me?" Mark asked, then laughed. "I suppose I am a creature of habit anyway. I haven't smelled one of your guys on my tail since that incident with Bigfoot up in Washington. How is Big Hairy doing these days?"

"He's fine. Doing some work out in Appalachia. This is about something else. I've got a suspected MAO problem in the area and I'm stretched a little thin. I could use some help."

"What kind of trouble? I'm getting a little old to be chasing people through the woods."

"Nothing like that, old friend. So many people turned out for the latest meteor showers, incidents are popping up everywhere. I need someone to pick up an item and hold it until my field agent gets there."

"I figured you guys would be busy with what's going on. What do you need me to pick up?"

It's a camera, one of those newer digital ones. The original owners disappeared the night of the event. Someone found it, posted it and some of the photos online to try and locate the owner. Now they aren't responding to requests for information."

"What makes you think the camera is an MAO? People go missing all the time, sadly."

"One of the pictures... moved."

"What?" Mark sputtered, sitting up in his old chair. "What do you mean the picture moved?"

"It's hard to tell in the image, but it looks like someone is trapped inside the photo. We think the camera transported the original owner inside. If we can get our hands on it, we think we can get them out."

"You've always been good to me, Leonard. Ever since we met. Send me the details. I'll see what I can do."

Mark pulled an old suit out of his closet. He checked the pocket, finding his fake FBI credentials still where he left them. "I'm just picking up a potentially dangerous camera. What's the harm?" He said to himself.

His hip protested the rushed manner in which he got dressed. Despite his self assurances this would be an easy job, he pulled a faded canvas from his closet as well. Concentrating on the images, he pulled a holster and service pistol as well as an extra clip out of the painting. He checked his appearance in the mirror one last time, adjusting the tie and jacket.

***

The address took Mark to a middle scale apartment complex not too far from the ocean. The faint salty smell to the air always felt like home. He took a deep breath before approaching the building.

Mark on the office manager's door. A balding man of advancing years opened it slowly, eyeing his suit. "Excuse me for bothering you, sir," Mark said politely. He pulled his Collective provided fake FBI badge from his coat, making sure the manager saw the gun hanging under his coat. "I'm Special Agent Campbell with the FBI. I need to speak with one of your tenants. We believe they may be in danger."

The older man nodded. "I'll grab my keys. Which apartment?" Mark gave him the number and the man returned a moment later. "Right this way." He led Mark to the door. Before trying his key, he knocked several times. When no one inside answered, he unlocked the door and stepped out of the way.

"Thank you for your assistance," Mark said to the manager. "I'll take it from here." He waited while the old man shrugged and headed back to his office before entering the apartment.

Mark stood in the silence of the small, one bedroom apartment. A desk in the corner held a folded laptop and piles of papers. On top of the papers stood a digital camera like the one Woolley described. Mark approached slowly. This wouldn't be his first Meteor Affected Object, but the effects could be unpredictable.

He stood to the side and pointed the lens away from him. The charger cord extended to a surge protector on the floor. The small LCD screen on the back lit up, showing the last picture taken with the camera.

Mark inspected the scene. It showed most of the body of a male, probably the occupant of the apartment. As he stared at the picture, it flinched, like the figure was moving. Mark held it up to his face to get a closer look, cursing his developing nearsightedness.

A sound at the door startled him. A young blonde woman froze in the doorway, Mark saw a small object in her upraised hand. She smiled. "Looks like you beat me here, but that's ok. I've got time." She started to squeeze her hand.

Expecting a bomb or flash grenade, Mark flinched and dove towards the couch. The camera in his hand clicked. Mark groaned as his entire side hurt where he hit the floor. When nothing happened, he poked his head up above the edge of the couch. The woman was gone.

He looked down at the camera. A picture of the woman, silhouetted on the doorway showed on the little screen. A look of surprise alternated with one of anger on her face. "Is this thing taking video?" he muttered to himself as he pushed the menu button.

The menu readout indicated the camera only took still photos, though it would take bursts of three to ten pictures at a time. Mark pulled his phone from his pocket, dialing Woolley's direct line.

"Mark, what did you find?" Woolley's voice came through the line as soon as it connected.

"I've got the camera. No sign of the kid who posted about it. But we've got a problem," Mark said. He winced, pulling himself up on the couch. "Someone showed up here. I think she was after the camera too."

"She?" Leonard asked, remembering the recent break in at Director Adams' house. "What did she look like?"

"Blonde, youngish. Twenties I guess. I managed to get her picture with the camera. It's weird though. The photo does seem to move, but this model at best does bursts, no video."

"How fast can you get to the airport?" Leonard asked, already pushing the button to call his secretary into the office.

"Hour or two, unless I'm allowed to go home and pack a bag," Mark said resignedly. "But you know I hate DC."

"I know, old friend," Leonard replied. "I don't trust handing this thing off to anyone else. Be careful who, or what, you point it at until you get here. Don't let it out of your sight." Leonard hung up after Mark agreed to bring the MAO in.

His secretary stood in the doorway. "Please arrange flight and transport for Mark Campbell from Santa Monica to DC, then here. Also, have the Vault ready to receive an MAO of unknown powers. Make sure Dreyer is there. When Campbell gets here I'll need Adams and Jackson up here for a meeting." His secretary nodded and returned to her desk. Leonard sat back in his chair. "Does StarHacker have anything to do with this too?" he wondered aloud. His empty office offered no advice.

***

Mark sat in a chair against the wall of Leonard's office, his suit only a little wrinkled from the flight. Director Jackson sat stiffly in a chair across from the desk while they waited for Adam's to arrive. As soon as the Director of Astronomy entered, Leonard pointed to the second chair in front of the desk.

"I think you've both heard of Mr. Campbell," Leonard pointed to Mark. "He's brought us an interesting MAO, as well as a lead on the girl who broke into your house, Anthony."

"I didn't realize the Artist was an agent of the Collective," Anthony Adams said. He sneered at his colleague. "You've got civilians doing your work for you now, Jackson?"

"Don't start, Adams," his boss scolded. "I've got the camera in question down in the Vault with Karl Dreyer right now. Preliminary review indicates the camera is capable of capturing not only images, but whole people. We're unsure as of yet how to retrieve anyone captured inside, but we may have captured an agent of the Star Children."

Leonard turned his monitor to show a transferred image from the camera. It showed a blonde woman in a doorway.

On the larger screen, Mark noticed something more in the image. Before either Director could speak, he stood up. "Leonard, I think I can retrieve the people from the camera."

"What makes you think that?" Leonard asked.

"I couldn't see it on the smaller LCD screen, but if we can blow it up to life size," Mark said, his thoughts racing back the previous attempts to paint and pull live animals from his art. He shuddered. "It's never worked before, when I painted, but these photos are different."

Leonard thought only a moment before nodding. "Jackson, take some agents and go to the vault with Mark. They should have a way to enlarge the image. I hope you're right. If this woman is the one who stole files from

Adams, she could lead us to StarHacker. One less concern while this Event is going on. Dismissed."

***

Down in the Vault, Mark was introduced to Karl Dreyer. The astronomer had the same cornered, overwhelmed look Mark remembered when he first started working with the Collective. He patted the younger man on the shoulder. "Where'd they find you?" he asked.

"I can hold objects and see what they do," Karl replied softly. Campbell glowed. "Are you wearing a bunch of their items?"

"No," Mark said before laughing. "I guess you could say, I am the object. With luck, I'll be able to get these people out of the camera."

A pair of lab technicians wheeled a cart with a small projector into the room. One of them reached for the camera, picking it up gingerly. As she started to turn it over in his hand, Mark grabbed his arm. "Don't point it at anyone. It might go off. Making my job worse."

The man paled. He carefully arranged the camera to point at the wall while he hooked it to the projector. The blank white wall served as the perfect backdrop as the last image appeared.

Mark reached down and dialed it back to an image of a couple on the beach. Neither one looked at the camera, involved in kissing each other. He watched how the edges of the couple wavered and blurred. "Here's hoping." He took a deep breath before reaching towards the wall and laying a hand on the woman's shoulder.

He concentrated, feeling his power react to the image. The similarities to his paintings reassured him. He pulled, as he had thousands of times before. He felt the image solidify. The feel of the woman's shoulder firmed before she and the man appeared in the room. They looked up. Before she could scream, Mark whispered, "Everything's going to be alright. These nice gentlemen will help you get home."

Shock set in as two agents led the couple from the room. A wave of dizziness washed over Mark, stronger than anything he'd ever felt from using his power before. He leaned on the wall. Director Jackson took a step towards him, but Mark waved him off. "Never done that before," he said. The image on the wall showed the beach, without the couple any longer. A faint smell of the ocean wafted through the room.

Mark pointed to the camera. Karl reached down from his spot behind the projector to dial the camera to the image of the man's side in his apartment. He adjusted the frame until it appeared normal size. Mark went to work again, grasping the edge of the man's image and pulling him out of the wall.

This time an agent approached immediately, as Mark dropped to his knees. Nausea rolled over him like an ocean breaker. It took several minutes for the feeling to pass. Jackson knelt at his side with a bottle of water. Mark drank deeply and accepted the offer of a hand up.

Standing on wobbly legs, Mark looked at the Director, then Karl and the other agents in the room. "I just need a minute." The weight of tons of dirt and cement above and around him pressed in from all sides, squeezing the air from his body. Mark clung to the Director's arm as the panic attack spun his head.

Jackson looked the older man in the eyes. "We can wait until you're feeling better if you'd like. I don't think she's going anywhere."

His heart rate slowed with each successive deep breath he took. Mark shook his head, standing up straighter. "Let's get this over with." He waited while Karl flipped the image and adjusted the size of the projection.

Mark looked deep into the eyes of the woman, remembering how she held something in her hand when they'd met. "Be ready for anything. I don't know what she had in her hand but it could have been a flash grenade or something."

Mark watched as Jackson whispered something to an agent. The younger man exited the room and they all heard the door lock click before the sound of a bar slid into place in the door. The Director then moved everyone to the far corner of the room.

Mark reached out towards the woman's image, steeling himself for the after effects. He chose to latch onto her upraised wrist, in hopes of disabling whatever it was she was planning to use on him back in California. As he get her skin in his palm, he reached up and grabbed her still forming hand with his other. He pried the object from her fingers. As agents moved in to take her into custody, he looked down at the watch in his hands.

"Give that back your creep," the woman said, struggling against the agents handcuffing her. "That's mine. You have no right to take it."

Director Jackson stepped into her line of sight. "You aren't in charge here, miss. What's your name?"

Mark handed the watch to Karl as she answered resignedly, "Katherine Zurowski. But everyone calls me Kat."

"Well," Jackson said. "Welcome to the Collective, Kat. I think we need to discuss a friend of yours by the name of StarHacker. As well as whatever that does?" He pointed to the watch in Karl's hand.

"It stops time," Karl said in wonder, staring at the watch.

"You," Kat said, looking at Karl. "He talked about you. Said he was hoping you'd come around to his side."

Karl put the watch in a small bag he pulled from his pocket. He began packing the camera into a box before responding, "There don't have to be sides in this. Some of these things are dangerous. Someone has to keep the public safe." He placed the watch on top of the box, picking them both up. "I'll get these logged and put away. If you'll have your men open the door, Director Jackson."

Jackson knocked on the door in a series of quick taps. They heard the bar slide out of the way and the lock click. The agent on the other side opened the door and Karl left quickly with the two MAOs in hand.

Mark watched him leave. Then the room swam before his eyes and he collapsed as everything went black.

***

He woke up sometime later in a comfortable bed. Wires monitored his vitals, feeding a machine that beeped as he opened his eyes. A woman appeared in the doorway a second later. "Mr. Campbell, please stay in bed. Curator Woolley is on his way. I'll bring you something to drink. You're probably thirsty." She disappeared before he could respond.

She didn't say anything when she returned with a cup with a straw. Leonard Woolley arrived right on her heels. "Mark," he said, pulling a chair next to the bed. "You gave us quite the scare, my old friend. What happened to you?"

"I'm not sure. I've never pulled live people from an image before. I'm still surprised it worked."

"Has this ever happened before? I don't remember seeing you pass out when you used to pull supplies from your paintings."

"No. This is new. I... got a headache a few times when I created a lot of items in a short time. Maybe I'm getting old." He laughed, his voice hoarse. He drank from the bottle of water. "How long have I been out?"

"Couple of days," Leonard replied, patting his friend on the shoulder. "I'm afraid I have to ask for your help again. We have a plan to capture StarHacker using the camera, but once he's secured, I'll need your help retrieving him from it so we can have a chat."

"I don't think I'm up to pulling anymore people out of images."

"Oh, don't worry about that. He's not a person, per se." At Mark's raised eyebrow, Leonard continued, "He is a part of the internet now. He left a physical body behind a long time ago."

"So, how am I supposed to help?"

"We'll go over that when you're up and about. Take a day to really rest. I'll have some food sent. Whatever you like." He squeezed Mark's shoulder gently. "Is there anything else you need?"

"An open window, some sunshine." Mark grinned at his friend. "The smell of the Pacific Ocean."

"Soon. Then you can go home." Leonard smiled before leaving Mark to his thoughts. The nurse brought him a small booklet to order something to eat. While Mark perused the options, she pulled back the curtains and opened the window. A breeze flitted in, bringing fresh air and muted sounds of the city into the room.

The Sins Of Fathers And The Sons

by James Pyles

November 20, 1978, Las Vegas, Nevada, 1212 Hours

It was after midnight when the Ghost and the Gambler faced off standing ten feet apart like a couple of western gunslingers. They were in the parking lot behind the loading docks of the MGM Grand Hotel, but this was Las Vegas. In the city that never sleeps, they might not be alone.

"I won't let you do it, Jack." Rafael Story balled his fists not sure what would happen if he actually threw a punch. He stood six foot two, built of hard muscle and grit like the Marine he had been before this. He was a black man facing a white man. It sometimes seemed as if that was all there was to his existence, except this time it wasn't about race. He kept his hair short and had long since shaved off the mustache he'd had through three wars. A black t-shirt under a washed-out denim jacket and matching jeans filled out his appearance.

"Once again Rafe, you stand between me and what I want."

"To kill thousands of people in that hotel with what this time, some sort of meteor mutated virus?"

"What? You didn't hear about that Legionnaires' Disease in Philly a couple of years back? That was me and this is it." He patted the right breast pocket of his jacket. "Oh, they'll all get sick, but not all of them will die."

"Or I can stop you and no one will get hurt at all."

"You don't want to face me, not now. Neither one of us knows what'll happen." Jackson Higgins seemed perpetually tanned to Rafe. He didn't know exactly how old Jack was, but probably old enough to have seen an actual western gunfight. He was a sliver under six-foot, full head of hair just now showing some gray, and the trimmed beard was grayer than that. His face was a model of charisma but marred by a half-closed right eye. Still, no matter how dirty his life had gotten, his clothes were clean and expensive. There was a reason they called him the Gambler.

Rafael quickly scanned the parking lot. Too many cars but no one nearby. However, Higgins saw him tense up.

"I think you're missing the point of our lives, Rafe."

"What point is that?"

Jack's voice dropped down to a low, feral growl. "There is no point."

Rafe reacted an instant after Jack began his leap and they met in mid-air.

The explosion leveled a quarter of an acre of the parking lot. Cars were reduced to molten slag and lamp posts were flattened like trees in a hurricane. Thousands of windows on the hotel-casino shattered, sending glass hurling inward like shrapnel.

The concrete loading dock shattered but didn't crumble, and fortunately, there weren't any people outside to be hurt. Inside, hundreds of tourists and hotel workers were slashed, cut, and nicked, but there were no deaths, or at least that's what Rafe would read in the papers the next day.

Rafael Story woke up almost half an hour later in the men's room of a hotel several blocks away, his head ringing like a proverbial bell. He was alone in the bathroom and dashing out to the lobby of the Circus Circus, saw no sign of the Gambler among the meager number of people. But then most must have rushed outside to see about the explosion.

"At least I stopped him," he muttered, rubbing his temples and nursing a headache. But how could he really be sure when he didn't understand what had just happened? And even if he were gone now, where would the Gambler strike next?

***

The Present, Washington D.C., 2002 Hours

"Here you go, driver. Thanks." Rafe paid the taxi driver with cash through the passenger side window adding a generous tip. Even in the so-called enlightened 21st century, the middle eastern cabbie seemed reluctant to have a black man as a passenger. Whenever he had to, he took cabs. At his age, Story still wasn't sure about using Uber or Lyft.

"Thank you. Have a good evening, Sir." He took the money, smiled, and then quickly rolled up the window.

Rafe was watching the taillights disappear into the relative darkness of Pennsylvania Avenue as he stood in front of Lafayette Square Park across from the White House. He checked his wristwatch, he still used analog, and saw it was just past eight. He cursed the traffic because it had taken almost an hour to get here from Dulles, and the Gambler had probably been on the grounds for almost that long. Then his latest burner phone chirped.

"How the hell does he keep finding me?" Pressing the Home button, he opened the text app.

"Hurry. He's already out there and using the device."

"Fine. I just got here." He issued a surly whisper rather than texting StarHacker back. He thought it was a dumbass name. Why not just keep Vincent? Then he remembered what the Collective called him.

Oddly, there wasn't any traffic, so Rafe trotted across the street. The sun was just setting, and it was getting dark. He knew following the Gambler onto the White House grounds wouldn't be easy, even for someone named the Ghost.

***

"Pierce to Solomon." The young Collective agent, built like a brick, whispered into a small mic hidden in his suit jacket's lapel. He'd hear the older agent's reply over his wireless earpiece. "You're not going to believe this. I just marked the Ghost." Pierce had been pretending to stroll by the General Marquis de Lafayette Statue near the intersection when he saw Story in the middle of the block running across the avenue.

"Good work. Looks like our intel was right for once. Try to keep up without him seeing you. He'll lead us right to the Gambler and we can nail them both. I'm driving north on 15th just approaching the Treasury Building. I'll be at your location in less than a minute. Notifying other units."

"Roger that, Solomon. What about the Secret Service and the White House police?" Pierce made it across the street and was pacing behind Story who seemed to be looking for a way over the barrier.

"Don't you ever listen at briefings?" The older man snarled at his partner. "The Secret Service received info from an NSA chief that foreign terrorists were going to use a directed energy weapon at the White House. Secret Service evacuated the grounds as a precaution and cordoned off the area to everyone except us." Both of them knew that the Collective engineered that "tip" so they could have the run of the block. Their manufactured FBI "Division Six" ID got them past the barriers.

"Yeah, I remember the briefing. I just didn't think anyone would buy it. But I saw a cab pulling away from the park. How did it get in?"

"We picked up the Ghost at Dulles and informed the Secret Service to allow the cab through. Cabbie thought it was some sort of drunk driver checkpoint. The Service was told this is a sting and that the cab was transporting an accomplice we're here to pick up along with the perp."

"That's actually not a lie...oh crap."

"What?"

"I lost the Ghost."

"What? Did you stop to tie your shoelaces?"

"No, I was looking right at him. He stepped into a shadow for a second and then he was gone."

"I'll join you in fifteen seconds. Hold your position. All other units are converging."

***

"There's nobody here, Jack. You're wasting your time." Rafe had caught up with him just past the fountain on the North Lawn facing the White House.

The Gambler's back was turned to Rafe as he spoke. "I don't think these people would consider themselves nobody, Rafael." In spite of the dire pronouncement, his voice was light, almost comical. With a wave of his free hand, he swept toward their left.

Rafe saw three uniformed police officers, two men and a woman, on the ground. The female officer was on her hands and knees vomiting on the grass, while the two men were more or less in a fetal position. One was clutching his middle, while the other kept trying to stand up, but kept losing his balance.

Jack slowly pivoted to face his opponent. In his right hand was a Caduceus, maybe a foot long, made of brass or copper. It was what the Collective called an MAO, meteor affected object. The sheer number of them had multiplied like lemmings since the "event," and according to StarHacker, both the event and its results were driving the Collective crazy. There was no way anymore for them to keep a cap on the meteors and what they'd been doing for centuries.

"Want to see if your trinket can protect you against mine?"

Rafe involuntarily touched his shirt and felt the long necklace underneath. "Let's not."

He feigned a leap toward Jack and then suddenly rolled to his left. The woman was already sick, and Rafe figured he didn't have much of a choice. He used her as a shield while grabbing the service revolver from her holster.

Jack opened his mouth to hurl some taunt, but Rafe started firing. He might not be able to injure the other immortal, but if he could hit the Caduceus...

The first slug struck Jack just below the sternum and the second grazed his right shoulder as the Gambler was spinning away. Jack took off at a sprint southwest in the general direction of the Oval Office. Rafe released the weakly struggling officer and let her fall into her own puke. He felt briefly sorry for her, but knew she'd recover now that Jack and the object were gone. Besides, stopping Jack was more important than helping any one person. In the second it took him to get on his feet, his phone chipped again. The text read, "Collective agents converging. Run."

Reaching out with an uncanny sense of his surroundings, he could feel them coming closer. Dropping the revolver next to its owner, like Jack, he took an unusual exit. The female officer was barely conscious when she thought she saw a tall, black man step through a non-existent edge in thin air and then vanish.

**

Pierce was the first to get to the three officers who were still faintly struggling on the grass. "Damn, I don't believe this. Not again."

The older Solomon, puffing like an ancient steam engine and thin as a chimney, arrived seconds later. Leaning over, hands on knees, he managed to gasp. "Got away."

"Yeah. Maybe the other units…"

"Forget it, kid." Solomon stood, still trying to catch his breath as two more Collective operatives joined them. "I mean we'll try, sure, but we blew it. Without the element of surprise, we haven't a prayer to capturing them."

"I still don't understand how they get away each time, Sol."

Solomon slapped Pierce on the back and then grimaced. It was like hitting a wall of granite.

"Call Paramedics for these three. Once we're sure that the Gambler and the Ghost really are gone, I'll sound the all clear with the Secret Service and then we'll blow. They can do a sweep of the grounds for anyone else who was caught in this mess."

"What do you think did it?"

"Be at the briefing tomorrow at 0800. We're upping the ante. It's time we brought this game to an end. One way or the other, they're both going down for good."

***

A Business Complex Near Washington D.C., a Briefing Room at Collective HQ, 0802 Hours

Solomon was tapping the top of the podium in irritation. Sitting in front of him, eight members of the team he requested had arrived on time or earlier. He expected Pierce to be late, but where was the specialist?

A man who looked like a defensive linebacker in an expensive suit rushed through the open doorway. "Sorry about being late, Sol." Pierce hurriedly took an open seat in the front row slightly to Solomon's right.

"Relax, Pierce. We're still missing one more…"

The clicking of leather heels announced her presence seconds before she entered. All heads turned toward the person, who for them, was an unexpected visitor.

"Good morning, Agent Solomon. A pleasure to meet you." She extended her hand. He'd expected the Australian accent, but not the sense of charm her voice carried.

Solomon took it politely and moved back a bit so they could share the rostrum. Sol had been married for nearly thirty years, but her celebrity good looks captured him, even though he had memorized her dossier, including her ID photo, the night before.

"Good to meet you, Ms. Marquess. I'm glad you could join us." He hadn't meant it as a dig, but he saw her momentarily wince.

Putting a worn attaché case on the podium top, she softly uttered, "I'm sorry for being late. I've just moved into a condo in Arlington and I misjudged the commute time."

"Well, no harm done." He smiled courteously, trying to let his annoyance bleed off. Turning to the agents, he casually gestured, "Ladies and Gentlemen, this is Collective Special Agent Olivia Marquess. Obviously, she's not from around here." That drew a few chuckles from the group, mainly from Pierce and Nick Graves who was sitting in the back row at the far left. His collegiate good looks and neatly coiffed dark hair made him appear like Cary Grant at 26 when he was more like 36.

Solomon took a seat at the head of the room to Olivia's right. After he set up the nearby laptop which she would use for her presentation, he gave her respectful attention, still feeling her strong magnetism.

Her official record said she was 37, born and raised by her parents in Sydney until age 7. Then her parents were murdered and her 15-year-old brother, the only suspect, disappeared. She went to live with an aunt and uncle in Bendigo, north of Melbourne until she entered the University of Melbourne. At age 22, right after graduation, she was recruited by the Collective. They had been watching her since high school.

She was five foot nine and a half, Caucasian, although her great-grandfather on her mother's side was an Aboriginal. Her hair was just over shoulder length, the color of raw, dark honey. Her eyes were a pleasant doe brown. She had done a bit of modeling in her high school and Uni years to supplement her scholarship and had been approached by several agents to make modeling a career. She turned them all down, but it wasn't hard to see why those offers were sincere.

She was dressed in a dark blue pencil skirt and jacket with an off-white top slightly revealing her cleavage. The high heels matched her suit. In contrast, as she opened her case, Sol saw that it was severely scuffed and worn, with some patches of the outer leather having flaked off.

While she was dressed professionally now, field work consumed her career and she spent most of her time attired casually and living out of a suitcase. She'd been transferred from the Hong Kong branch to D.C. the previous week. Today was the first day of her new job.

"Good morning, Agents. As Agent Solomon already mentioned, my name is Olivia Marquess. I'm assuming my new position here in Washington as the Collective's Special Agent in charge of procuring Meteor Affected People. I'm here this morning largely because of what occurred at the White House last night."

"Interesting timing your starting here today then." Daniel Carpenter was a British ex-pat, 41, divorced, a cross between a gentleman snob and an introverted nerd. He also had a gift for dry sarcasm.

"Quite Agent…" Olivia briefly consulted her notes. "…Carpenter. In this case, I think it's just a happy coincidence."

Pierce raised his hand which made Solomon roll his eyes. "How much do you know about the MAPs we encountered?"

"An excellent question. Agent Solomon, can you start the presentation on the laptop?"

"Oh, yes. Of course." Sol turned on the screen and passed the remote to Olivia. Then he moved near the door, both to close it and lower the lights.

The first slide came into focus displaying what appeared to be an old sepia photo of a distinguished looking man with ruffled hair and a trimmed beard. The clothing dated back to the mid or late 19th century.

"This is the MAP known as the Gambler, also sometimes called the Joker or One-Eyed Jack. We believe him to be a man named Jackson Albert Higgins, born in Ohio sometime in the 1820s. Starting in his late teens, he made a name for himself as a prize fighter, con man, but mostly as a riverboat gambler, hence his codename. In his career he is reported to have won and lost millions in gambling. We don't know when he encountered a meteor, but it most likely affected the vision in his right eye. Witnesses over the past eighty years or so state that it seems to suffer from a progressive degeneration. We know he disappeared sometime in the summer or fall of 1903. Since then, there have been sporadic sightings. The ones we can confirm are 1922 in Alabama, 1944 in Okinawa, 1951 in New York City, 1978 in Las Vegas, and 1986 in Rio.

"On almost every occasion, the Gambler's been intent on causing some sort of disruption, usually resulting in extensive property damage, but particularly causing the illness, injury, or death of people."

"The three White House police officers…" Gordon Ng started to volunteer the relevant details like an overachieving student and looked disappointed when Olivia interrupted him.

"Yes, Agent Solomon was good enough to supply me with his preliminary report of the events of last night, so I'm familiar with the circumstances."

"Do you know what caused…?" Gordon began.

"You're getting ahead of me, Agent Ng."

Ng nodded and sat stiffly in his seat. Solomon felt a little sorry for him. He was a young and ambitious achiever. At age 30, he already had an eye on the Assistant Director position, but Collective internal politics probably wouldn't let that happen for years. No wonder though. He had a beautiful fiancée who was also one of the top ten pediatricians in D.C. He wanted to impress her. Pity he could never tell her what he did for a living.

"Agent Marquess, why does he do it? The property damage, hurting people and so on?" Nick was normally smiling and even playful rather than curious, so the question was unusual, Sol thought.

"It goes along with his other name, the Joker. You've probably seen the movie where a similar character is described as someone who just wants to watch the world burn. The Agents who have made a study of this man over the last century believe that's the most likely explanation."

"An agent of chaos," Daniel murmured, mining his vast mental repository of trivia.

"That's how we believe he sees himself." She paused briefly to see if there were more questions before continuing. "I'll get to the specifics of his attack in a moment, but first I want to introduce you to the other player in this game.

She advanced the next slide to show a black man in a U.S. Marine's uniform sitting at a desk. The photo must have been unexpected because the man with the sergeant's stripes seemed both surprised and annoyed. The name plate on the desk said Sgt. Maj. Rafael J. Story.

This is Rafael James Story, codenamed Ghost Story or just the Ghost."

Laughter burst out from all the agents, including the normally reserved Joyce Castro. Oscar Brown who had become quieter and occasionally morose since the tragic death of his wife and unborn child three years ago, even chuckled out loud.

"I know. I wasn't the one that hung the name on him. At any rate, we know a great deal more about Mr. Story than we do Higgins.

"Born May 9, 1909 outside of Tupelo, Mississippi. Mother was Grace Bathsheba Story. Father unknown. Raised by his mother who died of tuberculosis in 1933. Story held a series of odd jobs helping to support the two of them from age 9 until she died when he was 24. After he buried her, he took to the road. Held a variety of jobs. Taught himself the guitar and played with a small blues group from '39 to '41. A week after Pearl Harbor, he volunteered for the Marine Corps."

Olivia had tapped through a series of slides of Rafe including one of him at church with his mother when he was seven. The most recent one showed him with four other black men in wrinkled suits, each holding their instruments and posing, probably before a performance.

"Without going into exquisite detail, Mr. Story was one of the most decorated African-American Marines in the history of the Corps. He was the first black man to become a drill instructor in 1942, eventually promoted to Gunnery Sergeant, served in Saipan, Okinawa, and in North China."

"When was he in Okinawa?" Sandra Kirkpatrick was 26, dedicated to the Collective and an eager agent. Being career minded gave her a keen sense of detail and the ability to make unusual associations. She also seemed to have her eye on Daniel Carpenter, but Sol didn't think Daniel had bothered to notice.

"Good. You made the connection. Yes, we believe both Story and Higgins were in Okinawa at the same time. Also, there are some reports that say an unidentified object, probably a meteor, crashed near where Story was stationed in November of that year."

"If the Gambler had been born some eighty years before, it's not likely this event also resulted in his exposure. Are we sure both men are MAPs and not using some sort of object to extend their life spans?" Brown's wife had been killed by an MAO, a curio on a silver necklace she had found in an obscure antique shop. Oscar had been away on a weeklong assignment only to come home to find his wife's corpse. She had miscarried and her metabolism had been wildly accelerated. She had died of extreme old age. The Collective physicians estimated her physical age at around 120. It broke Oscar's heart when they had to cover up the "incident" by faking a fatal car accident. Her body had to be burned beyond recognition. Now he was almost obsessed with MAOs.

"Correct, the Gambler was exposed much earlier, but somehow the second event, Story's exposure, must have tied the two men together, which I'll get to in a few minutes. As to your other question Agent Brown, we aren't sure in Story's case. On two occasions, witnesses say they saw him wearing a rather odd medallion along with his old dog tags, made of some roughly chiseled metal. Yes, it's possible this is an MAO, but we won't know for sure until we manage to capture and hold him. As you all saw last night, that isn't easy.

"To continue, after the end of World War Two, Story remained in the Marines. As you'll see in this next succession of slides, he appears to age very little if at all, and yet he served with distinction in both the Korean and Vietnam Wars."

"What?" Even Solomon was surprised at that one.

"As far as his service file is concerned, he performed with a perfect record in the Marine Corps for nearly 29 years. He was declared MIA in October 1970 at the siege of Firebase O'Reilly located south of Quảng Trị in Quảng Trị Province. He was 61 years old when he vanished. Of course, the Collective had been interested in Story for quite some time, but he never seemed to display any unusual abilities besides his youthful appearance, strength, and stamina. It wasn't until he encountered the Gambler in Las Vegas on November 20, 1978 that we realized he was a lot more, or at least his pendent is."

Olivia advanced to the next slide showing a crater a quarter of an acre wide in a parking lot. The photo had been taken early in the morning and it was still smoldering. Emergency fire crews and police were at the scene with a crowd of spectators behind the police line. The caption said November 21, 1978, MGM Grand Hotel.

"Security cameras in parking lots weren't common in the late 1970s, but a witness inside the hotel looked out her room window sometime past midnight and saw two men apparently about to get into a fight. The witness, a Mrs. Gretchen Lamb, was in the process of dialing the police from her room on the fifth floor. The lighting in the parking lot was excellent and Mrs. Lamb managed to give a good description of both men to officers later that evening. They matched those of Story and Higgins."

"What made...that?" Joyce's mouth momentarily hung open.

"Mrs. Lamb's initial statement was that both men advanced on each other and when they came into direct contact, there was a violent explosion. Of course, we managed to change the official story, explaining that a gas main had ruptured. We can only theorize that something in the...nature of both men is incompatible when they come into physical contact. Fortunately for the witness, an instant before the explosion, she heard her husband opening the door to their room and moved away from the window. She was still covered in broken glass but only sustained minor injuries. A lot of other people inside weren't so lucky."

"That's fine for Mrs. Lamb, but those two should have been killed." Agent Jeanette Schultz looked like she should have been a young suburbanite going to PTA meetings, bake sales, and shopping at budget clothing stores. In fact, the 25-year-old was single, though in a live-in relationship with her partner Emilio Mendoza. Unlike Ng's fiancée who never seemed to quite believe his cover, Mendoza was perfectly satisfied with her story of being a security consultant required to work a long and unusual schedule.

"You'd have thought so. We don't know what happened to the Gambler afterward. We wouldn't spot him again for years, but a security camera in the hotel lobby of Circus Circus clearly showed the Ghost exiting a men's room." She advanced to a slide depicting a slightly blurry but recognizable Story. "He appeared in some sort of minor distress but otherwise healthy. Unfortunately, he pulled his disappearing act before we could move in."

"Besides last night and presumably in 1944, have there been other occasions when they were in proximity?" Christina Cooper, the only other African-American agent in the room besides Kirkpatrick, was in her early 30s. Unlike most other agents, she was married to an "outsider" and had a five-year-old son. Somehow, she managed her career as an agent and maintained a close family relationship. Sol still wasn't sure how, even though he had the same thing with this wife Rachel. In his case, the kids were older and had plenty to keep them busy while their "workaholic" Dad was away from home.

"We suspect they may have met sometime in June of 1986, but it's unconfirmed and we can find no unusual events that occurred in or around Rio de Janeiro in that time frame."

"Could they have had some sort of common history before 1944?" As Sandra finished asking her question, Solomon saw Daniel turn in his seat, give her a gentle smile and a thumbs up. Sol mentally corrected himself, seeing that Carpenter had noticed her after all.

"None that we can find, but naturally we can't rule anything out."

Pierce started to raise his hand, saw Solomon scowling at him and put it back down on his tabletop. "You said you were going to explain about the MAO the Gambler used last night."

Marquess pressed the button on her remote advancing to the next slide. It was a photo of a foot-long brass representation of the Caduceus medical symbol. The note beneath said, The Cuban Object: MAO.

***

Collective HQ near Washington D.C., the Private Office of Curator Woolley, 1846 Hours

At 67 years of age, Collective Curator Leonard Woolley felt perpetually tired. After a decades-long association with the organization, initially as a junior agent and then working his way up the ranks, he was tired of it all. He was tired of the unending meteor strikes, tired of artifacts emitting unpredictable and sometimes deadly results, tired of people mutated by these mysterious objects from space, tired of budget meetings, tired of office politics, and tired of what he'd become. All he wanted to do now was retire and go fishing with his grandchildren.

It was late afternoon and he was going over what seemed to be an endless stack of reports. Woolley could have reviewed all the material on his computer, but he was old fashioned enough to still prefer hardcopies. They'd all go back in his secure office safe when he was finished.

He paused to look out of the window of his corner penthouse suite. Rank hath its privileges, he mused. He could see the light from a dying sun setting in the west glinting off the surface of the Potomac River. In the far distance, he could even pick out the Washington National Cathedral. It was a lovely view, but he'd rather be in his vacation cabin in Idaho's Sawtooth mountains enjoying a late spring afternoon, a fire roaring to keep him warm, and fresh trout frying on the wood stove.

Sighing, he returned to the documents on his desk. He'd already reviewed the Olivia Marquess file three times, and it contained confidential material he could never reveal to the agents, even those he trusted like Solomon.

He set it aside and opened the Cuban Object folder. This is what the Gambler had used at the White House yesterday. He frowned. These MAOs were becoming more menacing all the time, and now that the event had let the proverbial cat out of the bag, the whole world knew or at least suspected the true nature of the meteors. Worse, the Collective had been obligated to contact the various security groups of the world's nations, but only at the highest levels. If they were going to contain this disaster, the Collective could no longer afford to do so alone.

Woolley was familiar with the file. He'd even helped compile some of its data. The Cuba Object, also called the "Havana syndrome attack" because its first documented use was in 2016 in Cuba. That's when diplomatic and intelligence staff began reporting strange symptoms of ear popping, headaches, nausea and vertigo accompanied by a piercing, high-pitched sound. It was discovered that a heretofore unknown MAO was the cause.

After its initial use, diplomats, CIA operatives, and other US personnel experienced the same "illness" in Russia and China. Unusual tactics for the Gambler who, as far as anyone knew, was apolitical. Then again, his latest target was the White House.

A wave of dizziness overcame the old man and his heart started pounding. He let the papers fall from between his fingers as he broke out into a profuse sweat. "Oh God, not now. Don't let me go like this."

Then Leonard realized he wasn't alone in his office.

"Fear not, Mr. Curator or whatever you're called."

A strong hand grabbed Woolley's wrist as his fingers reached under this desktop for the panic button. If he could press it, a dozen agents would come running through his door in just a few seconds. There were two surveillance cameras in here, but no one was monitoring the live feeds. They'd only see what happened by viewing the tapes, and by then it would be too late.

"None of that now." The hand released Woolley's wrist and spun him around in his chair. Leonard froze in terror. He was face-to-face with the Gambler and he held the Cuba Object in his left hand pointing it at the Curator's chest.

"Oh this? Not to worry. I'm not going to kill you, not yet anyway. Why I just thought the two of us should become better acquainted, seeing as how you've been searching for me so long."

The world became a whirlpool and dimmed, and then for Leonard Woolley, it faded to black.

***

When Woolley regained consciousness, at first, he thought he was still in the dark. Then his eyes adjusted, and although the lighting was unusually dim, he recognized the room. It was one of several surveillance stations in the major MAO repository called the Vault located deep below the central building in the Collective's business campus. He sat up, still feeling dizzy, and braced his back against a wall.

"How did I get here?"

He was talking to no one in particular, but a voice answered. "Oh, I get around, and I can sometimes take others with me." The Gambler stepped out of a shadowed doorway to Leonard's right.

The first thing Woolley noticed was that he no longer had the Cuba Object.

"You liked that thing. Probably wanted to examine it further. That's quite alright. You have it. You see, I've hidden the Caduceus somewhere within your Vault complex. Problem is, only I know where."

"What do you want from me?"

"What does a cat want from a mouse? Not just a dinner, but to play."

"Leave the old man alone, Jack."

Higgins looked to the floor and chuckled. "I was wondering when you'd show up." Then he looked at Story who was standing at the opposite end of the room. "Care to tell me how you always seem to know where I am?"

"I have friends in strange places." Rafe was wondering how, even with his extraordinary abilities, StarHacker always managed to keep track of Jack and text his location to him.

"So now that you're here, Rafe, what do you plan to do?"

"Let Woolley go and give up the Caduceus."

"You've always had a dreadful sense of humor. I can't imagine why I should do that. Besides, this man is as much your enemy as mine."

Seeing an opportunity, Leonard raised a hand. "Wait. It doesn't have to be this way. I can…"

"Shut up," Higgins growled. "Can't you see I'm in the middle of a conversation." Then he directed his attention back to Rafe. "You can certainly see the monitors in this room. There are three ways in and out, and the Curator's valiant agents…" Jack's voice was soaked in disdain. "…are stationed at each one, trying to gain entry. You learn a thing or two if you live long enough. I activated a timing mechanism on the locks. It will be over an hour before they get in, unless they manage to override the instructions. We'll have plenty of time to play our game."

"What game is that?"

"I want something…that trinket you wear around your neck."

"How will that help you and what do I get out of it? The Caduceus?"

"The Collective will have to deal with the Caduceus all by themselves. No, I mean I want the object you've worn ever since Okinawa."

Woolley kept quite still realizing that even without the Caduceus, the Gambler was a lethal threat. He wasn't sure what to make of the Ghost, but he didn't want to find out the hard way. The Gambler was right. The Collective would treat both of them the same way, as exhibitions and test subjects. There was no way he could appeal to either one. He just had to hope that the agents he could see on the monitor screens could get in before one or both of the MAPs decided to kill him.

"You still haven't told me why I should do that."

"Him. I can kill him at any time by sending him on a little trip through netherspace, that is, without me."

"He'd wouldn't survive a second."

"Oh, you've been paying attention, Rafe."

"You said it yourself. That man is my enemy. Why should I care if you kill him?"

"Not only do you have a poor sense of humor, you're a terrible liar. I should have stayed around to teach you poker, especially how to look a man in the eyes and bluff your ass off. Alas it was not meant to be."

"If I give it to you, then what?"

"I take it and go."

"You're just going to leave the Caduceus here, or is that a bluff, too?"

"Oh, I'm being sincere, Rafe. The Caduceus is actually hidden somewhere nearby, but it isn't exactly inert."

"Meaning?"

"I haven't always had it in my possession, but the freelance covert operative who had it before me no longer has to worry about how to spend the millions she earned. Ah, I see you grow impatient. Very well. The Caduceus can operate with a person willing it, but that's not strictly required. Once a set of commands is imparted, it can execute them independently."

Then to Woolley, he said, "You really are an idiot for locating your Vault directly beneath your national headquarters. A charge is building up within the Caduceus. Inside of the next thirty minutes, it will be released with such a force that everyone within a mile radius will become ill…deathly ill. Your agents have that long to find and neutralize it, if possible."

"But that could be thousands of people." The effects of the object had completely worn off, but the Curator still refrained from standing up or making any sudden moves. "We can work something out. The Collective protects the world from the knowledge of these strange events, but that doesn't mean we can't be partners."

"Thanks, but I value my freedom. If Rafe here wants to be your so-called partner…"

"Jack."

The Gambler turned his attention back to the Ghost, who had just unbuttoned his shirt and was taking off the chain around his neck. The fragment was attached with the dog tags. Jack's one good eye grew wide.

***

Agent Marquess was at the west entrance to Surveillance Room 13 with Ng and Carpenter. She'd ordered Solomon to cover the north entrance with Shultz, Cooper, and Brown, while Pierce took east with Graves, Kirkpatrick, and Castro. According to their records, Carpenter, Brown, and Kirkpatrick all had sufficient technical skills to override the timing locks on the doors to the chamber.

"How's it coming, Carpenter?"

"Almost there, Agent Marquess." His voice sounded strained, probably because he had to hold long fingers inside a very cramped open maintenance port.

"Hold off on opening until the other two teams are ready." She spoke into her mic. "Solomon, Pierce, what's your status?"

"Solomon here. Brown says he needs another few minutes. Don't pop your hatch open yet."

"This is Pierce. Kirkpatrick's ready. Just say the word."

"This is a coordinated effort. We have to open all three doors at once and keep the MAPs guessing. Then all agents rush in and fire your tranquilizer guns at them. Hopefully, we can incapacitate them both before they can escape. Stand by."

"Solomon again. Brown says another 60 seconds and we're in."

***

Jack lowered the necklace over his head, letting the fragment rest on top of his rather expensive tie. "What do you think? Is it my color?"

"You got what you wanted. Now take it and go."

"Seems a shame to leave you here to their tender mercies." Jack nodded at the monitor station depicting the agents, all now pulling out handguns. Then he looked again at Woolley. "But then again, you are not merciful."

Woolley was filled with both dismay and anticipation. The Gambler was about to escape, but without the MAO, the Ghost was theirs at last.

"You'll keep your word and leave him here."

"I may be a scoundrel but I'm also a gentleman. I made an agreement and I'll keep it. He will remain to take you prisoner, if he's able. Good-bye Rafe."

Several things happened at once.

To Leonard's astonishment, the Gambler seemed to walk around a corner in thin air and then disappear. All three doors of the surveillance room slid open simultaneously and almost a dozen agents raced through them brandishing what Woolley recognized as tranq guns. Then he heard Marquess screaming, "Hold your fire! Hold your fire!"

He looked back at where the Ghost had been standing, but there was only empty space. He was gone.

***

"This is Special Agent Olivia Marquess. This is an Alpha One alert. I repeat, an Alpha One alert. This is not a drill. All available agents report to the Vault for an immediate search of a rogue MAO. Rogue MAO is the Caduceus or Cuba Object. It is hidden somewhere in the Vault and will go live in…" She consulted her phone. "…twenty-four minutes. All units respond immediately."

She was at the main entrance of the Vault with Agent Mark Shepherd. He had been the Vault's chief administrator for the past ten years and one of the most trusted agents in the Collective. It was the first time they had met, and she found him to be completely professional, which was a quality she admired more than just about any other.

Watching dozens of agents rushing in and beginning a systematic search of the Vault's vast interior, she whispered to him, "What are our chances?"

"Not great," he responded sardonically. "Five levels, all subterranean, each level spanning several acres. Each level is separated into twelve sections, and each section contains hundreds of holding bays, quite a number of them still empty. We're looking for an object about the size of an empty paper towel roll."

"Surveillance footage?"

"I've got fifteen agents going over all of the tape for the time we estimate the Gambler was in the building, but you're talking thousands of cameras. It would be the wildest stroke of luck if we found the right section of tape in time, particularly because this MAP can teleport. He could have hidden the Caduceus anywhere. Did you get Woolley out?"

"EMTs took him to Walter Reed. He seems fine, but he should be checked out anyway. Building is evacuated of all but essential personnel, but if the Gambler makes good on his threat, it's not just the Collective that's in danger. Local law enforcement is clearing the surrounding area but there just isn't enough time. Thousands could still die."

"Including you and me."

"Our jobs, if it comes down to it."

"I'm at my post, Agent, as are you."

Olivia had read Shepherd's file and personality profile. He wasn't bluffing. He would willingly die in the protection of the Vault and the monstrous dangers it sheltered.

Olivia looked again at her phone. "Twenty minutes and counting. God damn the Gambler anyway."

"There's still hope." Shepherd's voice was soft and steady. "If by some miracle we can find it, the Asset is standing by."

***

Director Sanders paced at the bottom of the Pit, the Collective's communications nexus just one floor above the Vault. It was a round room and he was at its center. Several rings of consoles crewed by cybersecurity experts were monitoring all manner of communications, internet, cellular, land line, radio, television, any possible means of transmitting and receiving data. On the walls over those consoles were several layered banks of video screens depicting scenes from all over the Earth. Some of those rooms and buildings were heavily guarded and highly classified. They could watch almost anyone and anything.

The NSA would have been green with envy if they knew it existed.

He started to run his fingers through thinning dark hair, forgetting that he was wearing a headset. His jacket was over his chair at this supervisory console in the center of the Pit. He loosened his tie and unbuttoned his shirt's top button. Sanders picked out Eastern Standard Time from the row of digital clocks above the wall monitors.

"Fourteen minutes." He could feel coffee and acid burning a hole in this stomach. Sanders dearly wanted to give the evacuation signal, but if there was the slightest chance they could acquire some intel on where the Caduceus might be, he had to take it. It was just a damn shame so many good men and women would die with him.

He felt his personal cell vibrate in his pants pocket. Reflexively he picked it up. He had a text message from an unknown source. It couldn't be spam. He had it totally locked down, so then what? He opened the text app.

"You're looking in the wrong place. The Caduceus isn't in the Vault. Gambler put it in Woolley's personal safe in his office. Hurry."

"What the hell?" Should he hit the panic button? The message had to be real. No one could possibly have known…

***

Marquess was running down the hall toward Woolley's office with Ng, Castro, Solomon, and the Asset. There was less than five minutes to find and neutralize the Caduceus.

"It won't work, Agent Marquess," Ng was yelling at her as they got to the double doors. Solomon's key card had a high enough security clearance to open them.

"Woolley's safe has a combination code changed every seven days, plus it requires his retina scan, voice print, and galvanic skin response. We can't get him here from Walter Reed in time and there's no way to override the security before the Caduceus…"

His voice trailed off as the five of them entered and then slowed. On the top of the Curator's desk at the exact center sat the Caduceus. There was a single piece of paper beneath it and a marker to one side. Olivia snatched the note up without touching the object.

"You lost something that I found." It was signed with a simple "G" and Marquess had studied hundreds of samples of Rafael Story's handwriting.

"The Asset."

Fourteen-year-old Eden Alexandria Currie stepped forward. Her skin was pale and her stringy blond hair was almost colorless. She wore a superhero t-shirt and faded jeans on a string-thin body. Her facial expression was vacant but there was something behind her eyes that burned like fire. The color kept changing.

She took the Caduceus in her hands and pressed it to her forehead. For several seconds, the four agents held their breath watching subtle waves of some eldritch force shimmer through the Cuba Object and across Eden's face. Then she put it down on the desk again, turned to Solomon, and nodded. The vaguest hint of a smile crossed her features for a second and then she again became impassive.

"I'll take you home, Eden." Solomon extended his hand and she took it. He led her away, seemingly heedless of the remaining tension in the room. Very few people knew about the Asset, who she was, where she came from, and most of all how she could seem to control and even deactivate MAOs. Those who did know understood that Solomon was the only person in the Collective she trusted.

"Less than a minute," Olivia was looking at her phone, palm so sweaty she almost dropped it.

"But it's over," Castro protested. "You saw..."

"We don't know what we saw, Agent." Olivia shot Joyce a withering look. "Do the reading. The Asset isn't 100% effective. Not even close. If she were, we would have no active MAOs. We have to be sure. Forty seconds."

"Then if it didn't work..." Ng began. He saw if they were wrong, there was no place left to go, nowhere to hide.

"Thirty...twenty..." Olivia was counting in hope, not defeat. If the Asset had failed, then the timing of it didn't matter.

"Ten seconds..." She was tempted to count it down, but for what?

"Three...two...one..." There was silence. The three of them were still. The air conditioner kicked on with a subtle swirl. A gust of wind rattled the windows, facing a now darkened sky and the jeweled brilliance of the metropolis outside.

"One minute past," Olivia said. Then she sighed, her shoulders sagging. She got on her comm. "Attention all agents. Attention all agents. Alpha One alert cancelled. Repeat, Alpha One alert cancelled. We're in the clear." She heard cheering through her earpiece from their agency-wide channel. "Send someone up from the Vault to take charge of the MAO. I want this thing locked down fast."

Less than ten minutes later, Mark Shepherd appeared in Woolley's office to personally take custody of the Caduceus.

***

Solomon pulled his ten-year-old sedan in front of a modest suburban home in a housing tract outside of Arlington not half an hour's drive from the Collective. It was already dark, and he knew Eden must be hungry. She said nothing on the drive home, looked at nothing, and showed no interest in anything. Sol saw her breathing and blinking, but if not for that, she might have been a mannequin.

"We're home, sweetheart." She didn't react and he had the urge to reach over and stroke her hair in compassion. Instead, he unbuckled her seatbelt, got out, walked around the front of the car and opened the passenger side door.

He tenderly took her arm and she passively let him lead her. Halfway up the walk, the front door opened, and both Sam and Esther came out.

"Eden, you're home," Sam rushed up and hugged her. His wife joined them and only then did the girl start

283

breathing deeper. She hesitantly wrapped her arms around them and whimpered, "Mommy. Daddy."

Let's go inside, Dear. It's getting cold and you don't have a sweater. Esther took Eden's hand.

"Can you come in for a minute?"

"Sure, Sam. Got any of that Knob Creek left? After today, I could use a belt."

They both chuckled as Sol followed his nephew inside.

"Sure, but only one. You've got to drive."

"Are you hungry?" Sol could hear Esther talking to Eden in the kitchen. "I heated up the chicken soup when Sol called saying he was bringing you home. He could hear an inarticulate grunt which must have been assent, because then there were sounds of ladling soup into a bowl.

"Let's go into the den, Sol."

The two men walked across the living room and into what amounted to a small library. Whenever Sol visited Sam and his wife and walked into the study, seeing all of the Talmudic commentaries, he reminded himself that it had been far too long since he'd been in shul.

"Here you go." Samuel handed him a glass with two fingers of whiskey.

"Thanks." He took a sip while Sam poured a glass for himself. Sol sat on a small, cushioned sofa against one wall, while Sam put himself down in the chair behind his desk.

"How did she do?"

"She was a champ, Sam. No fear, focused on the task at hand. Tonight, she probably saved five thousand lives. She's a hero."

"She's a kid Sol, and a really messed up kid at that."

"I know it's been hard…"

"She's no burden, she's a blessing."

"You and Esther are the blessing. Ever since we found that poor child wandering naked down a Kentucky dirt road during an event…"

"You're sure her parents are dead, that she has no relatives. If I were in their shoes and she'd disappeared, I'd be frantic."

"We've been over this, Sam. She's got no one. No one except you and Esther."

"She's got you."

"At our age, with three kids in the house already, Rachel and I can't raise her. She needs so much more attention."

"She trusts us, and she trusts you. We're family, not a foster family, but just plain family."

"Here's to family, Sam." Sol raised his glass and in a silent, thankful toast, enjoyed the bourdon and the company for the tiny march of minutes God would allow.

***

It was almost midnight when Olivia, having christened her brand-new office just two floors below Woolley's, turned off the video feeding across a secure network to her company issued tablet.

Only one desk lamp was providing illumination, so she could have been sitting in a large, shadowed cavern. "How could we have been so blind and so damned stupid. Of course, the Gambler would think it was funnier than hell to hide the Caduceus in Woolley's office while we were chasing our tails in the Vault."

She'd convinced forensics to release Story's note to her. It was in a plastic bag, but the fingerprints, DNA, and all the other evidence had already been taken from it. "Why did you do this, Rafael?"

Olivia had also viewed the tape from the camera inside of Surveillance 13, the one thing the Gambler neglected to disable. "You must have believed the Gambler was right when he told you the Collective is your enemy, too. Why did you bother to save us and how did you know where the MAO was hidden?" It had already occurred to her that in spite of the Gambler relieving the Ghost of his own object, he retained his ability to teleport. But if the necklace, the metallic fragment attached to it wasn't an MAO, why did the Gambler take it?

"You two better watch your asses. This was the closest we've ever come to containing you. For every encounter with you, we learn a little more. It's only a matter of time."

Her beaten up attaché was sitting open on her desktop. Almost against her will, she found her right hand reaching inside and pulling away a small flap. She retrieved a faded and wrinkled photo of two kids, brother and sister. He was fourteen at the time, the same age as the Asset, and she was only six. They were hugging and making goofy faces for the camera. Dad took it or that's the way Olivia remembered.

"I loved you so much, Noah." Tears described uneven trajectories down her face. "Why did it have to happen to you? Why did the meteor turn you into a monster? Mom and Dad…" She pressed her palm against her face, not wanted to remember all that blood, their shredded flesh.

Then she wiped away the moisture and abruptly returned the picture to its hiding place. "I'll find you someday, Noah. Then we'll see what happens between you and me." Her voice turned to ice. "I'll never forget what you did to Mom and Dad. Never."

***

A Week Later, An Old Cemetery Outside of Tupelo, Mississippi, 1100 Hours

"Hi, Mama. Sorry it's been so long since I visited." Rafe briefly looked around. The landscaping in this part of the graveyard was poor, but then who had the money and the concern to take care of the last resting place for black people who'd died seventy, eighty, and ninety years ago?

"Sorry I didn't bring you flowers. I still remember daisies were your favorite." He dropped to his knees and pressed his forehead against the gravestone. Time had nearly worn away the inscription, but he remembered the words anyway.

"Here lies Grace Bathsheba Story, loving mother and child of God. Went home to her beloved Jesus September 21, 1933." Even Mama was never sure exactly how old she was or when she was born. She said, "Dem didn't make no records for us sharecroppin' colored folk in dem days."

"I can't stay too long. They're probably watching this place, but it will take a little time for them to call in the cavalry. I just wanted to say that I'll always love you and no matter what happens or how long I'm allowed to live on this Earth, I will never stop missing you. Of all the souls I've met, yours was the only one who truly loved me."

The new burner cell he bought the day before yesterday vibrated in his jacket pocket. "You've got to be kidding me. Now? Couldn't be."

Yes, he had a text message. He opened the app. "Look behind the gravestone."

Rafe put the phone back and moved around one side of the stone. It was a small package wrapped in brown paper and string. He picked it up but had already felt the familiar emanation from within. There could still be a risk because it was from him. How did he know Rafael would be visiting here just now? He didn't like to think of the answer.

Pulling a small knife from his pants pocket, he cut the string and sliced through one side of the package. Inside, wrapped in a cloth was his dog tags and the pendant he's made from a fragment of the meteor that changed him on Okinawa nearly eighty years ago. That was also the first time he met him, although Rafe didn't understand how they were related at the time.

He also found a note:

"Dear Rafe, Figured you'd visit Grace's grave at some point so I left this for you here. As you know, my health has been failing me for some time now and we both know about how these meteor things work for good and for bad. Your trinket seems to have picked me up some, but I don't know for how long. I can tell that whatever it had to give me is all it would give. Might as well send it back to you, son.

"I suppose I've had a whole bushel of children, but by now, they'd have been born, lived, and either died or be old folks. I know what your Mama and I had didn't last long. I never could stand to be in one spot for more than a little bit. I don't know what she saw in me. Maybe the kindness of my own Mama, who was just as black as Grace, though my Daddy was a white man. Your Mama had more love inside her than any woman I've ever known. It was for the best I didn't stay, and for the best I didn't try to raise you.

"You know I'm going to keep to my ways. I don't know any other way to live anymore. A life lived this long just isn't worth a nickel to me, except to thumb my nose at it and those stupid Collective folks. I'll keep on doing what I do, and you'll keep on trying to stop me.

"Someday whatever the meteor did to me will wear off and I'll pass like any mortal man to meet my Maker and have my soul sent straight to Hell. I'll never see your Mama in the afterlife, and that's for the good. If one day, you're privileged to pass from this world, I know she'll welcome you at Heaven's gates with open arms. That's for the good, too.

"She raised you right and you're doing what she'd want you to do. Well, that's all I've got to say. Guess I had more words in me that I thought.

"You take care, son. Don't let any man put you down, not even me.

Your Papa, Jack."

Rafe opened his shirt, put the necklace back on, and buttoned up. He stuffed the wrapping and string in his pants pocket, but carefully folded Jack's letter and slipped it inside his coat.

"Don't worry, Jack. I won't."

His phone vibrated again, but this time he knew why. "Thanks Vincent, but I can sense them coming."

They were professionals and well concealed behind surrounding trees, but the cemetery was an open field and they'd never get close to him. "Probably a sniper. They want me alive, so a rifle, .50 caliber with tranquilizer darts."

Rafe suddenly flattened himself on the ground behind the gravestone a second ahead of the dart as it whizzed over where his head had been.

***

Twenty agents had been airlifted by helicopter out of the field office in Memphis to support the two spotters who'd been assigned the unenviable task of staking out the rundown graveyard. Chief Agent Iris Cannon was watching Rafe through a pair of binoculars one instant, waiting for the sniper's dart to impact, and the next, Story was gone.

"He's rabbited! Advance," she screamed. "On the double! Move!" The black woman jumped up from the brush, cursing the extra twenty pounds on her hips she shouldn't be carrying and ran with the rest of the agents converging on Grace Story's grave. When they got there, only the dead greeted them.

"I don't fucking believe this. All these months, years of watching this hole in the ground and we missed our shot?" Cannon kicked at the dirt still cussing. Then yelled, "His file said maybe a few blocks. Fan out. Find him!"

Twenty-one agents spread out in a circular search pattern in a vain attempt to capture a man who could disappear at will.

***

Half a mile away, Rafe opened the door to his economy rental car resting behind the caretaker's shack. At the wheel, he turned the key and when the engine caught, put the vehicle in gear and drove up the service road to the rural route he'd taken to get there. In minutes even the dust being kicked up by the tires would be nothing but a mirage.

***

Atlantic City, New Jersey, a Private Room inside an Unnamed Casino, after 0130 Hours

The Gambler sat down once more with six other people at the table. A side bar held anything the players might want for refreshment or entertainment. That meant booze, drugs, everything that would give someone pleasure or end up destroying them.

For the past four hours, he'd been playing poker in a game that wasn't supposed to exist. His opponents were notorious gangsters, pimps, drug dealers, people guilty of money laundering, assault, kidnapping, and murder. "Just my kind of crowd," he thought to himself.

"Your deal, Higgins." Mariah Williams weighed 350 pounds and ran the numbers rackets up and down the Jersey coast. Every time she shifted her weight, Jack thought her chair would collapse from under her. Earlier that evening, he'd placed a side bet with Mickey "the Weasel" DeLuca as to whether exactly that would happen. He also loosened one leg of her chair when they all took a break an hour ago. He didn't like to lose, which was evident by the mound of chips scooped in front of him, much taller than any of the other players.

He shuffled the deck with hands that had been dealing cards when Zachary Taylor was the President. "Ladies and Gents, the game is five card stud, and one-eyed jacks are wild. Ante up."

Damage Control

by Andrew M. Ferrell

Todd looked over the lineup for the evening news. Talk of the meteor shower had dominated the last few weeks in preparation for the start. He thought over the strange documents and images sent to him months ago. "If I'd been able to keep those, they could make for some interesting reports."

An item near the bottom of the sheet caught his eye. "Flying people?" He skipped to the longer report. "Oh. We are leading with this. Crow people. Gotta be good for ratings." He stood and ran to find the producer.

"This is a Todd Jenson with the evening report. As the world enjoys the Great Meteor Shower, residents of the town of a North Fork are dealing with something else falling from their sky." He paused while a grainy cellphone video of two men with large black wings fight in the street. Before the one killed the other, the image froze. "That's right folks. Big black wings, flying men. Who are these bird…" He stopped as the studio went dark. The crew looked at each other as people turned on their cellphone flashlights.

"Someone check the generator," the producer yelled.

"That won't be necessary," a voice said. Everyone turned to see a man in a dark suit. He held up a government badge. "When the lights come back on, apologize for the technical difficulties and read the teleprompter. We don't want a panic over the filming of a secret movie project. Big name stars coming out of retirement and all. Carry on." The man turned to leave. As soon as the door closed behind him, power started to flicker back to life in the studio.

Todd looked at his producer as words appeared on the teleprompter. "Do you buy this crap?"

The producer was looking at his phone. "If we want jobs tomorrow, read the damned screen. Now." His voice shook with fear.

Unlucky Strike

by Ian Hugh Mcallister

The commuter jet bucked and dipped. "God, Spider, I hate these things."

"Move over to that seat."

"We can't move now, it's too rough and the sign is on."

He growled at her, "Jen, it's not an ask."

"Come on, you even hate it when people stand up before the plane stops at the gate. Look, we're crossing the freeway and we'll be on the ground in a minute. What the hell are you doing?"

"Saving your life." He flipped the buckle on her belt and pushed her. "That seat. I'll sit behind you. GO, NOW!"

The plane bounced again as the pilots corrected in the strong crosswind.

"SIT DOWN," the flight attendant hollered, strapped in facing them a couple of rows away by the door.

"Sorry," called Jen as she slammed into the sidewall, propelled by another lurch and her husband's pitching arm. She scrabbled at the side for the belt.

Spider reached forward and grabbed her arm so hard she winced. "You'll be OK. Now, get in the brace position."

"What the hell is with you? Nearly broke my skull, and now you bruised my arm." Airport buildings flashed by outside.

"Down, brace," he barked at her, then put on his training field shout. "BRACE, BRACE, BRACE, FOR IMPACT!"

The flight attendant started yelling back at him as the wheels slammed too hard into the tarmac. "You can't—

Something broke and shattered the right side of the fuselage as the plane bounced.

Spider felt a surge as the engines spooled up, but he already knew they were coming down again, banking to the right. A sudden twist, and the 25 passengers snapped right, then left.

"BRACE, BRACE, BRACE," he yelled again, this time in chorus with the attendant. The plane spun around, and an icy blast filled the broken cabin with swirling dust, grass and the smell of jet fuel.

Then Spider *KNEW*. *Nobody would be killed, and the plane would travel half a mile backwards to stop on a taxiway in a banshee screech of twisted metal, minus its landing gear and a wing. He knew that when he opened his eyes, the pair of seats he and Jen had jumped out of less than thirty seconds before would be gone, speared by the right main landing gear strut and wheels.*

***

"What happened, Spider?" She clutched the cardboard bowl as he wiped her face. "You're OK, Jen, it's adrenaline shock making you sick. We walked away, actually the paramedic said everybody walked away. I can't believe there wasn't a fire. You banged your head is all, but you'll be fine."

"You knew…those seats…I feel faint again…You made me…Oh, ugh!" She gulped hard as the paramedic swapped the bowl just in time. Spider held her hair.

The flight attendant sat opposite, cradling an arm. "Yeah, that was weird. You changed seats. How did you know?"

"I have no idea. I didn't even think, I just did it. I pushed her real hard too. Then I *saw* the plane going backwards onto the taxiway, with the wheels sticking out the side and one wing ripped off. Look, I'm with the FAA, and I work liaison between them and the NTSB on airplane accidents. I'm a rules and procedures nerd but I…I have no explanation. I should be outside right now surveying the damage."

"Not a chance." The paramedic handed Jen some more wipes and moved to shut the doors. "Somebody else's job on this one. You need stitches in that knee, Glenn. Your wife needs a check-up and a scan, and Lacey here needs that wrist setting. We're just closing up and we'll be taking a gentle ride to the emergency room.

***

"Your guys asked me to call this number if I ever heard about anything you might call paranormal." The local reporter was a sceptic, but the card he'd kept all these years said there was always a reward for good information on the paranormal. "This guy Glenn 'Spider' Robbs. I know him, but he told me he *saw* the accident before it happened, like a vision or something. The injured flight attendant says he threw his wife across the plane with seconds to spare, and called the passengers to brace before there was any clue it would crash. The seats they had been sitting in were the only ones destroyed. He collected his wife from the local hospital this morning, and they are on their way home."

"That's good work, Mr. Shapiro. We will need to talk to you and the other witness. Can I get some contact details?"

***

"I'll get it."

"No, Jen, stay there. You're more knocked about than me. Oh, good grief, that stings."

Spider opened the front door. "Oh, hi Paul. I should have guessed you'd turn up for further interrogation. Come on in." He called over his shoulder, "Jen, it's Paul Shapiro from the paper."

"Hey, Spider," breezed Shapiro. This is Dan Henridge, he's monitoring all press activities after the accident yesterday."

Henridge had a much firmer hand than Shapiro. "Good to meet you, Mr Robbs."

"I usually go by Spider, didn't he tell you? Paul and I were class of '04 at Mills High."

Shapiro laughed. "So how come you're a hotshot crash investigator and I'm still just the local hack?"

Jen appeared at the lounge door. "Tea or coffee, folks? And no, Spider, I'm done sitting on that couch for today."

***

"Jen, that guy Henridge. He wanted information I can't give up, because it could compromise the crash investigation. He wanted some very odd side-story stuff too, details about us. I dodged as much as I could. I asked both him and Paul what agency he was with, but I didn't get an answer. Now, if he was FBI he would probably have said so. I just called work and they have no heads-up on any investigation outside of their own. My hackles are up."

She treated him to her finest eye-roll. "All this and we nearly got killed over a few shooting stars. I haven't told you how much I loved flying all the way to Wisconsin in midwinter just to see a clear sky."

Spider couldn't tell if she was being sarcastic or joking, but she dispelled any ambiguity by pointing the finger of zero backchat at him. "But, for your information, it's the last time I ever go in a three-seats-wide commuter jet, just because it's a type you haven't flown on before." The anger dissipated as fast as it had gathered. "I do have to say it was quite a show, though. Hey, baby, I just thought. Did you rescue your meteorite off the plane?"

"It was in my pocket all along." He fetched his favourite jacket from the hall closet and pulled out a smooth black pebble, rolling it around in his hand. "Still safe. Wait . . . It's Henridge again. In two minutes."

"Huh? Spider, what?"

"He's coming back. Basement, Jen. We're not home." He set the house alarm and slipped the remote into a pocket. He'd put the Mustang away next to his classic Mercedes, so the drive was empty. "Come on, downstairs, we need to avoid these fellas."

"I don't understand this." She followed him down and shut the door.

"I picked that meteorite out of my pocket just now, and it happened again. I *knew*. He's with a shadow agency of some sort. He wants me because of the rock. Something about the meteor shower wasn't normal. What I do know is that I'm not playing along with him." He squinted, and then looked straight at her. "Jen, I just realised! After I shoved you on the plane, I put my hand in my pocket to check the rock was still there. That was when I *knew* how we would crash and that we'd be OK. What I need to know now is if I touch it, will he know I'm doing it? Like the ring, you know, when Frodo wore the ring and Sauron could see him. I must have touched it before that too, when I wanted to move seats, but I wasn't doing it consciously."

"Spider, whose head was it got smacked? Shit, is it something to do with the shooting stars? should I be scared? Is he an alien?"

"No, he's not. I don't think we should be scared, but I know I don't want to deal with these folks. At least, not

300

until I understand them. I don't do surprises, I do standard procedures and order."

He connected the alarm remote to the downstairs screen, and looked at Henridge ringing at the door. "Jen, I'm going to hold the stone for a few seconds. Watch him. If I get the vision, my eyes blur a bit. Watch and see if he gives any clue that he hears me or anything."

He touched the stone. Jen held his other hand, but dropped it. "Ouch! Static."

He put the stone on his desk by the screen. "He'll ring a few times, then leave. It's only him, but he's waiting for backup before they come to take me in. There's no danger to life here, but they use people somehow. I don't know what for, but they'll have to work harder for it before they use me. And no more cell phones, these folks listen. We don't want them spooked while we plan how to dodge them."

"If they're that determined, can we do it?"

"Oh yes. Let's pack some stuff right now and disappear for a few days. I'm still on leave next week and we'll take the Merc for a road trip. No modern tech in it to track. Let's visit Pete and Pam in 'Bama. They're almost off-grid. Fancy an adventure?"

***

The Mercedes purred along, lapping up the miles on I-65.

"Know what I've always liked best about this car, Spider? It's the smell. I suppose it's that stuff you feed the leather. Can we stop soon and put the roof down?"

He laughed. "You know an old V-8 always has to stop soon at twelve miles to the gallon, baby. I wonder how long we'll be able to buy gas though. Look at all these e-machines out here, I can't see another car with a working engine."

"You could probably charge up an electric car yourself, you know. You zapped me when you were holding that damn meteorite, last night, and—

"What?"

"Spider, you gave me a static shock, a real big one. Do you think this thing, this knowing thing, I mean the stone, has anything to do with when you got struck by lightning and--"

"NO, JEN, no! I mean…nah, no way, but…Baby, I still can't talk about that."

They drove another half-hour in silence, before gassing up and pulling into a Denny's near the Kentucky/Tennessee border. As the waitress refilled their coffee and cleared the table, Spider reached into his pocket and held the meteorite for a few seconds.

"Nothing new about us, Jen. We need to hang out around here for a couple of hours though, the southbound is blocked by a car fire a couple of miles down." He thought for a few seconds. "I think it only gives me a flash of the next minute exactly where I am. What I got off Henridge Tuesday night was a snapshot of his head, somehow, stuff relating to us directly. I wonder if it would do lotto tickets."

She laughed at him, loving those pale grey eyes. They were the first thing she had noticed about him. A few lines, and the odd grey hair in the black if you looked for it, but he still looked younger than his 47 years. "You look so relaxed."

"I'm not afraid, and you shouldn't be either. These folks looking for us, at least I presume they are, don't mean us harm. I know that for sure. In a way I'm having a game, and I intend to see if the stone can keep us one step ahead. Maybe we should buy that motorhome and go off-grid. You know we've talked about it ever since…" He shut his eyes.

Jen sighed deeply as she reached over the table and caught his hands in hers, like she always did. "Look at me, Glenn Robbs. It happened, it was the worst thing ever, and it always will be. We are healing, but it takes time."

"He would have been driving that Mercedes this year, not me." The tears came and he let them fall. "I mean, lightning, for God's sake. Who the hell gets struck by lightning? If it had been forecast we wouldn't have been out on the course. He should have lived, and I should—"

"No!" she snapped. "You know I won't hear that. Maybe you lived because that damn meteorite needed you to."

He wiped his face. "The stone? Nah. But, then again, I've heard weirder theories. Look, I'm done for today. I don't want to drive any more. Let's find somewhere around here tonight."

Jen nodded. "Good call. It's early, and the sign by the freeway said there was a golf resort."

"Not yet, Jen. It's too soon." It was a familiar retort.

"It's three years now, Spider. Would Todd have wanted you to never play again? Come on, honey, nobody here knows. Nobody will talk about it. Let's find the place and see if there's a driving range."

***

"Morning." Spider put two coffee cups on the stand.

"Uh, morning, honey. What time is it?"

"Nearly ten. I played nine holes with those guys we met in the bar last night. You were out, zonko, so I went for coffee real early at the clubhouse and they asked me to go out. I'm so rusty I quit at nine so they could get their round done. Jen, I told them why I'd not played for so long, and then something made me tell them about the lightning. It was hard. That fella James, he just hugged me while I cried for a minute. Something happened there though, and I think we broke the dam." She was out of bed to reinforce that hug. "Come here, you. What a good man he is, to know what you needed."

"It'll take time, but I think I'll be able to breathe today without regretting every lung-full. I want breakfast, and the clubhouse smelled like heaven. Love you, Jen."

It was her turn to shed tears. "Love you too. For a while I didn't think you'd ever get this far."

***

"Man! This yours? What a beauty. Nautic Blue and the Palomino leather, I've never seen an old Benz this good." Spider clicked the roof deck down and turned to see James pulling his golf trolley.

"Yeah, it's an '89 560SL, the last year model. We did a lot of work on it. It was supposed to be for Todd, and I've been hanging on to it since…the accident. I know I should have sold it, and this morning I've realised I probably will. I need to put some of this stuff behind me."

"No way, Spider! Have you ever been told it was your lucky day? We were meant to meet here last night, man. I'm a classic car dealer. My showroom is about five miles west of here in Shafersville."

Jen walked around the car and put an arm round her husband. "James, we're kinda running away from it all right now, and he told you why, I believe. Thank you for being there for him. Can I ask a favour? If we were to leave the Merc with you for a valuation, do you have a car we could borrow so we can finish our trip south? We're on our way to see some friends, and we'll be heading back past here up to Cincinnati next week."

***

"Smart thinking, Jen. Here we are somewhere west of nowhere, Alabama, in a loaned Ford, with the Merc garaged in a workshop hundreds of miles away. Nothing about this traces us. We're free and clear."

She laughed. "This is like a movie now, but I still don't know if it's a fun road trip movie, or a sinister frightener."

"I told you we're not in danger."

"It's next on the right, I think, and then it's a driveway on the left with white stones. I'm sad Pete and Pam aren't here, but it was generous of them to ask us to stay til they get back. Hope the keys are where they said."

They drove a quarter mile along the track, taking them out of sight of the road towards a cleared space in the woods. A black Suburban blocked the access road just inside the last of the trees. Henridge sauntered across as Spider got out.

"Afternoon, Spider, Jen. Good to see you again."

Spider took the offered hand. "You caught me out, Henridge, and that gets you points. But you get nothing from me until you tell me how, and I mean exactly."

"The miracle escape, folks. It caught our attention.

Jen stayed on the other side of the car. "Mr. Henridge, I'm so scared of what's happening here. We don't need any more drama in our lives. Leave us alone."

"Jen, please call me Danno. We owe you an explanation of course, but you didn't wait around to get it. We, meaning the organization I work for, think Spider may be important. For many years we've studied what is often considered paranormal, or at least unexplained. People lifting cars to save an accident victim, or doctors who can diagnose diseases accurately after just a handshake. I need to talk to you about all this, but it has to be kept very quiet."

"But…"

"If that's 'but why does it have to be kept quiet,' you need to consider the plight of witches. Since the Middle Ages, the odd ones out have been burned at the stake, or drowned, or worse. There's safety in conformity. Here in the 21st Century we'd rather avoid that. I work for a Collective that harnesses the possibilities of Altered People, and either keeps them safe, or teaches them to keep themselves safe. You came to our attention immediately after the accident the other evening, Spider. Random guy saves himself and his wife from certain death, and then issues brace instructions seconds before a freak jet crash nobody could have anticipated. Turned out you were a sky-watcher returning from a meteor shower watching trip. That was where our interest peaked."

"Paul Shapiro," Jen spat. "He must have called you, but…?"

Henridge grinned at her. "Well done, Jen. He did, and this time the 'but' is easy. We have a huge network of local reporters on the look-out for the unlikely. He hit a Grand Slam with you, Spider. We've never found a Prescient before. Well, not in living memory, anyway."

Spider studied Henridge. "That's how you knew we'd be here, too. Paul Shapiro is the only other person I can think of who knows where these folks live, they're old school friends who had stuff up north they wanted to leave behind, just like us now, I guess."

"I told you, we have people who can find things out. Paul is actually on his way here, you'll see him shortly. I've never been to Alabama. You have connections in beautiful places, my friend."

"FBI. You said you weren't, but it has to be. What do you want from me?"

Henridge shook his head slightly, and looked straight at him. "Spider, we don't want anything from you. I've been honest with you, and I need to tell you more about us. Can you suspend your disbelief and hear me out, now?"

Jen cut in. "I think it's time you did just that, Mr. Henridge, because I'm really scared of all this."

"You shouldn't be, Jen, and it's Danno, remember. You are not in trouble, you will continue to be safe with us, and I am not from the FBI, OK? I represent an organisation that draws in people with special skills. By skills, I mean unnatural talents, if you will. Spider came to our attention after the air crash this week, and Paul Shapiro was justifiably proud of his old school pal. You shouldn't blame him."

He reached out to place a hand on Spider's shoulder, but Spider moved away. "Go on."

Henridge shrugged a little. "We know you went to Wisconsin to watch the latest meteor shower. Is there any way you could have come into contact with dust from it?"

"Dust?" Spider queried. "No, not dust. In the morning there was a small meteorite in the snow on the hotel lawn. We heard it come down and thought it had hit a tree somewhere, but couldn't find it in the dark. In the light you could see a tree down, and the small melted snow patch. The stone is right here, in my pocket."

"Holy cow!" Henridge almost shouted, and then calmed down to speak quietly, giving Spider that unnerving direct look again. "What changed in you? This is why I am here, to ask you that."

"I *saw* the crash, Danno. I put my hand in my jacket pocket for some reason, to make sure my rock was still there, and as I touched it I *knew* what would happen.

Jen cut in again. "He touched me while he was holding it the next day. I got a big static shock. He has history with lightning, and that's one of the reasons I'm so scared. He and our 15 year old son were struck on the golf course three years ago. Todd died."

"Oh, for goodness sake, that's so…" Henridge put a hand over his eyes. "I am so sorry to hear that, sorry for your loss."

"We're learning to heal, I think," Jen said. "And now, out of nowhere, electricity comes back to taunt us, somehow. We've talked about selling the house and moving away. This trip was planned for later in the year, but we brought it forwards and just went."

"Yes, and I understand that. The Collective, the organisation I represent here, gathers people in who have had been altered. Recently it's been due to the meteors, but it's happened before, through the ages. Usually, where meteorites are concerned, it's from random dust contact, but holding a fresh meteorite and having a history with electricity is on a whole different level. We help people come to terms with what happened to them, and we encourage them to drive change in the world, for the common good."

Jen turned to her husband. "Honey, if Danno's offering us that life change, isn't it what we were looking for? I'll need more proof, but…"

Spider was staring vacantly into space. "Uh? He said I had a history with electricity. I just remembered I had a shock as a kid, off my Granpaw's old radio. It had loose wires and I tried to push them back in the plug. Maybe I do have history, maybe the lightning came looking for me that day. I'm so confused about all this."

***

Paul Shapiro sat in the shade with a beer. "Alabama is too hot after the snow at home. I'm melting."

"You do look warm," Spider laughed.

"I need to lose weight, but I can't seem to get around to it. I can't catch my breath out here." Paul rubbed at his pale chest.

"You OK?"

"Just overheated, man. I need a/c." He walked the few steps to the pool and sat heavily on the edge , dipping his feet. "Ah, that might help."

"Look, Paul, Danno wants us to fly with him and visit his organization. They want to look me over and see if they can figure me out. What do you think? Would you come?"

"He also said private jet, they're way too small. And you know I don't fly anywhere if I can help it. Hell, I drove all this way to find you when he told me where you were going.

"There's a good story in it."

"And there you have it. I jokingly asked you why I was still the local hack last week. Good journalist/doesn't fly. There was no way to go 'far' in that line, was there?"

"I didn't know that."

"Anyway, after I got here, Henridge said there wasn't a story in it. They're a bit secretive about their 'Collective'. I wonder if they kill people who know too much. All the way here to be told I can't tell your story. And then proceed to die of heat exhaustion. Spider, I really need to go inside and get cool. Lunch gave me indigestion."

"Kill you if you know too much; too many movies, that's your problem," Spider laughed again.

Paul heaved himself up, took a few steps, and knelt down. "Ah, that hurts."

"what is it?" Spider got down beside him.

"Chest. Oh, shit."

"Jen!" Spider yelled. "Danno! Jen!" He pulled at Paul. "Can you get into the shade here, buddy?"

Paul nodded, and managed to crawl the few feet, then rolled onto his back. "H.A…Ambulance," he gasped. He shut his eyes and his chest fell.

Henridge ran up to find Spider tearing Paul's shirt open. "Jen took one look, and she called an ambulance. "Is he breathing?"

"No. Can you do CPR for me? I need to get the stone."

"Go!"

It took thirty precious seconds to recover the meteorite and run back outside. Henridge was still pumping.

"Good job, Danno. Now move away and don't touch him or me. I had a brief vision of what I need to do."

Henridge moved, and Spider placed his hands each side of Paul's chest. His left hand was balled around the meteorite. He closed his eyes and his head drooped. There was a flash of light across Paul's chest between Spider's hands, and a sound like a sharp clap. The body went rigid, then limp.

Paul sucked in a breath and opened his eyes. "Am I dead? he asked faintly."

Henridge shook his head. "No, man. You're alive because of this guy's gift." He turned to Spider. "I think

311

the universe may be trying to make up for taking his son, by giving you the gift of life. That was incredible."

***

The business jet pulled to a stop, and the ground handler chocked its wheels as the door folded down and steps extended. In the executive terminal Spider laughed.

"Poor Paul, he said even coming this close to one of these things would give him a panic attack. It's a good job he's still resting up."

"That's why I asked them to come here and meet you, instead of flying you to them. Paul is a part of this deal." Henridge turned to the two men entering the lounge. "Hi, Greg, meet Spider Robbs, and his wife Jen." He turned to them. "Greg Jackson is my boss, and the head of recruitment. This is Karl Dreyer. He wanted to meet you as soon as possible, Spider, because he assesses folks' changes and abilities. We think you are something special. "

Dreyer clasped Spider's hand. "It's so good to meet you, Glenn Stuart Robbs, Spider. I've been following your case, and now I'm here I can see where the alteration resides in your head. It's not what I expected, and I want to run some tests on you when we get the chance."

"I'm still not sure about being a guinea pig, Mr. Dreyer."

"Karl, please. We're quite informal. I don't mean experiments and stuff, just to try and understand what it is that you have in there." Dreyer turned to Jen, indicating a lounge chair nearby. "Please come sit here and we'll get you some water. How are you feeling?"

"Thank you, Karl. Good to meet you. I'm a bit tired if the truth be known, I'm still confused by all this, and it's got me stressed. Am I ill?"

"Far from it, Jen. You are in first class shape for a 44 year-old, but you feel queasy today. Your body needs pineapple juice and more salt at this stage." He looked at Spider with a chuckle. "Oh, my, you guys have no idea, do you? Well, it's congratulations to the pair of you, because you're thirteen weeks pregnant, Jen. I think you are having a little girl."

Replica

by Sandy Stuckless

You've heard of the Invisible Man, right? Well, I'm like him except different. You can call me the Copier Man. Or, more accurately, the Copied Man. Allow me to explain.

It all started when I found that dumb sliver of rock on my Saturday morning jog in the woods near the mining site. The shard was warm when I picked it up, like it had been left in the sun for a few hours. Except, where I found it, the sun didn't reach. I took it thinking, hoping I'd have some time to study it.

I returned to the site field office. Sure it was Saturday, but a geologist's job ain't no nine-to-five. I almost tossed my cookies when I saw the black Beamer with the top down. Eaton Mason. A pain in my ass since the day I joined the firm. It should've been me running this expedition, but the man was such a kiss-ass. The bosses drank up all the crap he loved to talk.

I went up to my office and set the shard on the table

next to the core sample I dug up yesterday and turned on my laptop. New ground penetrating radar data had come in to help lock down the direction and size of this vein we were investigating. It was a career maker. For Eaton.

I had just started downloading the data when Eaton appeared at my door. "Didn't think you'd show up today, Irwin. There's still real work to be done, after all."

"What do you want, Eaton? I'm about to go over these new GPR readings. I think we're getting close to mapping out this entire vein."

"That can wait. I need these notes compiled. The brass wants a progress report and they're coming out here to get it in person. The chopper lands 10am tomorrow."

I pressed my fingers into my eyes. "Can't Claire do them? These new readings could really put us over the top." And finally get me my own field op.

"Claire is handling her environmental impact bullshit and I'm trying to arrange some explosives for the next round of excavation." Eaton dropped the folder on my desk. "Get it done before you leave today."

I spun my chair to toss the file on the table next to my field pack and did a double-take. There were two identical core samples sitting on the table. At first I thought I was hallucinating until I picked up the copy. It was slightly warm, but otherwise felt exactly like the original. Even 3D printed copies didn't feel this real.

I glanced at the strange rock I'd found less than an hour ago. Nah, it couldn't be. Could it? There was no known substance on Earth capable of cloning, but what if this substance was not of this world?

I ran my thumb across the shard again, contemplating

what I had in my possession. It was still warm. Warm rocks that hadn't spent any time in the sun meant heat generated internally. That meant radiation. I grabbed a lead-lined sample bag from the cupboard and dropped the shard inside.

I dropped a pencil from my desk drawer in with it. I had a hunch. Sneaking out of my office, I headed down to the microscope in the basement. When I opened the bag, three more identical pencils had joined the first.

Looking at the shard under the microscope nearly blew my mind. I'd never seen anything like it. The composition was highly complex. Maybe this was a piece of that meteor shower that happened last week.

"What are you doing down here?"

My heart nearly stopped at the sound of Claire's voice behind me. "I'm a geologist. I use microscopes. Didn't think it was that complicated."

"Okay, smartass. Be evasive if you want."

It wasn't Claire I didn't trust. She'd be obligated to tell Eaton everything I was up to. "Sorry, force of habit. What's your excuse? I don't think Eaton's coffee is down here."

"That's not funny. Eaton wants the last batch of stones from yesterday. He's doing some kind of presentation for the locals who still aren't onboard with the potential. They think we're going to destroy their beautiful land."

My Spidey Senses were going full red alert. None of that sounded like Eaton. No, Eaton was spying on me using the one person in this office I trusted. I took the shard from the electron microscope and dropped it back into the sample bag. "Tell Eaton that what I'm doing is not part of this project and none of his damn business."

"It's not like that, Donte."

"The hell it's not. He can't stand that I've got something his grubby little fingers can't touch."

I cared about Claire so I left before I said something I couldn't take back. The fact that she was willing to spy for him said perhaps this relationship wasn't destined to be long term.

Back in my office, I dropped the sample bag into my backpack and flopped down into my chair. I had to think this through. I knew I had something big, though exactly what, I wasn't sure. I did know I couldn't pass up the unexpected advantage. Eaton had all the power right now. That was about to change.

A quick Google search gave me the number to call about the meteorites.

"Porter Consultations, Eve speaking. How many I help you?"

"I think I found a piece of your rock," I replied.

"Is it secured?"

"For the time being."

"Good. Ensure it stays that way. Send us the exact GPS location of the shard and we'll send someone to collect it. Tell no one else you have it."

I figured I had at least twelve hours before they showed up. More than enough time to get rid of Eaton and take what should've been mine to begin with.

I flipped open Eaton's file. There were several maps, GPS coordinates, and sample reports right on top. None of this was for the main site vein. Something wasn't right here. Eaton's maps had an unmarked vein. It wasn't the largest one on site, but it was viable. At first, I thought it might be an oversight, but Eaton didn't have oversights. He may be a giant prick, but he was good at his job.

Why would Eaton intentionally leave a profitable vein off the official reports? Only one reason came to mind. He didn't want to share. I questioned these 'locals' Claire mentioned. I had a feeling Eaton wasn't being completely honest with her. I looked toward Eaton's office in time to see him grab his field pack and head for the door.

Of course, I couldn't take my assumptions to the suits without some hard proof. Eaton was their golden boy and they wouldn't take my word that he'd gone crooked. There was only one way to know for sure. I shoved Eaton's file into my backpack and followed him out.

The drive out to the trailhead took about forty minutes. I parked my car farther down the access road, out of sight of Eaton's Beamer. Whatever he was up to meant trouble for the whole expedition. I didn't want to see Claire get hurt and prison wasn't really my thing.

I hiked for almost an hour into the site of the sub vein that had been conspicuously left off the map. As I crested the ridge a smile touched my lips. The exposed rock glimmered in the afternoon sun. Eaton chiseled away at a rock outcropping before holding up a sizeable chunk of material. His cellphone was in his other hand.

"The first shipment is ready. Completely uncut, as agreed. I suggest arriving tomorrow at dawn. My bosses are coming later in the morning and your presence wouldn't be good. Don't worry. They won't even know to look for you. I've got a plan to take care of that."

Sonofabitch. Eaton really was selling company product to some unscrupulous folks. I knew the man was greedy, but I didn't think he'd go that far. And now, I was caught in the middle. Was Claire helping him in this little venture? I suddenly felt very alone in a place I was already an outsider.

The realization set in that I had to shut Eaton down completely and get him off this project. It wasn't enough to stop him from selling the gemstones to black market traders. He had to be caught in the act. An idea formed in the back of my mind. Eaton needed to get caught, but I wasn't willing to gamble with actual core samples. Enter my new little trinket. The Cloning Shard.

Eaton left after gathering up a few more stones. I stayed hidden amongst the trees until I was sure he was gone.

Thankfully, I didn't have to dig too deeply to come up with samples big enough to catch Eaton's attention. All he needed to do was take the bait. I loaded the samples into my backpack with the shard. All that was left now was to wait.

My stomach gurgled and flipped. It felt like I'd eaten some rancid meat or greasy fries. I normally had an iron stomach, but this definitely didn't feel right. I dropped to the ground, clutching at my fiery guts. I'd never been in this much pain before. Hopefully, I didn't crap myself out here in the middle of nowhere. The agony lasted almost ten minutes, but it felt like hours.

I rolled over onto my other side and came face-to-face with an exact replica of myself, right down to the stubble I hadn't had a chance to shave and the forehead scar from my first geology expedition. My chest clenched tight and I couldn't breathe. What the hell was happening here? I had to be seeing things. I had to be sick. Did I drink enough water today? Was the heat getting to me? Maybe it was a tumor.

"You look like you've seen a ghost."

Oh, wonderful. It speaks too! "Yeah, something like that." First thing Monday morning I was checking into a mental institution.

Slowly, clear thought replaced the panic. I wasn't actually losing my mind. I still had the meteorite shard in my pocket. Apparently, rocks weren't the only thing it could clone.

"You gonna be okay?" the clone asked with fake concern. "Do I need to slap you because I can do that?"

I held up my hand. "Not necessary. I just need a minute." A minute to figure out how to get rid of you.

"Oh come one. Why would you want to get rid of me? I'm a delight."

Great. He can hear my thoughts too. "You're not supposed to exist, that's why."

"Just think of it. Double the fun, double the excitement. You think Claire would be into the two for one special? Tell her I'm your long lost twin."

I dry washed my hands over my face. "Shut up and let me think."

"I got an idea. Let's grab a couple shotguns, get hammered, and pick up women. There's got be a couple around here desperate enough to be willing."

"Will you knock it off? I got bigger problems." I still had to deal with Eaton.

"Why are you thinking about black market diamond traders? And why wouldn't you want to take their money? They have lots."

"Ummm… because it's illegal and dangerous."

"Only if you get caught."

"Listen to me very carefully. We are not getting involved with black market traders. End of story. I'd like to leave this site still breathing."

"You're no fun."

"Alright, come on. You're coming with me until I can figure out what to do with you." We hiked back to the car, the clone mumbling about boring forests and ugly rocks the whole time. I shoved him into the back seat. "Keep your head down and your mouth shut."

"Sheesh, you sound like my mother."

I had to laugh a little. Clone Me wasn't wrong. My mother used those exact words more than once.

We returned to the office and went in through the back. It offered the shortest route to the basement and if Claire was still here, I didn't want her seeing me.

"Why are we at the office on a Saturday afternoon? We should be out drinking."

"Didn't I tell you to be quiet? Go wait in the corner until I'm done. And don't touch anything."

As expected, the stones we collected yesterday were gone from the safe. I opened my field pack to see the shard had done its job. Copies of the few sapphires and emeralds I just retrieved sat in the bottom of the pack. I put them in the safe case where Eaton would be sure to find them. The real stones, I kept in my pack.

I went back upstairs to my office. Claire wasn't ducked

out for lunch. I quickly logged the new samples into the registry. That ought to get Eaton's attention.

"Hey, what's this pile of dirt here on your table for? Probably should have a word with your cleaning service."

I turned to see what Idiot Me was talking about. The pile of dirt next to the sample used to be the clone. "It's nothing. Just another sample I'm studying."

The clone huffed. "When are you going to learn you can't lie to me? Why did the clone of that rock crumble like that?"

"That, I don't know." I went for the door. "Stay here. I have something else I need to do."

It figured Eaton would be arrogant enough not to lock his door. There was nothing in any of the desk drawers or the cabinets. No name or phone number of any sketchy people. The only thing I found was a folder with some topographical maps and satellite imagery.

"What are you doing back here? Where did you go anyway? You and Eaton tore out of here like a bat out of hell."

My heart leaped into my throat as I looked up to see Claire standing in Eaton's door. "Claire! This isn't what it looks like."

"Really? Because it looks like you're stealing Eaton's research for your own purposes."

"It's not like that. Look, I've found something. Eaton is planning on ripping the company off while selling the real stones on the black market."

"So, what? You can't have what he has so you accuse him of being a criminal?"

"This isn't about me. This is about your boss doing

something incredibly stupid. Where'd he take the stones you fetched for him this morning? They're not in the safe anymore."

"I can't believe you, Donte. I thought you were different than the rest. You were using me to get to Eaton." She stormed out before I could explain.

"That didn't go well. I don't think she'll be up for any freaky fun any time soon."

"Shut your damn mouth and let's go."

We followed Claire downstairs to the parking lot, hoping to catch her before she found Eaton. I hadn't counted on Eaton pulling into the parking lot as she was halfway to her car. "This is not good. Come one. If Eaton sees you, the shit will hit the fan."

I led the clone back through the corridor to a utility closet near the back door. "Stay in there until I come for you. Understand?"

The clone nodded with a smirk. "Whatever you say, chief."

I rushed back out to the front when Eaton was leaning against his car and Claire was talking quietly.

Eaton smirked at me. The arrogant bastard knew I knew about his side hustle and that there wasn't a damn thing I could do about it. "I hear you have a wild imagination, Irwin. Ever think about writing a book?"

"Give me the stones, Eaton? I'm not going to let you rip off the firm."

"I have to ask you to calm down, Donte. Your wild accusations could damage the firm."

"Screw you, Eaton. I'm done with you and your team. Pretty sure the cops would love to hear my wild accusations and get a good look at your phone records."

Eaton got in my face close enough for me to smell his onion breath. "You listen to me, you little shit. I've got a lot riding on this site. Do anything stupid and you'll regret it." He spun on Claire. "Get a leash on your little pet or you can find a new job too."

He disappeared into the office without looking back. I waited a minute before following him inside.

"Where are you going?" Claire called. "Let him go, Donte. You're going to get us fired."

I ignored her. I didn't give a damn about Eaton. I knew something was off before I reached the utility closet. Clone Me was gone. I spun about, but the corridor was empty. This wasn't good. Not good at all. I dashed out the back door and around the side of the building. Still no sign of him. I needed to find that idiot before he wrecked everything.

Claire was still next to my car when I got back. She tried to block me from getting into the driver's seat. "Donte, wait. Please."

"Save it, Claire," I snapped. "You made your choice. I guarantee you'll never have any sort of career as long as you work for him. You'll be lucky to avoid prison."

"I'm sorry, Donte. I had to tell him. He's my boss. You were acting crazy."

"I'm the only one here acting with any sort of sanity."

"Please, Donte. I don't want you to get hurt."

"You have a funny way of showing it." I gazed into her eyes. She seemed genuine and I had always been a sucker for those big blue orbs. "Do you want to see something cool?"

She shook her head, confused. "What are you talking about?"

"Get in for a minute and I'll show you."

"This isn't some creepy move to get me to make out with you in the car, is it?"

"Of course not, but I wouldn't pass up such an opportunity."

I fished the cloning shard and an ordinary stone from my backpack while Claire shifted around to the side of the car and got in. I held up the ordinary stone in my right hand. "Regular rock, right?" I waved my hand as if I were doing some fancy magic trick. I held up the other hand with the shard. "When you found me at the microscope earlier today, I was looking at this. I found it on my run this morning. Somehow, it has the ability to clone materials."

Claire threw her head back, cackling. "I thought you said you were sane."

"Your skepticism is understandable, but observe." I placed the shard and the stone on the dashboard. For the first few minutes, nothing happened. "Wait for it."

Then, there it was, the small stone had formed a second part, almost like a tumor growing out of another body part. After a few more minutes, a whole new stone, identical and separate from the original sat next to it.

"How did you do that?" Claire gasped.

"I told you. Cloning rock. I suspect it's a piece of the meteorite from the recent storm that's been causing all sorts of weird stuff all over the globe. I made some calls. I have a specialist of my own coming here to have a look."

Claire leaned in close to the shard. "This is amazing,

Donte. We have to study this."

"I plan to, but not with El Capitan Tyrant hanging around."

As Claire inspected the shard an ant crawled across the dashboard and stopped next to it. When it moved again, a second ant remained in its place. "Holy shit," she shrieked. "It can clone living organisms too."

"Pretty cool, right? That actually leads me into my next trick. There's a clone of me wandering around town somewhere."

The look on Claire's face would've almost been comical if I hadn't been nearly shitting my pants all afternoon. "Please tell me you're joking."

"I wish I was. I need to find him before he does something stupid in my name." I took a deep breath, dreading bringing up the next part. "You can't tell Eaton about this, Claire. Who knows what he'll try to do if he finds out."

My car door whipped open and Eaton stood there, mouth gaping open. "What the hell is going on here?"

We were so focused on the cloning shard we hadn't noticed Eaton return from the office. There was no way he hadn't seen the shard's unique ability. "A private conversation, that's what." I reached for the door handle, but Eaton jammed his hip in the way. "Get lost Eaton. This doesn't concern you."

"Oh, but it does. That little rock of yours solves so many problems."

"Problems you're responsible for creating."

"Donte, Donte, Donte, think about it. We have a golden opportunity here with your little gift. We can make a lot of money and still keep the golden goose. I'll even send a full recommendation to the brass for you to be the team lead on the next project. That's what you've always wanted, isn't it? Your own gig."

"Somehow, ripping off international black market gemstone dealers wasn't exactly the career advancement path I had in mind."

"Hey man, gotta take the opportunity when it's presented."

"I think I'll pass."

"Then we have a problem. That shard is my golden ticket and I'm letting a little pissant like you ruin it."

Eaton grabbed at the shard. I shoved my shoulder into his chest. I pushed him the rest of the way out of the car and slammed the door. I hit the power locks before Eaton recovered.

Eaton scrambled back to his feet and pounded on the window. "Open the door, Donte. Give me the shard."

I punched 911 in on my phone and held it up to the window for Eaton to see. "Walk away or I push it."

Eaton backed off with a snarl on his face. "You have to come out of the car sooner or later, Irwin. And when you do, I'll be waiting."

"Good luck with that."

Eaton stalked back to his car and tore out of the parking lot in a cloud of dust.

"This isn't good," I said. "Where do you think he's going?"

Claire threw her hands in the air. "I have no idea. I do know that he has a gun and he's not afraid to use it."

"Probably not a good idea to stick around here then.

We need to find the clone anyway." I pulled out onto Main Street. "Know any good bars close by?"

"Bad time to go clubbing, isn't it?"

"The clone was eager to go drinking tonight. It's really strange because I never touch the stuff."

"Maybe it only cloned the parts of you with a personality."

"Hey, wait a minute."

"There's only one place close by, but I hear it's a rough spot on Saturday nights. The loggers and miners like to blow off steam."

"I don't think that matters to the clone."

The parking lot of the Splintered Timber Bar and Grill was already full with Harleys and jacked up pickup trucks. The twang of country music filled the air. This was going to be fun…

A circle of the parking lot failed to locate the clone. I parked on the other side of the lot from the gathered revelers and headed for the front door. The bar was packed inside. With the lights turned down, picking out faces was going to be difficult.

"Maybe we should split up," Claire said. "We might find him faster."

"I considered that, but I don't want either of us getting ambushed in here. Let's stick together for now. If we don't find him quickly, we'll split up."

As it turned out, we couldn't get near the bar. Bikers and rednecks lined it from one end to the other. The clone wasn't among them. I turned to the dance floor, thinking he might've decided to cut a rug. Never mind that I looked like a wounded chicken when I danced. "He's not in here."

"Then where is he?"

"That's a damn good question. Come on. Let's see if we can find an answer."

We made it outside without anyone giving us a second glance. All that changed as we crossed the parking lot. Two mean-looking boys sat on the bumper of my rental Prius. I didn't think they were here to invite me to church. "Something I can help you boys with?"

"You're one of the ones out digging up our rocks."

"Sounds about right. Those rocks will bring a nice little windfall to your cozy little borough here. Everybody wins."

The thug pushed off the car and blocked my path, his arms crossed. "Yeah, we don't see it that way. We don't like outsiders coming here ripping up our land."

"I don't know what to tell you. We're being as gentle as possible and we have all necessary permits."

The thug staggered me with a hard shove to the chest. "I don't give a crap about your permits."

"You'll have to take that up with your government. They're the ones who issued them."

The thug answered with a fist to my jaw. His boot landed into my stomach before I hit the ground. Claire screamed as the other thug grabbed her and pinned her arms behind her back. Pain stabbed through my back and kidneys with every blow they landed. I tasted blood on my lips.

I lay on the ground for a while after the beating stopped. One of the thugs leaned down close to my ear. "You and your friends would leave town, if you know what's good for you."

I felt Claire's hands on me, probing for broken bones or other internal injuries. I was sure there were a couple.

"Hey buddy. You okay?"

I lifted my head slightly to see three or four others standing over me. Gingerly, I uncoiled from the fetal position, grimacing at the fresh wave of pain. "Yeah, I think so. Accidently stumbled into his fist."

"Take it easy, Donte," Claire said. "You could have some broken bones."

I managed to sit up and spit out a mouthful of bloody saliva. "Wouldn't be the first time. You should've been around in my first year of college."

"I'm serious," she said. "You need a hospital."

A few x-rays wouldn't hurt, I supposed. A starting car got my attention. I looked over in time to see my car tearing out of the parking lot. My clone was behind the wheel. "That's not good. My backpack with the shard was in the back seat."

"Where do you think he's going?"

"The clone can't survive without the shard and Eaton needs it to make his fakes. My guess is he's going to find him. We need to find Eaton first."

"My car is still at the office. Can you can make it?"

"Yeah. I'll be okay. Let's get out of here before someone else decides to take a swing at me."

Despite my bravado, I had some significant injuries. My chest was on fire and I couldn't rotate my left shoulder worth a damn. I really should've gone to the hospital.

We made it back to Claire's car and she eased me into the passenger seat. There was no sign of my or Eaton's car when we pulled into the office parking lot. "You're in no shape to go running up and down stairs. Stay here. I'll go check it out. There's a first aid kit in the glove box. Clean yourself up."

"Be careful. Eaton won't hesitate to hurt you if he's here."

"He can try."

She returned ten minutes later. In the time she was gone, the pain in my chest had eased some, but I wouldn't be running any marathons any time soon.

"He was here. All the samples are gone."

"He's likely heading for the dig site. He needs time for the shard to clone the stones. There's plenty of places to hide out there until that happens and his shady friends arrive."

We pulled up to the dig site trail head to find my car and Eaton's side by side. "This is not good. They're already linked together."

"I'm not sure about this, Donte. We're not equipped for trekking through the woods in the dark. Who knows what kind of wild animals are around? Let's call the police. They have handcuffs and guns."

"There's no time. Besides, you think the cops will believe there's a clone of me running around with a magic meteorite intent on ripping off black market traders with fake gems. I hardly believe it and I'm the one saying it."

Claire took out her cellphone and dialed 9-1-1. "Help me," she cried.

"Calm down, ma'am," the dispatcher said. "Tell me what happened."

"We're out at the geologists' dig site. We were chased by a bear. My colleague fell and hurt himself. He can't get up."

"Is he breathing?"

"For now. I think he hit his head pretty hard though. He's not making any sense."

"Okay, stay where you are. Help is on the way."

"Please hurry." Claire hung up and looked at me.

"Laid it on a little thick, don't you think?"

"What? I wasn't lying. I think you're freakin' nuts, but at least help is on the way."

We hiked into the main dig site, taking our sweet time so we didn't break our necks. I tried to hide the sheer agony experienced with every step, but doubted I was successful. We found the site empty. We worked our way deeper into the sub vein, hoping any noise we made was mistaken for wild animals. We reached the edge of the clear cut and hunkered down for a brief rest. A single flashlight beam danced around in the distance.

"There he is," Claire said, "but what the hell is he doing?"

"Oh shit," I gasped. "He told me he was trying to acquire more explosives for excavating. He must've succeeded. He's going to blow the side of this rock apart."

We moved along the tree line, closer to where Eaton was placing blasting caps at the opening to where they found the first gem lode. Off to the side, my clone sat on a rock, eyeballing Eaton with amusement.

"You still don't believe me, do you?"

"Let's just say I want a little insurance. I've known Irwin for a while. I wouldn't put it past him to pull a fast one."

"He's not smart enough for that. He has no

imagination, no creativity. He's so boring."

"You're not wrong there."

"Are you sure you've planted enough dynamite? They'll see the explosion from the space station."

"I don't plan on sticking around this shit hole after dawn and aim to squeeze every last nickel I can from it."

He finished planting the explosives and turned his attention back to the clone. The sample bag I put the shard in sat on the ground next to him. Eaton picked it up and peeked inside. A wide grin swallowed his face. "Looks like you weren't lying. This shard is authentic."

"So, do we have a deal?"

Eaton drew a pistol from behind his back and shot the clone twice in the chest. "No, we don't."

I almost choked on the gasp I took. I always suspected Eaton capable of coldblooded murder. Seeing it firsthand shocked the hell out of me. Claire trembled next to me. From fear or anger, I didn't know. I wrapped my arm around her shoulder and she leaned into me.

"We can't let him set off those charges," she whispered.

"Do you think you can disarm them?"

"With ease. What are you going to do?"

"I have to get the shard back."

"He'll kill you the first chance he gets."

"Yeah… Gonna try to avoid that, if possible. Give me a few minutes to draw him away and then do your stuff."

I shuffled along the tree line to the other side of the mine entrance. The downside was the amount of noise I made.

"That you, Irwin? Wondered when you'd show up.

Come out and let's parlay some."

I froze, not wanting to blow my cover just yet. Anything that served to disorient Eaton helped me. I found a fist-sized rock at my feet and hurled it back along the trail. A bit of luck went my way for a change as Eaton bolted after it. I fell in behind him, but stayed far enough back that he still couldn't see me.

"Come on, Irwin. Why the games? We can still work this out. I'm not a greedy man. I'm willing to share."

"Says the guy with the gun who just shot an unarmed man." I threw another rock and moved before Eaton could pinpoint my location. It didn't stop him from firing blindly into the trees.

"He wasn't really a man though. Just a carbon copy who'd get in the way. With this little shard, we could go anywhere, do anything."

"What about Claire. You just gonna toss her aside too?"

"Claire's a sweet girl, but she's only interested in saving the birds. I don't have time for that nonsense."

"Always knew you were a prick, Eaton. Never believed you'd be some kind of international criminal though."

Eaton fired again in my general direction, but I'd already moved. "Don't feel bad, Irwin. You had no way of knowing. When you're a world-renowned geologist like me, you meet some interesting people. Some of them just happen to be on the other side of the law."

"How long have you been ripping off the firm? This can't be the first side deal you've brokered."

"Long enough to know there ain't a goddamn thing you can do to stop me."

We'll see about that. I led Eaton away from the mine entrance. Hopefully, Claire wasn't having much trouble disarming those bombs.

Eaton grunted and began thrashing around the ground. "What the hell is happening to me?"

You're being cloned, you dumb shit. I ran back to him, and although I don't normally kick people when they're down, planted my boot firmly into his face. He tried to raise his gun, but I kicked it out of his hand and into the trees. "Game's not over yet, Eaton. You haven't won shit."

I dashed back into the darkness and hid behind a low berm. Claire needed just a bit more time.

"I'm going to kill you, Donte. You're not making it out of these woods alive."

"What's going on here?" The voice sounded almost exactly like Eaton, except for the tinny squeal. "Why are we in the middle of the woods in the dark? Someone could really get hurt out here."

"Shut up," the real Eaton snapped. "Go back to the site and make sure everything is ready. Dawn is less than an hour away."

"But what if I twist an ankle? We don't even have a medical kit with us."

The sound of someone being smacked followed. "Ow! That was rude."

"Go, or the next one makes you bleed."

Bushes rustled as the clone retreated back to the dig site. I was out of time. I stood and flipped on my flashlight. "Over here, Eaton. Come and get me."

Eaton started to give chase, but stopped. He chuckled. "I see what you're up to. Stalling me so your little girlfriend can defuse my bombs. The big question is, did she get them all?"

The mountain rumbled and screamed when Eaton pressed the detonator trigger. The sky lit up orange briefly as the hot wave of air smacked into me. "Claire, no!" I ran for the dig site.

Trees burned as rocks and gravel rained down. I couldn't believe that sonofabitch did it. How big would that explosion have been if Claire had not defused some of the bombs?

I exited the tree line to a much bigger crater than was there before. There was no sign of Claire. I tried to get down to the crater, but Eaton blindsided me. I regained my feet with a few more scrapes and bruises and went for the rocks where Claire was likely buried.

Eaton once again blocked my advance. This time with his gun. "Stay where you are, Donte. I won't tell you again."

"Claire'll die, Eaton."

"Then she should've kept her nose out of my business."

"I don't care about the shard or the gems. Take it all. Just let me get Claire out."

"Oh, I plan to. You're going to help me. The quicker we do this, the better chance you have to save your sweetie." He twitched with the gun. "Start picking up rocks, Donte. Anything pretty goes in a neat pile over there."

I worked quickly, fighting through the pain to finish this so I could find Claire. The sky in the east was beginning to brighten. One way or the other, we were almost out of time.

Before long, we had a small pile of precious stones. There was still no sign of Claire or Eaton's clone. Eaton knelt beside the pile and placed the shard on top of it. "By the time they realize what's up, I'll be long gone."

"You're insane, Eaton."

He turned and waved with the gun. "Stop talking and keep digging."

I moved a few more heavy stones and spotted Eaton's clone lying motionless nearby. I considered letting him die. Eaton killed my clone, after all. Turnabout was fair play. I wasn't going to sink to that level though.

"Leave him," Eaton ordered when he saw what I was doing. "On second thought, help him out. I may have a use for him."

I helped the clone sit up. "Just stay still."

I caught the sound of a helicopter approaching over Eaton's heavy breathing. My heart sped up a little. Things were about to get interesting.

"Sounds like my friends are about to arrive," Eaton said. "Run, search for your girlfriend, I don't care. Just don't be here when I get back." He pointed at his clone. "You, come with me."

"But I don't want to go see the scary men with the guns."

Eaton shot a round into the ground at the clone's feet. I took the opportunity to scoop up a fist-sized rock. I'd only get one chance at it so I had to make it count.

The helicopter pitched in toward the small landing pad near the main dig site. Eaton poked the clone in the back with his pistol. "Grab that satchel there and start walking."

Eaton and the clone started toward the main dig site as a second helicopter approached from the south. That was a search and rescue helicopter.

"How the hell did they know we were up here?" Eaton growled.

"You're not getting away as easily as you thought," I called.

Gunfire from near the first helicopter forced the SAR chopper to veer off. Eaton shoved the clone forward. "Hurry up. They'll be back."

As Eaton and the clone rushed to their meeting with the gem traders, I scrambled back over the rocks to find Claire. Hopefully, I wasn't too late. I hadn't thrown three rocks when I heard. "Psst. Donte. Over here."

I nearly threw up when my eyes settled on Claire's face. She was dirty, and a little bloody, but otherwise okay. "What the hell?" I wrapped her into a tight hug. "Are you okay? What happened?"

"I thought I got all of the blasting caps and moved away to wait for you. I guess I missed a couple."

"I thought you were buried. I thought you were dead."

"Yeah, I heard that." She kissed me on the lips. "Thank you for caring. More than I can say for that piece of shit Eaton Mason."

"Speaking of which. He'll be back any minute. You need to get out of here."

"I'm not leaving you."

"Yes, you are. Get back to the main road and bring the cops. Hell, bring the National Guard if you have to. I have a plan for Eaton. He thinks he's won. He's in for a rude awakening."

Claire kissed me again and backed off. "Be careful, Donte. I expect you to be walking out of here with me."

"That's the plan." I turned away before she spotted the lie in my face. The truth was, I fully expected to die here today.

Back down near the main dig site, Eaton's clone worked his way toward the still-running helicopter. I guess they weren't planning to stick around for the company picnic. Three mean-looking well-dressed men stood out front of the chopper expectantly. Two were armed with assault rifles.

I couldn't believe what I was watching. Clone Eaton was handing off fake stones to the black market traders while Real Eaton stayed out of sight with the originals. The black market trader never hesitated once his hands were on the satchel. He turned back to the helicopter and motioned to one of his henchmen who unleashed a burst of bullets into the clone's chest.

The helicopter took off and flew into the rising sun, thinking they'd just gotten away with the ultimate double-cross. They had no idea they'd been the ones double-crossed. They were the least of my problems though. Eaton would be on his way back here to finish me off by now.

The shadows were still long enough to hide me when Eaton trekked back up to the crater. I didn't see the pistol in his hand but that didn't mean he didn't have it. His cocky attitude probably told him he no longer needed it. He went about loading up his backpack with the most valuable rocks. There was enough there to ensure he never had to work again.

I clutched the rock I picked up earlier and moved in behind him as he secured the straps on his backpack. The rock left my hand and impacted the side of his head with a dull thud.

Eaton screamed and went down. I pressed my advantage and leaped onto his back. My fist connected four times before he was able to flip me off. Apparently, I misjudged how hard his head was.

"Gotta hand it to you, Irwin. Seems you have a bit of fight in you after all. Come on then. Let's see what you've got."

"There doesn't need to be a fight, Eaton. It's over. Surrender so we can all go home."

"Yeah, that's not going to happen."

Eaton charged. At the last second, I moved to the side. Eaton tripped over my foot and the uneven rocks, and fell into the crater. The sickly crunch of his head smashing against the rocks was unmistakable.

I sank to my knees and after throwing up, started shaking. I didn't know how long I was like that before feeling a hand on my shoulder. I looked up at Claire. Behind her, cops and wardens worked to get Eaton out of the crater. They confirmed what I already knew. He was dead.

"I told them what happened," Claire said. "We'll have to give full statements, but it doesn't look like we'll face any repercussions."

"We managed to get the tail number off that chopper and tracked them to an unmarked airfield. They won't be buying any more fake gems. You should've come to us, Mister Irwin. We could've helped you before it got to this."

No, I thought. You would've called me crazy and sent me on my way. The biggest thing I could do for myself now is hide that shard until someone came for it. The less people knew about it, the better.

Claire helped me down the trail towards where the cops and paramedics had set up base camp. We weren't expecting a figure to be blocking the way before we got there.

"Mister Irwin? My name is Nixon Lane. I believe you spoke to my organization regarding a piece of meteorite you found."

I shoved the sample bag with the shard into his chest. "It's all yours. I never want to see it again."

We stepped around him and continued on down the trail toward the medical aid I sorely needed.

The Vault

by Alex Minns

Jerome ran through the readings again, just to be sure. Everything in the Vault was as it should be: no temperature fluctuations, no energy flares. Everything was fine.

"You could go home you know."

Jerome peered over the top of his monitor at his new colleague. Rika was leaning back in her chair, twirling a pencil between her fingers. The pile of new acquisition reports he'd given her still sat untouched on the desk.

"My shift isn't over for another hour, we need full handover time. It's protocol to make sure you're completely up-to-date." He watched her eyes flick down to the pile of papers. She let her chair fall back onto four legs with a bump. With a tilt of her head, she flicked her fingers through the pages, skimming the headings.

"We put stuff in the Vault. All is fine. The end?" She gave a shrug. "Just like last night. Pretty samey."

"Nothing in here is samey." Jerome shook his head ignoring the groan from the young woman as she realised a lecture was forthcoming. "You need to know what is in there, what it does, where it is and what fail-safes there are."

"Oh come on J, it's mostly harmless, all the big stuff gets shipped off to the States."

Jerome gave an indignant sniff and lowered his gaze back to his screen. Perhaps he should ask for an appointment with the Director. She'd only been working down here two months but she clearly had aspirations of something bigger. Her disappointment at her assignment was clear. Jerome had spotted her writing various letters and emails off to different departments to see if there hadn't been some mistake and actually she should have assigned to an agent as a probationer. Maybe with some encouragement from him, he might actually get rid of her.

Twenty-two years Jerome had acted as a custodian to the UK Vault. He knew plenty of people thought it a rubbish posting but they didn't understand. The items stored just beyond the two-foot-thick walls beside him were the stuff dreams were made of; the power and magic lining the shelves was unimaginable. And where there was a MAO, there was a person ready to misuse it not far behind. He was a gatekeeper although he feared his time was nearing an end. Why else would they have assigned the young woman to work alongside him, to learn from him? Yes, perhaps some people found him, as one agent put, arrogant, pushy and other less repeatable words, but they just couldn't accept that there were protocols and procedures. He wasn't old; he had years to state retirement so why did he feel like a dinosaur? Already Rika had tried to update the computer systems, change his cataloguing, she'd even talked about using a drone to replace the scheduled security walks in the Vault. Thankfully, Director Harrison had knocked that one on the head. He had nearly cried with relief, walking through the stacks once a shift was the highlight of his day.

He wasn't sure who was more relieved when Rika's month of shadowing was over and she could work shifts alone. There were four custodians at the UK Vault and although no-one was more senior, Jerome had been there the longest. Everyone else seemed to get bored and move on. Their office, which he liked to think of as the antechamber, almost like in one of the Great Pyramids, was rather small. The Vault behind him had grown outwards but their little room had barely changed in thirty years. Two desks faced each other allowing a clear path between the outer door and the door to the Vault.

Some people complained about the stark strip lighting but Jerome didn't mind the lack of windows. Windows meant distractions, or worse, people gawping in as they went past. The walls were a dark grey, making the space resemble a bunker. The room itself was fairly sparse, not that you could fit much else inside. Their desks were the only furniture and the drawers were shared between the custodians. Only Jerome's drawer had a sticker with his name on. It was also they only one that was ever locked.

A familiar beep rang out on the main door. Both of them looked up in surprise. No-one was scheduled to come down.

The door catch released and it swung inwards as the custodians watched. Agent Mathieson did not show his usual carefree demeanour as he entered. Instead, his scowl outright dared anyone to challenge him.

"Agent Mathieson!" Rika jumped out of her chair at the sight of a field agent. Jerome really wished she could control herself better. The girl fawned over every agent that came in, hoping one would take pity and whisk her off to a more exciting life.

"I need a MAO putting in the Vault."

Jerome frowned, bristling at the agent's demand. "I'm sorry Agent Mathieson, it needs to go through the lab first, you know protocol."

"I haven't got time to take it to the lab and fill out all their paperwork. I need you to put it in there now and I'll come back and do the lab bit tomorrow." He swung a black case up and waved it at Rika.

"Rika, don't," Jerome warned. Her mouth hung open as she froze in indecision.

"Look, what you lot in here don't seem to realise is that things are going crazy out there." Mathieson dropped the case to the floor. The sound echoed around the small room, the metal walls only amplifying it. Jerome stared at the case, praying nothing fragile was inside. Mathieson's head tilted and his eyes glazed over for a split second before he took a deep breath. "I've got to go straight back out to another call. One of the Starchildren is running round with a device that lets them pass through solid matter. I haven't got time to do paperwork. I need this locked safely up so I can get out there before people get hurt. Or do you want to explain to the Director why I'm tied up in the lab."

"You could ask the lab to hold it. These protocols are here for a reason…"

"The protocols are out of date. You have no idea what it's like out there." The agent stared at Jerome, his eyes full of accusation and distaste. Jerome ran through possible retorts but all fell short so he just stared back.

Rika looked between the two men in a standoff. She glanced pleadingly at Jerome. "Surely one night in the vault can't hurt?"

"Out of the question. We don't even know what it is."

"It makes the wearer invisible. Now you know." Mathieson turned on his heel. Jerome tried to step over the case but Rika blocked his path.

"We'll look after it tonight Agent Mathieson, but just the one night yeah?" Rika put her arm out to stop Jerome getting round her. Mathieson waved a dismissive arm in the air, not bothering to look back as he swiped his card by the reader. As the door moved, he barely gave it time to open before he squeezed out of the gap, almost desperate to get away.

Silence descended as the door sealed them back in. Rika slowly turned.

"Look, before you yell at me…"

"I'll have to report this."

"Jerome. Come on man. We need to be a little more empathetic yeah? We can't just be robots every time. Those guys are out there risking everything, cut them a little slack."

"Those guys have a job. As do we. But breaking the rules and cutting through those failsafes puts us all at risk."

"It's an invisible cloak or whatever, how much risk can there be?" Rika's face went red and her jaw tightened. "I'm putting this inside so just get out of the way." She picked up the case and squared her shoulders.

He opened his mouth, ready to quote from the procedure documents when she spoke again.

"Move, before I move you."

The hairs on the back of Jerome's neck stood up as a shudder went down his spine. He tried to repress it so Rika didn't see but in that second something seemed very wrong.

Rika gave a shake of the head and took a deep breath. "Come on Jerome, are you going to take it up to the lab? You know they won't take it without the case agent's paperwork. You'll just be stuck there arguing until Mathieson comes back anyway. We'll just put it in the stacks for one night." Jerome didn't move, unnerved by her sudden aggression. They hadn't worked together long but this was new.

The case in her hands drew his eye. Every fibre of his being was screaming in indignation. This was not how it was supposed to be. There was a procedure. But Mathieson had gone and Rika did make a valid point. The lab wouldn't let him anywhere near them let alone take this from him. A lowly custodian didn't have the same sway as an agent, no matter how important Jerome knew his job to be, others did not agree.

"I'll have to write up a report. This needs to be addressed by the Director."

"Fine, write your report, I'll even counter sign it." She shrugged. "Now can we put it inside?" She gave the case a rattle, gesturing towards the door behind him.

"This is not right."

"You said already. Open the door."

Jerome's eyes lowered, wracking his brains for a way around this but he could come up with nothing. With an indignant huff, he turned to the Vault door, ashamed at himself for bending to her pushiness.

The Director would definitely be hearing about this. His hand hovered over the keypad, just to the left of the entrance. The whole door seemed unassuming, just like the door Mathieson had just made his quick exit through. A solid piece of grey metal but this one had all the bells and whistles. Jerome adjusted his position to make sure Rika couldn't see his unique code as he typed it in. The code was verified and a square above the buttons lit up, an outline of a hand glowing faintly green. He placed his palm over the cold screen as it read not only his palm print but his vital signs as well. Any signs of too much stress and it would refuse entry and lock it down until a top level official came and overrode the system. He half expected it would flash red now. A petty part of him wanted it to just so he could get one over Rika.

A happy sounding beep confirmed acceptance. Jerome's teeth ground together at the lock's treachery as the door popped open. Pressing his weight against it he pushed it forward and stepped inside.

The ceiling rushed away from him, opening out into a vast warehouse that no-one on the other side of that door would have expected. Rows upon rows of shelving stood in front of him. He allowed himself a small smile as he entered his domain. The strip lighting flickered into life, the clinking sound of bulbs sparking echoed around the cavernous room. Jerome stood in the open space at the start of the central aisle. Two equal banks of rows lined up either side of him, full to the brim of MAOs. Everything had its place and Jerome knew where that was. A rock that generated its own heat and light when you introduced water: section 7 row K. The skull that Shakespeare used for Hamlet, the one that talked back: Room B, shelf 3. The skull needed to be in a room; you could hear him all around the stacks out here once he got going. Ahead of him, through the centre of the stacks was the door to the strong room, where the really dangerous items were held.

"I'll just put it here so we can grab it quick tomorrow yeah?"

Jerome frowned as Rika immediately turned to exit. The case sat on the floor just to the left of the door. His colleague was already back in the antechamber, staring at him expectedly. He took a moment to take another look around before begrudgingly moving to the exit. His eyes flicked to the case as he passed by and he wondered if perhaps he should at least look inside to check the contents.

"Come on J, you'll let all the heat out." Rika cocked her head and gave a lopsided grin at her own joke. Her constant changes in demeanour were throwing him completely off. He had a hard enough job knowing how to respond to her at the best of times but this evening was impossible. He left the case untouched and crossed back into their office. Rika hit the door release and the metal door's pneumatics hissed as it swung into place with a thunk. Jerome couldn't suppress the thought that the noise sounded somewhat final.

***

"Your shift finished an hour ago. You stay much longer and my shift replacement will be here."

Jerome's cheek twitched as he leafed through some paperwork, doing his best to ignore her.

"Are you still angry about Mathieson?" She sighed and let her elbows drop onto her desk with a bang.

"I'm not angry," he sniffed. "More disappointed."

"Oh come on J."

"Rules are rules Rika. The standard operating procedure states quite clearly that under no circumstances should lab assessment…"

"I know what the SOP says Jerome. You made me read them all five times in the first week." She glowered at him.

"Apparently a sixth time was needed." His voice dropped low but by the raise of her eyebrow she still caught his words.

"The SOP also says that Vault custodians need to support the deployment of field agents. This can be by way of loaning out MAOs, assisting in specialist collection procedures in the field and other tasks as requested."

Jerome paused and chewed his bottom lip. "It does?"

"You know it does. I bet you recite those rules in your sleep. Now, did we not assist Agent Mathieson and facilitate his deployment by accepting the MAO for temporary storage?"

Jerome's hand reached up, his fingers danced in the air before he scratched nervously at his nose. "I suppose, that could be one interpretation."

"I think potentially refusing his request would have been in breach of the regulations in fact." Rika was grinning now, leaning back in her chair. Another minute and her feet would be up on the desk again, Jerome knew it.

"I need to check that process again. Submit an amendment I think, can't have vagaries in there." He leaned forward and reached for his notepad, scratching a note for the morning.

"You're just annoyed I actually read the thing aren't you." Rika shook her head and turned her attention back to her screen.

"Nonsense. It's shown us a potential error in the system if certain staff are going to bend the interpretation to their will." He nervously glanced over his monitor. She hadn't reacted. "I'm still going to have to write the report." Still nothing. "I said…"

"I heard you." She still didn't look up. A frown had etched itself on her face. Jerome immediately sat up straighter. Rika never looked concerned. Ever.

"What's wrong?"

"The sensors." She trailed off. Jerome immediately brought up the readings on his screen. Nothing was about to set off an alarm, but everything was in the amber – heat, vibrations, the lot. For one to go amber was not unheard of, but for all of them. Jerome dismissed the screens and brought up the live camera feed of the Vault. Everything was dark, the lights hadn't been triggered. Jerome clicked in the settings, switching to night vision and began cycling through the different camera feeds. His eyes took a few seconds to register each image, check for movement before moving on. There wasn't an inch of the floor that wasn't covered by at least one camera although primarily it was in case an MAO decided to do something new. It was always best not to get too close to an MAO when it was showing off, you never knew when it was going to get flamey.

The colours on the screen seemed to flare for second, like he had looked at a light for too long, but then it was gone. Jerome leaned in. He hit the arrow keys on his keyboard to adjust the angle slightly and zoom in. It happened again, just for a split second. "I'm going to have to go in and check."

"Seriously?" Rika's head swivelled between her computer and the steel door and then back again. "Should we not get back up or something?"

"What for? It's a bit too warm in the vault can someone send a swat team?" Jerome giggled at his own joke. Rika just glowered at him. "This is protocol. I need to check and see what if anything we're dealing with. I remember about five years ago we had constant tremors on one corner, we thought it was a stone grotesque that was moving around at night."

"And was it?"

"No, a mouse had made a home just above the sensor. Was putting the readings out completely."

Rika stared at him.

"My point is, no need to get worried until we know what we're dealing with." Jerome stood up and straightened his shirt. "Although, in this case, it probably is something to do with that MAO you allowed Mathieson to put in there. So if it kills me, could you make sure that goes in the report."

"If whatever's in there doesn't kill you, I might."

His heartrate was still climbing as he stood in front of the keypad. He unlocked it as always but even he couldn't deny the slight tremor of his hand. Whatever was going on in there, he sincerely doubted it was innocent.

"Jerome?"

He turned just as Rika threw him a headset. Both his arms grabbed at empty air before slamming into his chest. The device clattered to the floor. Jerome blinked slowly before bending to pick it up, refusing to look at Rika. He hooked it over his ear and adjusted the mic to point closer to his mouth.

"How's that?" He spoke quietly into the mouthpiece.

"Somehow still works, now hurry up yeah?"

"If you could alert the Director to the current situation." Jerome didn't wait for a reply. He stepped into the Vault and hit the close release on the inside. He waited until he heard the door shut into place. All noise died, the only sound he could hear was residual ringing in his own ears. He took a second to adjust.

The lights came on as it sensed his movements. The case was just where Rika has left it. He frowned. Nothing looked like it had been disturbed but he had never liked coincidences. Instincts warred within him. Protocol did not allow him to open up an unassessed MAO. But then again, it should never have been in here so this situation was not accounted for in the procedures. He needed to know what was going on. He held it breath and bent over to unfasten the case clips. Flipping it over to lay on the floor, he threw open the lid as if he was going to catch something by surprise.

He blinked.

The case was empty.

He knelt down and got closer to the case, almost pressing his nose to the insides. It was an MAO that caused invisibility he remembered, so he felt around the bottom, just in case he couldn't physically see it.

"Oh."

Static crackled over his earpiece. "What? Oh what? What did you find?"

"Nothing." Jerome snapped the case shut and stood, surveying the vault with increasing anxiety.

"But you said oh. Oh implies something." Rika sounded impatient.

"Agent Mathieson's case is empty."

"Oh."

"Exactly."

"I should come in with you."

"No, I need you to keep monitoring the feeds. Tell me if you see anything." Jerome thought for a second. What if there had been an MAO? "Even if it is just static or something similar." He thought back to the red glow he caught earlier. Perhaps the MAO could still be picked up on the camera somehow.

He mentally ran through which camera had shown him the anomaly and where it was. Section 3, category 1 weapons, he nodded to himself, nothing that should have been more dangerous than its more mundane form. The most spectacular object there was a dagger that emitted sparks. If he could find something from Section 5 then he would most definitely have the upper hand. He stepped forward just as the lights flickered out.

"J, I can't see anything."

"The lights are out." Static hissed through the earpiece. "Rika? I said the lights are out. Can you hear me?" Buzzing was the only reply. His eyes flicked back to the door, perhaps calling for back up would be the best idea. Two red lights glowed above the release. Jerome let out a groan. The door had moved to deadlock position. It would take someone from the outside to get that door open now. Rika would have spotted it but she couldn't do it alone. No lights, no communications, door power interrupted – Jerome cursed, there was only one object in here that could do that: a small, silvered discus that worked like an EMP, MAO FZ-45. At least he had confirmation now, someone was definitely in here.

***

Jerome fished in his pocket and took out his keys. He turned on the small torch hanging from the ring and held it out. It didn't give out a huge amount of light but it was just enough to see immediately in front of him and yet not give away his position. He suddenly felt very exposed standing in the middle of the entryway. Whoever was in here could easily have something to see in the dark with and could have been watching him. The thought spurred him into action and he started to move to the racks to his right, longing for cover.

The discus had been in a completely different section to where he'd seen the anomaly. How much had the intruder managed to look through already? Jerome placed his feet with precision and care, not wanting to make the even barest of noises. His hand ran along one of the shelves as much for comfort as for guidance. He knew exactly what sat in each position on the shelf. On his left were recordings of MAPs in action, ones that had been confiscated from members of the public. To his right was the section dedicated to psychic and telekinetic inducing artifacts. Perhaps he could make use of something here, the net of confusion would help to trap the culprit. If he could just get it over the intruder's head, they would be frozen with confusion long enough to get help. Or perhaps the Desborough Mirror? That was somewhere on this row. All he would have to do would be to show the intruder the mirrored side and they would be trapped in their own reflection. Jerome had often found himself wondering if Medusa had been real and she had just had one of the original mirrors before the Celts.

Jerome found himself getting carried away, almost forgetting why he was in the Vault. That was until his hand caught the edge of a box. Jerome halted and brought his torch up. Every box was perfectly aligned on the shelf. Nothing should have been sat that near the edge, Jerome made sure of it. The box that sat too far forward had a large yellow warning sticker over the seal which had been sliced open. There were two catches that needed to be released simultaneously to ensure that the box could not be opened by mistake. Jerome double checked the shelf location even though he already knew what it was: the Nemesis bracelet, as it had been dubbed. Earlier that year, Agent Soth had managed to talk down a member of the public who had gotten hold of the bracelet. Wearing it had allowed her to see all the sins of the people around her and gave her an insatiable need for justice. Soth had just managed to stop her before someone was killed. The object had been deemed highly dangerous. Even Agent Soth hadn't quite seemed the same since.

Now the box lay open and empty. Nothing else nearby had even been touched. Whoever was in here had taken it but not only that, they had specifically located it. A chill ran down Jerome's spine, they knew where everything was. Agent Mathieson? Would he have sold The Collective out? The man was a brute but Jerome found that hard to imagine. The faintest of noises drew his attention. It was a sound of stone being scratched. Jerome's chest threatened to burst with his hammering pulse. His attention turned to the end of the row, towards the secure room. Suddenly a net of confusion didn't seem like enough firepower. Leaving the empty box, Jerome headed for the secure room. There was empty space all around it, so you had to breach the Vault first to even get close. No drilling through a wall conveniently next to an alley running alongside the building. And as soon as you entered the Vault, someone would know; there would never be enough time to get this far. Well not for humans at least. Jerome pressed himself against the wall and made his way round to the side. The door would be deadlocked shut just like the entrance door, there was no way he was getting in anytime soon but there was always a failsafe. This time it was a failsafe very few people knew about; he hadn't even told Rika about it yet.

He slid down to sit on the floor before feeling around with his left hand until he found a grate at the bottom of the wall. Changing his keys to his left hand, he poked a key into the small metal grill and rattled it very gently. Even he could only just hear the noise. He retrieved his key out of the grate and waited. Seconds seemed to drag on and on. He found himself wondering if he was too late but then a low-level buzzing noise made him sigh in relief. Three small clouds of haze appeared before his eyes. Eventually he adjusted to the light and the images coalesced into three distinct beings. He smiled as they hovered before his face. Each one was no more than five centimetres in height. Anyone else would have dismissed them as dragonflies and, quite often in the outside world, others like them were. The product of a meteor fall hundreds of years ago, there were very few of their kind left in existence. They tended to fight amongst each other, their Celtic heritage giving them rather fiery tempers. Laymen would call them pixies but it was a mistake you would only make once to their face. they called themselves Aossi.

"What's going on Jerome?" The figure in the centre was giving off an amber glow. Jerome squinted and could just make out the features of, Talin, the defacto leader of their band of Aossi.

"We have an intruder, looting the Vault. They know what they are looking for and seem to know where to find it." All three of them gasped in shock. Eoin hovered closer to Talin; he had always been the more nervous of the three, being the smallest by over a centimetre. They had come to the Collective looking for asylum. Having been cast out by their own tribe of Aossi, they were unprotected and easy pickings for others. Jerome wasn't entirely sure of the details, they had been here longer than him, but he knew they had been given sanctuary in exchange for consenting to working with the lab. Somewhere along the line, they had set up home in the secure room and become the unofficial last line of defence. They might have come for protection but they were far from defenceless.

"They have knocked out all the power so we are currently trapped in here and have no light except for this." He held up his keyring torch and Saphi snorted in derision. Talin shot her a warning glance and she stooped instantly.

"You need recon." Talin gave a nod. He folded his tiny arms across his chest and flew slightly higher. His set of double wings vibrated more quickly, sparkling in the light from Jerome's torch. Jerome twitched; you could just about hear the wingbeats and as Talin sped up, the frequency shifted slightly, just into the edge of Jerome's range. It was akin metal scratching on metal. "Eoin, you stay with Jerome, give him a better light than that. Saphi, you're with me, we will locate the intruder and report back." Saphi gave a decisive nod and was gone in the blink of an eye off to Jerome's left. Talin darted to the right leaving Jerome with the nervous Eoin. The small creature was centuries old but to Jerome he still looked younger than himself, no more than thirty. As far as they were aware, the Aossi could not reproduce so the only ones alive were the ones created by that original meteor strike back in the days before the Collective existed in its current form. It was part of why Jerome came down here so often. Rika had given up trying to figure out why his rounds took so long, but he always made a stop to check in on the Aossi and question them a little more on the things they had seen over the years. To have lived throughout history must have been incredible.

"Where to Mr Jerome?" Eoin hovered in front of Jerome's face. A range of scraps of material covered his frame, at least that's what it looked like at first glance. On closer inspection you could see the pieces had been carefully stitched together, Jerome knew, by Eoin himself. Had he been full size, Jerome theorised he would look like an elf-lord of popular fiction or similar.

"I'm going to need something to face the intruder with, we can't have him stealing the artefacts."

"But he'll never get out surely?" Eoin was the only one of the three that still had a lilt in his voice of his Irish homeland.

"Whoever this person is seems to know a lot and had an excellent plan for getting in. I must assume they also have an excellent plan for getting out."

"Is the Director going to come?" Eoin's eyes widened and his tiny hands clasped together.

"Rika called her. She must be on her way to open the Vault. I only hope she has enough agents to spare to bring other reinforcements."

Eoin's brow furrowed in concentration before he jerked up in the air and started to glow. "I know what you need! You wait here, I'm certain I can get it out." Jerome didn't even have time to enquire. The Aossi was gone in a flash back through the grate into the secure room. Jerome fidgeted; he wasn't supposed to touch anything in the secure room. And Eoin was definitely not supposed to be able to bring anything out. He made a mental note to mention to the Director at some point that perhaps they should look at that hole in the security. Clanging noises echoed through the grate. Jerome was about to lean down to have a look when a sharp, silvery point shot out of the hole in the wall perilously close to his eyebrows.

Stunned, Jerome watched as the spear emerged from the grate, all three feet of it. Eoin was almost invisible half way down the weapon, balancing it effortlessly in one hand.

"How did you..?" Jerome looked back into the hole and tried to figure out how the small man had manoeuvred the spear.

"This spear is so well-balanced it would take a special kind of idiot to drop it."

"That's AE-5 isn't it?" Jerome reached out hesitantly and waited for Eoin to place it in his grasp.

"You mean Gae Buide?"

"The spear given to Diarmuid Ua Duibhne?"

"You know your history well." Eoin grinned and puffed out his chest proudly.

Jerome winced. "Well, that is one theory. Although we haven't actually had a chance to test if it causes wounds you cannot recover from."

"You have a chance now." A mischievous look crossed the small man's face.

"Yes, quite." Jerome looked away awkwardly. "Some believe it is Gungnir, Odin's spear. And others think it could have been Vel, a javelin possibly belonging to Karthikeya, the Hindu war god."

Eoin opened his mouth to argue when a blur of motion distracted them both. Talin stopped short and raised an eyebrow when he saw what Jerome was holding before giving an approving nod.

"He is not in the right wing. He must be somewhere to the left. I will find Saphi and concentrate our efforts…" His words were cut short as a tiny orange dart sliced through the air and straight into him. Eoin gave a startled cry and flew to Jerome's shoulder. Jerome did his best to ignore the buzzing that accompanied the small man's presence. The orange dart flared red and paused mid-air. Jerome's eyes widened in shock as he realised it was Saphi. She turned her attention to him, her eyes flicking to the spear; assessing it she drew her own miniature daggers.

"Saphi?" If Jerome had had anywhere to retreat to, he would have but his back was against the wall. He put his other hand on the shaft of the spear and held it across himself as a weak form of protection. Her short, spikey hair seemed aflame as she slowly inched forward. Hatred was etched into her every feature. She held the daggers ready at her sides, palms outward as if inviting attack.

"Enemy." Her voice was strained, crackling as she spoke.

"Who is? Me? I'm not your enemy Saphi, I'm your friend." Jerome looked around for the fallen Aossi leader but he was nowhere to be seen.

"She's been brainwashed." Eoin's voice squeaked in his ear. "She'll kill us."

"Brainwashed?" An idea sparked in Jerome's head just another flash of movement erupted from the floor as Talin reappeared and knocked Saphi sideways. The two gripped each other and started to fight mid-air. "Eoin, section 4 just over there, artefact EJ-7 can you get it. Eoin gave a sharp nod and was gone. All Jerome could do was wait and watch the battle go on in front of him. Tiny sparks flew as their weapons clashed. The glow of their bodies was mesmerising as they vibrated faster and fought harder. Talin's blade struck Saphi but she would not stop. Blood dripped from her wound but still she launched another attack at Talin, her blades dancing in arcs as she spun and dove at her leader. She gave a warcry as she forced Talin backwards, defending her blows, unable to get any of his own in.

"Mr Jerome!" Jerome's head snapped round towards the voice. Eoin could not been seen behind the glass he carried. Reaching out, Jerome grabbed the artefact.

"Talin, make room!"

The airborne warrior hesitated but heard the urgency in Jerome's voice and flew backwards as if he was being snatched by an invisible string. Seizing the gap and Saphi's momentary confusion, he launched forward and thrust the piece of glass in front of her forcing her to look into the reflection. Initially she snarled and tried to launch forward but then froze, her face going slack. Waves of confusion reigned as the mirror went to work cutting through the tangle of manipulation that had weaved on the Aossi's mind.

"What?" Her voice sounded hers again even if weakened. Her arms dropped to her sides, the daggers hitting against her legs. The colour seemed to drain out of her, her brain suddenly registering the pain and trauma of her injuries. Saphi tilted before losing consciousness, her small body beginning its plummet to the ground. The two other Aossi both darted forward but she was falling too fast. Jerome let go of the artefacts and launched forward to catch her in the palms of his hands. Vaguely, he was aware of the sound of the spear clattering to the ground, followed closely by shattering glass. His eyes widened in horror.

"Damn."

The sound of laughter echoed across the Vault, slowly increasing in volume as if it were creeping closer and closer. Jerome locked eyes with a bruised Talin as he tried to suppress a shiver. Saphi stirred in his hands. Eoin fluttered down to hover beside her.

"Saphi?"

"I didn't..." she jerked uncomfortably in his hand. "I didn't want to." Her eyes snapped open, she sat up and looked side to side until she saw Talin. "I'm sorry, I, I couldn't stop. He made me. He told me you were my enemy."

"He told you?" Jerome cut in.

Saphi wobbled as she turned her attention back to Jerome. "He knew I was there. Knew what I was." She held a hand to her forehead. "He asked me who was here and I just told him." Jerome frowned, that would explain Mathieson. He wasn't just dealing with someone using an MAO, the intruder was a MAP too. He thought back to

Rika's strange behaviour too. They had been in the room with them, invisible. He shivered. He hadn't noticed a thing.

"I'm so stupid." He shook his head. "I opened the door and let him walk right in."

"You can't stop him." Saphi's voice was so intense, it snapped Jerome out of his self-flagellation. Fear widened her eyes and made her glow almost white. "He said we were nearly as old as him, wanted to know about the woman."

"The woman?"

"I don't know. I asked if he meant the Director and he just got angry and told me I had to attack the enemy and before I knew it, I was here, attacking you." The small woman began to sway in the palm of his hand.

Footsteps echoed across the floor.

"And now he knows where we are." Talin hefted his sword back up. "And how many we number. Eoin, get Saphi back inside." Eoin swooped onto Jerome's palm and lifted Saphi up, draping one of her arms over his shoulders. He gave a last look at Jerome before launching the pair of them back towards the grate.

"Talin." Jerome stood, picking the spear up as he did. "Stay close, but stay hidden." The winged fighter met his instruction with a stoic nod, his face set with grim determination before all his light went out. Only the occasional feint buzz let Jerome know his companion was still there.

The footsteps rang out again, clear and deliberate. They were taunting him. Jerome edged round the back of the secure room, away from the steps. He just needed to stay away until the others arrived. A row of shelves stood ahead of him. Row F. His mind ran through the inventory and landed on one. He smiled. He took a deep breath before making a dash for the cover of the shelves just as the footsteps rounded another corner.

"There's no point in running." Jerome's eyes scanned the shelves furiously by torchlight until he spotted what he was after. He pulled a mahogany box forward and fumbled at the catch. A small drawstring bag lay inside which he snatched and put into his pocket. Movement at the end of the row made Jerome turn. A figure stood holding a sword, the sword was glowing incandescent red, casting an eerie glow upon the suited figure. He had forgone the invisibility. He lifted the sword, the red highlighting his features. Black hair was slicked over to one side complimenting his Wall Street banker clothes. The man held a case in his other hand which he put down on the ground beside his feet. As he stood up again, he gave Jerome an appraising look. His piercing, eyes seemed to penetrate through to his very soul. Jerome withered under his gaze. The man took a deep breath and lifted his chin. He had an aquiline face, sharp angles and pale skin. There was something strangely familiar about the man. With his free hand, the man adjusted his tie.

"Now, tell me, what's in that room?" He indicated behind him, towards the secure room.

"Brooms, mops." Jerome shrugged.

The man stepped forward, smiling. "Why don't you come a little closer?"

Jerome stepped backwards. So, he had to be close to weave his magic. He definitely needed to keep his distance then. A gap had opened between the shelves to his right but he didn't look just yet and give the position away.

"Come along Mr Porteous. I'd just like a little look." Jerome faltered as the intruder used his name. How much did this man know?

"This isn't a jumble sale you know or a library. You can't just take these things."

"But that's exactly what you did." His voice had turned to ice. "This for example." He held the sword out in front of him. Jerome didn't recognise it, nothing in the weapon section glowed like that, if it did, it would not have been on open shelves. "This is mine. You should not have it." He tossed the sword into the air and it spun a full rotation. Jerome watched in shock as the glow went out. As soon as it landed back in the man's grasp, it lit up like a firework.

"Amazing." Jerome muttered. He did know the artefact KM-51, carved from garnet. A whole barrage of tests had revealed nothing special about it and yet the Director was adamant it should stay in the Vault, apparently Director Woolley had insisted.

The man stepped forward again. His face had lost the charming smile, instead twisting into a grotesque snarl. The red lit up his eyes, filling them with fire. He dragged the blade across the edge of the shelf causing the paint to bubble and peel. Jerome heard a tiny gasp from over his shoulder. Jerome could only just drag his eyes away from the melting metal as the man spoke again.

"You are thieves, no more. Now it is time to redistribute these items to those that will make proper use of them."

"Like the Nemesis bracelet?"

That brought a smirk to his face. "Is that what you call it now? How quaint. The scales were my brothers and now they will be wielded by someone worthy. My last choice was a disaster." He glanced down at the case. Panic fluttered in Jerome's chest. How many other things did he have in there? "Now, how do I get in that room?" Jerome gripped the spear tighter in his right hand and brought it in front of him, hiding the movement of his left hand into his pocket. He wiggled his fingers into the bag and grabbed hold of the marbles within. He gripped them tightly, feeling a vague static buzz through his arm. Once it finally settled, he pulled his arm out and let the marbles scatter on the floor watching as five other Jeromes appeared out of nowhere and all scattered in different directions. He used the confusion and darted through the gap, hearing the man curse behind him.

The illusions created input for all the senses, slaps of feet against concrete echoed out in all directions as the versions of him split up. Jerome didn't go too far, he wanted to keep his quarry within eyesight even if he did now feel like the hunter that had quickly become the hunted. Pressing against a set of shelves, he could just see flashes of movement. He sidestepped to a larger gap and saw the man catch up to a copy. Jerome watched himself try and put up a fight against the intruder. A hollow feeling emanated from his gut as the copy of him weakly held the spear out in front of him. The intruder knocked it aside with a swipe of the sword, reaching for the fake Jerome's throat and lifting him in the air.

At his vantage point, Jerome covered his mouth, horrified at the macabre scene. The copy was an exact replica, so his abilities were the same too. If the copy didn't stand a chance, then neither did he.

"So very lifelike." The man hissed through gritted teeth. Without warning, he drew back the glowing blade and thrust it into the stomach of the dangling copy. Jerome recoiled as he heard his own scream echo throughout the Vault. The sword seemed to glow even brighter, including the handle. The faint scent of burning flesh reached Jerome's nose and he nearly gagged instantly. The illusion reached critical damage and suddenly the copy disappeared into a cloud of smoke. Jerome wondered whether his other copies felt a surge of fear as well.

"One down." The man's gaze swept round, not catching sight of Jerome peering through the stacks. The glow of the blade illuminated the man's immediate area, casting him in a fiery haze. Flames danced on his face. Jerome had never seen true evil, but this had to come close. "Come along Porteous. Defying me is pointless, I am the devil on your shoulder, the dark thought at the back of your head, you cannot deny me." Jerome watched as he edged forward, searching for the slightest movement. He dare not even breath lest it give away his location. The man's voice rose to a shout. "I'm the bogeyman your mother told you about. My time has come and I shall not be denied!"

A familiar buzzing noise echoed overhead as the lights spluttered and coughed back into life.

"That's a good sign right?" The tiny voice whispered in his ear. Jerome didn't dare answer him. Instead, he retreated moving back further between the rows, nearing the back wall. A hissing noise sliced through the air followed by a howl of pain. Out of the corner of his eye, Jerome caught the sight of flames licking up between the shelves before dying down out of sight.

"Jerome!" The woman's voice echoed in horror.

"Not a good sign." Jerome's eyes widened in fear as he near-crawled to the end of the row. He could just peer through the shelves to see the man back near the secure room. Rika appeared at the edge of his peripheral vision, staring down in horror at what was left of his copies. The man grinned, his pale skin becoming pearlescent in the harsh lighting. He looked like the devil himself. Jerome suppressed a shudder as he watched him take a step closer to Rika.

"Hello my dear." His voice dripped with false sincerity, making every inch of Jerome's skin crawl.

Movement behind Jerome nearly made him tip forward into the shelves.

"Steady," a woman's voice whispered. Jerome's heart leapt in relief as he turned to see the Director crouching down behind him. Her gaze looked straight past him and fixed on the intruder. He could almost see the calculations and theories whirring behind her eyes. She was wearing a business suit, the jacket button now undone but Jerome couldn't help but notice the flat shoes. She may have been Director for several years but clearly the field agent part of her was still very much active. Explained why it was always so hard to find her in her office.

"Director Harrison." Jerome struggled to keep his voice in check. "I'm afraid to report that a MAP has infiltrated the Vault and he is currently using it as his personal kit room."

"That sword?"

"Yes Director, it's KM-51. We've never seen it do that before." Jerome glanced over his shoulder. He was getting closer to Rika who seemed to be frozen in place. "He also seems to be able to influence people, talk them into doing things. Like Agent Mathieson to escort him in and Rika to convince me to put an empty case into the Vault. I apologise Director, I should have.."

"Not now Jerome eh? Bigger fish to fry I think. Now, that spear, if I may?" She held out her hand and Jerome automatically handed it over. "I'm going to try and get round behind him. If you could find a way to keep his attention focused this way. I resealed the door behind us, so he's not going anywhere." Jerome felt the relief dissipate as the Director rolled her suit jacket sleeves up and started to make her way back the way she came, keeping low at all times. She didn't even make a sound.

Keep his attention this way, she'd said. That sounded distinctly to Jerome like sticking his head above the parapet. Something he felt less than keen about. He peered through the gap again and found the space between Rika and the intruder was now worryingly small.

"Now, is there any chance you could get me into that room?"

"You can't let him get in there," Talin squeaked down his ear. Jerome flinched at the high-pitched noise.

"Yes, thank you, I'm aware of that." Jerome leaned away from the frantic Aossi. He managed to keep the light he was giving off to a minimum but the flapping of his wings was quite intense. An idea formed. "Oh, I wonder. Talin, I'm going to get their attention, I need you to get to Rika unseen and just fly right beside her head." Talin frowned but didn't question him. After a split-second pause, the small man disappeared without a trace.

Once he had given Talin a head start, Jerome stood not feeling incredibly confident. "Don't let him in Rika."

He saw Rika's head snap towards the source of his voice in shock. "Jerome? But?"

"A copy."

The intruder moved with incredible speed taking them both by surprise, grabbing Rika from behind and turning them both towards Jerome's hiding place.

"Let her go, she can't even get you in," Jerome stepped to the side to reveal his position.

"I don't believe you." He leaned over Rika's shoulder and moved closer to her ear. So he literally had to whisper in your ear to compel you, Jerome noted. "Thankfully, I don't have to rely on your word." He leaned in closer. From his distance, Jerome couldn't hear what he was saying to her but he could see the man's lips moving even as he kept his gaze locked on Jerome. Rika's eyes seemed to glaze over. Damn, Jerome thought, if he had to get between them and the secure room he didn't stand a chance. Then her eyes flicked over to her other side, and her head twitched. The man kept speaking to her but he was so focused on Jerome, he completely missed her flinching at some unseen annoyance just by her left ear.

Jerome couldn't suppress a smile. Talin was doing an excellent job drowning out his manipulations.

The man drew back, a grin on his face. "Well, Rika. The Room?"

Rika looked to her left. Jerome could see her eyes widen, as she got a glimpse of Talin. Jerome could just make out a tiny pinprick of light dart off out of sight.

"Rika." The man's voice was harder this time, displeased she was hesitating.

"The Secure Room," she moved a sidestep towards it and away from him. "Er, yeah, I don't have clearance." Her eyes locked with Jerome as he willed her to move faster.

"Impossible!" He lunged forward, grabbing Rika by the shoulder and pulling her closer. His sword flared red as he pressed it against her throat. She screamed out in pain. Jerome moved forward but at the same time there was a rush of activity behind the man as a flash of silver arced through the air. The spear pierced him in the side making him howl in pain and fury. He tossed Rika to the floor. Grasping at her burned throat, she slid across the floor towards the secure room.

The intruder reached behind him and pulled the spear out of his back, throwing it to the ground with a clatter. He touched his side, his fingers coming away red with blood. He looked confused for a second before fury took over his features. The wound barely seemed to have fazed him. He turned to face his hidden assailant as the Director came out from the shelves behind him. Jerome hurried across to Rika, crouching low beside her. Her fingers were wrapped around the wound but he could see no blood. At least he hadn't cut her, the burns were going to need serious attention, however.

A cry of rage drew his attention back to the Director and her opponent. The man held his glowing sword out in front of him before sweeping it in an arc, testing the Director's range and speed. She moved backwards, just out of the reach of the blade and then dived back forwards to kick him in the side before he could bring the sword back round again. Her foot connected precisely with where the spear had pierced him. He howled in anger grabbing his injured side. She dove forward again and wrapped her arm around his, twisting the hand that gripped the sword, barely keeping out of the way of the superheated object. He dropped the blade but brought his other hand up to smash into her jaw. The Director released him and backpedaled. He didn't give her space and moved in again, attacking with a fierce backhand that took her off the ground. She went careening backwards into one of the rows; boxes cascaded down off the shelves on top of her.

The intruder turned back to see his sword laying on the ground. The spear lay a little way away, near the case of items the man had looted. Jerome launched himself forwards and grabbed the spear bringing the point up towards the man's face just as he came forward too. They locked eyes. Jerome daren't blink. Then the man broke first, his eyes flicking to the spear.

"Where did that spear come from?" His voice was full of malice.

"I forget. Did it hurt?"

The man snorted. "A scratch. Already healing." Jerome couldn't help but glance at the man's side. The bleeding had stopped already without any intervention. That was not good.

"Better not chance another blow though." Jerome jabbed the point of the spear forward. The man recoiled instinctively. He stepped back and looked over Jerome's shoulder at the case. "I think not." Jerome sidestepped so he was between him and the case.

The man growled. "Next time Porteous. You can't keep them from me." The man moved backwards, pausing only briefly to gather up his sword before spinning on his heel and running towards the door. Jerome turned back to Rika, looking between her and the Director, still buried under boxes.

"Get him." Rika ordered, her voice strained.

"The door's closed, and the Director…"

"I'll check on her. That door might not stop him."

Jerome gripped the spear to his chest. She was right. He cursed, he was a Custodian not a field agent, he wasn't supposed to give chase. With a shake of the head, he turned and made after him.

He moved carefully just in case he was headed for an ambush but as he got closer to the door, his pace sped up. A hole had been cut into the door, a glowing circle highlighting the molten exit. The sword had managed to cut through solid metal. Jerome's grasp on the spear tightened as he squeezed through the hole, trying not to touch the superheated edges. The next room was empty. Jerome headed straight for the next door and out into the hallway and straight into the barrel of a gun.

Agent Mathieson held the weapon steady even as Jerome yelped in surprise. The back-up plan, Jerome cursed himself, he'd known he'd have one. The man stood just behind Agent Mathieson, whispering in his ear.

"If he tries to follow, shoot him won't you."

Jerome looked behind him, where were the other agents, the Director would have brought someone else.

"They've been stood down. Agent Mathieson was kind enough to tell them this was all a drill." He looked so pleased with himself. "You'll be seeing me again. A lot more of me. When the others are free, we'll ride again. Now you tell your Director, that I'll find the woman, and I will end her, no matter where she hides."

"Woman?"

"Shoot him in the head if he tries anything Mathieson."

"Bit harsh." Jerome felt ridiculous holding the spear as he stared down the gun.

"My nature I'm afraid." He shrugged, his sword starting to fade. Jerome started as the man blinked out of sight. The gun followed his movement, encouraging Jerome to freeze. The custodian cursed: the man still had the MAO that made him invisible. The man's voice seemed to reverberate, coming from everywhere at once. "Be seeing you. I do hope your precious Collective is ready for War."

Return Of Maia

by Andrew M. Ferrell

A female voice whispered, "Remember…" Woolley's eyes glazed over, the tumbler landed on his desk with a muffled thunk.

***

He thought about his predecessor's last words when he retired. "Leonard," his old mentor said, laying a hand on his shoulder. "The Collective is older than anyone believes. Though we didn't call ourselves that in the beginning."

"What do you mean, sir?" Leonard asked respectfully. His head still swirled from the promotion and all the added responsibilities he now held. A history lesson on top of the celebratory drinks didn't sound exciting. Still, he knew when to pay attention to his superiors.

"Deep in the files accessible only by the Curator is a record of our founding," the older man continued. "This tribe of nomads witnessed the first recorded meteor shower. Their leader, an intelligent man, became imbued with knowledge from the stars. It says he knew from then on he and his people had to protect the world from the effects of the meteors. He imparted his knowledge to his sons, and sent them to the four corners of the Earth, seeking any remnants from the meteor showers. These objects and people were to be brought before him to determine how much of a threat they posed. Or so the record says. I think it's a load of pomp and circumstance written by men who wanted to puff up their own egos." The old man took a drink from his glass.

"So what happened to the man and his sons?" Woolley asked. "How did they go about gathering up everything affected by the meteors? With all the technology we have today it's still difficult to get ahead of the events."

"Well, as the sons brought back the objects, their father became greedy and cruel. He used the people as test subjects to safely determine what the objects did. Those with strength or useful abilities, he used in a war of conquest," he said.

"So he became the threat he was supposed to stop," Woolley noted grimly. "An empire founded in such a way should have been in all the history books. Why haven't we heard of it before?"

"His own son saw what his father had become and put a stop to it. Something to do with a woman who turned out to be an MAP. I haven't read the file since my early days as Curator," the elder man paused, sipping his drink. He blinked back tears. "It's been a good run. I've helped a lot of people." His face turned serious as he locked eyes with his protégés. "No one who isn't Curator sees those files, Woolley. Promise me that. There are things in there. Things we've done. Things you can't unsee. Promise me you will uphold the tradition."

The intensity in his mentor's gaze shook Leonard. His voice came, shakily, "I won't let you down, sir."

The old man's face softened. "No more of that Sir business, Leonard. You're the boss now." He tipped his glass to Leonard and shuffled off in the direction of the bar.

His first few days in the office had been hectic, as with any changing of the guard. When Leonard finally sat down at his desk to review the secret Curator Only files, he grabbed the one with the origins of the Collective first. His fingers shook as he carefully opened the seemingly ancient file.

"This thing reads like a fantasy novel," Woolley muttered to himself a half hour later. "The Star King. An empire ruled by a powerful MAP wouldn't have fallen to a single man or woman. I think he was right. Bunch of puffed up nonsense to make the original Curators feel good about themselves. No way there was some family of MAPs that built an empire and then fell apart from the inside." He closed the file and turned to drop it in the safe.

"Sometimes what you think is fiction is more true than you know," a female voice said. Woolley looked up, taking in the robed figure standing across from his desk. She pulled back her hood, revealing tanned skin and dark, flowing hair. Her eyes shifted from violet to a deep red before settling into a swirling grey, like that of a thundercloud.

"Who are you? And how did you get in here?" Woolley asked, reaching for the alarm under his desk. His hand stopped a scant two inches away. Try as he might, he couldn't make his arm move closer.

"Relax," the woman said, a smirk flitted across her features before they settled back into a blank expression. "If I were here to kill you, you never would have seen me." She waited for the tension to leave Woolley's body before she released her hold on him. He settled back into the chair. "My name is not important. I've been called many things since I brought down the Star King and three of his sons. You may call me, Maia."

The field agent in Woolley picked up on something in her speech. "Three? What happened to the fourth son?" His brain kicked into gear, watching for micro changes in her expression. He was satisfied to catch the hint of a smile.

"He sacrificed himself to help me trap his father for eternity," Maia replied. "I visit each new leader of the Collective. Though that's not what I called you when I charged you with your mission."

Her words shocked him. His brain went back to the file he'd read. "So you're telling me you're the woman the son brought back? I find that highly unlikely."

"Believe me or not," Maia said, "You won't remember this conversation when I leave. All you will remember is to do your job, protect humanity. Do not become like the Star King."

"What do you…" Woolley cut off, the woman gone. Filled with a sense of purpose he began going over the latest reports from Astrology on the likeliest locations for an Event. He signed off on the deployment of Agents before sending it off to his Director of Operations.

***

Woolley snapped out of his memories to find Maia standing across from his desk again. Though over 30 years had passed, she still looked the same. Tanned skin with dark hair framing a face that could belong to a woman in her late 20s or early 30s. "I never forgot my purpose," he stated to the apparent immortal.

"I'm not here because you've failed. I'm here because the Star King's prison is in danger. Someone is playing a dangerous game with objects imbued by the stars. They must be found and stopped. Immediately." The command in her voice seared into the marrow of his bones.

"I understand," Woolley said. Fear, an emotion he thought he'd buried beneath discipline long ago, reared its head. "I'll have my top people on it." He mentally prepared a list in his head as he reached for the phone on his desk. When he glanced up, Maia was gone.

His momentary confusion shattered when his phone rang with a direct call. Only the Directors, and a handful of trusted top agents, could call his office directly. The display indicated it was Director Harrison from the UK division. "Harrison. I may be behind on your reports. There was an attack from the Gambler. Put me in the hospital for a day or so."

"I'm glad you're back at the helm, sir." Her voice leaked concern. "We had an individual just break into our vault and cut his way out with that sword you had us keep here. As you'll recall, we never found anything unusual except why would someone craft a sword out of garnet."

Memories from a conversation with Maia some years previously flashed in the Curator's mind. "What else was taken?"

"Near as we can find, just the Nemesis bracelet. One of my custodians managed to utilize the vault's objects to prevent further theft. The intruder referred to a woman. And his brothers. Is there something I need to know, Curator?"

A woman's voice interrupted, "Yes. War rides again. He will come for the items of his brothers and father. Items he will use to break them free."

Woolley looked up to see Maia standing in his office again, unchanged. Harrison's voice fell into the background as the immortal continued. "He is still too weak to face me directly. But he will seek to brew as much chaos as he can."

"Will you be helping us stop him?" Woolley asked, remembering everything about the original four horsemen and their StarKing father's empire of conquest.

"I will be nearby. But I must find a more permanent solution to him," Maia said. Almost on the edge of his hearing, Woolley heard her add, "Even if it costs me my love." Maia disappeared.

Harrison's voice finally broke through Woolley's thoughts. He turned back to the speaker on his phone, "Promote and commend your custodian. I think we're going to need his expertise in safeguarding the Vault. Any suggestions he has I want on my desk right away."

Woolley ended the connection. He rested his elbows on the desk and rubbed his temples. "Now I've got immortals with a grudge to deal with." His computer screen sparked to life, drawing his eyes.

A chat box opened. "I hear you've been looking for me."

Woolley stared at the message. He didn't need the screen name to know who it was. He typed back, "Hello Vincent. I have. I think it's past time we had a conversation."

"Are you ready to admit your organization mistreats those affected by meteors?"

Remembering the Curator only files locked in his safe, Woolley bit back his initial reply. Instead, he typed, "The Collective may not be completely innocent, but I've tried to lead in a way consistent with our original mission. To protect humanity from meteors and their affects. Sometimes that means we have to do things we may not like."

"Sometimes, people just want to be left alone to live their lives, Leonard. Why can't you see that?"

"I'd like to respect that Vincent. But here in the real world, there are a lot of bad people, affected or not, and someone has to stand between them and the rest of humanity. Take your friend Stavros for one."

"He was yours first. And never really mine. But I hate to admit I see your point."

"We've got something bigger to worry about at the moment. So if we're calling a truce. I could use your help. Yours and Sofia's, if she's around."

"She's in cyberspace with me. What is it you need my help with?"

"I'm sure you've heard the story of the four horsemen." Woolley didn't wait for any sort of confirmation. "War is real. He's trying to free his brothers, and his much worse father. If he succeeds, I doubt there will be much left of our world, or the digital one."

Several minutes passed while Woolley worried he had lost his one chance to recruit StarHacker and the rest of his followers to the cause. Then he received a reply. "We're in."

About Our
Authors

Andrew M. Ferrell is a lifelong fantasy and science fiction lover who lives in Northeast Wisconsin with his wife and three children, plus two attention seeking dogs. He splits his time between a factory day job, family commitments, his own writing, and running a small press. He currently has two full length novels and a novella published and can be found occasionally blogging on his site, http://www.andrewmferrell.com

Alex Minns is based in England and is a self-professed Jack of all trades (and still a master of none). Her background includes forensics, teaching, PR and custard flamethrowers. She writes sci-fi, fantasy and steampunk stories. Currently working on a time-travel steampunk novel, you'll find her tied up in timelines, getting thoroughly confused (so nothing new there) and making her mother listen as they try and figure out how to untangle it all again. You can find her obsessively creating blog stories and micro-fiction on https://lexikon.home.blog/ and on Twitter under @Lexikonical

Previous publishing credits include: *Spring Into Sci-fi* 2019 and 2020, *Fall Into Fantasy* 2019 and 2020, *Fantastical Stories* and *Harvey Duckman Presents Volume 5*.

James Pyles is an information technology textbook author, editor, and technical writer as well as a published author of science fiction and fantasy tales. Since 2019, he has had numerous short stories appear in indie SciFi, Fantasy, and Horror anthologies. He won the 2021 Helicon Short Story Award for his science fiction tale "The Three Billion Year Love" which appears in the Tuscany Bay Press Planetary Anthology *Mars*. His first science fiction novella, *Time's Abyss* was published in October 2021.

James has worked in a variety of careers, including as a Marriage and Family Therapist, a Child Abuse Investigator for Child Welfare Services in Southern California, and a Computer Desktop Support Technician. He has been married for overthirty years, raised three children, and is the proud Grandpa of three grandchildren. He lives with his wife in Southwestern Idaho.

Find out more about James at http://poweredbyrobots.com/, https://www.facebook.com/jamespylesauthor and https://twitter.com/jamespyles

Sandy R. Stuckless, born on the Canadian East Coast, now lives in the 'big city' with his wife, two teenage children, and two cats, Blueberry and Cinnamon. Growing up in a family of hunters and outdoorsy types, that passion has rubbed off on Sandy and he spends much of his downtime avoiding confined spaces. When Sandy isn't writing fantasy, sci-fi, paranormal, or anything else his twisted mind can conjure, he can be found at his day job as a technical communicator in the traffic management systems.

Twitter: @SandyRStuckless
Facebook: https://www.facebook.com/SandyRStuckless
Redemption's Beacon By Sandy Stuckless

Molly Neely is a life long reader of everything from history and theology, to politics and vampires. She is the author of the Paranormal novel, *The Sand Dweller*, (Black Opal Books) as well as its sequel, *The Orcus Child*, to be released in April 2020. Molly's a contributor to the anthology, *Fall into Fantasy 2017* & her short story, "An Heirloom Spirit," is one of 108 stories in the collection, *CEA Greatest Anthology Written*, which is currently a contender for a Guinness Book of Worlds Records title.

When she's not writing novels, Molly enjoys Pre-code films, bacon and dabbling in poetry. Molly lives in the San Joaquin Valley, with her husband Lyle & their Whippet, Devo.

Ian Hugh McAllister is a UK based author who's first work was a biography of his grandmother, Hilda James, an Olympic swimmer in the 1920s. This book, *Lost Olympics*, really launched his writing bug. He would later write the foreword for Spring Into SciFi 2019. This led to Cloaked Press launching his hard science fiction novel, *To Visit Earth*. A sequel is in the works. You can find him on Facebook at https://www.facebook.com/SciFiMac/